The Sundance Revenge

A Belle Bannon Novel (No. 1)

By Mike Pace

Foundations Book Publishing
Brandon, MS 39047
www.FoundationsBooks.net

The Sundance Revenge
By Mike Pace
ISBN: 978-1-64583-065-8

Cover by Dawné Dominique Copyright© 2021
Edited and formatted by: Steve Soderquist

To Anne, of course

Table of Contents

"When you begin a journey of revenge, start by digging two graves: one for your enemy, and one for yourself.

Jodi Picoult – Nineteen Minutes

"Anger is an acid that can do more harm to the vessel in which it is stored than to anything on which it is poured."

– Mark Twain

Chapter One

Isabella Bannon braced against a near gale force wind, fighting to keep her balance at the top of the ski lift tower.

Twenty minutes earlier a small earthquake had knocked out the power, stopping all of the resort's ski lifts. With the Sundance Film Festival in town drawing more people to movie screens than ski slopes, Belle and her fellow ski patrollers thought they might get lucky and the lifts would be mostly empty. They didn't get lucky. On this single lift alone, sixteen night-skiers had to be evacuated using the resort's cherry picker. The first fifteen evacs were routine. One skier remained and he presented a problem because he hung at least eighty feet over a rocky ravine where the normal picker couldn't anchor. The resort had sent for a special picker from Deer Valley that could adapt to unusually rugged terrain, but the chances it would arrive before the skier achieved ice-sculpture status were slightly less than zilch.

Belle had practiced the monkey crawl maneuver many times

during Marine Recon training, but that training didn't include the wind doing its damnedest to dislodge her while she clung to an ice-encased steel cable eighty feet in the air.

Her walkie crackled. Carrie calling from the ground below.

"Belle, you have to wait for the special picker."

Belle knew she was right. Waiting was the smart thing to do rather than risking two lives—one of them her own—attempting a crazy circus stunt rescue. But the smart thing to do wasn't always the right thing to do. Any delay increased the chances of the skier dying from hypothermia. Unfortunately, the stranded skier hadn't responded to Belle and the others calling up to him. Probably in shock. Which was why she now found herself about to do something pretty high on the stupid meter.

"Belle, do you read me?"

"No time to wait. We'll have to use the T-Bar."

"Too dangerous in this wind," Carrie's voice crackled over the wind. "Kip and I think we should hold off till the picker arrives."

"This guy will turn into a popsicle if we don't get him down now."

"Not the time for macho Marine heroics."

"Girls can't be macho."

"I'm serious, Belle."

"We don't have another choice."

Carrie's voice crackled with tension even the static on the walkie couldn't hide. "At least secure yourself to another safety line in case you slip."

A single safety line had been looped over the haul cable to snap under the shoulders of skiers being lowered to the ground. Belle didn't have a second safety line for herself, but she figured they'd already spent too much time talking. She locked her elbows around the frozen cable and was about to swing her legs up when a wind gust as powerful as a shotgun blast blew her off the lift tower into the icy night air.

"*Shit!*"

The howling wind whipsawed her back and forth as she dangled from her elbows eighty feet above the rocky gorge.

She'd always assumed her end would come at the wrong end of a bullet to the brain. Or an IED bomb mushing her body into bloody oatmeal. But now her ability to continually pressure her forearms against her biceps was the only thing keeping her from falling to a certain death. *Everyone considers me tough. Kick-ass Belle Bannon. Belle the ballbuster. What bullshit.* Fear pulled a cinch around her chest so tight she could barely wrench in a breath.

She struggled to keep the cable locked into the crook of her elbows and slid as fast as she could down toward the relative safety of the chair. But after only a few yards she couldn't maintain the pressure.

"*Nooo!*"

The cable slipped free and skidded across her glove. She clamped her fingers around the cold steel and squeezed.

Her grip momentarily held and her breathing moved from a few deep breaths to a *rat-a-tat-tat* of rapid gasps. She needed to reach the chair fast and swung her legs to accelerate the slide down the cable. The violent movement strained her grasp to the breaking point.

The man in the chair flung a pair of snowshoes into the swirling wind. *What?* Only reason for snowshoes was to reach the double diamond expert runs at the very top of the mountain, a spot the lift didn't—*What the fuck?* The idiot now ripped off his jacket, his sweater, and his thermal undershirt, exposing his bare skin to the driving wind and ice.

The cable slipped to the last knuckle in her hand. Only one option remained. Hit or miss. Live or die. *Isn't this the point where your whole life is supposed to flash through your mind?* At only twenty-nine, she figured the show would be short.

She swung both legs back as far as she could then shot them forward full force just as the cable slid across her fingertips. For a moment she flew through the air—

One hand touched, then curled, around the back of the lower chair frame. Her other hand grabbed ahold and she scrambled up into the chair. *Safe!* For the moment.

She slid her legs under the safety crossbar and tried to slow her rapid breathing with little success. That crossbar was all that kept them from falling as the shrieking wind threatening to rid the chair of its occupants. She turned her attention to the bald, paunchy, middle-aged man sitting beside her. He stared straight ahead with unblinking eyes as if Belle were invisible. *Definitely in shock.*

"Sir?" She jostled him. "I'm going to get you down."

The wind had twisted the man's parka around the chair's armrest, exposing the weekly lift pass ID hanging from the zipper: Walt Harrison. He turned toward Belle and studied her face, curious, like he was examining a museum specimen. He didn't say a word.

She tried guiding his arm into the jacket sleeve. "We need to get your parka—"

He jerked his arm free and swept the jacket off the chair. Corkscrewing his body hard, he flailed his arms and head violently in all directions like a two-year-old throwing a temper tantrum, almost knocking Belle off the chair.

"Gotta ski Black Lightning! Promised...rover...rover..." He yanked off his gloves and frantically scratched all over his exposed skin, drawing long, ragged streaks of blood. "The bugs!" He raked his nails across his forearm. *"Ahhhh!"*

"Mr. Harrison, you have to hold still and remain calm."

The walkie crackled again. "We saw you hanging from the cable," Carrie said. "Good thing you wore a safety line. You okay up there?"

No time to answer. With his bare skin exposed to these conditions Belle only had a minute, maybe two, to get him down. She pulled a knit cap from her inside jacket pocket and yanked it down over his head and ears. The T-Bar, a rescue seat shaped like an upside-down T, tossed in the wind. She grabbed it, used one arm to fend off Harrison's flailing arms, and slid under the safety bar onto the seat. She turned back to the lift chair for Harrison and saw ice caking not only the chair seat, but also the T-Bar.

Harrison became even more frantic and she feared he would slip under the safety bar at any moment. If she had time, she would've unlatched his skis so they didn't get in the way, but time had clocked out.

Though only inches apart, she had to shout to be heard through the wind. "Reach under the safety bar and grab onto the T-Bar so you don't slip!"

Harrison didn't move a muscle.

Shit. Belle saw the safety line blowing by. Zero time to fuss with it. She flipped up the safety bar, grabbed Harrison in a bear hug, and dragged him off the lift chair onto her lap, facing her.

Down below, Kip belayed the T-Bar rope. A few inches shorter and a few years younger than Belle, Kip was broad-shouldered and very strong from pumping iron four days a week. Yet the weight of two adults twisting in the wind caused him to struggle. The rope jerked violently back and forth. She tightened her hold.

Harrison leaned his head back and for a moment held Belle's gaze. She couldn't tell for sure, but sensed a flicker of recognition, like the man finally realized his dire situation.

"Hang in there, Mr. Harrison. We'll have you down in a—"

He punched her in the jaw, and she momentarily saw stars. The lizard door in the back of her brain cracked open and she glimpsed the intoxicating white light on the other side. *No! I'm the doorkeeper...I'm in charge.* She concentrated as hard as she could, took a few deep breaths, and willed the door closed.

I'm in charge...

It resisted, but slowly swiveled shut.

Harrison tried to swing again, but this time she blocked his arm. His head snapped forward, head-butting her full force. Even wearing a helmet the blow stunned her. Her grip loosened.

"Ski Black Lightning... Promised her...rover...gotta hurry... Gotta go *now!*"

Harrison slammed both hands against Belle's chest and shoved hard, propelling himself off the seat and backward into the black emptiness. She reached out to grab him but was a split-second too late. No scream, no cry, as Harrison fell eighty feet to the rocks below.

Without Harrison's extra weight Kip was able to lower her quickly to the ground. Carrie had already descended into the ravine and was checking the man's vitals. Belle held Kip's gaze. His usual affable demeanor and easy smile had given way to shock. She rushed over to Harrison's crumpled body.

Carrie looked up, visibly shaken. "No pulse. Good God, Belle, what happened up there?"

Belle averted her eyes and directed her cell flashlight toward Harrison's head. His lifeless blue eyes matched the color of his lips. She inched the light down. The man's neck was clearly broken. Her spine instantly iced, and it wasn't from the cold. *What happened up there?* Good question.

Carrie activated her radio. "Mick, this is Carrie. We—we have a fatality."

***

Her eyes bright with excitement, the Sword of Justice witnessed the asshole's fall. From her vantage point she couldn't hear what was being said, but judging from the ski patrollers' body language there was no urgency. Sally had been avenged. Harrison's brains were splattered across a welcoming bed of sharp black rocks. An even more satisfying result than the one she'd planned.

She slipped back through the trees onto an adjacent run and skied down the mountain.

The earthquake was an act of God—unassailable evidence her cause was just. Did God support her mission? The only logical answer had to be yes. His words guided her.

I walk in the way of righteousness, along the paths of justice.

She skied faster, adrenaline pumping.

It had begun.

Chapter Two

Two burly bouncers stood outside the door of the No Name Saloon managing the unruly crowd lined up to enter the already crowded restaurant. Belle had called ahead and asked Molly the bartender to save a couple of seats at the bar. Carrie arrived on time, and people in line were none too happy when the two of them were waved through. Belle figured she owed Carrie lunch for sticking up for her in the morning debrief meeting with the suits.

Carrie, Kip, and Belle had been summoned by the resort's attorneys to tell the Walt Harrison story. Belle figured showing up in jeans, buckskin, and boots might not make a great first impression, so she'd worn her official meet-the-suits clothes: knee-length navy skirt left over from her Marine dress uni, white cotton blouse starch-stiff after years encased inside plastic, and sensible low heels that insensibly pinched her feet.

At first the lawyers focused on her failure to secure Harrison with the safety line, but Carrie aggressively convinced them Belle had no choice. They learned Harrison was a councilman from a small eastern Wisconsin town who came to Sundance every year with his buddies for a little partying without the wives. He'd taken a ski lesson and was rated as a high beginner, meaning he had absolutely no business heading up to ski Black Lightning, the most dangerous expert run on the mountain. Skiing Lightning would've been suicidal for even an accomplished skier in the previous night's storm conditions. Fortunately, the tox screen results arrived at the end of the meeting. It appeared that Councilman Walter Harrison, Midwestern white bread, had been sky-high on crystal meth when he decided to execute a perfect eighty-foot back-dive into a pool of deadly black rocks.

Over a hundred years old, the saloon was a Park City institution. It had never been named from its early days as a watering hole serving silver miners out to seek their fortune, and providing liquid solace when they weren't successful. NoName—locals slurred the name into one word—was a Park City institution. The mixed aromas of grilled buffalo, draft beer, and smoky barbeque sauce seasoned the air. Rough-hewn dark oak walls rose from weathered wide-plank floors to a tin tile ceiling twenty feet high. A brown vintage Harley hung suspended over the service bar.

Carrie had been excused from the meeting early and was able to change into more comfortable clothes—jeans and a baggy red and black sweatshirt bearing the crossed pickax logo of the Park City High Miners. Her day job consisted of teaching AP chemistry to upperclassmen at the high school. The school was closed for its winter break, purposely scheduled to coincide with Sundance, and Carrie, along with several other teachers, spent the downtime making a few extra bucks on ski patrol. Barely over five feet tall with short red hair and freckles lightly dotting her nose and cheeks, she could've stepped out of a Saturday morning Disney so-sweet-I-might-puke TV show.

Belle removed the "reserved" signs at the end of the bar and they nestled onto the narrow wooden stools. Molly approached. Belle guessed Molly Hovenden to be in her early twenties, and had long ago concluded any further description of her would require use of the word "medium." Medium height, medium build, medium brown hair. On the quiet side, she wasn't someone who would stand out in a crowd. Maybe that's why Belle liked her.

Carrie had moved to the area only four months earlier and this was her first visit to NoName. After introducing her to Molly, Belle ordered an elk burger with extra cheese.

Carrie frowned, not hiding her disgust. "You don't feel at least a teeny bit guilty that a defenseless animal had to be murdered just so you could eat that burger?"

"Working as a hunting guide is my day job and pays the rent." Belle did her best to drain the sarcasm from her voice. "How many vegetarian hunting guides do you know?"

"Why can't your clients just take pictures?" Carrie groaned.

Belle took a deep breath and modulated her response so she wouldn't sound defensive because as far a she was concerned, she had nothing to defend. "I've led hunts in many states. You name it—moose, elk, deer, bear, bighorn sheep, wild hog. And every hunt is fully licensed by state gaming officials who manage wildlife control and enforce very strict gaming laws. In most states if you kill a wild animal without a license you go to jail. So long as we eat what we kill, God is okay with us taking the life of one of His creatures to feed ourselves. At Peabody, whatever the hunting party doesn't eat goes straight to local soup kitchens. Ironclad rule. Guilting me won't work."

"I've heard this from you before."

"You hear, but you don't listen."

"I listen, but I don't approve," she said sharply, then paused and softened her voice. "Belle, those animals you murder have just as much a right to live in peace as we do." She looked up at a bemused Molly. "Field greens salad with goat cheese would be fine."

Molly stifled a laugh. "You got it." She entered the order into the computer.

"How's Fred?" Belle asked Molly, anxious to change the subject.

"Fine."

"Who's Fred?" Carrie asked.

"Molly's saguaro cactus. When she took a trip last year she worried about Fred. I pointed out that a cactus can live for long stretches without water because, well, it's a cactus."

"Let me guess," Carrie said. "Fred's the name of an ex-boyfriend."

"Nah. The cactus was a birthday gift from my mom when I was little." Molly's eyes briefly glazed and her voice softened, no doubt retrieving a memory from her past. "She fed me Flintstone vitamins every morning, and my favorite was Fred, the red ones." Molly paused, back in the present now. "I didn't want to take a chance of losing him. Fred may not need water, but plants have feelings, especially cactuses, and he feels much better when someone reads to him every few days."

"Didn't realize cactuses were so sensitive," Carrie said, trying to keep a straight face.

"So I volunteered to stop by several times and read to Fred," Belle said. "He seemed to like *Bowhunter* magazine."

"And he appreciated it," Molly said.

The crowd mingling near the bar tightened around us.

"I can't believe how busy it is in town," Carrie said.

"Sundance," Molly and Belle responded in unison.

"During the festival, the town's population swells from eight thousand to over one hundred and twenty thousand visitors," Belle explained.

"Good for the economy," Carrie said.

"Undeniable, but the crush of traffic in the streets and the mobbed sidewalks make everyday life almost impossible for those of us living here," Belle said.

Biggest problem's the attitude," Molly said with a resigned expression. "Completely unnecessary."

"We locals call the Hollywood invaders the "Woodies," Belle added. "It's not meant to be flattering."

Belle excused herself to wash her hands, slid off the stool, and headed back to the ladies' room. NoName had painted life-size images of Popeye and Olive Oyl on the two restroom doors.

Though none of today's regulars knew their origin, the quirkiness fit right in.

***

Carrie watched Belle head to the back of the bar, easily knifing between the crowded tables in her slim navy skirt. Probably 150 pounds or so, she still moved with the light step of a ballerina.

Like she could instantly dart in any direction if need be. Her dark golden hair, released from its normal restrained ponytail swished in perfect time with the rhythm of her gait. The eyes of every male she passed flashed the familiar *I'd-like-to-slow-dance-with-you-naked* look. Carrie could hardly blame them; she wouldn't mind a slow dance herself.

A server brought their lunch to the bar, and Molly delivered it.

"That was fast," Carrie said.

"Salads are pre-made," Molly said, "and at lunch the kitchen already has burgers ready to go."

"Thanks. So how long have you known Belle?"

"Long as I've been working here, probably over a year now. A little secret? She may come across tough as nails on the outside, but inside she's as soft as an ice cream sundae. Enjoy your salad." Molly returned to the end of the long bar.

Carrie had only known Belle for a few months, but there seemed to be something lurking behind those big green eyes. Something much darker than an ice cream sundae. Kip told her Belle had been in the Marines and served in Iraq where she'd no doubt witnessed death and destruction almost on a daily basis. Obvious explanation.

She noticed a commotion at the door and turned to see a small group enter wearing matching black jackets and baseball hats, each emblazoned with a red logo—the initials PJ inside a star.

The other Woodies crowded around the bar parted, allowing the PJ group clear passage.

Carrie figured PJ must be pretty important. She leaned toward a young woman dressed in black sitting to her right. "What's PJ?" The woman looked at her as if she'd asked, What's a pope?

"Piper Jones. The biggest, most powerful talent agency in the world. They rep everybody—all the biggest stars, directors, and producers in town."

Carrie assumed the town she was referencing wasn't Park City, Utah. A young, broad-shouldered guy led the PJ group to her end of the bar. He pulled out Belle's stool.

"Sorry, that's taken," Carrie said.

"Funny, I don't see anyone sitting there." He flashed a smile revealing yellowed teeth—odd for her impression of the typical self-absorbed Hollywood hipster—then removed his jacket and tossed it on the stool. Maybe late twenties and at around six feet, he was about Belle's height. He wore a black T-shirt several sizes too small to accentuate his thick bodybuilder physique. At school, all teachers had received mandatory training on how to spot a student on drugs, and he displayed the typical characteristics of a meth user: flushed face, dilated, bloodshot eyes, twitching movements, and skin glistened with sweat. Bad teeth were the final clue.

"I think you were saving this stool for me because look, there's my jacket on it." With a quick jerk he spun around to his posse and grinned. His PJ buddies responded with laughter and gathered tighter around him. A gaunt, fidgety young woman said, "She doesn't know who you are, Gavin."

Carrie hadn't finished her salad, but suddenly she wasn't hungry. "We'll be leaving shortly, and we'd be happy to give you our seats."

Gavin reached across her chest, purposely brushing her breasts and grabbed Belle's burger. He took a big bite, not bothering to wipe the barbeque sauce dribbling down his chin. "Seems like your friend's almost finished with his lunch right now."

Like many women, Carrie had stood on crowded subways and buses where men "accidentally" brushed up against her boobs while innocently staring off in another direction. But this idiot didn't even bother with an attempt to appear innocent. She looked for back-up, but Molly was still at the other end of the busy bar. Her gaze returned to Gavin. *God, the man doesn't even blink.*

Gavin swallowed another huge bite and smirked. "By the time your man gets back, his burger will be history. He won't need the seat." Again he reached across her, this time rubbing his arm up and down against her chest as he dropped what was left of the burger to the plate.

"Mmmm—"

Carrie felt her face flush. "Listen, mister. I realize mentally you're still in junior high school, but if you touch me one more time—"

"You mean like this?" He grabbed her right breast. Carrie grimaced. He turned back to his pals. "Hey, it's small, but I think it's real!"

Carrie glanced anxiously toward the front door, but the bouncers were still outside dealing with crowd control. The posse dutifully laughed, although Carrie noticed a few females squirm and only force a smile.

Gavin announced, "I haven't felt a real tit since—"

Carrie snatched the remains of Belle's burger from the plate and shoved it in his face.

Gavin and his gang froze, apparently unable to wrap their mind around what they'd just witnessed. To Carrie, they looked like mannequins in a museum tableau. Then Gavin's eyes glazed over, his face flushed and his nostrils flared. He grabbed her by the shoulders, whipping her off the stool, and shoved both of his barbecue-covered hands up under her sweatshirt.

***

Belle wound her way back to the bar and noticed a small gathering of people near Carrie, all wearing the same colored jacket. Probably grunts from one of the L.A. talent agencies, she thought. Every year they infiltrated Sundance like a swarm of—

Holy shit. Some asshole just pulled Carrie off her stool!

Belle's heartbeat hammered then slowed almost to a stop. Then cranked up into the red zone again. The lizard door in the back of her brain cracked open. *No! I'm in control, I'm the doorkeeper...*

She watched him jam his hands up under her sweatshirt. *I'm the door—*The lizard door burst open. White light flooded into her brain, engulfing her, cleansing her of all meddlesome controls.

Belle's vision blurred around the edges, tunneling to the guy in the black jacket. The sounds around her muffled to almost nothing. She felt both serene and angry at the same time. *Is that possible?* Can one's rage be so natural, so *comfortable,* that its normalcy acts as a calming effect?

She kicked off her sensible heels, ran as fast as she could, and launched her body full force into the jerk, easily knocking him to the floor. His head snapped back against the wood planking, momentarily stunning him. That moment was all she needed. She hiked up her skirt to thigh level so she could straddle his chest and wrapped her fingers around his throat, ignoring his bulging eyes and his bucking body. He'd assaulted Carrie and needed to die.

At the bare edges of Belle's mind, she heard muffled voices fighting through.

"Belle, stop!" Maybe Molly.

The white light floated Belle above the earth on a puffy cloud. Music—violins? She thought probably violins—surrounded her, caressing her body with each note.

One set of hands then many sets of hands tried to pull Belle off, but she continued to squeeze.

Her pulse remained placid. The deeper her thumbs dug into his windpipe, the more euphoric she felt.

"Are you crazy?" Carrie?

Belle paused for a moment.

"Stop, you're killing him!" Carrie, definitely.

Belle felt what seemed like a hundred hands pulling her off the asshole. She closed her eyes, took rapid deep breaths, and focused. *I'm the gatekeeper... I'm the gatekeeper....*

Belle's cloud fell away, the white light slowly receded, the lizard door closed, and she fell back to the worn plank floor of the No Name Saloon.

Chapter Three

The Sword of Justice pulled down the blind to block the glaring streetlights. She suffered no regrets for Harrison's death. He'd earned his sentence for the way he'd treated Sally. In the end, they all will have deserved it. Just like her real daddy deserved it.

The voices of her mom's friends burst into her head, screaming *"Don't go in the bedroom!"* They'd tried to reach for her, but she'd scooted past them and opened the door...

She squeezed her eyes and forced a deep breath to collect herself. Tomorrow's mission; that's the only thing she should be thinking about. She would strike again, and Pretty Boy would be next. She could hardly wait.

She attributed the lingering unease in her stomach to hunger pangs, certainly nothing to do with Harrison's demise. That was a cause for celebration. She maneuvered sideways into the kitchen so her back remained facing the blue entry foyer wall. She hated the color blue but the asshole landlord wouldn't let her repaint it.

The blue wall tugged at her from behind, lightly at first, then pulled hard, trying to twist her around. She resisted, only risking a quick glance over her shoulder. Immediately she had to grip the edge of the chipped, butt-ugly Formica counter to steady herself, trying without success to block the Blue Room from her mind. *No more blue rooms.*

The official title was Visitors Lounge, but the residents, also a euphemism, uniformly called it the Blue Room.

Aunt Lucy always reminded her of a sugar doughnut—round, pasty white, and sickeningly sweet. They sat in chairs that years ago had been upholstered in a red floral grandma print before the grease stains and the passage of time muted the red flowers to blurry shit brown smudges. The chairs smelled vaguely of bodily fluids—probably from residents pissing themselves—but she'd become used to it. The only good thing about the lounge was the staff usually stayed outside and didn't hover over them with their little tattletale notebooks, like they did in the dining hall.

She doodled on the cover of a five-year-old People *magazine while Aunt Lucy stared at her with a pathetic smile. Though only in her early fifties, Lucy seemed a lot older to her. She was certain her aunt's heavy powder makeup would crack at any moment and the woman's entire face would break apart, the pieces clattering down onto the chipped coffee table. And what would be behind the broken face? Another pasty white mask of course. There was always another doughnut in the box.*

Lucy slid a brown paper bag across the table. "I made you some chocolate chip cookies."

Again? Doesn't she know her stupid cookies make me vomit? "Thanks." She pulled out five cookies from the bag, stood up from the chair, and juggled the cookies. "How's Uncle Ralph?"

"Fine, I'll tell him you asked about him."

"And my brother?"

"Don't hear much from him, but I'm sure he's fine." Lucy lowered her eyes and took a deep breath, obviously gathering courage to continue. *"And Mayor Yaeger—"*

"You mean my real daddy?"

"I heard the skin grafts on his face seem to be holding and the doctors think he might regain some sight in his left eye."

The bastard. She hoped the pervert writhed in unspeakable pain for the rest of his life.

But Lucy would be debriefed by the staff at the end of her visit, and any sign of contrition might increase her chances of an early release. *"That's good news. And my brother? How's he doing?"*

Lucy's expression clouded at being asked the same question twice, within the span of a minute. *"Haven't heard from him in a while. I got a card from him on mother's day, but I accidentally saw a text from Ralph reminding him to send a card. Hey, boys are always bad at those things. He's a good boy."*

He's more than good, Luce, he's great. Popped my cherry at the ripe old age of fifteen. Didn't know that, did you?

"Your counselor says you're making good progress."

"He's very nice." Dick-face Harold was a toad. She let him feel her up in return for keeping his mouth shut during their private sessions, but lately he'd been hinting the price was about to rise. Was an hour of freedom from his idiotic yammering worth screwing the asshole? Probably. Maybe she could get away with just a BJ.

"Honey, you're going to be twenty-one in six months."

Five months, twenty-eight days and—she glanced at the institutional clock on the filthy blue wall—fourteen hours to be exact. *"Can't wait."*

Lucy dabbed her eyes. *"Which means, of course—"*

It means I get out of this gulag and never have to see any of these assholes again. *"I know. I'm excited."* Uh, oh. Old Lucy was looking down at her doodles, twisting the damp tissue in her hand. Auntie had something on her mind.

"Your pictures are interesting, dear. Are they swords?"

Of course they're swords. *"Crosses. You know, Jesus on the cross. I've been spending a lot of time reading the Bible."* Try reading the Book of Job, Luce, you might learn something. Be ye afraid of the sword: for wrath bringeth the punishments of the sword. *"It's helping, you know, spiritually."*

"That's wonderful, sweetie." Lucy lifted her eyes. *"Dr. Estes has reported that lately you've become more engaged in your education, and he's very pleased. Chemistry, American history. Very impressive. You know, after you leave here the state will pay tuition at the community college for the first year as part of the rehabilitation protocol. Maybe you could continue your interest in science."*

"That would be nice." Except she had much more important things to do than sit in a classroom where she knew more than the idiot teachers.

"He also reported you're still, uh, consumed with Maria, and with your mom's... accident."

She caught the cookies in midair and replaced them in the paper bag then sat back down and leaned forward. Ready for the perplexed, innocent look, Luce old girl? Okay, here you go. *"Jeez, not sure what you mean. I have great memories of her."* Especially that one of Mommy sprawled naked on the filthy shit-brown shag carpet with a hole in the side of her head. How about that memory, Luce? Should I add a tear? Maybe a pitiful smile?

Lucy was shredding the tissue now, sending tiny white auntie tear flakes floating down to the piss-stained carpet. *"I stopped by the cemetery Sunday. Laid a fresh bouquet of red roses."*

Red? You idiot. She hated red. Yellow roses, bitch, yellow. *"That's nice. Thanks."*

"Doctor Estes is also concerned, we're all a little concerned with the, uh—"

C'mon, Luce, spit it out.

"You know...the revenge thing."

The noise coming through the apartment's second story window snapped her back. She kept it cracked open for the fresh air and didn't mind the chill. She walked to the window and when she raised the blind, noticed her hands were shaking. From her memory of Aunt Lucy's Blue Room visit? Nothing that a swig or two of vodka wouldn't fix.

She looked across the street to NoName and Frannie's Nail Emporium. The Woodies, along with gaggles of local teens, were everywhere, clogging traffic on Main Street, all for a chance to see a silly movie star.

She noticed several spots along the street where fans congregated in tight circles, presumably around a celebrity, phones held high in the air. Good. She was counting on the fan swarms to continue the next day. She also saw heavy traffic moving down the street's steep decline. Stopping, then speeding up, then stopping again to avoid the crowds. She smiled. The setup was perfect.

God had helped her beat long odds in her mission to exact justice on Harrison, so she'd decided to make the plan for Pretty Boy even more spectacular, and even more unlikely to succeed. If God were on her side, Plan A, no matter how unlikely, would work. A part of her cautioned against testing God, but she had confidence He would come through again. And if not, no problem. She always had a reliable, but boring, Plan B.

She wondered what Danny was doing now. She hadn't told him about her mission yet, but soon the time would be right. He cared deeply for her and in her heart, she believed he would understand.

She opened the closet door and pulled three knives from the cardboard box. Tossing them into the air, she juggled the knives easily, practicing for the big show tomorrow.

A show where Brad Banks himself would be the star.

Chapter Four

T he arrow pierced its target dead center.

Shooting classic bull's-eye paper targets tacked to hay bales in the enclosed field behind Peabody Outfitters kept Belle sharp for her day job guiding big game hunts for Peabody. She made $11.50 an hour for her ski patrol gig; her job at Peabody paid the bills. Belle much preferred leading bowhunting excursions to rifle hunting. She found the weapon intrinsically fair because despite technological advancements to improve its power and efficiency, the bow remained primitive and offered a wild animal better odds for escape than a high-powered rifle with a sophisticated scope.

She made her way through the light snow to retrieve the arrow from the target. Hardly surprised by her accuracy, she'd been bowhunting since she was nine, and would've been alarmed if the arrow had not found the center ring. She smiled inwardly and thought back to her first hunt. Her dad had taken her turkey hunting the day before Thanksgiving. She still remembered the thrill when she saw the bird emerge from the underbrush. Her hands had shaken so much that the first arrow missed by a mile. But the second one didn't.

The arrow point stuck deep in the bird's breast, and she had to yank hard to remove it and still recalled struggling to hold back the tears. The day before in school her teacher had read a book to the class called *Tommy the Turkey* where a little boy helps Tommy escape the hunters and persuades his parents to have a vegetarian Thanksgiving. She'd stared down at the dead bird in the snow— only moments before Tommy had been alive, and she'd killed him. She could still feel her dad resting his thick hand on her bony shoulder. *You did good, Belle.* Those were his exact words—"You did good."

The next day, she'd seen her first kill plated on her mom's only-for-special-occasions silver platter resting in the center of the Thanksgiving table. She remembered her unease, staring at the bird she'd felled. Her grandma had patted her on the knee and told her, "So long as we eat what we kill, sweetheart, God is okay with us taking the life of one of His creatures." Soon the aroma from the roasted bird overcame her misgivings, and she'd consumed two helpings of Tommy the Turkey.

She stepped farther back from her previous spot and nocked another arrow into the chip on the string of the sixty-five-pound Hoyt compound. The single target-point arrow was mostly used for competitions, which she didn't do. Nothing against them, just wasn't her thing.

She'd hoped a little target practice might help her relax. In a few hours she'd be meeting up with Carrie again on the mountain, and after the NoName incident, she had to admit she wasn't looking forward to it. She tried to focus on the hay bale target. *Melt your mind, Marine. Let everything drain away. Your only thought is the target.*

She didn't use a release aide, instead preferring the old-fashioned three-finger grip. She pulled the bowstring back partway, and the eccentrics—gears on the top and bottom of the compound bow—tripped in, reducing the pull from sixty-five back down to thirty-five pounds. She lined up the tiny sight-hole on the bowstring with the lowest of the three pre-sighted pins on the bow itself. The pins translated into the distance the bow needed to be raised to reach the target. By lining up the sight-hole on the bowstring to the lowest pin the bow would necessarily rise and launch the longest shot. Her fingers released, and the arrow again pierced the target dead center. *Dead* center.

Yeah, Belle really liked the bow. Maybe part of the attraction was the ability to effect a silent kill. She knew that thought should've bothered her, but it didn't.

And that thought bothered her.

***

Carrie and Belle cruised silently down Silver Moon, an advanced intermediate run. During patrol Carrie's comments had been perfunctory, only the bare minimum to do their job. Belle could tell Carrie remained upset about what happened at NoName. Belle could hardly blame her.

Ahead they saw a young girl, maybe nine or ten, crisscrossing the slope in a maneuver indicative of someone who might've bitten off more than she could chew. Belle didn't mind skiers who challenged themselves; that's the only way to improve.

Belle sensed movement behind them, glanced back, and saw a skier clad in solid black blurring down the slope at high speed. Behind him, a tall woman with long red hair swished by. She couldn't tell if they were together, but she was worried about the girl. With the slope lights and the young girl's fluorescent green jacket, Belle felt certain they'd see her and slow down. She was wrong. The man in black clipped the girl's skis, sending her flying, then kept going with the redhead following.

Belle and Carrie zipped down to the girl and helped her to her feet.

"You okay?" Belle asked.

She was visibly shaken. "I...I think so."

Belle turned to Carrie. "Stay with her." Without waiting for a reply, she fired down the slope after the skier in black. He was fast. Belle was faster. She shot past him, stopped, and spun uphill, blocking his path. Belle had hoped he wouldn't be able to stop. Big guy, powerfully built, obviously athletic. Made no difference. She lowered her body and prepared to pound a hard shoulder into his gut, knocking him on his ass.

Unfortunately, he stopped in time while the redhead zoomed past and disappeared down the slope.

He didn't hide his anger. "What the hell—?"

The man's transgression was very common, mostly caused by a skier unable to control his speed, and Belle usually went out of her way to project an understanding tone. But she could see this jerk was well in control, and she didn't try to hide that she was pissed. "You realize you ran into a young girl back there?"

"Yeah. No. I mean I saw her, but I thought I missed her." He assumed a defensive air. "She shouldn't be on this run anyway. Crisscrossing the entire width of the slope, she's the one who's creating the danger."

"Let me see your pass."

He paused for a moment then fished his pass out of his jacket pocket. The threat of losing his season pass must've had an effect because his tone changed. "Look, I'm sorry. Is she okay?"

Belle didn't answer right away and studied the pass. "Daniel

Pagano from Denver. Please remove your goggles."

He complied and she saw the face matched the photo on the pass. Thirties, dark hair, thick brows, and brown, almost black eyes that projected intelligence and, despite the moderated tone of his voice, a condescending smirk.

"People call me Danny Pags." He offered a smile that didn't reach his eyes.

"The answer to your question is, yes, she appears to be okay."

He reached into his pants pocket and withdrew a thick roll of bills. "I'd be happy to compensate her for any injury she sustained as well as any damage to her equipment." He held Belle's gaze as he removed a small glassine bag from his pocket. It contained white powder. "And for any other needs you might identify. By the way, I can get you as much of that as you want. Or anything else that might fit your appetite."

Danny Pags was about as subtle as a proverbial freight train. Belle had never been offered a bribe before, much less a drug bribe. She had every justification to pull his pass and call the cops, but doing so would require spending time in the resort office filling out paperwork. The amount of coke in the bag would at best result in a light slap on the wrist. The patrollers had agreed to meet for a late dinner at The Snake in Heber, and Belle wanted to use the opportunity to maybe mend things with Carrie. Besides, Belle was partial to the restaurant's famous spareribs.

She snatched the glassine bag from his hand and dumped the contents into the snow. "This is your lucky day for two reasons. First, I'm going to pretend I didn't hear that last comment or witness you offering me a bag of extra salt for my French fries. Second, I'm not going to pull your pass. But I will circulate your name, and if you're stopped for any infraction including butting to the front of the lift line, your pass will be pulled for life. I'm going to pass your name on to the local authorities and encourage them to throw the book at you if you're caught jaywalking in my town. So whatever you're doing, stop. And I strongly suggest you consider heading back to Phoenix. Got it?"

He held her gaze and offered a cold smile. "Oh, I definitely 'got it.' By the way, didn't catch your name."

"Bannon." She handed him his pass.

"I promise I'll remember you, Ms. Bannon." He turned and mumbled something that sounded a whole lot like "bitch."

She watched him glide down the mountain until he disappeared behind the abandoned silver mine located near the base of the Silver Moon lift. Something told Belle she'd run into Daniel Pagano again soon.

She hoped so.

***

At eight-thirty p.m. the Summit House restaurant at the top of the Silver Moon lift seemed busier than normal, probably because of the milder temperatures. Carrie and Belle decided to take a short coffee break before going back outside for end-of-night sweeps. Belle wasn't happy that the Summit only offered the basics for coffee flavoring—cream and sugar, but at least the cream was real and not that foul, white powder crap that came in a cardboard tube.

Belle didn't particularly want to revisit the Noname incident but knew she had no real choice if she was going to continue working with Carrie. She took a sip of coffee and shifted uncomfortably in her chair. "Look, I'm sorry about what happened at the saloon this afternoon."

She didn't say anything for a few long seconds. "The guy was a jerk. Beyond a jerk. But Belle, you almost killed him. Does an explanation even exist?"

Belle lowered her eyes and remained silent.

Carrie took a deep breath and rested her hand on mine. "I owe you a debt of thanks for defending me, and I don't want you to think I'm not appreciative. But I abhor violence. I'm mad at myself for rubbing the burger in Gavin's face."

"Christ, he'd just shoved his hands under your clothes and was groping your breasts."

"No excuse. Violence begets violence. I'm sure I could've apologized and reasoned with him if given the chance. But I was never given the chance because you took it upon yourself to strangle the man to death and would've been successful if three guys hadn't pulled you off."

Neither of them spoke. Finally, Carrie broke the silence, lowering her voice. "All people are born good. I really believe that. And as a gay woman, that's not easy for me to say. I've been exposed to some very hurtful people in my life, but I nevertheless believe good lies in everyone, admittedly in some people buried very deep. I also believe that someone has to break the cycle of violence before it escalates beyond control. I don't feel comfortable around violent people, and I tend to stay away from them."

Her words cut deeper than Belle expected. "Like me."

Now it was Carrie's turn to look away. "I know you thought you were doing the right thing. But..." She lowered her voice to just above a whisper. "I'm sensing you have...issues."

Issues? Yeah, Belle had issues. She considered taking Carrie up on her offer but at that moment, a teenage girl with purple streaks in her dark hair walked by their table carrying a cup of hot chocolate in one hand and an iPhone in the other. Describing her gait as walking wasn't completely accurate. More like bouncing. When she saw the two patrollers her face brightened into an infectious smile.

"Hey, Belle. Ms. Palmer?"

"Hi, Markie." Belle waved the girl to an empty chair at their table. "Join us. I gather you two know each other."

"Markie's in my senior AP chemistry class," Carrie said.

Markie Dodd took a seat. "I didn't know you, like, worked patrol, Ms. Palmer. Totally awesome."

"Just started. So, I read about you in the *Beacon.*"

Belle noticed Carrie's tone had changed on a dime thanks to Markie's irrepressible sunny disposition.

"Yeah. Dad kind of roped me into it. He said..." She exaggerated a deep voice. "'The human-interest story of an upcoming graduate dedicating her last months at home to bonding with her parents before leaving for college would be like a big hit with my constituents.'" She giggled.

"Markie's dad is Deputy Mayor," Belle explained.

"I'm well aware of that," Carrie said. "I particularly enjoyed the part of the story where you started this tradition of skiing together every Friday night, then sharing an order of nachos at Baja afterward."

"Mom would usually meet us there, but that part didn't make it into the story."

"And you'd ski the same last run—"

"Double Jack."

"Right. Double Jack. You'd always let him lead you down the mountain."

"Dad called that part a heart-tugger. His constituents totally loved it. He's a skier." She said the word the same way any snowboarder would—as if her mouth were filled with thumbtacks.

"I could beat him down the slope blindfolded riding backward. But I decided to let him lead on the last run every Friday. You know, kind of a little symbol of respect for, like, putting up with all my teenage bullshit over the years. Dad said that part of the story was totally major. Lots of tweets from his constituents."

Belle really liked this girl. They'd met during Belle's first day on patrol when she had to chase Markie down for speeding through a slow-ski zone. After that, they'd see each other frequently on the slopes and over time became friends. Often we'd join up for a hot drink at the Summit during the night-ski. Her bubbly personality and bright-eyed enthusiasm never failed to make Belle smile. She'd watched the girl grow and mature over the last couple of years. Markie would ask Belle about typical teenage stuff—family problems, boy problems, fitting-in problems. Belle would do her best to advise the girl after making sure she understood that as someone who'd spent a year in a juvenile detention facility, Belle was hardly a role model, and she should take Belle's advice with a healthy dose of skepticism.

A few weeks earlier Markie told Belle she was the only girl in her family, and she'd come to think of Belle as her big sister. Belle got the sister-bonding thing; when she was a kid her little sister, Jenny, would attend Belle's ballet classes and gymnastic meets and say when she grew up she wanted to be just like her big sister. *Fortunately for her, that didn't happen.*

Markie checked her phone. "Time for one more run." She gulped down her drink. "See you later." She popped up and bounced toward the exit.

Belle shook her head. "Did we have that much energy at her age?"

Carrie smiled. "Wasn't that long ago, but still hard to remember."

Belle paid little attention to her words, instead focusing on the smile. It appeared genuine. Maybe there was hope Carrie would soon come to understand Belle's behavior at NoName. She sighed. That could only occur if Belle revealed her "issues." *Am I ready for that?*

***

Danny Pagano sat on an old milking stool in an abandoned barn, breathing the dank musty air.

Where the hell were they? For a moment he thought something might've happened. A mistake? A slipup? Jello and the Dane were two of the best, particularly when it came to disposal.

A blur of light briefly crossed the filthy window then quickly extinguished. A minute later the barn door creaked open and the rat, hands tied behind his back, stumbled in and tripped onto the plastic sheeting. Jello and the Dane followed. The Dane lit a battery-powered lantern that cast long rippling shadows across the plastic.

Paul Stein attempted to stand but with his hands bound, he fell flat on his face. Forties, short, scrawny, with a pock-marked face, watery eyes, and a prematurely receding hairline. "Paulie the Jew" had been working for Danny for over two years, and Danny had considered him one of his most loyal employees. Then he'd learned from his Salt Lake sources that the Feds had gotten to Paulie and were about to flip him. Consequences needed to be administered.

Danny spoke in the calm voice of a disappointed parent. "Your disloyalty saddens me."

Paulie crawled to his knees and hung his head.

Jello and the Dane stood behind him looking bored. Angelo "Jello" Biondi had been in the muscle business for thirty of his forty-five years. Just under six feet, he'd recently added a small paunch to his sculpted 250-pound body and there were now silver streaks in his black hair. Danny had used him on two earlier jobs, one in Florida and one in New York. The Dane weighed almost a hundred pounds less than Jello but stood well over six feet tall with thinning blond hair and dead blue eyes. Danny had never seen the man frown or smile, and he rarely spoke. At Jello's suggestion,

Danny had brought the Dane in on an enforcement matter in Provo, and he'd proven very helpful.

Danny knew Paulie understood how this would end. How it had to end. He'd broken the code, and the consequences for ratting were universal and unequivocal.

"I only ask that you make it quick," Paulie whispered.

Danny again spoke in a soft, almost conversational tone. "I need to know what you told the Feds."

"Nothing. I didn't tell them nothing, I swear!"

"But you were about to."

Paulie didn't speak for a long moment, then his voice lowered further. "They had me cold and promised if I cooperated, they'd give me money and set me up in witness protection. I didn't want to spend the rest of my life in jail. I got a kid, Danny. Only eleven, lives with her mother in Ogden. Thinks I travel a lot working construction."

"Doing a little time would've been better for the kid than the alternative."

Paulie's silence signaled his agreement.

Danny prided himself on his ability to read people, and he was reasonably certain Paulie the Jew was telling the truth. He nodded to Jello, and Jello held Paulie's arms tight behind him so he couldn't move his body, while the Dane locked Paulie's head tight so it couldn't move. Paulie tried to struggle to no avail.

Danny stood up and saw Paulie's eyes widen. He'd spotted the grilling fork lying next to the milk pail, a gift from Felix Ross. The two-pronged fork had been modified to about the same length as a hammer and its handle was thick and shaped with finger grooves like a ski pole grip. Danny scooped up the fork and stepped forward to face Paulie.

"Danny, please, a bullet."

Danny's placid expression instantly contorted to that of a raging predator. He stretched up on his toes and held the fork high. Paulie screamed as Danny roared then savagely thrust the fork straight down, burying it through Paulie's left eye deep into his brain.

Jello and the Dane released their hold, and Stein's body collapsed to the floor. Danny wasn't certain, but the fading glimmer in Paulie's right eye suggested the man had not died instantly. Hopefully, the traitor would experience a last second of terror as he witnessed his blood and brain matter ooze out onto the dirty plastic.

Chapter Five

Brad Banks forced himself to maintain the cool, calm, collected image that had not only shot him to the top of the Hollywood A-list, but allowed him to remain there longer than the normal celebrity shelf life.

He checked his phone. Almost noon. In less than an hour, his writing and directing debut, *Two to Go,* would be premiering at the Egyptian. Funny, in a month he'd be walking down the red carpet in the heart of Los Angeles as a favorite to win that famous gold statuette for his role as Rhett Butler in the remake of *Gone with the Wind.*

According to the tabloids, he and Laura were officially considered Hollywood royalty, to the point where the pending birth of their first child was treated with the same level of anticipation as a new birth in the British royal family. Not bad for a kid born Isaac Rosenfeld from Sandusky, Ohio. Millions of people from around the world would be watching that Oscar stroll. And yet he had to admit the idea his little indie flick was about to be seen by an audience of only a couple hundred people amped him up higher than all the Oscar buzz. He'd actually *created* the film—wrote it, directed it, produced it—and didn't simply recite memorized lines written by someone else according to the directions of another someone else. He'd purposely decided not to take an acting role in his movie so the film would be judged completely on its own merit and not be tagged with a "Brad Banks movie" label.

They drove up Main Street, slowed by the crowds spilling over from the narrow sidewalks. Along with the driver, two bodyguards accompanied him, Al sitting at his side and a new guy in the front seat. With Al's assistance, Brad snorted his last line to keep the excitement level elevated and made a mental note to contact Sonja for a new supply. He smiled inwardly as the image of his local supplier flashed through his mind—jet black hair falling to her shoulders, tight body, great rack, and the best blowjob he'd ever had. A bonus, she had called it. He knew he could've fucked her, but he'd learned his lesson on that front. He also knew she wouldn't go blabbing to the press because doing so would expose her to the cops. He assumed another bonus would—

"Where you want the driver to let us out?" Al asked, interrupting his pleasant chain of thoughts.

Brad sighed and returned to the present. "A couple blocks from the theater."

"You sure? All these people see you, might be a problem."

"Al's got a point," the driver said. "Tough to maintain security in that crowd."

When Brad had hired Al he'd made it clear the guard was expected to speak his mind when it came not only to his security but, even more important, to the safety of Laura and his unborn child.

The need for care had been heightened over the last three months when the tabloid story broke about the waitress's suicide. Jesus, he'd made one lousy mistake. The stupid Kupchak bitch had sworn to him she was on birth control. Two months later, she sent a message through his agent that she was pregnant with his kid and she intended to keep it. Brad suggested throwing some money at her in return for a signed statement that he wasn't the father, but because of all the #MeToo hysteria—thank you, Harvey Weinstein—that plan hadn't worked. Someone in the doctor's office dropped a dime about the kid, and the tabloids had a field day.

Upon his lawyer's advice, he'd denied paternity and branded the woman a crazy money-grubber. Then three months ago she'd overdosed on sleeping pills, killing both herself and the fetus. Enough negativity against her for killing the unborn child blunted the #MeToo crowd, and he'd weathered the storm. That Laura had continued to stand by her man was key to his survival. And now, footage of him walking a few blocks up Main Street surrounded by swarms of adoring fans couldn't do anything but help the public forget all about the crazy bitch.

"Pull over here," he said.

The two bodyguards emerged first, opened the door, and he stepped onto the slick pavement. In less than fifteen seconds, the air was filled with shouts of "Brad!" In an instant a horde of screaming starstruck fans holding cell phones high in the air surrounded him. He smiled and waved while Al and his buddy tried to clear a path to move him up the hill.

By the time they reached a spot across the street from the Egyptian, the crowd had tripled, spilling off the walk and taking up half the street. Excited faces leaned into him.

"Brad! Brad!"

Fans fought for an opportunity to position themselves shoulder-to-shoulder with him so they could snap a selfie. The crowd's light jostling soon morphed into serious pushing and shoving. He could hardly breathe. Maybe the walk through the crowd wasn't such a great idea.

***

Belle sat with her feet soaking in the little pool at the base of her padded chair while Frannie worked on her nails. She'd descended from the members of the substantial Chinese colony that had settled in Utah after working on the transcontinental railroad in the late nineteenth century, and her nail salon had been a fixture on Main Street since before Belle was born. Carrie's nails and toes had already benefitted from Frannie's attention, and she sat in a facing chair waiting for Belle.

Belle had always preferred her own company, but though she hadn't known Carrie long she now considered her a friend. Belle had made the appointment—something rare for her—because she had this crazy idea that if she arranged a two-gal mani-pedi outing maybe Carrie would forget the NoName incident, and they could return to normal. But Carrie was one of those people who wore her feelings on her sleeve, and while she did an amazing job attempting to hide it, Belle could tell she remained disturbed.

Belle attempted to push her back to normal with gal-pal chatter and nodded to a vial of polish on the counter. "I'm thinking that green for my toes."

"The color is Pine Maiden's Breath," Carrie said, gamely participating in the banter. "I can't believe you don't know the difference."

"Oh really. And what exactly is a pine maiden?"

"A fairy that lives among the conifers," Carrie responded.

"If her breath's green, not sure I want her blowing on my toes,"

Belle said, eliciting a polite laugh.

Frannie scolded Belle like she did every time Belle came in to see her. "Your nails have taken a beating since I saw you last. From your job. Hunting is man's work." She pointed to Carrie. "Why don't you teach children like Ms. Carrie?"

Belle didn't tell Frannie she'd tried teaching for a little while. Didn't want a prolonged conversation on that subject, so she changed to another one. Maybe a more substantial discussion would divert Carrie.

"Have you happened to run into that jerk Pagano again? The one who almost ran into the girl on Silver Moon and offered me a thinly veiled bribe?"

Carrie was somewhat startled by Belle's abrupt change in subject. "No, why? Belle? I see the wheels turning."

"Nothing." Now Belle was the one trying to hide her thoughts. She held up her nails for inspection. "I'm thinking something bright and sunny."

"I have the perfect color," Frannie said as she pulled a tiny bottle from the rack on the wall.

***

They emerged from Frannie's, and each held up a hand to assess their manicures in sunlight.

Frannie had selected a sunny yellow Chanel shade called Giallo Napoli for Belle. She said it would cheer Belle up. After Belle's experience with Harrison and her uncomfortable conversations with Carrie, she was in dire need of anything to cheer her up.

They walked downhill through the thick of the annual Sundance Main Street spectacle toward the parking garage. The street more resembled a carnival midway than the chief artery of a sleepy Western town. Queues forming to enter the historic Egyptian

Theater spilled out into the street, and every few minutes they'd hear a horn honk and the screech of brakes as a car traveling down the steep incline had to avoid the mostly young revelers. A bare-chested male unicyclist wearing a purple top hat and purple tights, seemingly oblivious to the cold, threaded his way in and out of traffic tooting a kazoo. On the balcony of an upscale Asian restaurant, beautiful young bodies packed into two hot tubs splashed nearby partiers who tried with little success to keep the tub water from polluting their mai tais.

Farther up the street, a kid dressed as Darth Vader blasted away on his trumpet. A girl in full goth regalia slowly eased a cart downhill. In the cart, an African American dude played the Stones' *Jumpin' Jack Flash* with his feet on an electric piano. North of the Egyptian, a guy in a black hoodie wearing silver face paint and large sunglasses juggled what looked like rusty knives, entertaining a small crowd gathered under the clock next to Café Terigo. The juggler finished his set, put his knives in a case, and disappeared into the crowd.

Carrie shook her head. "Crazy. Is it always like this?"

She'd arrived in town at the start of the school year, and Belle realized it was her first Sundance. "Each year it gets a little worse, and like clockwork, the organizers moan about how Hollywoodization is pulling the festival away from its original independent roots. Yet the glitz keeps growing."

"Is Hollywoodization even a real word?"

"Take a look around and you tell me."

They wound their way through the crowd, and at various spots along the way they saw pockets of people circling a celebrity caught outside on the street. The time a celebrity lingered for photos was inversely proportional to the level of fame that celebrity had achieved. Most of the fans weren't Woodies who would consider themselves too cool to display excitement at seeing a fellow "artist." Instead, teenagers comprised the bulk of the crowd. Not only townies, but also kids who annually drove up from Salt Lake for the chance to see real live movie and TV stars.

Ahead, another crowd quickly gathered around someone—Belle couldn't make out who—drawn like iron filings to a magnet. Young arms holding cellphones strained to catch a photo for instant posting.

Belle stated the obvious. "Looks like we have a roadblock."

"Who is it?"

Belle could tell by the excitement in her voice Carrie was not immune to stargazing, and in fairness, Belle couldn't blame her. She remembered as a little kid seeing Hayden Christensen, Anakin Skywalker from *Star Wars, Revenge of the Sith,* walking past her on Main Street so close she could've touched him. She'd been so excited that night she couldn't eat her dinner. They moved closer to the gaggle and spotted the object of all the fuss.

Carrie's eyes lit up. "Brad Banks? Is that really Brad Banks?"

Belle couldn't muster the same enthusiasm for another in a long line of Hollywood actors that invaded Sundance every year, but she tried not to sound jaded. "Yeah, that's him. Probably in town to burnish his true artist cred with an indie flick. You see that a lot."

"I can't believe it's him. He looks older than his pictures."

A breathless teenage girl came up behind us. "Is that Brad? *Oh my God, it's Brad!*"

The girl drew her cell from her back pocket with a speed that would make Wyatt Earp envious. Holding it high, she turned in an attempt to position herself for a selfie with Banks in the background and puckered her lips. The unruly crowd surrounding him now took up half the street and his two burly bodyguards struggled to keep the fans at bay.

Carrie hesitated. Belle knew she itched to snap a picture of the movie star too, but didn't want to come across as some stupid groupie.

"Why don't you get a little closer and take a photo?" Belle suggested.

"Oh, I'm not sure..."

Belle was sure she was sure. "Go ahead, you know you want to."

Carrie shrugged with a sheepish grin, pulled her phone from her pocket, and snapped the picture. "Got it. Let's get out of here, I can hardly breathe."

Walking away, Belle bumped into someone wearing dark clothes—the silver-faced juggler with the big sunglasses—and mumbled an, "Excuse me."

The juggler said nothing and moved closer to Banks. Probably hoping for a selfie like everyone else.

Chapter Six

"**G**et me the fuck out of here," Brad whispered to Al through a forced smile. His crazy fans were now actually clawing at his jacket, and it would only be a matter of moments before it was ripped from his body.

"You got it." Al took the lead and cleared a path to the street while his buddy stayed back to block the fans crowding from behind. Brad noticed a truck driving down the hill carrying porta-potties and sneered inwardly. *Don't want the rabble pissing in the streets.* He glanced up at the ornate marquee above the Egyptian and smiled with pride. *Two to Go – Directed by Brad Banks.*

He heard a whisper close to his ear. *"Hello, Grover."*

What....? He turned to see a man wearing sunglasses and silver face paint, inches away from his own face, smiling at him. The guy reminded him of the typical villain in a cheap slasher flick. He shuddered. "Excuse me, but—"

Silver-face glanced uphill at the oncoming truck. "This is for

Annie, asshole."

Brad felt the blood drain from his face. "Who the hell are—?"

Silver-face jutted out his leg, tripping Brad forward on the slippery pavement. He stumbled then fell, smacking the back of his head hard on the icy street and blacking out for an instant.

He shook his head and glanced up. A huge, dirty truck tire inches away rolled toward—

***

Belle and Carrie had broken free of the crowd and headed down the street when they heard the deep blast of the truck horn and screeching brakes followed by hysterical screams from the fans surrounding Banks. They glanced back to see Banks's two bodyguards knock fans aside and rush to the front of a delivery truck stopped in the middle of the street. Hurrying back up the hill, they ran into a teenage girl with tears streaming down her face rushing past us.

Belle raised her voice above the shrieks and wails filling the air. "What happened?"

"Oh, my God! Brad was like trying to cross the street and his bodyguards were major shoving people out of the way, and some of the people shoved back, and all of a sudden Brad tripped into the street when this truck..." Overcome with emotion, the girl couldn't finish her story. Immediately the sound of sirens pierced the air.

The girl tried to gather herself. "Can you believe it? *Brad Banks is dead!*" Not bothering to dry her tears, she turned and snapped a photo of the chaos before continuing down the street, telling all she passed that "Brad Banks is dead!"

It seemed every soul in town now converged on the scene. The crowd appeared as a single organism; alive, swaying, pulsing around the front of the truck. With Carrie following close behind, Belle knifed through the mob until she was blocked by a distraught bodyguard.

"Ski patrol!" she shouted. "We can help until the ambulance arrives."

The bodyguard paused for a moment then cleared the way for them to get through.

Banks lay crumpled next to the left front wheel of a portable toilet delivery truck. A shorter bodyguard hovered over him. The bodyguard had stripped off his coat, pulled off his shirt, and pressed the shirt against a deep gash on Bank's cheek. The driver was a wreck, standing to the side of his truck babbling on about how Banks tripped in front of him before he could put on the brakes.

The driver instantly became the object of the shocked fans' collective grief and anger. The crowd charged at the driver. He jumped back into the cab and locked the door. A big kid in a red ski jacket came out of a ski shop carrying a new helmet just as someone pointed to the driver and yelled, "You killed Brad!" Momentarily confused, the kid paused a few moments to take in the scene. Suddenly, his face flushed with anger. He rushed the truck and swung his helmet as hard as he could against the driver-side window, shattering the glass.

Covered in glass shards, the frantic driver shouted, "I got a gun!" temporarily holding the mob at bay.

Up and down the street chaos reigned.

Belle crouched down to Banks and quickly checked his throat for a pulse. "Weak, but it's there." Judging from his position, it seemed Banks had tripped headfirst into the path of the truck. A deep gash to his cheek was the only obvious sign of bleeding, and Belle kept the bodyguard's shirt pressed tight against the wound while Carrie ran her probing hand over the man's body, giving a running inventory of his injuries.

"Broken clavicle, three, maybe four ribs on his left side—"

Belle didn't want to move him because he'd likely suffered neck damage, but she also needed to see if the back of his head was bleeding. She gently slipped two fingers under his neck and followed up along the contour of his skull hoping to find nothing. Her hopes were dashed when she felt the thick sticky wetness. She pulled her hand away to see not only blood, but tiny chips of bone.

A young hysterical female voice shouted, "Ambulance is here!"

Someone behind Belle, maybe one of the bodyguards, shouted, "He moved! I saw him move!" A TV cameraman bullied through the crowd to record the gruesome scene.

Banks emitted a low groan, barely audible. Belle doubted the man could hear her, but she whispered, "Don't worry, you're going to be fine. Ambulance is here." She heard the squeak of gurney wheels as the paramedics approached from just a few feet away.

Banks's mouth moved in an odd open kissing motion, like a fish lying on a pier, struggling to breathe. Barely audible sounds—more squeaks than speech. Carrie bent close, her ear to the man's mouth.

"Back away!" the authoritative voice of one of the paramedics commanded.

Carrie and Belle stepped aside to let the paramedics do their work. They immediately snapped an oxygen mask over the man's nose and mouth and professionally immobilized him so he could be lifted onto the lowered gurney.

Banks's eyes flew open wide in an expression Belle could only describe as stark terror. For a moment, she was certain he focused on her. Then his eyes fluttered and closed. The paramedics and emergency room doctors would try their level best to save him, but in her gut she knew. Brad Banks was already dead.

Belle led Carrie through the crowd. "You okay?"

She appeared stunned, glassy-eyed, and spoke as much to herself as to Belle. "I was probably the last person in the world to hear Bad Banks's voice."

"What did he say?"

She turned to stare at Banks's body being lifted into an ambulance. "A name. Annie Grover."

***

The Sword of Justice nestled naked under the warm covers and spooned tighter to her man.

Like everyone else in the country, she'd spent the last few hours watching the TV coverage of Brad Banks's accident. She realized she'd gotten lucky. Again. Banks could've decided not to walk up the street to the theater and been delivered directly to the Egyptian's front door. Traffic could've been temporarily held up by the cops or been so clogged nothing moved. When devising her plan, she wanted a spectacle, but she knew the chances of Banks being in position at the exact moment a car drove down Main Street was a stretch.

She wasn't a fool, and as was the case with all of her targets she'd developed a Plan B for Banks—tainted champagne at the after-party. Not as spectacular, granted, but sufficiently effective. That Harrison's death was triggered by an earthquake, and Banks tripped into an oncoming truck—not a car but a *truck carrying shit and piss*—was continuing evidence God was on her side. Was she testing God's support by stacking the odds higher against herself? She had to admit the answer was yes. But her cause was just, and she trusted in Him to make it happen. And He did. She hadn't thought about the TV coverage, but fortunately, so far she'd seen no footage showing the crowd below the waist. No evidence that Banks had been intentionally tripped. Again, evidence of divine support.

She slowly rubbed her hips against Danny's butt, first one way then the other, signaling an invitation for a third round. She couldn't remember when she'd been so happy.

Her step-brother—step-cousin?—had been part of her life ever since Lucy had taken her in after her mom died. Six years older, Danny had stayed around after high school and supported himself by dealing drugs. Of course, Lucy and Ralph didn't know that because they were too stupid to notice that a kid supposedly working as a pizza delivery boy wouldn't make near enough money to buy an almost new Dodge Charger. *Could he be delivering something in addition to pepperoni pizza, Luce old girl?* Tall with dark, smoldering black eyes, Danny was gorgeous. He reminded her of a jungle cat—silent, lethal, ready to explode unmercifully at any provocation. She idolized him and considered him her true brother, a brother with benefits. He'd only visited once when she'd been enslaved inside the Juvie nut house, and it had cost her two packs of Marlboros to keep her roommate outside long enough for them to fuck each other's brains out.

When she'd been released, there'd been no doubt where she'd go—Utah. Danny had considerably expanded his business and operated out of Salt Lake. He also maintained a small condo in Park City both for pleasure and business, especially when the Hollywood assholes swarmed the place every January for Sundance.

His drug supplies proved a boon to her mission. Having sex with the disgusting jerk Harrison last year during his stag ski vacation had been a high but necessary price to pay. She hadn't told Danny, not because she was worried about him being jealous. She knew he had sex with women from time to time as part of his business. And that was all Harrison was; the business of imposing judgment on deserving scumbags. She'd known Harrison would be back this year like a panting puppy dog looking for more, and she'd need to be ready. Hooking him on crank was critical to her plan.

Danny stirred. She reached over his hip to help ready him but discovered he needed no assistance. He rolled over onto his back, eyes still groggy from sleep, offering a half-smile. She mounted him.

"You are insatiable."

Then a loud knock at the door.

"Sorry, Sis, business."

"You don't want to stay and play?" she cooed.

He gently rolled out from under her and, not bothering to dress, answered the door.

Danny's enforcers, Jello and the Dane entered—she called them the two stooges—along with Sonja, one of Danny's street sellers. She didn't like Sonja with her strung-out gaze and her fake tits, and the girl didn't hide the fact the feeling was mutual. She knew Danny had sex with Sonja but firmly believed it was only for physical relief. Like a massage, that's how Danny had put it. No big deal, he'd assured her. Not like how he felt about her. After all, they had a history going back over ten years. They were family.

"Sorry for interruptin', boss," Jello said.

"No problem."

"Hi, Maria," the Dane said.

She offered a slight nod. It was Danny's idea not to use her real name around the help. She chose "Maria." Danny knew why. He didn't know about the Sword of Justice. She hadn't been sure he would approve.

While he dressed, the two stooges couldn't keep their eyes off her naked body. She resisted the instinct to cover up. Let them see the fruit they'd never taste.

Danny slipped on his jacket and slid his stubby grilling fork into an inside pocket. She had never seen him use it, but she knew its purpose wasn't to flip steaks. While part of her found his use of the weapon abhorrent, she also understood that for him to be successful he needed to enforce strict loyalty.

Another moment and the four of them were out the door. No goodbye kiss, no "see you later." She knew Danny had to project a certain image to the stooges, and she was okay with that. In her heart she knew someday soon they'd be lying on an Italian beach with no one to bother them. Were there beaches in Tuscany? She'd have to check, but no matter. The key was they'd be together forever.

Scrunching down, she pulled the covers back up around her shoulders and breathed deeply. She could still smell him in the sheets and allowed herself several minutes to luxuriate in his essence before focusing on her next target.

So far, God passed each test she'd thrown at Him. The challenge to devise a mode of death even more unlikely, even more outlandish, was great fun. The plan for her next target would really push the envelope, and she was counting on the fact he, like most people, was a creature of habit. While God hadn't let her down yet, the timing and positioning of the weapon would need to be perfect. A million things could go wrong. This one would truly challenge Him.

She held the sheet up to her face and again breathed in Danny's scent. She wondered if her target might enjoy a little quickie with the wife tonight before nodding off. Part of her, the merciful part, wouldn't deny him that.

After all, it would be the asshole's last night alive.

Chapter Seven

B elle and Carrie were both glad to be back at the resort, surrounded by the relative solitude of the mountain at night, away from the media circus taking place in town after the death of Brad Banks.

Belle still hadn't resolved her situation with Carrie and hoped maybe witnessing Banks's death might've triggered a life-is-short moment in her mind, and she'd move on from the NoName incident. But she hadn't forgotten. During the patrol, their conversation could best be described as clipped and Belle could tell the "issue of her issues" hadn't disappeared.

They took a break for a quick coffee at the Summit. The lifts were about to close shortly, and they had the place to ourselves. Belle figured it was up to her to break the ice.

"You okay?"

Carrie cast her eyes down and didn't speak for a long moment. "I've tried over the last day or so to forget your...*reaction* when that jerk got pushy with me at NoName."

"*Got pushy?* Mauling you and grabbing your boobs seems a little bit beyond—" Belle stopped and mumbled, "Sorry."

Carrie's voice lowered to barely above a whisper. She peered down into her coffee. "I guess I need to know if I should worry about my safety."

Belle's first instinct was to blow her off, feed her some bullshit, apologize profusely, and swear it would never happen again. Except she knew she couldn't make that promise. Did she trust Carrie Palmer enough to tell her the truth?

Yeah, she did. Belle took a deep breath. "Have you ever heard of IED?"

Carrie raised her gaze, curious. "Sure. Improvised explosive device. Homemade bombs used by terrorists to blow up stuff in Iraq and Afghanistan."

"Actually, there are similarities." Belle paused. Did she really want to continue?

"Belle?"

Another deep breath. "IED stands for Intermittent Explosive Disorder. It's a condition where a series of stimuli can trigger disproportionate, uncontrolled rage in a person. Rage that usually continues unabated unless stopped by an outside force. Something or someone makes a normal person angry, and they turn into this raging monster. Some people call it the Incredible Hulk disease."

"A raging green monster that rains down death and destruction? Never much liked the Incredible Hulk. So, you have this IED?"

"Mild form, and for the most part I'm able to control it." Belle squirmed a little in her seat. "Sounds weird, but I feel like there's this...door in the back of my head. I call it the lizard door because it leads to the reptilian or limbic section, the oldest part of the human brain. It's what controls our primitive instincts of survival and aggression."

She paused and looked away. "I have to ask, Belle. Did you ever seriously hurt anyone?"

At first, Belle couldn't answer. *Did you ever hurt anyone?* Yeah, she hurt someone. Hell, she was responsible for the death of three of her best friends. "You knew I was in the Marines, but maybe you didn't know I spent time there in Force Recon."

"That's like Special Forces?"

"Kind of. Its motto is *Celer, Silens, Mortalis.* Swift, silent, deadly. That pretty much sums up its mission. Our primary job is gathering intel behind enemy lines, which sometimes includes capturing enemy combatants and interrogating them. I was one of only two women in the unit."

Carrie's eyes widened. "I assume by 'interrogate' you don't mean so-called enhanced interrogation."

Belle's throat tightened. "What constitutes enhanced can involve a lot of blurry lines."

Carrie appeared stunned. "Are you serious? My God. How could you—" She stopped, took a deep breath, and struggled to gather herself. "What happened?"

"Not sure you want to hear this."

"You're right. But at this point, I think I need to know."

Belle wrapped her hands around the porcelain coffee mug bearing the resort logo, blind to the possibility that the steadily increasing pressure might shatter it. "We were operating in the Zagros Mountains north of Mosul. One of my friends in the unit, an American son of Iraqi-born parents, spoke the language fluently. They sent him into town to snoop around. A bomb in the marketplace blew him to pieces. Happened the week before he was to ship home for good. We caught the man who planted the bomb.

"The C.O. planned to send three platoons through this narrow mountain pass the next day, and we'd received orders to make sure the pass was safe from an ambush. We needed to know from the prisoner where his fellow rats were positioned so we could clean them out that night. Our success rate was quite high in extracting this kind of information quickly and efficiently."

Carrie couldn't look at her.

"You want me to go on?"

She paused, then nodded.

"They tied up the prisoner inside a tent at our makeshift camp and I'd drawn guard duty to watch him before the questioning was to begin. After about ten minutes, the prisoner, Ahmed something-or-other, told me in broken English he had to take a crap. I pointed over to the corner of the tent. He lowered his pants, grunted a few times, then reached back and pulled a small knife wrapped in plastic out from his rectum. I was stunned and froze for a second. That was all he needed. He lunged at me and reached for the pistol on my hip. His knife missed my throat by a hair. He tried another slash, but this time I blocked his arm and the knife went flying. I leveraged his body, twisting him under me and pinned him to the ground. I was about to call for help but then he looked up at me, smirked, and said, 'I hear they serve your friend as hamburger tonight for dinner.'"

"You had to know he was baiting you."

Belle eased up on the coffee cup a bit. "You're right, of course. He wanted to die, collect his seventy-two virgins, and not provide us any useful intel. I should've waited for help but my IED tripped in. I beat his face to purple mush. By the time someone heard the commotion and entered the tent, Ahmed was dead."

All the color drained from Carrie's face. "Dear God."

Belle was no longer offering a sterile sit-rep to her CO. She took a deep swallow of coffee to loosen the growing lump in her throat. "The CO was livid and threatened a court-martial, but my platoon mates stood up for their sister and the CO decided he needed my gun—I was one of the best marksmen in the unit—if we were going to find the hostiles and clean them out. That night I led seven men up into the rocky terrain bordering the pass. Thanks to me, we had no intelligence concerning their specific whereabouts, and we walked into an ambush. Three of my men—my friends, my brothers—were killed. If I hadn't strangled Ahmed, there was a strong likelihood we would've learned the location of the hostiles, and three good men—boys really—would still be alive today."

"I'm sorry," Carrie said softly. "I know you were acting in self-defense."

She cast her eyes down and her voice lowered to just above a whisper. "But I could've stopped. Ricky Cohen, Sean Zielinski, and Charles Washington paid for my actions with their lives." At that moment Belle was talking to herself, not Carrie Palmer. "Ricky, he was the camp clown. Loved playing practical jokes. Charles was a big kid, always had a smile on his face. The Marines offered him an escape from the mean streets of Detroit. Sean joined because he couldn't afford college, and the Marines provided a ticket to an education. After he died I found his journal and kept it safe so I could return it to his parents. In his last entry, he wrote he was going out on another night patrol, but wasn't worried because his sister, Belle Bannon, would make sure he returned safe and sound."

Carrie didn't say anything immediately. She seemed to be downloading everything Belle had said, piecing it all together.

"Please say something," Belle said, still not looking at her.

Carrie finally murmured, "What happened at the court-martial?"

"Didn't happen. The politics of court-martialing one of the first women assigned to frontline combat didn't fit their PR narrative. But they needed to get me out of there because they couldn't take a chance on my condition putting my fellow Marines in danger again. And they were absolutely right. So they gave me an early medical discharge. I returned to Park City and took a job teaching high school English. One night after being there only a few months I caught the girls' softball coach behind the bleachers buck naked about to have sex with his fifteen-year-old star pitcher. I stopped him without the IED tripping in, but it was close. I reported what I'd seen to the principal and resigned on the spot for personal reasons. I couldn't take a chance I'd injure someone again."

"Then you became a hunting guide?"

"I figured not too many people I could hurt out in the wilderness." Belle drained the dregs of her coffee.

"Isn't it kind of rare for a hunting guide to be female?"

"Our numbers are growing every year, but, yeah, it's still unusual."

Carrie pushed. "And you never attacked anyone who didn't deserve it?"

"My dad moved us from Park City to a tough part of Pittsburgh when I was thirteen. Didn't take me long to get mixed up with the wrong crowd. When I was sixteen I bloodied up a gangbanger when he tried to force me to give him a blowjob."

Carrie's nose wrinkled in disgust. "Sounds justified to me."

"Problem was, my IED tripped in and I smashed his head in with a rock, almost killing him. He survived, but suffered permanent brain damage. Last time I heard he was bagging groceries at a Safeway. Landed me in juvie for a year. That's where I was diagnosed. The shrink tried to put me on drugs but they made me feel loopy, so I didn't continue."

"Wait. You're telling me you don't take any medication?"

"I keep a bottle of Prozac in the medicine cabinet but for the past year or so I haven't needed to open it. I use mental exercises they taught me. Then there's my quilting."

A half-smile creased Carrie's face. "Quilting? Really? Somehow, you don't strike me as the quilting type."

Belle chuckled. "I don't strike me as the quilting type either. "But the Marines made me go to these group therapy sessions, and several of the other participants recommended quilting as a way to keep the IED under control. The shrink said quilting would allow me to clear my mind of...of other stuff. I gave it a try and found I actually enjoyed it."

"Does it work?"

"Sometimes."

"And Peabody didn't have a problem with your...affliction? I'd think putting an armed employee with IED out in the wilderness alone with clients would raise liability concerns."

"I told Harlan—he's my boss—about the IED before he decided to hire me. I assured him that even an elevated level of pissed-off wouldn't trigger it and that I was working hard to keep the condition under control."

"Through quilting," Carrie said dryly, "and medications you don't take."

"He actually liked the quilting thing. After thinking about it for a few days, he decided to hire me on a probationary basis. Since then there have been no incidents. Nothing even close. And I've had to deal with more than a few assholes since I started." Carrie shifted in her chair and Belle sensed she was both fascinated and repulsed by Belle's story.

"What about your ski patrol gig? The resort's owned by a major corporation and I'd think they would have zero tolerance for any possibility of someone being injured or worse due to a rogue employee."

"I Didn't tell them. I figured the chances of a triggering event occurring on the ski slopes would be practically nil."

"But my life wasn't in danger at NoName, yet you almost killed that jerk simply because he grabbed my boobs."

"My trigger level is a little lower when I see people I care about being hurt or threatened." Belle locked eyes with her. "Carrie, listen. If you don't want to hang around me, I fully understand. But I swear I would never hurt you."

She turned away and gazed out the window, obviously deep in thought. Friendships always fascinated Belle. You can know lots of nice people who share your interests, yet they never become close friends. Who knows? Maybe it's primal. Like everyone has his or her own unique genetic undetectable pheromones that somehow only connect with a certain limited number of pheromones released by others. Length of exposure has little to do with it. Belle had only known Carrie Palmer a short time, yet their pheromone imprints fit. But after revealing her IED condition, Belle figured the chances were good that Carrie would now tell her it might be best if she kept her distance. Belle hoped she was wrong.

Finally, Carrie said in a kind voice, "Thanks for confiding in me. I know it wasn't easy. You gave me a lot to think about." She squeezed Belle's hand and glanced up at the clock. "We better get going."

Chapter Eight

Belle and Carrie waited in the gathering area at the top of the Silver Moon lift as a few snow flurries blew lazily around them. It was almost 9 p.m., and they'd need to start their sweep shortly, making sure all stragglers were off the slopes. Night skiers were particularly guilty of boarding the lifts at the last minute to squeeze in a final run.

The lift moving overhead was empty except for a man and woman riding together. The couple dismounted, a teenage girl riding a board and an older man on skis. Belle recognized Markie Dodd as she zipped down to the gathering area with the man straggling behind.

"Belle!"

"Hey, Markie."

"Hi, Ms. Palmer."

"Good to see you, Markie. It's Friday night, so I assume the gentleman following you is your dad." The man came to a stop next to Markie.

"This is my dad, Virgil Dodd. Dad, this is Belle. She keeps an eye out for me on the mountain, and Ms. Palmer, I'm in her chemistry class. They're both major awesome!"

Virgil appeared to be in his late forties, short like his daughter with a paunch. Hands were shaken all around. "Nice to meet you both. I've heard Markie talk about both of you. You've clearly made a positive impression. Since Markie's going away to college soon we've set aside these few hours every week for some father-daughter bonding."

"We read the story," Carrie said. "Heartwarming."

"It was supposed to be. Right, Dad?"

The deputy mayor shrugged, a bit embarrassed.

"I saw you both in the TV footage showing Brad Banks's accident," Markie said. "Wow, so horrible."

"And not the kind of publicity the town needs," Virgil added.

Belle was weary of hearing and talking about Brad Banks and wanted to change the subject. "So, Markie, what are you riding tonight?"

"Burton Custom X. A Christmas present."

Judging from Markie's gleeful expression, Santa's gift had been well received. "Cool. Well, you better get moving. We're going to start the sweep in a few minutes."

Markie bent over and buckled her boot to the board bindings. She waved, and daughter and father maneuvered across the flat terrain toward the top of Double Jack.

"Kids like Markie," Belle said, "they're what give me hope the future won't be completely fucked up."

"Careful," Carrie said with a half-smile. "People might think Belle Bannon's turning sentimental."

***

Markie Dodd loved night riding. Those who enjoyed the night sessions were mostly young snowboarders like herself, not the old, over-thirty skiers who didn't like the drop in temperature at the end of the day. Night riding meant freedom, an awesome feeling she never experienced during the day while having to navigate through the ancient ski crowd.

Except her dad was a skier, and she didn't consider him stodgy, not really. Their relationship had definitely improved over the last few months. Before that, the negative vibe at home had been super heavy. She wasn't stupid and knew her parents were having problems. She asked her mom about it several times and had been brushed off. But from overhearing snatches of conversation here and there, she suspected another woman could've been involved. She hoped not. She loved her dad, and the idea he might've cheated on her mom made her sick to her stomach. Thankfully, her parents must've patched things up because over the last two months her home life had returned to somewhat normal.

She'd spent most of the day working on her backside flips in the half-pipe then met her dad for a cup of hot chocolate at the base. They'd spent the last couple of hours running the slopes together. The official Dodd Friday night tradition, one she promised her dad they'd continue when she returned home from winter breaks. All her friends knew about it and after the article in the newspaper, all the locals knew about it, too. As deputy mayor, her dad took every opportunity to get his name in the papers, something she didn't particularly love. Still, she'd decided if the whole politico thing made him happy, so be it. A mark of maturity? She giggled to herself. She hoped not. Markie Dodd had every intention of maintaining her decidedly un-mature personality until she was way past the ancient age of thirty.

Much faster than her dad, she'd relish flying past him, then waiting impatiently at the bottom of a run for him to catch up. But since she was off to Boulder in August, she wanted to savor her remaining time with him and was surprised to discover she really did enjoyed the slow cruises.

She'd been riding since she was old enough to walk and preferred men's boards as they were stiffer and allowed her to be more aggressive. Now that she was a senior she wanted the best, and when she'd asked for a new board for Christmas, she knew her parents wouldn't disappoint. The Custom X could rip hard and fast, shredding the groomers, but was particularly designed for off-trail back-country powder. The X was totally awesome.

They reached a gentle slope, and she was able to gain a bit of momentum, cruising past her dad toward the top of Double Jack. Despite his pudgy body, Virgil Dodd was an excellent skier. Markie had fond memories of him teaching her how to ski when she was still in diapers.

The Double Jack run itself consisted mostly of moguls, rounded mounds of snow and ice the size of Volkswagens. During the day, Markie enjoyed zipping around and over these moguls but at night the long shadows from the lights sometimes made it difficult to see her cut line, slowing her down. Markie Dodd didn't do slow.

She led her dad down the Double Jack run for about forty yards then veered off to the right and slipped under the red out-of-bounds rope at the entrance to the trail running through the woods, parallel to the run. In a few moments, her dad followed.

Each afternoon before the night session started, the ski patrol strung the red rope across the entrance to the trail. They didn't want anybody accessing the trail through the trees because the lack of direct lighting could prove dangerous. The poor lighting didn't bother Markie. She'd ridden the trail so many times over the last decade she could do it blindfolded. Late that afternoon, they'd received a six-inch dump and from what she could see, no one else had ridden the trail since. She couldn't wait to carve some major phatties in the virgin snow.

When she first suggested the trail run to her dad she'd been surprised he had agreed. Bad enough for anyone else, but really daring for the Honorable Deputy Mayor of Park City, Utah to violate the rules. Markie suspected her dad might have broken more than a few rules when he was younger. She'd have to ask him about that one day. Markie slowed and allowed her dad to take the lead. "Age before beauty."

"Just remember, hotshot, you'll be old someday."

Markie laughed then followed him down the trail.

Bits of diffuse light from the Double Jack slope-lights filtered through the trees, and the dancing snow flurries created, in Markie's mind, an amazing fantasy world that grew more magical with her every turn. She loved it.

The trail run zigzagged around the thick pines as it steepened down the mountain. The Custom X was sick, allowing her to make sharp, quick cuts with little effort. The board seemed to have eyes of its own as she flowed easily down the trail.

Dead, broken branches jutted out from the trees like stubby arms. She loved the tree people, that's what she and her friends called them, as if they were old pals watching her pass by. The ski patrol made sure none of the branches impeded the trail. She'd taken a warm-up run first thing that morning and the trail had been clear. Out of the corner of her right eye she saw something move. Someone hiking through the thick underbrush at night? No way. Possibly a deer, but they usually didn't make it up this high and no one had seen a bear on the mountain in years. Probably just the broken fragments of light from Double Jack playing tricks.

She came around a familiar turn and saw her dad stopped, fiddling with his ski boot. "What's the problem?"

"Left boot's a little loose," he said. "Go on ahead, I'll catch up."

"Okay, see you at the bottom." She fired off, easily navigating the next sharp turn. Again, she sensed movement off to her right, and this time she was sure she saw a pinpoint of light. Someone up here with a flashlight? Suddenly, her isolation didn't feel so good. She decided to finish the trail quickly and turn back into the well-lit run. She shifted her weight and pointed the nose of her board forward, increasing her speed as she approached a mini-ledge defining a steep drop-off, her favorite part of the trail run. She prepared to launch from the ledge and catch some awesome air. For the moment she forgot about the light in the trees and decided to see how high she could go. She bent her knees then sprang up at the perfect moment. She felt the board leave the ground effortlessly like it was born to fly.

The exhilaration from sailing through the air past the thick dark pines lining her path like soldiers at attention was major awesome. She felt like a bird. Or maybe a superhero. Night Queen of the Forest.

She glanced down to pick out her landing spot. The tall pine on the left was familiar. The broken limb aiming at her like a thick, pointed spear was not.

Oh my God.

She tried to shift her weight mid-air, fully prepared for a controlled fall. She might suffer a few bruises, maybe even a cracked rib, but...

At first she felt no pain.

Curious, she looked down and saw the branch had impaled her gut clean through. She wiggled a little like a fish on a pike.

Then she felt the pain.

Black blood bubbled up into her throat, and her first scream came out more like a gurgle.

Her second scream was a rasp.

There was no third scream.

Chapter Nine

B elle's walkie buzzed. "Where are you guys?"

She quickly pressed the transmit button. "Near the top of Double Jack with Carrie. What's up?"

She heard urgency in Mick's voice. "Just received a call from 9-1-1 dispatch. The Deputy Mayor, kind of hysterical. Apparently his daughter's seriously injured. They're on the Double Jack side trail. We have a couple of sleds on the way up."

Markie? Every nerve in Belle's body snapped to attention. "On it."

They moved as fast as they could and reached the trailhead in less than two minutes. The red boundary rope lay in the snow.

"Markie's an excellent rider," Belle told Carrie. "Fast, but not reckless."

They sped off down the trail and stopped at the base of a crest leading to a steep drop-off. Belle was very familiar with this section of the path and loved to fly down the trail and use the crest to catch some serious air before landing on the downslope.

She led Carrie to the top of the crest. At first they didn't see anything, then in the shadows created by the dappling light filtering in from the main run she spotted—

Oh God, no!

She raced ahead and reached the girl who was completely impaled on the frozen dead pine branch, her board dangling from her feet. Virgil Dodd had his arms wrapped around his daughter and struggled frantically without success to pull her free. A thin film of snow covered Markie's body. Her goggles had been knocked aside and her eyes were wide open. Blood caked around her mouth and chin. With her arms askew and her body twisted, she looked like a marionette cut from its strings. *Wait. Did she blink? Or was the flickering light playing tricks?*

"She's still alive!" Virgil Dodd screamed. "Help me! Can't get her down! My baby girl..."

"We need to break the branch!" Carrie shouted.

Both she and Belle wrapped their hands around the branch. It looked like it had already been partially broken where it intersected with the trunk. The heavy wind at this altitude twisted and turned tree branches all the time. In this case, the tear had redirected the branch's lethal spearpoint into the trail. The branch felt slick and Belle knew it wasn't just from the ice. They summoned every ounce of strength and pulled down hard, but the branch wouldn't snap.

Belle returned to Virgil and they wrapped their arms around the girl's body. Belle's face was next to hers. She heard gurgling. Markie was trying to talk. *Jesus.*

"Markie?"

"Belle?" Her eyes tried to focus. She mumbled, "Tell Dad—"

"He's right here."

"...love Dad...Mom...lights. Someone in woods." Then another gurgle. Her body stiffened and her eyes sharpened, boring right through Belle.

"Belle...help me."

Belle bit her lip and struggled to hold back the tears. "Don't worry, honey. I will."

The girl's eyes dulled. She shuddered twice then fell limp.

"Get her down!" Virgil shouted. "Oh no...oh, God!"

Belle couldn't look away and struggled to stifle her tears. She'd seen death up close and personal. Too much of it, to be sure. Yet there was something about staring into the lifeless doll eyes of this innocent young girl that grabbed deeper into her gut.

"I said get my baby down!"

"I'm so sorry," Belle whispered. "She's gone."

Virgil pushed Belle aside and tugged on his daughter's body. The gnarled branch must've been caught on something, probably the girl's rib cage, causing a sickening but muffled tearing sound. Belle didn't want to try again. The last thing Virgil Dodd needed was to witness his daughter's body being further mutilated. In the distance, she could see the lights of the approaching snowmobiles.

Virgil cradled Markie's drooping head in his arms. He struggled with his words, a confession forcing its way through his heaving sobs. "I love you so much... My fault... God punishing... Should've been me."

"It was a horrible accident," Carrie whispered.

"Last run. She...she always let me lead for the last run. It was our little thing."

Belle thought encouraging him to talk might be a good idea. "What happened this time?"

He took a deep breath and tried to gather himself. "I had to stop to adjust my boot and she sped ahead. Jesus, it should've been me. We weren't supposed to go under the rope. If I'd only been a little more responsible. Oh, my baby girl..."

"Lots of people do it," Belle said.

His mood suddenly flipped to anger. "Someone could've warned her!"

"I don't under—"

"Somebody else was here ahead of us. Over there, with a flashlight." He pointed to the right where the darkness was all but complete.

"No one can ski there," Carrie said. "The underbrush is too heavy. What was this guy doing?"

"Who knows? But he could've warned her. When I find out who it is, I'm gonna kill the son of a bitch!" His demeanor flipped back to suffocating anguish. He dropped his head into his hands. "Dear God. I'm so sorry, baby. What am I going to tell Linda?"

The pain in his eyes could've eaten through a steel door. He buried his face into his dead daughter's shoulder. He was done talking. Within a few moments two snowmobiles approached, one pulling a sled that would transport Markie's body down the mountain to a stunned, grieving family.

The snowmobiles' headlamps lit up the scene. Belle spotted something she hadn't noticed before and made her way toward the base of the tree. Hard to tell, but it looked like letters scratched in the snow. An L, or could be an I, then either an E or F, an X, and what might've been an I. LFXI? LEXI? Maybe LETI? The lines were so crude they just as easily could've been imprints from dropped branches. She pulled out her phone and snapped a photo to check out later.

"What did you find?" Carrie asked.

"Probably nothing."

The snowmobile pulled directly over the markings, obliterating them before coming to a stop. Two medics jumped off the seat and rushed to the girl. A patroller from the second snowmobile shot photos of the scene while a fourth pulled an ax from the sled and, with a few whacks, cut off the branch at the trunk. Markie's body dropped into her father's arms. Belle couldn't look away. The soft falling snowflakes dusted her long eyelashes for a moment before melting. Her wide eyes stared straight at Belle, unblinking. *Belle... help me...*

Belle used her sleeve to wipe away the wetness from her cheek. It wasn't from the snow.

***

The Sword of Justice strapped her snowshoes to her back, stepped into the pair of skis she'd left on the edge of the unlit run, and moved quickly down the mountain, taking care to remain close to the bordering tree cover whenever possible. She'd already seen one ski patrol snowmobile moving up the mountain toward Double Jack. A second one approached, and she cut into the treeline behind a thick spruce. The snowmobile came so close she could almost reach out and touch it. Her whole body shook, and she struggled to hold back the tears. She paused to catch her breath.

Fuck! Virgil Dodd, not his daughter, was supposed to die. Virgil always skied first on the last run down the Double-Jack side-trail. Their tradition. Their thing. *It was in the fucking newspaper!* When Virgil paused to fix his boot—who the hell fixes his boot mid-run?—and the girl shot ahead, there was no time to rearrange the branch.

The idea for the branch came to her in the middle of the night. Virgil had caused the girl's destruction by screwing her, and the penetrating branch was meant to be a phallic symbol of his evil deed. She really didn't expect it to work—the odds seemed near impossible—and she had her Plan B ready as a backup. But it *did* work. *On a teenage girl.*

She gasped and paused to take a sip of vodka from the flask, her second and last. She was so distraught she could easily drain the flask dry, but denying herself what she wanted at any given moment was a good exercise to maintain self-discipline. She allowed the liquid to drizzle slowly down her throat. It didn't help. She was not a child killer, *she loved children.* My God, the whole point of her mission was to exact justice against those who hurt women and children. She tried to rationalize that Markie wasn't a child. The newspaper article said she was eighteen. If you're eighteen you can vote and sign shit, and if you mess up you go to big girl prison.

But it didn't help. She bent over and vomited into the snow.

God, that poor girl.

She stood up, her whole body shaking, and wiped her mouth with her sleeve. She had to talk to someone or she would explode. But who? There was only one person she trusted.

She hoped Danny would understand.

Chapter Ten

O nce she'd decided to unburden herself, the Sword of Justice couldn't wait an extra minute and drove straight from the resort.

She'd hinted a few times to him that maybe it would be convenient if she had her own key, but he hadn't responded. Probably she'd been too subtle. Or, given the nature of his business, he was hypersensitive about security. No problem, she understood. She knocked again, and this time heard someone moving inside. The door opened a crack. He was tense, his expression severe. She'd stood behind him when he answered the door on several occasions and knew he held a gun behind his back. When he saw her he relaxed, but only partially.

"I wasn't expecting you."

She promised herself she wouldn't cry, but the tears came anyway. She threw herself into his arms. "Oh, baby—"

He yanked her inside. "What's wrong?"

The words spilled out. "There's something I need to tell you, and I know I should've told you sooner, but I was worried—"

She looked over his shoulder and saw Jello, Sonja, and the Dane standing in the kitchen gawking at her like she was some kind of babbling idiot. She forced herself to stop crying and gently pushed away. "Sorry, didn't know you had company. I can come back."

Danny said nothing. Instead, he took her hand, led her into the single bedroom, and closed the door. Did the door click? No matter. The stooges wouldn't eavesdrop if they knew what was good for them.

He sat on the edge of the bed and pulled her close, his face, just inches from her breasts,

"Talk to me."

She bent over and kissed him. Suddenly she was overcome with a compelling desire to have him inside her, pounding away the pain. She pushed him back onto the bed. In seconds she was out of her clothes and astride him, reaching for his belt buckle.

He rolled out from under her and held her at arm's length. "Sis, talk to me."

Now she wondered if coming here was a good idea. She'd assumed because of his feelings for her he would be understanding and supportive, but maybe she'd miscalculated. Too late to go back. She took a deep breath. Her cause was pure, and her actions in furtherance of that cause were just. He would see that. After all, he was family.

"The Bible is the word of God. God says in the Book of Job, 'Be ye afraid of the sword: for wrath bringeth the punishments of the sword, that ye may know there is a judgment.' I am the Sword of Justice."

Then she told him everything.

***

She slid off him and gulped for air. Sweat oozed from every pore. *Holy shit, that was the best sex of my life. Period, end of sentence.*

When she'd explained the reasons for her mission and told him about Harrison and Brad Banks and the girl, he hadn't said a word. She didn't know whether he was going to strangle her or screw her. Fortunately, he chose the latter.

She absently trailed a fingernail along the length of him. "So, you're not mad? You don't think I'm crazy?"

"Maybe a little." It seemed like he was speaking to himself.

"You're a little mad, or I'm a little crazy?"

"Both." He grinned for the first time since she arrived, a signal she hoped meant everything was good. "And don't feel too bad about the girl. Her father will experience that pain every day for the rest of his life, much better than a quick death."

Now she knew coming to see him was the right thing to do. She nestled her head against his chest. "Thank you."

"Why did you choose now to kill these people?" His tone had changed. Businesslike.

She had no problem answering. "I knew Harrison and Banks would be here for Sundance. The others I could've chosen anytime. But I figured it was better to do them all together, to exact justice with one single sweep of the sword, and then move on with my life."

"I need to know if you are under suspicion. Is there any chance the cops are on to you?"

She could respond to that question quickly, without reservation. "No. I've made them all look like accidents." The image of her carvings in the snow where Markie Dodd was impaled flashed through her mind. Maybe she shouldn't have done that, but she wanted Virgil to see the name as life sapped out of him. She purposely made the letters look like they'd been formed by dropping twigs and doubted anyone would—

Belle. The hairs on the back of her neck locked to attention. Belle might notice. She hadn't mentioned carving the name of Virgil's victim to Danny, and now she was glad. He wouldn't be happy if he knew she might've left a clue. But she did need to warn him about Belle. "The only person who's been sniffing around is Belle Bannon."

He showed his surprise. "From the ski patrol?"

"Yeah, although that isn't her main job. She's a hunting guide. Belle was first on the scene. Now that I think of it, Belle's been on the scene in each case."

"If Bannon gets too close, we can deal with her for you."

She was about to respond when he rolled over on top of her. Her body stepped in front of her mind. "Mmmm, ready so soon?"

"That's what you do to me." Definitely not businesslike.

She locked her legs around him. She wanted to talk to him about Tuscany, but that could wait for another day.

***

Danny Pags kissed his step-sister goodbye, closed the door, and turned to his crew. "You heard?"

They all nodded.

Jello seemed the most concerned. "I don't know, boss, taking out three people in a few days, that could be a problem. We know you like her, but if she gets caught some lawyer could get her to dime us. And let's face it, she's an amateur."

Danny said, "Problem is, she's a little—"

"Nuts?" Sonja offered.

The Dane, who rarely spoke, asked, "How many more?"

"Who the hell knows? She thinks she's on some kind of mission from God exacting revenge for what happened to her mother and her great-great-grandmother."

The Dane shook his head. "Jello's right, boss. *Helt Vildt.*"

"What's that mean?"

The Dane actually flashed a half-smile. "Nutso."

"Unpredictable ain't good," Jello said. "What would make her stop?"

Danny stopped spinning. "Let me think about it."

"What about this Bannon bitch?" Sonja asked.

Danny hadn't forgotten their run-in on the slopes. The woman wasn't hard to look at, but she thought she was the fucking FBI. "I'll think about that, too. The Hollywood assholes will only be in town another week or so. Time for you all to get back to work."

Without another word, Sonja and the stooges left, and Danny Pags resumed slowly spinning back and forth, his mind racing. Bannon sniffing around his sister could ultimately be a problem for him. His lips curled into a cold smile. But a problem easily solved.

Chapter Eleven

T he butterflies had taken up residence and were flapping their wings like crazy inside Belle's stomach. She felt like she was teetering on the edge of a skyscraper roof as she looked straight down Black Lightning's vertical drop.

An hour earlier, during their usual coffee break at the Summit before the final sweeps, the patrol office had called. They'd received a report of what appeared to be lights along Jupiter Ridge leading to the Black Lightning run. Last year Belle had been the only one willing to attempt Lightning at night to search for a missing skier. She'd found him unconscious and mangled, sprawled up against one of the menacing black boulders lethally positioned in the middle of the run. If she hadn't made the rescue, the man would've died. Even got her picture in the paper posing with the skier and the smiling mayor handing her a citation.

So when the call came reporting suspicious lights on the ridge, she understood why she was the one they'd dispatch to check it out. Despite Carrie's strong protests, Belle had sent her back down the mountain then headed for the patrol cabin where the patrollers kept backup gear. The liftie reported only a few skiers had used the lift during the day before he shut it down. The night was unseasonably warm with little wind, so Belle supposed it was possible for someone to remain on the mountain for five hours, but she fully expected I'd find nothing.

At the patrol cabin, she'd switched skis and strapped snowshoes to the back of her pack then skied the short distance over to the Jupiter lift. The lift provided the only access to the top of Jupiter Ridge for anyone wanting to ski the bowl or the Black Lightning run from the top of Jupiter Peak. To access the Peak a skier had to hike along a narrow ridge uphill through heavy powder. That's where the lights were reportedly seen. Expert skiers brave enough to attempt Lightning couldn't make the trek on skis, so they carried snowshoes to travel along the ridgeline.

Belle strapped on the snowshoes and began the trek up to the top of Black Lightning. Night skiing was never permitted on the Peak, and only the moonlight reflecting off the snow allowed her to see ahead. Her trek up the slope slowed as the ridge steepened, and she had to pause several times to catch her breath. The hike also offered more time to think about everything that had happened.

After leaving the scene of Markie's accident, she and Carrie had been herded into the resort's offices where they met with police and company officials. Markie's mom arrived soon after and along with her husband was understandably inconsolable. Belle felt so sorry for both of them and repeatedly assured Virgil the accident wasn't his fault.

Belle had decided not to tell the police about the scratches in the snow. After checking the photo, what she thought could've been intentionally drawn letters appeared to be nothing more than simply irregular markings caused by dropping branches. Virgil Dodd said he might've seen somebody off the trail, but that was highly unlikely. Was it even possible someone could've intentionally redirected the tree branch? Again, highly unlikely.

But possible?

Markie's voice echoed inside Belle's head. *"Help me...."* One thing was certain. If by any chance someone murdered Markie Dodd, Belle wouldn't rest until the bastard responsible was brought to justice one way or the other. If she had her way it would be the other.

Three deaths in four days. Though Belle knew of no evidence to suggest the deaths were related, she couldn't shake the feeling in her gut telling her maybe they weren't accidents.

No more time to think about anything else than surviving Black Lightning. Belle inched closer to the edge. The run was never groomed, and the few who skied it weren't looking for a safe groomer anyway. To them the allure was the death-defying drop, the challenge of the uneven, sometimes shoulder-deep powder, near impossible sharp cuts, and the ominous boulders jutting up through the snow like shark's teeth, thrusting toward you at every turn, ready to smash your body to dust if you made one split-second mistake. The problem was the unexpected. You could blast out of powder so loose it sprayed up into your face then suddenly slide into uneven crud filled with "chocolate chips," small sharp rocks protruding up from the snow that would fillet your skis tip-to-toe in a nanosecond then find yourself skidding down "bulletproof" —sheet ice so called because it was hard enough to repel a bullet.

Belle scanned the continuation of the ridge and the first part of the drop but saw no sign of life. The ridge ended shortly beyond the ski run in a thick stand of pines. Beyond the trees were an unmanned weather station and a narrow maintenance road leading down from the station to the base. But no skier would've gone beyond the run. The patrol office had confirmed no one was visiting the weather station, and the light sightings were in all likelihood a false alarm. Certainly not the first time.

One other possibility existed. —an adventurous skier embarked down Lightning and didn't make it. Cell phones didn't work well up here, so if someone was hurt, waiting until daylight could easily mean the difference between life and death even in the milder temperatures. Black Lightning was the only way down so no use wasting any more time.

Belle rode a pair of Dynastar Cham 107s. The Chams, her shortest pair, also contained side-cuts to make quick turns easier. She shuffled the skis until the tip extended out into the air over the edge of the vertical drop. Not sure why she was so hesitant. She'd skied the run before and intended to proceed very carefully.

Something caught her eye in the treeline. Movement? Probably a crit—

Crak.

The left side of her helmet blew apart.

She froze for a moment, unable to process what had just happened. Then another shot pinged into a rock at her feet. Her heart raced from zero to warp speed in an instant. Instinct took over. She locked her fingers around the pole grips and propelled herself over the crest into the night air.

The drop seemed to last forever before her skis touched the surface. She couldn't see. The remaining portion of her helmet had twisted, covering her right eye and her goggles had been knocked askew. Muscle memory took over and she dug the ski edges into the uneven ice, effecting a sharp right turn to avoid what she remembered to be a boulder on the left. She planted her right pole to make the turn and the sudden movement caused the helmet to slip around, covering more of her face. She used her left hand to rip off what remained of the helmet and tossed it into the darkness. Because her goggles were attached to the helmet, they went sailing as well, and she had no ability to protect her eyes from flying powder and ice.

Ping.

Another shot ricocheting off a boulder on her right. Only one option—race down the mountain as fast as she could. Even with the moon lighting the scene, the shooter would have a difficult time gaining a bead—

Crak.

The sound came from below her. *Two shooters.* She was caught in a crossfire.

Normally she'd be able to see powder stashes ahead and adjust her ski pressure in anticipation. Now she could barely make out the boulders looming on each side of the run, much less see abrupt changes in the snow conditions.

Her skis hit a wall of deep powder and it felt like someone reached up out of the snow and grabbed her ankles. She tumbled forward, her head planting in the snow. Fortunately, the powder acted as a cushion. If she'd landed on the ice without a helmet her head would've split open. She rolled down the hill head over heels for thirty yards before she could swing her feet below her, dig in her edges, and skid to a stop. The only good news was the high spray of snow caused by her fall prevented whoever was shooting from taking dead aim.

Belle rolled to an upright position. Her pulse raced even faster. Somehow her skis remained on her feet, but she lost a pole. *Great. What else could go wrong?*

Ping.

Stupid question.

She swept down the slope shooting through the powder to more crud—uneven snowpack littered with ice chunks the size of baseballs. The descent steepened further. She made out the blurry image of the "Sentinels" up ahead—two boulders seemingly forming an impregnable wall across the run. She'd skied the run before at a much slower speed, and without bullets flying in all directions about to pulverize her brain at any moment. She knew the boulders were slightly staggered, so it was possible to carefully navigate through a narrow icy passageway between them. Normally, skiers would come to a complete stop well in advance of the boulders then slowly slide through the passageway before continuing down the mountain. But this was hardly a normal situation.

The passageway ran left to right, which meant she'd have to execute a sharp right turn. After switching her remaining pole to her right hand, she decided to risk slowing down a little—

Ping ping ping. Bullets ricocheted off the Sentinels.

She tried to swallow, but her mouth was too dry. Blood pumped through her body with the force of a firehose.

Slowing down wasn't going to work.

The first Sentinel rushed toward her like a huge black monster ready to crush every bone in her body. She looped to the left as far as she could then planted hard. The right edges of her skis cut deep into the snow, snapping her around the pole and hurling her into the narrow passage. The speed of the turn widened its radius, preventing her from entering the passage clean. She yelped out in pain as her left shoulder slammed into the side of the second boulder then bounced her back against the first boulder like a pinball. The sharp edges of the rock ripped through the white cross on the shoulder of her red patrol jacket and sliced across her cheek. Ironically, the narrowness of the passage kept her upright—there was no room to fall— and she whooshed through the Sentinels to an icy drop. Her skis skidded in opposite directions, but by lifting her left ski she was able to regain her balance. This part of the run started wide with no boulders, but it also left her completely exposed.

Crak.

Best she could tell that shot came from her left. She figured it highly unlikely shooters lined the entire run, so her best chance was to ski to the bottom as fast as she could and hope that the speed and the poor visibility would make it difficult for whoever was trying to kill her. Looming ahead, the slope funneled to the steepest section of the run—Bode's Chute, named after Olympic skier Bode Miller.

Another shot. Could be her imagination, but the sound seemed farther away. She felt a moment of elation. Maybe she'd outrun them.

Ping.

Maybe not. The bullet smacked into a boulder just ahead, guarding the entrance to the chute. If she could make it to the chute, the severe drop should protect her from the shooters. All she had to do was survive the chute with one pole...

Then the moon slipped behind the clouds; someone turned out the lights.

The black was blacker on her right. Had to be the entrance boulder. She veered left, her skis dropped, and for a moment she was airborne in the chute. *Where are the boulders? The cuts? How many seconds do I have before my first turn?* She knew she was moving too fast and needed to slow down, but the chute wasn't wide enough to slow her speed by traversing the slope. She whipped her skis around so they were perpendicular to the fault line and attempted a hockey stop, but she hardly slowed and skidded fast down the chute, heading toward another vague round black shape directly ahead. Breaking out of the stop at the last moment, she cut right, bounced off the boulder, but remained upright. Again her skis dropped. She now was in the steepest part of the chute, a vertical plate of ice streaked with heavy crud. No time or room for stops or turns. She simply skied.

What seemed like hours but could've only been a few minutes later, the slope leveled out. She felt as much as heard the rip. Her left ski slid across a chocolate chip slicing the ski down the middle from the binding to the tail. The ski shot out from under her. She flipped into the rock-studded hard-pack and rolled fast down the slope, losing her other ski in the process. Another boulder rushed her...

Her scream diffused into the wind as her body smacked into the rock. Sharp pain beginning at her ribs and hip immediately washed over her whole body. Momentary blackness, then the blackness faded into scattered points of light swimming in all directions as if searching for purchase. She opened her eyes and gasped for breath. Her entire body felt like a giant bruise, but a quick inventory suggested all extremities were still attached and seemingly in working order. Using her remaining ski pole as a crutch, she crawled to her feet. When she reached for her walkie, every muscle in her arm and shoulder protested. She pressed transmit.

A voice, tinny and small, responded to the walkie's squawk. "Belle?"

She could barely speak, and her voice came out as a ragged whisper. "Hey, Mick."

"You okay?"

She couldn't believe she was still alive with all of her key body parts attached.

"Belle? You okay up there?"

"Not exactly."

Chapter Twelve

B elle plucked another nacho from the dwindling mound in the center of the table.

"I can ask for another order," Carrie said wryly.

"Only if you want more."

She chuckled. "Uh, I've only eaten two so far."

Belle's laugh was cut short by the ripples of pain washing through her bruised body. "Sorry." She drained her second vodka down to the ice, eliciting a slurp much louder than she expected.

"No problem," Carrie said, this time more sympathetically. "You probably burnt a couple thousand calories up there. Sure you're okay?"

"That's the hundredth time you asked." Belle tamped down the urge to roll her eyes. "I appreciate your concern, I really do, but again, I'm fine."

"Fine" might be a stretch. After hearing Belle's story, Mick had radioed ahead to the police. Kip picked her up on Pioneer Ridge and transported her down to the resort's on-site clinic. Despite her loud protests, he'd strapped her into the gurney sled rather than allowing her to ride behind him on the snowmobile saddle. The young doctor on duty had determined the cut on her cheek wasn't deep enough for stitches and fortunately, her aches and pains resulted from muscle trauma.. Nothing broken and even more important, no bullet holes. After a couple of butterfly bandages and three prescription-strength ibuprofen, he'd released her with instructions to take it easy for a few days.

Take it easy? Belle was pissed.

Carrie had been there with a couple of Park City's finest to greet her when she exited the examining room. The police advised they couldn't send anybody up to Jupiter Ridge looking for clues till daybreak due to the treacherous conditions. They'd blocked off the maintenance access road and officers were posted at the bottom of the runs, but it was too late. The bad guy guys had gotten away.

Despite Carrie's pleas that she go home and rest, Belle wanted food and a stiff drink more than sleep, so they ended up at the Baja Cantina at the resort base to address her immediate needs.

"I still can't believe it," Carrie said. "Why would anyone try to kill you?"

"No idea."

Carrie pointed to the widescreen TV hanging behind the bar. "Belle, look. It's us."

Because CNN happened to be on the scene for a Sundance premiere, the network appeared to have the most extensive coverage of the accident and now re-ran footage of the crowd hovering around Banks's body sprawled on the pavement by the truck wheel. The camera avoided showing the body, but through the crowd, Carrie's back could be seen as she bent over Banks. The face of one of the bodyguards filled the screen. Belle had seen the video that morning but this time watched more intently.

The interview began with a question from a breathless blonde reporter, her makeup impeccable, who could hardly contain her excitement. Belle suspected she normally covered the entertainment beat and was in town for the festival when the story of the century—at least for this week—fell into her lap. "Al, can you tell us what you remember moments before the accident?"

The bodyguard clearly wasn't used to being the one in front of the cameras. "Uh, we did our best to keep the fans back, you know, close enough for pictures, but not too close, but there was so many fu—friggin' people it was impossible, and when Mr. Banks decided to cross the street he didn't tell us so we was a few steps behind and then he tripped just as the truck was comin' down the hill. The driver, he tried to stop and he wasn't goin' fast or nothin', but it happened so quick and..." The bodyguard shook his head, trying to find the right words. "Bad juju, man. Real bad juju."

The picture changed to a slow, frame-by-frame progression of the scene showing the crowd moving along behind Banks, as he tried to cross Main Street. The HD picture quality was very good but showed nothing below the waists of the tightly packed fans. All the networks had broadcast the moments leading up to Banks's death in slow motion, and there was no shortage of fans from the crowd anxious to appear on TV as witnesses to the event. Yet even with witness testimony, video of the scene from both the network cameras, and over three dozen cell phones, no clear camera shot emerged showing how Banks tripped. Some believed he tripped over the legs of crowding fans, others saw the press of the crowd pushing the bodyguard into the star. CNN continued its frame-by-frame presentation while their go-to forensics expert offered his profound opinion: "In the end, Marcia, we just don't know."

The video showed Banks pausing for selfies with several fans as he moved toward the street. Carrie again pointed to the screen. "Directly behind the bodyguard. Is that the guy who was juggling knives?"

The juggler, part of the crowd pressing behind Banks's bodyguard, appeared only for a few seconds before the bodyguard tripped forward. For a moment, Banks dropped below the screen then the camera picked him up again as the star fell forward directly into the path of the truck.

Carrie couldn't pull her eyes away. "The juggler's hood and makeup make him impossible to identify. This is going to sound crazy, but could he have intentionally tripped Banks? Or tripped the bodyguard into Banks?"

"Anything's possible," Belle murmured, not particularly interested at the moment. She'd seen all of the Brad Banks videos and interviews and analyses she needed, thank you very much, and was more consumed with identifying who wanted to blow her head off.

Carrie pressed. "Belle?"

Belle glanced up at the screen. She didn't want to get sucked back into the Brad Banks incident but Carrie seemed insistent. "There's no video footage below the waist, so no way of knowing for sure. And if the juggler intended to kill Banks, he'd have to know Banks was going to be on the street at the same time a truck would be coming down the hill. That's a hell of a huge stretch."

Carrie snatched the last nacho from the plate. "Actually, not completely far-fetched. Banks's movie was premiering and his appearance at the premiere was common knowledge. The news report said he spent the night at the Park City Hotel, so again it was predictable his driver would be coming up the hill, meaning Banks would at least have to cross the street to the theater."

Belle had to give her that. A knot of disquiet twisted in her gut. "And traffic on Main is crazy that time of day during the festival. Whether Banks fell into a truck or a car, the result would likely have been the same. Best case, he would've been seriously injured.

Now, does that mean he was murdered? Highly unlikely, but maybe you're right. Not completely impossible."

"So should we suggest the police question the juggler?" Carrie asked. "Just to make sure."

"They'd have to find him first. The hoodie, silver makeup, and sunglasses would make a facial ID impossible. And then there's the issue of motive, which brings me to the name Banks whispered to you before he died—Annie Grover."

"I *thought* that's what he said," Carrie corrected. "Look, we were in the middle of a human tornado of screaming people. Horns honking, sirens blasting. Total chaos. I easily could've been mistaken."

"Three deaths in four days," Belle said. "Harrison does a back dive off a chair lift and says a woman told him to ski a deadly ski run while he's tweaked on crank. He repeats the word, 'rover.' Then a big Hollywood star trips into an oncoming truck and whispers the name of a woman, Annie Grover. I don't know whether he was high, but—"

"*People* magazine reported last year he's been in and out of drug rehab."

"*People* magazine? Really?"

"Hey, when I'm waiting at the dentist's office I like to read Hollywood trash as much as the next person. But Annie's last name raises an obvious question. When you heard Harrison say, 'rover,' could it have been Grover? Is it possible this Annie Grover is somehow connected to both Harrison and Banks?"

Belle shrugged. "The only possible common denominator is drugs. During the festival drugs, mostly cocaine and meth, are as easy to obtain as an ice cream cone. We know Harrison was high on meth, and thanks to your impeccable source, we know Banks was no stranger to drugs as well. Both Harrison and Banks mentioned a woman. Maybe Annie Grover was their local supplier."

"But that doesn't account for Markie Dodd," Carrie said.

The simple mention of Markie's name flashed the image in Belle's mind of an amazing young woman dying on the cold, snowy mountain, her last words begging for help. Belle shivered, but didn't think Carrie noticed.

"And none of it explains someone trying to kill you unless they thought you were getting too close to the truth," Carrie continued.

"Truth about what?"

"My point is, who kills people whose testimony can put them in jail?" She jabbed her finger toward the tabletop between them. "Bad guys. And who are our most likely bad guys? Drug dealers. This guy Danny Pags has a run-in on the slope with you. He thinks about it and decides you might encourage the cops to bird-dog him for drug charges. It's possible the two shooters were instructed not to kill you but to spook you so you'd have a fatal, or at least debilitating, accident on Lightning. There would be no evidence of shots fired, and you'd be either dead or out of commission."

"If they were just trying to spook me, they're lousy shots. The first bullet almost tore my face off."

"That said, other than the fact maybe two of the victims could've been customers of Danny Pags, there's still no evidence that the three deaths were anything but unfortunate accidents."

"Logically, it's hard to argue. But my gut is sending contrary signals."

"How accurate is your gut?"

Belle waved at the server to order another plate of nachos and a vodka refresher. "Fifty-fifty."

"Not exactly overpowering odds," Carrie said dryly. "And the threshold question. Why aren't you leaving the detective work to the professionals? As you learned tonight, getting involved can be very dangerous."

Belle... help me...
Don't worry, honey, I will.
"Just something I need to do."

Chapter Thirteen

Belle and Scout wound their way through the crowds down Main Street. The town had an old leash law on the books, but nobody followed it, and Scout stayed tight at her heels with no problem. They reached the familiar weathered sign overhanging the narrow sidewalk: *Salvatore G. Marino, Attorney at Law.*

They entered to see Sal's secretary at her familiar post behind her desk in the small reception area. The aroma of fresh coffee and sugar doughnuts filled the air. Scout headed directly for Dora's desk drawer where she always kept a bag of bacon treats just for him.

She scratched his head and offered two strips. He devoured them almost instantly. "You look more like your mama than that white ruffian who violated her in the dead of night."

While Dora expressed outrage that one of her prize Newfie bitches had been set upon by the local riffraff, she adored Scout and though she wouldn't admit it, Belle believed she liked him as much as her Newfie purebreds.

"Morning, Dora."

In a town where exercise and good eating habits resulted in one of the nation's healthiest populations, Dora was the exception. She was big, loved doughnuts, and didn't care what anybody else thought. Bell slumped down into her uncle's uncomfortable reception chair.

"Please don't take this the wrong way, sweetie," Dora said, "but you look like..." Her voice dropped to a whisper. "S-h-i-t."

Belle shifted in the chair to get more comfortable and winced from muscle pain radiating down her back. "I look better than I feel." She hadn't been able to sleep. After several hours of tossing and turning, as a last resort, she tried a few selections from the vodka family of clear liquids. She figured while the hooch might dull her senses and make her more vulnerable to the people wanting to kill her, trying to function with no sleep would be worse. Unfortunately, her senses remained un-dulled, and now along with lack of sleep she had a bitch of a headache and pain from what seemed like a single body contusion running from head to toe.

Dora nodded toward her computer screen. "Story on Markie Dodd's accident is trending."

Belle wasn't surprised. The human-interest element of Markie's tragic death would naturally spark curiosity. A vivacious young girl about to head off to college, her future bright, her whole life ahead of her, is skewered by a dead tree branch like a shish kebab. The story was ready-made for combat cable news: *Was she wrong to ski in a roped-off area? Was Deputy Mayor Dodd responsible? Was the company liable? Is the Park City ski resort safe? We have experts on all sides of these issues. Stay tuned!*

Belle's thoughts were interrupted when the front door opened and Sal entered. "Morning, Isabella."

Uh-oh. When he used Belle's full name she knew he wasn't happy. After pouring himself a cup of coffee, he plopped down in the second reception chair.

Dora must've sensed something was wrong because she quickly tried to lighten the mood. "I swear, every time I see you two together I can't believe you're related."

Belle could see her point. Sal barely stood five and a half feet tall and looked so Italian he could've starred in pizza commercials. By contrast, she was almost six inches taller, and her light complexion evidenced that her late father's Irish DNA had ruled her gene pool. "Hey, my mom looked even more Italian than Sal."

Sal ignored the genealogy analysis, and his stern expression didn't alter. "So, is there any reason why you didn't call me last night to say someone tried to kill you on Black Lightning?"

Dora's eyes bulged. "What?"

Belle cringed. "Sorry. I intended to tell you this morning. The police said the chances of finding evidence are nil. It's also possible they didn't want to shoot me, just spook me."

"Sure you're okay, honey?" Dora asked.

"Fine." *Well, sort of.*

Sal motioned her back to his office, closed the door, and took a seat at his desk. "Okay, at the risk of asking the obvious, why would anyone want to kill you?"

"I honestly don't know. Probably mistook me for someone else."

Sal's eyes bore into her. "In my experience, violence usually partners up with sex or drug problems. I highly doubt you're having an affair with another woman's husband, which leaves drugs."

"I'm not involved with drugs," Belle said stiffly.

"What about your IED? Did you hurt or embarrass someone, someone crazy enough to want to kill you? I understand you had a confrontation with a Woodie at NoName."

"He was a bully who assaulted my friend. I doubt if he would go that far."

"Do the cops know about him?"

"Probably not."

"Then tell them." Sal leaned back in his chair and sighed. "Your aunt and I love you very much. Every day when you were overseas we were worried sick you might not come back. Now that you're here, we want you safe. Not to mention with both your parents gone you're the only immediate family your little sister has. Promise you won't take any unnecessary risks."

Depends on one's definition of "unnecessary." "Promise."

"Okay, change of subject. Markie Dodd. How do you think it happened?"

Given her just-granted promise to steer clear of risk, she decided to keep any suspicions, however small, to herself for the time being. "She must've jumped, not seen the branch, and landed full force. The branch protruded out onto the trail like a spear, and because of the hill, there was no way to see the branch until it was too late. Even if she hadn't jumped, there's a good chance she would've run into it." Belle sounded like she was reciting a police report that completely ignored the hurt she felt inside.

"Likely the wind pushed the branch over into the trail before she reached it," Sal said. "Branches are always shifting in those pine woods."

"The trail was open during the day and no one was injured, so it's likely that—"

Dora's shrill voice pierced the office door. "Dear God, look at this."

Belle and Sal returned to the reception room and gathered around Dora's computer where a full-color photo of Markie Dodd's impaled body filled the screen. The harsh light of the police flash camera gave the image a cheesy, surreal look. Belle's stomach wrenched.

"You okay, honey?"

"Not really."

Dora removed her Bible from a desk drawer, held it in both hands close to her face, closed her eyes, and mumbled what must've been a prayer.

"Who posted it?" Sal asked.

"Amen," Dora murmured before setting the Bible down on her desk. "GAB."

Glitter and Blood was a website that somehow obtained shock-value pictures, mostly of celebrities in trouble, but now and then would throw in a grisly crime scene photo.

"How could they get that photo so quickly?" Sal asked.

"That's their job," Dora replied. "It's already gone viral."

Belle turned away and swallowed hard in a futile attempt to dissolve the growing lump in her throat. "Bad enough to lose a child. Then the whole world sees the grisly remains of what once was a young, beautiful girl. Her parents must be in agony." She assumed the patroller who took the photos of the scene sold his pictures to SAB for big bucks. If so, he'd never show up on the mountain again because he'd have to face his colleagues, and that conversation wouldn't be pretty.

"Right on top of Sundance," Sal added. "Crazy."

Belle's muddled mind returned to the scratches in the snow. Maybe she should've shown the photo to the police. Harrison, Banks, and now Markie. Could it even be conceivable there was a connection? None of the victims had anything in common. Her eyes drifted around the room and landed on Dora's computer screen: *Deputy Mayor's Daughter Killed in Freak Accident.*

"Story says Virgil was supposed to be skiing ahead of his daughter," Dora said. "If he hadn't stopped to tighten his boot, he would've been the one killed. My God, can you imagine the guilt that man must feel?"

Belle remembered Carrie's description of the newspaper article where Virgil detailed their new last run tradition. Which meant if the three deaths were connected by something other than proximity of time, two of the "intended" victims were politicians and the third was a well-known celebrity.

Belle reviewed the cases in her head, trying to conceive of a way they could've been homicides instead of accidents. Harrison only killed himself because he was hopped up on meth. Someone could've given him the drug, but there would've been no way of knowing a small earthquake would hit, much less hit at the exact time Harrison was on the ski lift. But he'd told Belle that he was on his way up to ski Black Lightning, a promise he'd made to a woman. As Carrie said, a beginner skiing Black Diamond, even with the clearest of minds, would've likely been killed or suffered serious injury. So if a woman jacked Harrison up on meth and somehow persuaded him to ski down Black Lightning at night in heavy winds and blowing ice...yeah, that constituted murder in Belle's book. Unlikely, but possible.

"Belle?"

Brad Banks fell into a moving truck. Could he have been intentionally tripped? Yes. And someone who learned from the newspaper that Virgil Dodd would be leading his daughter down the trail on the last run Friday night could've maneuvered the pointed tree branch so it would spear the man coming over the hill.

"Either your mind's churning or you're in post-traumatic shock," Sal said.

Belle put her train of thought on hold and turned to Sal. "Virgil Dodd told me he thought he saw someone along the trail as he skied by."

Sal's gaze sharpened. "What are you suggesting?"

"Too crazy to discuss now," Belle muttered. . "But if someone *was* there, then footprints might still exist."

"What about the snow last night?" Dora asked.

"The trees are pretty thick along that trail and can act as an umbrella. It's possible remnants of any footprints could remain visible." She headed for the door. "Scout, let's go."

He didn't move and by his expression made plain that he was sticking close to the lady with the bacon, thank you very much. Belle offered the only thing he loved more than bacon. "Want to go for a snow ride?"

His tail thumped a steady beat on the wooden floor.

She saw her uncle was about to speak, so she beat him to it. "Don't worry. No unnecessary risks. I remember." Belle flashed a smile and was out the door before he could respond.

***

Scout sat in front of Belle on the snowmobile seat. She had to stretch around him to reach the handlebars and her arms acted as a restraint to keep him from falling if she needed to make a sharp turn. Last year she'd experimented a few times having the dog ride with her and after the first several attempts, he never fell once.

They rode up along the edge of Double Jack, avoiding the moguls and turned into the trees at the top of the side trail. Driving slowly down the trail they soon reached the incline, the jump-off point where Markie had caught air for the last time. Belle pointed in the direction of a few broken branches in the underbrush near the landing spot.

"*Uomo.*" Dora had suggested most professionals use German commands when training a dog, but speaking German gave Belle a sore throat so she used her mother's native tongue.

Scout followed her order and headed into the underbrush, his nose almost touching the snow. She stayed put, not wanting to contaminate his search and watched him weave in and out of the tightly bunched trees. Five minutes passed, and she was about to call him back when he barked a single time. She'd lost sight of him, but headed toward the sound of the bark and found him next to a thick spruce maybe fifteen yards from the trail. The snow had been disturbed at the base of the tree. The churned-up snow easily could've been caused by a critter, except for one thing.

The clear imprint of a snowshoe.

Chapter Fourteen

B elle and Carrie found the coffee shop at the resort base nearly deserted at 3:15 p.m., except for a young couple who looked like they'd just come off the slopes, and two young women. A hard-looking young woman with long black hair and boobs out of proportion to her thin body huddled alone over in the corner, her eyes glued to her phone as she tapped a message with one thumb while lifting her coffee cup to her lips with a shaking hand. Belle thought, the living definition of strung out. Interesting. Didn't get many druggies up here. Two tables away, a young, tall, redheaded woman flicked her thumbs over her phone screen. Was that the same woman who might've been following Danny Pags down the slope when he almost crashed into the young girl? Belle couldn't tell for sure. The redhead glanced up at Belle then quickly refocused her eyes on her phone. *Might've been following.* If anyone was associated with the drug dealer it likely was the black-haired druggie.

Belle returned her attention to the matter at hand. Belle had brought Carrie up to speed, and now Belle needed to share what she found with Sal. Their patrol shift started in forty-five minutes. And he was fifteen minutes late. She was about to reach for her phone when she saw him enter. He waved then handed the girl behind the counter a few bucks, picked up an empty paper cup, and filled it from the coffee urn.

He weaved through the mostly empty tables and slumped into a chair. "Sorry. Sundance traffic."

"And it doesn't help that you have a media truck on every street corner," Carrie said.

Sal nodded. "With the photo of Markie Dodd skewered on the pine branch, on top of the Brad Banks accident, on top of Sundance, you have the proverbial three-ring circus."

"And that doesn't even count Harrison doing a back dive from a ski lift," Belle added.

Sal sipped his coffee and his face instantly scrunched up. "Don't think they've drained the urn since... forever. Now I remember why I never come here."

Belle introduced Carrie. Sal expressed his condolences that she was assigned to work with Belle. *Not in the mood.*

"So, what's up?" he asked.

Carrie shifted in her chair. "What we're suggesting... well, *suggesting* is too strong a word. What I mean is—"

Belle took over. "We think it's possible the three fatalities in the last few days were homicides."

Sal didn't respond immediately, and I could see he was trying to wrap his mind around what I'd just said. "I'm listening."

Belle knew she had a near-impossible case to make and leaned her elbows forward on the table, speaking faster than necessary. "Okay, first we need to stipulate that Virgil, not Markie, was the intended target. Anyone reading the story about him and his daughter knew they skied Double Jack as their last run, and he always skied down first. That means two of the three victims were politicians, Banks being the only exception."

Sal didn't hide his skepticism. "Pretty big exception."

Belle forced herself to slow down. "Harrison told me he promised a woman he would ski Black Diamond, a likely suicide run at night in those conditions for even a sober expert, much less a beginner sky high on crank. Banks tripped into the oncoming truck. We've already seen that a juggler performing on the street just minutes earlier could've pushed the bodyguard into Banks, and given his Halloween getup, finding the guy is virtually impossible. Then there's Markie." She pulled out her phone and showed him the photo of the lines in the snow. "I snapped this when we first arrived on the scene before it was obliterated by the rescue team."

Sal took the phone from her and hand and studied the photo closely, turning the phone back and forth. "LFXL?"

"Or maybe Lexi," Belle offered.

"Or nothing but snow imprints from falling twigs," Sal countered. "Something you can find all over the mountain."

"True, but the proximity of the markings to Markie's body, what would've been Virgil's body, seems more than a coincidence."

"If there weren't coincidences there'd be no need for the word."

Belle took the phone back, scrolled to the next photo, and handed it to him.

He didn't so much as raise an eyebrow. "A snowshoe imprint. I can see that."

"Scout and I found the print just off the trail close to the landing area where Markie died. And remember, Virgil said he thought he saw someone up there."

"With light flickering through from the other side of the trees, it would be easy to think you saw movement."

Carrie didn't hide her exasperation. "And the snowshoe print just happens to be there at that exact spot?"

Sal paused, the wheels turning. "Other than the fact two of the victims, counting Virgil as an intended victim under your theory, what links them? What links an A-list movie star to a small-time politician from Wisconsin? What's LFXL? In short, what's the motive?"

Nobody said anything. Finally, Belle stated the obvious. "We don't know." She noticed both the druggie and the redhead had stopped texting. Because of their proximity, they likely could hear most everything that she, Sal, and Carrie were saying, and she lowered her voice. "But Harrison was high on meth, and Brad Banks's drug use is hardly a secret," Belle added, conveniently leaving out her reliable source for this information was *People* magazine.

"And Virgil Dodd? Are you saying he's a druggie, too?"

Belle squirmed in her chair. "No. Don't know one way or the other."

Sal spread his hands wide. "So what would you like me to do?"

Belle exchanged glances with Carrie. "We've run into someone who might be dealing drugs in town." She explained their contact with Danny Pags.

"Mighty thin, Belle."

"Agreed. But we think there's something here, and if you agree we'd like you to take it to the police. Given your reputation and connections, much more credible coming from you."

Sal paused for a long moment then pushed back his chair. "I'm sorry, I don't think there's near enough here to take to the authorities. Look, I'm not completely discounting what you're telling me. But I know even you agree calling these accidents murder is a huge stretch." He paused, thumbing his chin. "Still, send me those photos. Let me think some more on it."

"What about Pagano? There's got to be information on him out there?"

After a long pause, Sal said, "There's a new DEA agent assigned to Salt Lake from the Denver region. Name's Longabaugh. Met him once. Impressed me as pretty savvy. I'll give him a call. But no promises after that."

Belle figured they'd probably gotten all they were going to get out of her uncle, but she softly nudged a bit further. "Thanks. What about Virgil? You must know him, you know everybody. Maybe show the snow imprints to him. Those letters might mean something."

Sal's voice sharpened. "Virgil's deep into grieving for his daughter. Suggesting Markie was murdered with absolutely no evidence would be cruel. If you find anything more, let me know. But we really need something solid, Belle." He waved goodbye, thanked the girl behind the counter for the crappy coffee, and left the shop.

Carrie held Belle's gaze, scowling, not saying a word. They both were pissed because Sal was right. They had nothing.

Belle noticed the redhead's thumbs picked up speed again, sending a text to someone. Danny Pags? *That's ridiculous.* She was probably just communicating with a boyfriend.

***

At five p.m. the Summit was about half full of night skiers. Belle was working solo at the moment while Carrie was paired with Kip cruising the Silver Moon run. So far, quiet night, Belle observed. Quiet was good. With the drop in temperature she'd stopped in for a quick coffee. She checked out the laminated dessert card on the table by the window and contemplated a piece of the Summit's famous key lime pie.

In the last day or two, the restaurant had added a coffee

creamer flavoring—vanilla. There's a reason they call a boring choice "plain vanilla," Belle thought. Still, vanilla was better than nothing, and she helped herself to a healthy pour.

She peered out the window and watched skiers dismount from the lift. A majority of ski accidents actually occurred during lift dismounts rather than on the mountain itself. Inexperienced skiers would fall and twist an ankle or knee or fail to fan out properly, causing a fellow rider to run into them. Never really serious, but twists and pulls earned you a free sled ride down the mountain to the clinic at the resort base.

As she returned her attention to her coffee, she spotted the tall redheaded girl alone at a table by the window, the same one who trailed Pagano down the slope, and the same one who was seated within eavesdropping distance at the crappy coffee shop. The table was empty. The redhead checked her watch a few times, then looked up when a couple entered—Danny Pags and the skinny girl with long black hair, also an alumnus of the coffee shop. Did Pagano and the redhead exchange glances? Hard to tell for sure. The redhead rose and scanned the restaurant. Belle was pretty certain the girl's eyes paused for a split second when they reached her. The redhead left abruptly, and Belle tried to follow her through the window. Seemed like she was heading to the lift that would take her up to Jupiter.

Distracted, Belle didn't realize she had company until she heard the sound of chair legs scraping against the wooden floor. In a moment, Pagano pushed aside the dessert menu resting on the table and sat down with his coffee. The skinny girl leaned against the table behind him. Probably one of Danny's dealers. She noticed a bulge under Danny's jacket. Maybe gloves. On the other hand, there were no metal detectors installed at ski lifts.

Danny flashed a cold smile. "Taking a little break?"

Her first instinct was to push away from the table. Okay, maybe that was her second instinct. Her first instinct was to reach across and strangle the son of a bitch. Instead, she decided maybe she could extract some information that might help nail the bastard.

"What do you want?"

"I just needed to thank you for stopping me on the slope the other day. My skiing was reckless and I could have hurt that girl. Even more important, I'm embarrassed by my juvenile attempt to placate you with the coke."

"Placate? Big word."

He shrugged. "Again, I apologize."

He sipped his coffee without moving his eyes from hers. "I saw you on TV at the scene of that horrible accident. Very tragic. Brad Banks was a true star. And word is that you were the one who found that poor girl speared by the errant pine branch."

"'Word is?'" Belle held his stare.

"And then there is that unfortunate fellow who, *word is*, fell off the lift despite your heroic efforts to save him." He allowed a thin grin to slowly crease his face. "No offense, but I'm not sure I would want to hang around with you right now, Miss Bannon."

"Then I've got a great suggestion for you. Why don't you find a table elsewhere?"

A slight bow of his head. "Of course. Just thinking if I were you, I'd want to be careful where I went and whom I associated with."

"Your concern for my well-being is touching, particularly given the fact someone tried to blow my head off on Black Lightning last night." She didn't hide her sarcasm. "Don't suppose you know anything about that?"

He took his coffee cup and stood. "Of course not, and I'm glad to see you survived. But I wonder if this last incident might underline my suggestion about laying low? Have a good evening. Where are you off to now?"

She stiffened. "Why do you ask?"

He offered a humorless chuckle. "You are awfully jumpy, Ms. Bannon. Quite understandable, but I was just making polite conversation."

Her walkie crackled. Carrie's voice. "Belle, Kip had to head down. If you want to join up, I'll be at the top of Home Run shortly."

Belle tilted her head to speak into the walkie, her eyes locked on Pagano's face. "Roger that."

He held her gaze for a few long seconds, his face devoid of expression, then left without another word, followed by his grungy associate.

Pags didn't find another table. Instead, after tossing his paper coffee cup into the trash receptacle they exited the restaurant.

***

Belle skied down the Silver Moon run on the way to the green beginner slopes where she planned to meet Carrie. In the distance ahead, she saw Pagano skiing effortlessly, his henchgirl struggling to follow with wide beginner turns back and forth across the slope. The light cast by the nearby lift allowed her to see him stop, cut behind the abandoned building housing access to the old silver mine, and disappear into the deep shadows behind the structure. The mine was located mid-mountain, across from the Silver Moon lift that took skiers to the top.

A minute or so passed, and the girl followed her boss behind the mine. Another figure, short and wide, emerged then disappeared back into the shadows behind the abandoned mine. Belle fought a strong temptation to investigate, but she'd already extended her break and Carrie was waiting for her.

Maybe later.

Chapter Fifteen

Belle and Carrie cruised over to Pizza and French Fries, patrol slang for Home Run, a beginners slope that began at the top of the mountain and followed the winding switchback road to the bottom. "Pizza and French Fries" referred to the way instructors taught beginner skiers—point your feet inward like a slice of pizza to stop, point your feet parallel like French fries to go. They stopped at the crest of the slope, and Belle filled her in on Pagano's visit.

"He's definitely up to something," Belle said. "And the answer might be in the old mine. After he left me, I watched him disappear behind the mine building. I worked as a guide there one summer during college before they ended the tours, and there's no door back there. But a broken window could provide easy access."

"Don't know what he could be doing. Maybe stashing drugs there?"

"Possible."

"Should we let the cops know?"

"Nothing but speculation at this point. I'm pretty familiar with the place, so maybe one day soon I'll check it out."

"Hard to picture you as a guide. They're usually so bubbly."

"I can be bubbly. I can be very bubbly."

Carrie chuckled. "Why'd they end the tours?"

"A few years ago a woman became claustrophobic, went nuts, and took off running down the maze of tunnels screaming like a banshee. They eventually found her, but the lawyers got involved."

"What a shock."

"After that, the resort couldn't get insurance, so they closed it."

"As a high school teacher, I've learned there are two immutable laws of nature," she said lightly. "First, teenagers do stupid things. Second, teenage boys do really stupid things. I'm surprised some enterprising teenage boys haven't tried to break in."

Belle gazed down the run. The lights bathed the twisting slope in a soft white glow. Very few skiers. Hardly surprising. Night skiing targeted mostly experienced skiers, but the resort felt obligated to light up at least one beginner run. "About a year ago a couple of boys on a dare broke open the power box behind the mine, turned on the power to the lift inside, and entered through a broken window."

"So there's still power going into the mine?"

"It's on the same circuit as the Silver Moon lift. The incident with the boys convinced the owners to keep power access to the mine alive in the event of another rescue situation. They switched to security code access instead of a lock and key. By the way, the code's 1963, the year the resort opened."

"I assume they found the boys?"

"Once inside, the rescuers descended using the elevator and began exploring about a thousand miles of interconnecting tunnels running under these mountains. No surprise, they got lost."

"A thousand miles? That's like the distance from here to Dallas. It's amazing they were found."

"The search party got very lucky. Finally located them down the Keetley tunnel. Cold, wet, and bedraggled."

"The tunnels have names?"

Belle smiled and shook her head. "Just one. Miners were constantly blocked from reaching the deepest silver veins by the interference of underground water, so they built a giant drain tunnel about halfway down. That way they could dig deeper and only have to pump the water up to the drain tunnel instead of up to the surface. The drain tunnel emptied miles away into a basin down in the valley near a small town called Keetly. Back in the late eighties, that basin was intentionally flooded to form what's now the Jordanelle Reservoir."

"Ahh, I hear the tour guide speaking."

"Please exit single file, and tips are appreciated."

They skied farther down the slope and stopped where an older man had fallen. He looked to be in his late sixties and in great shape. Belle recognized him as a night ski regular.

"You okay?" she asked.

"Fine, thanks." He waved to a woman down the slope who held the hand of a young boy bundled up in a blue snowsuit. Couldn't be more than four or five years old. "My daughter brought Jack up to ski with Grandpa. Thanks, guys."

They watched the man zip down to join the woman and little boy. The woman took his poles and skied away. Grandpa positioned the boy between his legs and the two of them began to take wide turns down the gentle run. In a few minutes, they'd disappeared around a bend.

Belle found herself smiling. "Every time I see little kids learning to ski, I feel better about the future of—"

Crak.

Belle looked up, startled. "What the hell was that?"

Carrie looked over Belle's shoulder with widening eyes.

Belle turned... *impossible.* her entire body shook. *Avalanche?*

For a long moment they both stood frozen, unable to process what they were witnessing. A thick slab of snow had broken apart from Jupiter Peak and was now tumbling down toward the Home Run slope at breakneck speed.

Belle glimpsed Grandpa and Jack ski a wide turn back into sight. *Oh, my God, they're in the direct path.* He glanced up the hill and froze. A moment later he snatched the boy up off the ground, held him close, and skied frantically down the run, gamely trying to outrace the rumbling sea of white rushing toward them at nearly eighty miles per hour.

Carrie had to shout above the crescendoing roar. "Belle, move!"

The avalanche thundered their way.

Belle spun around searching for cover and spotted a small copse of spruce off the trail just below them. It only took a few seconds to reach the trees, but the edge of the avalanche arrived at the same time. No time to unsnap skis. The avalanche's roar sounded like a jet plane revving its engines. Belle grabbed Carrie around the waist, pointed to a low hanging branch, and mouthed the word, "Jump!"

She jumped and Belle lifted her at the same time. She looped her arms around the branch and struggled up just as the crashing wave of snow, like some powerful white monster, grabbed Belle's skis and violently yanked her down. Before she could take a breath, the snow crashed into her chest, knocking the air from her lungs.

A split second later she was buried alive.

Chapter Sixteen

B elle instantly recalled Rule One if you're buried in an avalanche—don't panic.

Yeah, right.

Rule Two: Create an air pocket. Belle frantically moved her head hard left and right then backward and forward hollowing out a small space so she could breathe. For the moment. She tried with only partial success to thrust her arms skyward. Once the avalanche stopped completely she'd have less than a minute before the compacted snow and ice would lock her in like concrete.

Breathe slowly. She remembered to face a different direction when she exhaled. Hypoxemia—poisoning caused by breathing back oxygen-depleted air—often caused death in avalanche victims before asphyxiation.

The statistics rushed through her brain: ninety-one percent of all avalanche victims who are rescued within eighteen minutes survive, while only a third of those rescued between nineteen and thirty-four minutes lived. All patrollers carried a beaming locator device. More importantly, Carrie knew exactly where Belle was buried.

Despite being locked in ice, Belle began to sweat. Her pulse pounded. Her hamstrings knotted tight, and the cramps sent pain shooting down her legs. She strained every muscle to move without success, but she was frozen solid. *Rule One, remember?* She wondered if whoever came up with Rule One had ever been encased in an ice coffin.

She thought I heard a scraping sound coming from above her head. Already she felt lightheaded from the combination of low oxygen and increased carbon dioxide. Maybe her mind was playing tricks on her. *If I shouted would anyone—?* This time she was certain she heard something.

The avalanche had smacked them with its outer edge so Belle figured the depth over her head should be significantly less than anyone in its direct path. The image of the little boy in the blue snowsuit flashed through her mind. She needed to get out now.

Something hit her hand, and in a moment she could wiggle her fingers. She heard Carrie's muffled voice. "Belle, if you can hear me, hang on!"

The sound of her portable shovel scraping the ice increased in intensity. Less than half a minute later Belle felt Carrie's gloves on the top of her helmet. Carrie tapped twice then frantically clawed away an air passage in front of Belle's nose and mouth. When the ice was brushed from her eyes, Belle could see Carrie's face hovering close to hers.

At that moment, the most beautiful sight in the world.

***

They zigzagged over the new snow that now covered the Home

Run slope.

She'd rejected Carrie's attempts to have her transported down the mountain for observation. The few other patrollers on night duty were now on their way up to join in the search for buried victims. Their greatest obstacle was time. Over ten minutes had passed since the avalanche hit, and with each passing minute, the likelihood of survival decreased.

Both Belle and Carrie had their scanners flipped open. The Ortovox S1 was the latest buried victim technology with a range up to fifty meters.

Belle called over to her. "Anything?"

Without taking her eyes from the screen she shook her head. Then, "Hold on." She stopped and pointed the scanner to her right. Belle quickly joined Carrie and saw the image of the supine body on her screen above the number twenty. Twenty meters away.

With the scanner guiding them—it reminded Belle of the childhood "hot and cold" game—they quickly moved close enough for the image to be replaced by a circle with the number 3.5 inside. Three and a half meters away. Using both scanners they narrowed the location down to 0.7.

They pulled portable shovels from their backpacks and Carrie immediately began frantically shoveling straight down into the now hard-packed snow.

"Stop. The shovel could hit their heads or compress the boy's chest." Belle assumed this was Carrie's first avalanche rescue and she was visibly shaken. Belle fully understood.

"Sorry."

"Dig laterally into the hill."

They worked at a frenzied pace, making sure to dump the snow downhill. Belle could hear her teeth chattering. Her fingers stiffened around the shovel handle. Being buried in snow, even for a relatively short time, seriously increased the chances of not only hypothermia but shock.

Carrie noticed. "You're going to go hypothermic on me, Belle. Stop and wait until—"

"Forget it." She dug faster.

The snow was rock hard and heavy, and they consumed almost ten minutes to excavate about six feet.

"When you were in the tree did you get a sense of the snow depth?" Belle asked.

"My eyes were squeezed shut in prayer, but we should've reached them by now. My God, where are they?"

Belle jumped into the hole and flipped open her scanner. The image on the screen now showed two bodies. "Uphill! Maybe a couple yards!"

Together they dug laterally into the wall of the excavation. Belle paused to pull a collapsible probe from her pack and extended the long thin tube—it reminded her of an old car antenna—and carefully inserted it into the uphill sidewall of the excavation. Feeling no obstructions, Belle immediately removed the probe and tried other places around the excavation's walls. No luck. Carrie yanked the probe from Belle's grasp and repeatedly inserted it rapid-fire into the excavation wall. "They've got to be in there!"

Belle heard the sound of snowmobiles and saw Kip leading the cavalry down the hill toward them. She shouted, "We're close!"

"We pulled out three so far," Kip said. He hopped off the seat and ran toward them with a larger shovel in hand. "Two are okay except for a few bumps and bruises, one was unconscious but it looks like he's going to make it." Kip called out to three other rescuers, each pulling an empty sled. "I'll help here. You continue scanning down the slope." The three snowmobiles revved up and turned downhill.

"How could this happen?" Carrie wailed to no one in particular.

"Can't figure it out," said Kip. "Hasn't been an avalanche on

Jupiter in years, and even then the fall began at the 9,000-foot elevation and only ran to the top of the treeline, not all the way down here to the friggin' bunny slope. Jesus."

Belle pointed to a spot just uphill and off to the side from where we were digging. "Start there."

"And be careful with that big shovel," Carrie ordered. "There's a little boy down there."

"Along with his grandfather," Belle added.

Kip held Belle's gaze. "How long?"

She checked her watch. "Going on thirty-five minutes." Kip didn't say anything. He didn't have to.

"Stop talking and dig!" Carrie shouted.

Belle suddenly felt dizzy and leaned on the shovel to keep from falling over.

Kip took notice. "Belle, you okay?"

Carrie, covered in ice sprayed from her frantic digging, spoke without looking up. "I had to dig her out."

"Are you kidding me? Belle, we need to get you down the hill. You're probably suffering from hypothermia and—" He grabbed her shovel.

She jerked it away. "No." She took a deep breath. All she could think about was Jack in the blue snowsuit. He and his grandfather had to have been hit by the thickest part of the avalanche. Her head hurt and she felt waves of dizziness. Her body temp kept switching wildly back and forth from too hot to too cold, and the muscle aches from her Black Lightning adventure had ratcheted up a few notches. "I'm fine."

Belle again tried the probe and this time felt something. She yanked out the probe and planted it next to her earlier insertion point. "Found 'em!"

The three of them worked with a renewed vigor, none more so than Carrie. In less than a minute a blue mitten flopped free from the snow wall.

"Use your hands!" Carrie shouted.

Kip threw down his big shovel. They used their hands to scoop out the hard-packed snow and quickly cleared through to little Jack's head. Carrie clawed away the snow and ice from around his face. He was unconscious. Kip ran to his snowmobile to retrieve the resuscitation kit. Belle pulled off her glove and used her forefinger to clear snow from the boy's mouth. With the rest of his body still encased, she stretched out prone in the excavation and covered his mouth with hers, breathing in and out.

Carrie whispered, "Come on, baby. Breathe for us, sweetie."

As Belle worked, Carrie used a combination of her hands and the small shovel to clear the snow and ice from the child's chest.

They could see the grandfather's ski parka above Jack's head.

Carrie said, "Looks like the grandfather used his body to create an air pocket for the boy."

"He's still not breathing," Belle said.

Kip appeared with the R-Kit, a bag containing oxygen masks, small green oxygen tanks, and OPAs—oropharyngeal tube devices—to clear airways. Carrie pulled the kit from Kip's hands and picked the smallest OPA. She lifted the boy's tongue forward and carefully inserted the tube into his mouth. Carrie gently blew into the tube while Kip and Belle dug furiously to free the grandfather's face. In less than a minute they'd exposed his head. Kip selected a larger OPA and inserted it.

As Kip and Carrie worked, Belle used the shovel to free the two bodies. "Anything?"

Carrie tearfully shook her head and kept blowing.

Kip wasn't getting a response either.

Once Belle had freed Jack's body, Carrie scooped the boy into her arms and continued blowing into the tube while she rushed to the sled. Suddenly the boy gagged then coughed. Carrie quickly guided the tube from his mouth then turned his head so he wouldn't choke.

"He's breathing!" Carrie attached the child-sized oxygen mask to his head and adjusted the intake to account for his age and weight.

Kip kept working on the man with no positive results. Almost immediately another snowmobile appeared, and the driver hopped off to help.

"You two take the boy down," said Kip. "We'll handle the grandfather."

For the first time, Belle took a hard look at the man's face. His skin color was as blue as the ice that had encased him. There was no doubt in her mind. Jack's grandpa was dead.

Belle searched his pockets for ID and located a local driver's license in the name of Judge Wilson Maddox. She hopped on the snowmobile, and Carrie, not even bothering to hold back the tears, climbed behind her onto the seat, clutching little Jack close.

"Sure you're okay back there?" Belle asked.

"Move!"

Chapter Seventeen

Belle curled up on the couch in her tattered robe sipping her second cup of dirty gray coffee.

She'd waived her no-couch rule and allowed Scout to snuggle up next to her. He dozed contentedly, taking full advantage of this special dispensation. After being checked out at the base clinic and benefitting from a good night's sleep, but for a slight headache and soreness in muscles she never knew existed, she felt as close to normal as she had a right to expect.

Someone had called her Aunt Helen and Uncle Sal. Helen had been understandably upset and to calm her down Belle promised to relax and drink lots of lemon tea. With her quilting pouch beside her, she ran a running stitch along a red arrowpoint appliqué on the Navaho blanket quilt. She knew it sounded crazy, but quilting really did calm her mind.

She heard a knock, set down the quilt, and shuffled to the front door to find Carrie standing on the porch.

"Just came from the hospital and thought I'd stop by. But if you're still recuperating or busy..."

Belle was glad to see her. "Come on in." She entered the tiny living room, and Belle closed the door behind her.

"How are you feeling?" she asked.

"Fine. Come on back." Belle shooed Scout off the couch and she sat down.

"I see you're working on a quilt," she said. "That's a good sign. You're self-aware enough to know you need to veg out for a while. It's beautiful."

Belle didn't buy into her self-awareness crap but kept her thoughts private. "Can I get you something?"

"If you have hot tea, I'd love some."

Belle took the three steps required to enter the kitchen and popped a green tea K-cup in the machine. "What's the latest on Jack?"

Her face softened into a wide smile. "He'll fully recover. His parents were beyond thankful for the rescue. So sad. Judge Maddox gave his life to save his grandson."

A few moments later Belle returned with the tea and sat next to her. She seemed fidgety. Something was on her mind.

Carrie looked down at the mug of tea. "I know I maybe lost my cool a little bit last night on the mountain, and I want you to know it won't happen again."

"Lost your cool? Are you crazy? First, you saved my life then you helped save the life of a young boy. You had every right to get emotional."

"It was different with Jack." She looked up from her cup. "I have a daughter just a few years older than him, and all I could picture was Lilly buried under all of that snow."

For a moment Belle was too stunned to reply. Not that it would be unusual for a young woman of her age to have a kid, or even unusual that the kid wasn't living with her. But she'd never mentioned it. "Oh? Where is she?"

"Back in Crenshaw, Wyoming, with her dad and his new wife." Her voice was neutral, no hint of bitterness or regret.

"Get to see her much?"

"Couple of weeks in the summer. Every other Christmas."

An attractive young gay woman has a daughter and a former husband. On one hand, Belle knew Carrie's personal life was none of her business. But she really wanted to know what happened. So she asked, "What happened?" Belle figured she'd either tell her or change the subject.

Carrie heaved a full body sigh. "Paul and I were young, too young. Crenshaw is a small town in the middle of Wyoming coal country. Most everybody knows most everybody. Church is big, and not only on Sundays. In Crenshaw, the church is the social center seven days a week. Girl Scouts, choir practice, Wednesday potluck dinners, youth fellowship. Heck, each church had its own basketball team and competed in a town-wide league. They informally called it the Jesus League."

"I'm sensing not the most progressive environment for gays and lesbians."

"That's an understatement," she said with a cold chuckle. "You have to understand, the LGBTQ community has made amazing strides. Still, people forget that it wasn't that long ago when things were quite different. I suspected I was gay as far back as grade school and by my sophomore year in high school was certain. Like any teen the most important thing was fitting in, so I went on dates and even had sex with boys a few times. Paul was my boyfriend in my senior year. We both were accepted at Colorado, and after our freshman year we did what everyone back home expected us to do. We got married. Lilly came along a year later. As far as Paul, his family, and my family were concerned, everything was wonderful.

Then I met Max."

"I assume Max is of the female persuasion."

"Maxine was in pre-law and, well, stunning. We started a secret relationship, and when I was with her I felt truly happy. But then, of course, I'd come home to Paul and Lilly, and the guilt was overwhelming. I didn't know what to do. One day Paul had classes all afternoon and I was home with the baby. I invited Max over. It was stupid, I know, but love makes you do stupid things."

"And your husband came home early."

"Old story. It was kind of hard to come up with an innocent explanation since we were both naked on top of the bed in, shall we say, a compromising position. I honestly believe if Paul had a gun handy, he would've shot us both. I didn't blame him for being angry, I really didn't. I'd not only cheated on him, I'd turned his world—a world defined by Crenshaw, Wyoming—completely upside down."

Scout must've sensed something in her voice because he arranged himself so he could rest his massive head on her lap.

"You don't have to tell me this," Belle said quietly. "None of my business."

She continued as if she hadn't heard. "To say I created the biggest scandal in Crenshaw probably ever would be an understatement. Paul's dad owned the mining company, and his uncle was the most influential lawyer in town. I think we set a record for the fastest divorce in the history of Campbell County. Not only was the whole town against me—I swear if it were lawful I would've been stoned to death in the town square—but my own family sided with Paul. At that point I was such a wreck I would've signed anything. Paul was awarded full custody of Lilly, and I received very limited visitation rights. Paul transferred to the University of Wyoming and two years ago married my best friend from high school. My relationship with Max fizzled, but in some weird sense I'm glad it happened because I no longer had to live a lie."

"What about your family? Have they softened with the passage of time?"

"With my mom, some. Not my dad. Paul will sometimes take Lilly over to see them for an afternoon, which I appreciate. And as she's grown older, I feel Lilly does sense a connection the few times I do see her. But she calls me Carrie. Paul's new wife is 'Mommy.'"

"I'm so sorry."

"If I were coming out of high school today, my whole life might've been different. But hey, in life, timing's everything."

"Profound."

She smiled and took another sip of tea. "Sorry, didn't mean to tell you my sordid life story."

"Glad you did."

"So, there's something I want to show you."

She reached into her pocket and pulled out a baseball card.

At that moment they heard a knock.

Carrie set the card on the end table next to the lamp and rose from the couch. "Sit still, I'll get it."

Chapter Eighteen

A man filled the doorway. Slim, broad shoulders, mid-thirties, sandy blond hair, blue eyes, thick mustache, two-day beard. He wore jeans, a beaten tan leather jacket, a black cowboy hat, and heavily scuffed boots. From where Belle was sitting, she guessed he'd have her by a couple of inches even in his bare feet. She thought, stick a dangling cigarette in his lips and he'd look like he'd just stepped out of an old Marlboro cigarette commercial.

"Hi, I'm Alonzo Longabaugh. Looking for Belle Bannon."

"That's me," Belle said. "Come on back."

Alonzo glided in, and she felt a twinge at the base of her spine, which pissed her off. Admittedly, he wasn't hard to look at, but she wasn't some doe-eyed schoolgirl swooning for the hot boy in history class.

He removed his hat and set it on the coffee table. "Hope I'm not bothering you, Belle, but your uncle called and told me you've had some run-ins with Danny Pagano, and that you have reason to believe he might be involved in several fatal accidents that occurred in the last week. I also understand you've been shot at and buried in an avalanche. He shook his head and flashed a smile. "Your life clearly doesn't fall into the boring category. Are you okay?"

She was far from okay but didn't want to come across as a wimp to the hot boy in history class, particularly since he just flashed his pearly whites at her. "Just fine."

"Want some coffee, Alonzo?" Carrie asked.

"Thanks, that sounds good."

Carrie waved him to the spot on the couch next to Belle where she'd been sitting and, after picking up Belle's coffee mug, headed for the kitchen. For some unknown reason, Scout abandoned his coveted spot on the couch and followed her, almost like they were in cahoots. Belle shot them both a "what-the-hell" glance. Carrie offered an expression flat as a computer screen.

Belle turned to Alonzo, whose butt maintained a respectful distance from hers. "So, you're a DEA agent."

"Yep. Worked out of the division office in Denver until a few weeks ago when I was transferred to Salt Lake."

"And I assume from your presence here that Danny Pags is on your radar."

"He's only in his early thirties, but he's shooting up the ranks fast. Already he's probably the largest meth supplier in the state. We suspect he reports to an outfit in Vegas headed up by a notorious drug who goes by the name of Felix Ross."

"CEO?" Belle asked.

"In the old days, we would've referred to him as a kingpin. Ross doesn't get his hands dirty. His men take possession of the drugs, mostly coke, heroin, and fentanyl from the cartels at the southern border, then his organization distributes the product to regional managers located across the mountain west. Colorado, Utah, Arizona, New Mexico, Nevada, Wyoming, Idaho, and the Dakotas. The managers fan it out to frontline street sellers. Ross is like the CEO; Pagano's a regional manager. He's very ambitious, and Ross looks on him as the golden boy."

"CEOs and regional managers...sounds like an insurance company," Belle observed.

"Except this company will torture and kill at the drop of a hat."

"Why don't you arrest Pagano?" Carrie asked from the kitchen.

"Love to, but he's very smart and very dangerous. We thought we had one of his dealers flipped, but the guy's disappeared and is presumed dead. Pagano's people are afraid of him for good reason. When Mr. Marino called and said you might have information that could lead to nailing him, we paid attention. So, talk to me."

She realized that what she was about to say might trigger a call from Alonzo to the men in white coats, but took a deep breath and dove in. "You've probably seen on TV all the stories about the deaths of Brad Banks and Markie Dodd."

"Hard to miss. Tragic." He shook his head. "The photos of that young girl...I've seen some nasty stuff in my business, but that was difficult to look at."

Carrie returned with his coffee, and a refill for Belle, along with a container of chocolate toffee flavored creamer. Belle added a healthy dose of the creamer while Alonzo watched with a bemused look on his face.

"During the days preceding Brad Banks tripping into a toilet truck, a local politician from Milwaukee died in what appeared to be another tragic accident when he executed a back dive off a chair lift," Carrie said.

"We don't think they were accidents," Belle said. "And the avalanche that killed Judge Maddox and almost took his grandson? That, too."

They paused to see if Alonzo would react, but he remained quiet, which Belle saw as a good sign.

Over the next few minutes, Alonzo listened intently as they brought him up to speed, including Belle showing him the photo of the scratches in the snow by Markie's body. When they finished, Belle could see the wheels turning.

Finally, he said, "Are you suggesting someone intentionally set off the avalanche to kill Judge Maddox? Is that even possible? If so, the odds of it being successful have to be extremely low. There are so many other ways to kill a man and make it look like an accident. And what's the motive? Are you saying Maddox was somehow in bed with Danny Pags and Danny killed him because...because why? Maddox decided to ruin his life and reputation by ratting him out? Sorry, that's beyond a stretch. And Belle, I didn't hear you identify any connection between Maddox and the other three."

Carrie slid the baseball card across the coffee table toward them. On the cover was an old-time photo of a pitcher named Grover Cleveland Alexander. Belle flipped to the back of the card and read out loud. "Hall of Fame pitcher for the Philadelphia Phillies, played from 1911 to 1930."

"I Googled him," Carrie said. "He was named after President Grover Cleveland. Back in the fifties they made a movie about Alexander's life starring former President Ronald Reagan. The judge's daughter gave me the card at the hospital. She found it in his ski jacket pocket. When I saw the card, I told her I was a big baseball fan, hoping she might give it to me. She did, saying it was the least she could do for helping to save little Jack."

"Are you really a baseball fan?" Alonzo asked.

"No, but I wanted the card," she said with a flicker of guilt. "Think about it. One of the last things Walt Harrison said to Belle was 'rover.' "

"Yeah, at the time I assumed I misheard him. Or maybe he was telling me his life was 'over.' "

"But you said he'd promised this mysterious woman and needed to get up the mountain to ski Black Lightning," Carrie said. "Not the words of someone planning a suicide. Brad Banks's last words were, 'Annie Grover.' So couldn't Harrison have said Grover, not 'rover?' "

In Belle's mind, she tried to recreate those moments on the lift: Harrison thrashing about, the heavy wind, the squeaking chair. "Yeah, I guess it's possible." She passed the card to Alonzo. "What do you think?"

"Maybe Judge Maddox was a collector," Alonzo said.

"According to his family, no," Carrie said. "In fact, his daughter said he complained about baseball. Thought it was too slow. He was a big football fan. She had no idea what the card was doing in his jacket and never saw it before."

"So, you're saying someone else slipped this card into his jacket pocket?" Alonzo asked skeptically.

"At the Summit, most everyone takes off their ski jackets and leaves them hanging over a chair to save a seat while they go order food," Belle said. "It would've been very easy for someone to slip the card into Maddox's jacket pocket."

Alonzo continued to study the card. "And you think this someone is a woman named Annie Grover?"

"Is that name familiar to you?" Carrie asked.

"No, but Pagano, like others in his business, recruits street dealers all the time. She could be new. What about Markie? Or more specifically, Virgil Dodd?" Alonzo asked. "The scratches in the snow, if they say anything, don't read Grover."

"I don't know," Carrie said. "There's obviously something we're missing."

"The Grover connection can't be a coincidence," Belle said.

"You understand what you're both suggesting?" Alonzo said.

Belle nodded. "Premeditated murder."

After a long pause, he shook his head. "I'm sorry guys, but again, I keep coming back to the theory that the avalanche was intentionally triggered and targeted to hit Judge Maddox. To say that's a reach is an understatement."

Carrie said, "The judge's daughter told me over the last six months or so the family would gather at the base for an early Sunday dinner at Baja—Jack loves nachos—and before dinner, he would take the boy down Home Run a couple of times."

"Tradition, just like Markie and Virgil Dodd," Belle said. "So if someone were targeting the judge, it's conceivable he could've learned about the Sunday dinner habit."

Alonzo sipped his coffee. "I assume from your theory that it's technically possible for someone to trigger an avalanche?"

"Absolutely," Belle responded. "Whenever there's a serious accumulation of snow we send a team up in the morning before the lifts open to plant dynamite and trigger a controlled avalanche. But the snow never comes close to the trails, much less the beginner runs. Never happened. The killer would've had to time the avalanche perfectly to hit Maddox. You're right, highly unreliable. But impossible? With a pair of binoculars, you can see Home Run from Jupiter."

"I don't suppose the judge's family offered any information that might suggest a motive," Alonzo said.

"The issue never occurred to them," Carrie stated. "As far as they're concerned, Maddox was the victim of a tragic act of nature."

"*If* these accidents weren't accidents at all but premeditated murder," Alonzo said, "I have yet to hear your theory of a motive or your theory of Pagano's connection."

Belle swallowed the dregs of her coffee. "We know Harrison died because he was high on meth, and Danny Pags or his people could well have been the supplier. Maybe Harrison owed Pagano and was late in payment."

"But no apparent connection between Brad Banks and Pagano," Alonzo said.

"Not necessarily," Belle said. "Harrison's bent on skiing Black Diamond in a blizzard high on meth to satisfy a woman. He says 'rover' which could've meant Grover, and Banks's last words were 'Annie Grover.' Maybe the connector is a woman working for Pagano named Annie Grover. And according to..." She glanced at Carrie. "... reputable sources, Banks's recreational drug use was an open secret. This Annie Grover could've been his local supplier."

"And you combine that with finding the Grover card in Judge Maddox's jacket," Carrie added.

"But what about Virgil Dodd?" Alonzo asked.

"If we assume the victims were murdered," Belle said, "we also have to assume Virgil, not Markie, was the target."

"Do you know of any drug connection to Virgil? Any mention by him of this Annie Grover?"

Belle lowered her gaze and her voice. "No. But we do have the scratches in the snow that could spell out someone's name—"

"But not Annie Grover's name, and they just as easily could be random imprints from branch droppings."

"You're right," Carrie agreed. Scout had curled up at her feet, and she absently rubbed the head of her co-conspirator. "Virgil Dodd is the outlier. But don't forget Pagano's not very veiled warning to stop snooping around, and the fact somebody or a group of somebodies tried to blow Belle's head off. Also, if we assume the scratches were a name, unless the deadly branch just happened to blow into the ski path right where some lovelorn kid wrote his girlfriend's name in the snow, the existence of the name strongly suggests Markie's death wasn't an accident." She turned to face Belle. "I think we need to go to the police."

"If we do, they'll immediately begin preparing commitment papers for both of us. Besides, we kind of have the police sitting here."

Carrie faced Alonzo. "Then what do we do?"

"I can run Annie Grover's name through our database to see if it sets off any bells."

Belle remembered the woman she'd seen with Pagano, the one who'd likely been eavesdropping at the crappy coffee shop. "At the Summit, Pagano had this woman with him. Thirties, long black hair, gaunt. Maybe she's Annie Grover."

"Sounds like Sonja Valek. She has a history with Pagano. Her family owns a construction company in Salt Lake. Remodels, modestly priced single-family homes. Nothing big. She worked for her dad doing everything from managing the books to driving trucks. Then she got hooked first on coke then meth. She quit her job and began working for her supplier."

"Danny Pags."

"Exactly. We thought she'd be a ripe target to flip on Pagano. We even enlisted her family. But she wouldn't crack. We suspect they have a personal relationship. I firmly believe Sonja Valek would jump off a cliff for Danny Pags."

Carrie pressed. "So, again, do we just forget the whole thing?"

Alonzo paused, then said, "Maybe if you could find some powder burns at the avalanche trigger site, that would at least show that the avalanche could've been intentional."

He was right, Bell thought, and it hadn't snowed since yesterday's avalanche so if any burn evidence existed, it should still be there. She rose to her feet. "I'm going up to Jupiter Peak and check it out."

"The snow could still be very unstable after the avalanche," Carrie warned. "Not to mention that part of the mountain's closed and you're hardly in a condition to ski Jupiter Peak."

Belle grinned. "That's why I need someone to go with me."

"Sorry," Carrie said, "but I have a teacher's meeting I can't skip."

Alonzo locked eyes with Belle. Upon her closer examination, calling his eyes blue was like calling Secretariat a horse. His eyes burned with the heat and brightness of a blue gas flame, and if provoked she sensed the heat from that flame could immediately rise to dangerous levels.

"I'll go," he said. "If you promise to take it easy."

Belle could deal with that.

Chapter Nineteen

Belle observed that Alonzo was a good skier—probably high intermediate, low expert—and he had no trouble keeping up as they skied down to the Jupiter lift. She'd loaned Alonzo a pair of her Dynastars, and they'd stopped at the base so he could rent boots and have her bindings adjusted for his weight. She also gave him her extra walkie, and at her suggestion, he brought along a flashlight and hiking boots in a backpack just in case they had to trek into wooded areas. He insisted on carrying his sidearm. She didn't object.

The Jupiter lift closed to the public at 4 p.m. but continued running for an extra half hour so the ski patrol could access the bowls for sweeps. Belle recognized the tall, curly-haired liftie with the soft brown eyes and easy smile. Sweet guy. A year earlier they'd both consumed too much vodka at NoName. She had an itch. He was handy. He scratched it. The next morning they were both embarrassed, and after that, they'd never spoken of the hookup again. His eyes lit up— not because of her, I suspect, but working the Jupiter lift was a lonely job.

"Hey, Belle. Didn't expect to see you so soon after the avalanche. You okay?"

"Fine."

"What you guys did to save that kid. Amazing."

"Thanks. Not too busy today I assume?"

"Never busy. Couple of singles, that's it. I saw both of them come down, so you probably don't have to sweep."

"We need to make sure no one entered from a cross-trail."

"What about yesterday?" Alonzo asked. "Did you have much afternoon traffic?"

The liftie's eyes narrowed. He didn't know Alonzo and probably was curious why this stranger was asking him questions. "No. Half a dozen maybe. Why you asking?"

"Happen to recognize any of them?" Alonzo asked, ignoring his question.

The liftie paused for a second. "No, but remember, they were wearing a helmet and goggles. You a cop?"

"We need to go," Alonzo said.

Without a further word, they stepped to the line, and the next chair lifted them off their feet into the air. Even on the busiest of days the traffic up to Jupiter's expert terrain was light, so the lift was old and slow. The chairs were tight two-seaters—a full shoulder-ribs-butt connect. She didn't really mind.

"Seems like there's at least a *possibility* Pagano or one of his men rode up to Jupiter yesterday," she said. "They could've hidden from the afternoon sweep and remained up there to do their thing."

"Could've?"

Belle knew he was right. Her mind twisted in a hundred directions trying to connect all of the victims to the damn dots—drugs, Grover, Pagano—but the dots kept moving. She held no illusions about Pagano's capacity for violence. Buried in the snow somewhere up on Lightning was her bullet-shattered helmet to prove that. But the avalanche could've killed many innocent skiers, including young children. If Danny Pags was interested in nothing more than trying to make money in the drug trade, she wasn't sure it made good business sense to put that many innocent civilians at risk.

"Remember, the odds are strongly against the avalanche being intentionally triggered," Alonzo said. "Mother Nature never ceases to surprise."

"Is that a fact? Ever think of auditioning for the Discovery Channel?"

He chuckled. "So in addition to being tough and attractive, ex-jarhead Isabella Bannon also has a sense of humor."

The "attractive" comment didn't go unnoticed. "You serve?"

"Spec Force 18F."

"Intel. Ah, it all connects. See action?"

Alonzo's expression clouded. "Yeah."

Clearly he didn't want to discuss it. She knew the feeling.

They reached the top of the lift, skied off, and stopped to tighten their boots. She pointed along the ridge of the south-facing slope. "If someone intentionally triggered the avalanche he would've had to set the charge along the south ridge."

Like all ski patrol members, she'd gone through avalanche-control training, including the intentional detonation of small bombs to trigger a controlled avalanche. What appeared to be a single sheet of snow was, in fact, a stack of different plates. Because of the variation in temperature with each snowfall, the snow pack resembled a lasagna casserole—various layers, each with a different consistency and thickness. These layers sometimes slid apart, triggering the avalanche.

Most patrollers enjoyed the often-daily avalanche assignment. Someone was paying you to ski through deep powder and throw bombs. Belle was no exception. The charge usually consisted of two pounds of dynamite packed into a red container about the size of a can of corn. They'd usually light two fuses sticking out of the bomb like antennae to make sure one of the fuses wasn't a dud.

She took the lead, moving very slowly, and Alonzo trailed behind. With the scarcity of skiers on this part of the mountain, she hoped they'd find suspicious ski prints.

A half-hour passed, the sun was about to completely disappear below the mountains, and they hadn't found anything unusual.

"We probably should go back," she said. "Damn. I thought for sure we'd find something."

They turned and headed back toward the lift. If it was still running they could hop a ride on a chair going down to the base. If not, they'd have to carefully make their way across to a lighted slope.

She glanced along the slope line and thought she saw something they might've missed earlier. Shadows from the few trees had lengthened, and the light and dark contrast was more pronounced. While probably a product of her imagination, she thought an area about the size of a typical living room rug appeared different from its surroundings. Smoother?

"See that smooth area there? Almost circular?"

"Yeah, looks like the snow melted there for some..." He got it.

They skied toward the patch for a closer look. Small black patches dotted the snow.

"Powder," Alonzo said, excitement leaking into his voice.

"Had to be from an avalanche bomb."

"That's why the snow's melted. The sun heated the bits of gunpowder here on the south slope melting the snow."

"If it snows tonight, the evidence will be gone. Avalanche bombs can't be that easy to obtain. The police might be able to trace back."

"If not, maybe DEA can help."

Belle pulled out her phone and took a flash photo of the smudge.

"That'll look like a great picture of dirt," Alonzo said.

She switched to video mode and handed him the phone. "Record me removing a sample of the powder from the site and depositing it into a plastic bag to preserve the chain of custody."

"Uh, Belle, I know a little bit about evidence preservation."

"Right, sorry." She found a plastic bag in her patrol kit, marked it with the date and time, then signed it.

He signed his name and recorded Belle carefully scooping about a quarter of the powder into the bag. She stared at the bag like it was a bloody knife. "Whoever triggered the avalanche murdered Judge Maddox and almost took the life of an innocent child."

"Not to mention a third life—yours. None of it makes sense, but I called in Annie Grover's name and I should have something shortly." He slipped the plastic bag into a zippered pocket, and they headed off to the top of the Jupiter lift.

***

By the time they made it back to the lift, it had closed. They'd have to ski partway down the mountain in near darkness to a lit run. "I know a cross-trail through the trees that should get us to Double Jack. It's lit. Follow me, but be careful."

She led Alonzo along a narrow trail that formed a crazy zigzag through the woods. Some of the turns were so sharp they had to hold a tree and jump around it, pointing their skis in the opposite direction.

He called ahead. "Sure this is even a trail?"

"Just stay close."

Twenty minutes later, the lights from Double Jack flickered through the trees making the going easier. Ten minutes after that, they popped out onto the run.

Alonzo skied up next to her. "For a while there I thought we might have to send up a flare."

From their position, Belle could see the abandoned mine off to the right at the base of the Silver Moon lift. The image of Danny Pags disappearing into the mine entrance flashed through her mind. What interest could he have in the abandoned mine? Could that be where he hid his drug stash? The more she thought about, it the more it made sense. He'd make sure the drugs would never be found anywhere near where he lived. Storing in a warehouse or any other property could allow investigators to trace a link back to him or one of his dealers. But no one accessed the mine. Even if the police did somehow discover the stash, it was unlikely they'd be able to link the drugs to him.

Alonzo asked, "What's wrong?"

"You go on ahead. I want to check something out."

"Check what out?"

"I saw Pagano and one of his dealers disappear behind the old mine building the other day. Maybe he's using the abandoned mine as a drug stash of some sort."

"And you think you might find evidence that could nail him?"

"Possibly. And while I haven't figured out a motive yet that would apply to all four victims, my gut tells me Pagano's somehow involved. If we find evidence that connects him to a drug stash, the police can make an arrest and interrogate both him and his men. Faced with a multiple first-degree murder charge, there's a chance one of his underlings might flip. At the very least we will have put a temporary dent in the local drug trafficking business. While it's highly unlikely I'll find anything, since I'm here—"

"I don't know. The mine's dangerous. Why don't we wait till daylight?"

"I used to work there as a guide and know the place pretty well."

"I'm not letting you go in there alone."

Part of her welcomed his chivalry, but she could handle it on her own. "You go on down to the base. I'll be fi—"

She found herself talking to the back of his head as he skied toward the mine.

Chapter Twenty

Belle and Alonzo stopped outside the wood-slatted shaft house, heavily grayed from over a century of weather and neglect. Snowdrifts reached almost up to the windows, many of which had been broken for decades.

Inside the shaft house, the tallest of the two structures on the mine site, the head frame and elevator hoist lowered men down a shaft extending hundreds of feet to hack out rock chunks suspected of containing silver. The same hoist brought buckets filled with the excavated ore back up to the surface. The second building contained the coal-fired boilers that generated the steam necessary to operate the hoist. Illumination from the nearby Silver Moon lift cast enough light for them to see the padlock on the front door.

"How do we get in?" Alonzo asked.

"Same way as the teenage boys."

She led him around the back of the structure to a thick blue spruce. The tree camouflaged a window located a bit over six feet off the ground with the glass panes missing. They both made sure their walkies worked. Belle removed her cell phone from its zipped, watertight pouch and checked. Almost fully charged. Alonzo did the same.

"Will we be able to get a signal in there?" he asked.

"Not sure. Why don't you stay here while I do a quick check of the top floor? The building's over a hundred and thirty years old. There could be loose beams, weak floors, and—"

"No way."

He bent over and unlatched his ski boots. She did the same, and they changed into hiking boots. No use causing an unnecessary alarm, so they hid their ski boots and skis under the spruce.

Alonzo leaned against the wall of the building and lowered his hands to form a stirrup.

Belle stepped one foot into his hands and sprang up high enough to insert her torso through the open window then wiggled through and thumped onto a dusty floor sprinkled with snow blown in from the open window. After unleashing a sneeze loud enough to wake the dead, she poked her head back outside. "The dust in here's as high as my ankles. Need a hand?"

Alonzo shook his head, reached up over the sill, grabbed onto the window frame, and leveraged his body up and through the window headfirst with the ease and grace of a gymnast.

A strong musty odor permeated the room. The ambient light from the lift outside filtered weakly into the space but only extended a few feet from the window. They both turned on their flashlights and scanned the area.

Having spent time in the mine during her tour guide stint, the space looked familiar. The main room extended about twenty feet wide and forty feet long. The elevator hoist to the tunnels below took up most of the space. At the end of the room, a door led to a storage area.

Alonzo focused his light on the floor around the elevator. "Prints."

"They don't seem fresh." She glanced up. "Watch your head." He followed her gaze to the rusted cables dangling from a pulley system. "The miners hooked up the ore buckets to those cables then pushed them through there." She pointed to a portion of the front building wall that resembled a rickety old garage door. "The cables connected to outside lines. Gravity would take over and pull the buckets down the mountain to town."

"Those dangling cables look like snakes," he said.

"I hate snakes," she said, almost spitting out her words. "I doubt if there are any snakes in here."

He coughed from the dust and pointed his light at the floor. The outer edges of the beam caught another set of much fresher footprints leading across the floor to the storage room door.

"Could be Pagano's prints," she said, not hiding the excitement in her voice. She led him around the shaft access then across the room toward the door. "Watch out for loose flooring." The last thing they needed was for one of them to step on a rotting plank, fall through the floor, and break an ankle. She immediately noticed that someone had placed a modern-day padlock on the door.

Alonzo examined the lock. "Still has the Walmart sticker. Don't think they had Walmart back in the late nineteenth century."

Belle checked the hinges on the door, but unfortunately, the pins were located on the inside.

"Can we get in through an outside window?" Alonzo asked.

"The only window faces the lift, and we'd be spotted in a second by the operator. Maybe we come back tomorrow with bolt cutters."

Alonzo's eyes seemed glued to the padlock. The stainless-steel bar of the lock threaded through two matching rusty brackets—

one on the door and one on the wall framing. After examining the screws attaching the brackets, he asked, "Happen to have a screwdriver?"

She pulled her Leatherman combo tool kit, smaller than a deck of cards, from the backpack. "Nineteen tools total."

"All I need is the screwdriver."

Three of the four screws came out easily, but the head of the fourth broke off. Alonzo had to twist the rusty metal back and forth a few times before he could snap off the remaining corner of the bracket still attached to the door. The door swung open, and once inside Belle examined the hinges.

"They've been oiled recently."

Electric lights had been added for the tours, but she didn't want their presence advertised so she used her flashlight to scan the room. Other than the thick layer of dust, nothing appeared to have changed from her tour guide days. A couple of crude workbenches rested up against the walls, and several old tools were scattered around the floor. In the far corner, she spotted a couple of rust-crusted ore buckets containing small rock chunks. An old chest rested next to the buckets.

Alonzo said what she was thinking. "No dust on the chest."

She followed him across the room to the chest. Each step caused the floor to creak. She warned, "Careful—"

Crak. Her right ankle dropped between the ragged planks, twisting hard. She fell forward. Instant pain shot up her leg.

"Shiiiit!"

He hurried back to me. "Are you okay?"

She gingerly pulled her foot free of the broken plank. "Damn. A little tender, but don't think it's broken."

Alonzo helped her to her feet. She wrapped her arm around his neck and carefully eased her weight down on the ankle. Sore, very sore. But at least she could put weight on it.

"Sit back down, and I'll wrap it."

"It's fine."

"Sit."

His tone left no room for argument. She carefully lowered herself to a sitting position on the floor and untied the laces on her boot. Alonzo found a new Ace bandage in her patrol backpack and eased the boot off her foot, trying to avoid any movement that might send pain shooting up her leg. After slipping off her sock, he wrapped the ankle with the compression bandage, replaced the sock and boot, and pulled the bootlaces as tight as possible so the high-top leather would act as a modified splint.

"There's some ibuprofen in a side pocket," she said. He found the packet, and she swallowed three of the painkillers. "Thanks." She attempted to get vertical on her own and was pleased to see the pain had already subsided a bit.

"We need to get you down the hill and have a doctor look at it," Alonzo said.

A battle between pain and curiosity raged. Curiosity won. "Okay, but while we're here, let's check out the chest."

Before he could protest, she limped across the room. The chest lid was padlocked, but unlike the door to the shop, this lock appeared original. Rust caked the body of the lock, yet Belle didn't see an easy way to break it. She checked out the hinges on the back that connected the lid to the body of the chest. The hinge pins, while rusty, appeared solid. She again pulled the Leatherman multi-tool from her pack and found the large, flat-head screwdriver. After inserting the flat-head underneath the head of the hinge pin, she pushed hard. Nothing.

Belle pointed to the ore buckets. "Hand me one of those rocks."

Alonzo lifted a chunk of ore from one of the buckets and checked it out. "So why would they leave these ore chunks if they contain silver?"

"Very low chance of any silver in that rock." She repeated the statistic she'd given daily on the tour. "A typical ton of ore contained 167 pounds of lead, ninety pounds of zinc, seven pounds of copper, and only one pound of silver."

"Impressive." He tossed her the rock, and she used it as a hammer, tapping the screwdriver against the head of the hinge pin. Because the screwdriver was part of a multi-tool, there was no solid handle to pound against like a regular screwdriver, making the maneuver more difficult. She tapped harder, the pin moved. A few more taps and the pin fell to the dirty floor.

The second hinge pin was easier to dislodge. They could open the chest from the back.

"If Pagano's drugs are in here, what are you going to do?" Belle asked.

"Not sure. We need to not only find his stash but also hard evidence tying him to it."

The lid stuck for a moment then popped up. They pointed their flashlights inside.

Empty.

Alonzo broke a long moment of silence. "Enough Sherlock Holmes. We need to get you down the hill where your ankle can be treated."

"Maybe he keeps his stash in the tunnels."

"No way we're going down there." He slipped her arm around his neck. "Let's go."

They shuffled back to the door. She was missing something. Why put a padlock on a door to a room where there's nothing to hide? She stopped for one last look and again swept her flashlight around the room. The light beam skimmed to a stop when it reached the ore buckets.

"The bucket on the left. No dust. The other buckets are covered with dust." She pulled away from him and limped back across the room to the bucket.

"Jesus, Belle, watch your step."

When she reached the bucket, she noticed the ore chunks were much smaller. Easier to remove? She carefully settled into a crouch, pleasantly surprised that she felt no additional pain in the ankle. Probably adrenaline, she figured. She removed a single layer of ore, and there they were—six brick-shaped blocks wrapped in aluminum foil. She lifted one of the bricks and observed a second layer of six bricks underneath.

Alonzo whistled softly as Belle peeled back a corner of foil on one of the bricks exposing the plastic-wrapped white powder.

"You were right," he said. "Danny's using the mine as a distribution safe house to store his product. But how do we prove it's his? I'm sure he wore gloves, so no prints. Then again, you did see him enter the mine."

"I never saw him actually enter the mine itself."

He grimaced. "Then we have nowhere near enough to tie him to the coke."

She pulled out her phone and snapped several pictures of the exposed cocaine brick as well as the stash inside the ore bucket. After rewrapping the opened brick, she wiped it down and replaced it inside the bucket then spread the layer of rocks on top. "Let's go."

Maybe it was the adrenaline or the IB or both, but this time she could limp without his assistance. They exited the storeroom and closed the door then slowly made their way across the main room, again passing the open-air hoist leading down to the tunnels.

"The broken lock, the cracked floorboard, he'll know someone was in here," she said.

"I'm hoping he'll panic and remove the stash. The mountain's our home court. Maybe we can spot him removing the coke. Then we pick him up with the drugs on him, before he finds another hiding place."

"Dangerous."

"Don't see another—" He froze. "Did you hear that?"

Belle listened hard. Nothing. Then she heard a faint sound filtering up the lift shaft from the tunnels below.

Hard to tell for sure, but it sounded like a human voice.

Chapter Twenty-One

Settling back on the torn maroon couch, the Sword of Justice drained her beer, eyes locked on the near-continuous local coverage of the avalanche on the secondhand TV. From an operational standpoint, she was quite proud of her work. The placement of the dynamite had to be precise for the avalanche to target Home Run.

After arriving in town a few years earlier, she'd joined the ski patrol. She'd only worked one year but saved five lives, including two children under ten, during that single season of service. She'd volunteered for avalanche duty. There was no way back then she could've known how she might make use of her experience, but she'd felt certain the skills she developed would definitely come in handy someday.

Admittedly, much more reliable methods existed to clear the world of the dishonorable Judge Maddox, and she knew going in that the odds of success were shaky at best. But the sheer artistry of the event could not be diminished. She'd intentionally devised the toughest test yet for God to prove his support. And He passed. With God on her side, it worked out better than she could've hoped. She hadn't seen the little boy and would not have triggered the avalanche if she had. The thought that her action could've taken the child's life sent a chill down her spine. *The Sword of Justice and God didn't kill kids.* Fortunately, the boy had survived, thanks to Belle and her trusty gal pal.

What about Markie? She was a kid.

The horrific image of Markie Dodd's body sagging low on the icy black branch flashed through her brain. She knew Markie hadn't died instantly, and it broke her heart. Could God have wanted Markie to die in pain? But God allowed wars to be fought, right? And innocent people suffered painful deaths in war, right? *And Markie wasn't a kid!* Eighteen was old enough to do a whole bunch of adult shit. No, she wouldn't allow herself to feel guilty about Markie Dodd. All great enterprises included a necessary element of collateral damage. And Danny was right. Virgil would feel pain every day for the rest of his life. She felt certain the slime bucket saw the name scratched in the snow, so the bastard had to know he was responsible for his daughter's death. Still, the poor girl.

She pushed Markie Dodd from her brain and focused on Maddox. Did she feel even a little bit guilty? No, of course not. Then what was that tiny burning sensation in her stomach? *A touch of indigestion, that's all.* The judge was a pig, and something had to be done. That was the problem with the #MeToo movement—no action, only shouting and waving signs and marching around wearing pink vagina hats, which was appropriate since they were all a bunch of pussies. She smiled at her little joke and forced herself to ignore the ache in her belly. She popped open another beer and turned up the volume.

They were coming to the good part.

***

Belle and Alonzo stared down into the shaft, trying to detect any sign of movement. They stood completely still, listening.

Silence.

"Must've been the wind," she whispered.

"Really? Does wind blow in mine tunnels?"

"Okay, maybe a critter."

"Sounded human to me."

She scoffed. "That's imposs—"

"Shhhh."

This time the sound was fainter.

"Somebody could be down there, Belle." Alonzo scanned the room as if searching for a solution. "We need to call the locals. Not to mention Pagano could be using one of the tunnels for his drug operation, so that somebody could be one of his men."

"If someone's hurt we don't have time to wait for help. And if it's a false alarm and the cops post, they'll see the broken door, find the drugs, and we've lost the chance to catch Pagano red-handed." She limped toward the lift. An idea had formed, and already she didn't particularly like it.

"What are you doing?"

"Stay here. If I find anything, I'll contact you on the walkie, and you can make the call. If nobody's there I'll come right back up, and we'll leave. Loan me your gun just in case."

"If you're going, I'm going. And if it is a kid, unlikely he went down there on his own. There could be multiple injuries."

He beat her to the hoist. The passenger compartment more resembled a cage than a traditional elevator. Three of the walls were completely open; the back wall consisted of a solid piece of water-resistant plywood installed several years earlier to accommodate the tours. Four steel pipes provided the compartment's frame.

"Sure this thing's safe?" he asked.

"No."

He scowled. "Not funny."

"It's been working for over a hundred and thirty years. They switched from steam to electric in the early 1900s, and local elevator inspectors checked it regularly back when they were giving tours. If anybody's down there they had to ride the lift."

Belle hobbled into the cage and opened a metal box mounted on the back wall of the compartment revealing two switches. "Top one turns on the power," she explained. "Bottom one's a toggle switch—up means go up, down means go down. No automatic stops, so you stop it wherever you want by returning the toggle to neutral." She flipped the power switch, and a dime-sized green light flashed. "Last chance to stay here."

She sensed his hesitation. Her guess, claustrophobia. Very common. During her tour guide stints, they had to deal with visitors who, once down in the tunnel, freaked out and insisted on returning to ground level immediately. "I still think you should stay up here. It will only take me a few minutes to check out the tunnel."

"You can stop it, right?"

Belle heard the tiny catch in his throat. "Absolutely." She instinctively rapped her knuckles against the plywood.

"You think knocking on a piece of dirty plywood will protect us?"

"Why tempt fate?"

Alonzo sucked in a deep breath and stepped onto the lift. The dusty, warped flooring planks creaked as soon as he put his weight on the open platform. "Do it."

She toggled down.

A few seconds passed then the grinding screech of gears that hadn't been lubricated in some time pierced the quiet. The platform lurched and shook side-to-side.

"Belle? Are you sure—?"

The platform dropped at a speed far faster than a modern-day elevator. Their flashlight beams ricocheted off the sharp, ragged surfaces of the black rock as the hoist descended the vertical shaft.

Alonzo shouted over the noise. "How will you know when to stop?"

Belle pointed to the wall as we passed a crude gray X painted on the rocky surface. "The X is a marker showing the first horizontal tunnel is coming up. Like I warned the tourists, hang on." She looped an arm around one of the pipe struts, and Alonzo followed her lead. She counted to three then flipped the toggle back to neutral. The hoist stopped immediately, and both of them would've tumbled to the platform floor if they hadn't been prepared.

They remained in the shaft. The gray X signaled a three-second delay before the toggle was supposed to be triggered. When she'd worked as a guide, it had taken several tries before she mastered the timing to the point where she was permitted to take tourists down on the lift by herself. It had been a while, and she'd obviously counted too fast.

"The horizontal tunnels were dug about every hundred feet or so into the vein. There are more tunnels shooting off from this shaft below us."

"So the voice could be coming from any one of those tunnels. Great."

She flipped the toggle switch back and forth, lowering the lift down slowly like a captain carefully maneuvering his ship to a dock. Two opposite sides of the shaft walls opened up. She quickly flipped the toggle back to neutral, and the lift shuddered to a stop about four feet above the tunnel floor.

"We're not sure it was a voice, but yes, the sound could be

coming from the eight or nine horizontal tunnels below us. The tour only descended to this first level." Belle trained her light beam along the tunnel wall. The beam illuminated an old ore cart, some equipment, and a few signs now too faded to read. "That stuff was part of the tour." She called out, "Hello?" No response. She tried again. Silence.

She toggled down, and the lift lowered about a hundred feet until it reached the next tunnel. They heard the sound again, almost certainly human, and definitely below them. Maybe more than one human voice.

When they reached each tunnel level, they called out but heard no response. At the fifth level, she finally said, "Maybe it's time to go back up and get help."

Then they heard it. Someone speaking. This time coming from the horizontal tunnel, not the lift shaft.

Her imprecise toggling left the platform a few feet above the tunnel floor. Alonzo jumped off first then assisted her. By purposely focusing almost all of her weight onto her good foot, she was able to reach the floor with almost no additional pain.

The air was dank, the walls damp. Belle pointed her flashlight down the long tunnel.

For a split second, a figure crossed the light beam then disappeared into the darkness.

Chapter Twenty-Two

Neither of them spoke for several moments before Belle broke the silence. For reasons she couldn't explain, she kept her voice low. "Did you—?"

"Yeah."

"Wasn't a critter."

"No."

"Did he look injured?"

"Couldn't tell. Why are you whispering?"

"Why are *you* whispering? The kid's probably scared to death."

"How do you know it was a kid?"

"I don't, but he or she could be hurt. Wait here, I'll check it out."

"No way, I'm coming." His tone left no room for argument.

Belle couldn't escape a feeling of apprehension. Made no sense. After all, they were here on a rescue mission. Probably just the darkness and the close quarters. She called down the tunnel. "Hello? Don't be scared, we're from the ski patrol here to help you."

They heard a thin, reedy voice, barely audible, but I couldn't make out the words. "Did he say, 'Help?' "

"Not sure."

"Don't think it's a bad guy." She was trying to convince herself as much as Alonzo.

Alonzo pulled out his gun. "Just in case."

She took a deep breath. "Okay, let's go."

They panned their flashlights back and forth as they moved away from the lift and headed down the tunnel. After a few steps, the damp mustiness mixed with an odor she couldn't place.

"Smell that?"

"Yeah, like urine."

Belle again shouted down the tunnel. "Hello? Are you hurt? Please say something so we can find you!"

No response.

They moved forward quickly, and she noticed shorter side tunnels—little more than excavations, really—on either side of the main tunnel. Had the shadowy figure emerged from one of these cut-outs?

The rock ceiling brushed Alonzo's hair, and the tunnel's dimensions narrowed, leaving little room for the two of them to stand side-by-side. The tunnel made a thirty-degree turn to the right, and Belle noticed his steps shorten. He glanced over his shoulder. The lift was now out of sight. She'd seen claustrophobia disable the toughest of men. "Why don't you go back to the lift and wait? Just in case the kid appears from one of the side tunnels behind us."

He offered a brief smile, barely detectable in the dim light from their flashlights. "Here's a suggestion, Belle. Don't ever play poker. You can tell I'm claustrophobic, and even in the dark, I can tell by the tone of your voice and your body language that you're trying to protect me. Thanks, but where you go, I go."

He pulled out his phone and turned on the video record function. "In case we get lost." He held the phone out in front of them with one hand, his flashlight in the other. Eyes straight ahead, he moved forward, forcing himself to lead the way.

They'd only progressed maybe another twenty yards when they heard the voice again: *"Mahhhhh."*

"Maybe it's a kid asking for his mother," Alonzo said.

The figure who'd crossed their light beam looked too big for a kid. Maybe a teenager. *Maybe not.* She called out, "Don't worry, we're going to take you back to your mom, just tell us where you are?" No response.

"We should've reached him by now," Alonzo said. "Must be in one of these side excavations." He directed his light into the next side tunnel, maybe twenty feet deep. Nothing. The main tunnel continued to narrow, and Belle assumed the lead. She saw another side tunnel entrance up ahead, and this one appeared a bit wider than the others.

A hand grabbed her collar, jerking her back. Alonzo released his grip and pointed his flashlight down to a hole roughly cut into the rocky floor, maybe thirty inches in diameter, a step ahead of me.

She gulped. "Thanks."

"What's that?"

"Vertical drain shaft. Remember, nine or ten horizontal mining tunnels extend out from the principal vertical lift access shaft. About halfway down is the Keetley drain tunnel. Water from tunnels above Keetley drained down through vertical drain chutes like this one."

"Like a storm drain next to a street curb."

"Right."

He stared down into the dark shaft. "Looks dangerous."

"I'm sure the miners who worked here every day knew the exact location of each drain chute."

They carefully inched their way around the hole in the floor and continued down the tunnel. The tight confines created an echo each time they breathed, and the shrinking ceiling now brushed her head. Even with the flashlight, she felt a weird sense of floating, like the floor was her only anchor.

She raised her voice. "Hello? Hello? Please say something so we can find you!" No response. "We should've found him by now. I'm getting a weird feeling. Maybe we should both go back. Get help. More people to search. Let me see your phone."

"I already checked. No signal."

"I want to see the video."

He handed it to her and she rewound the video then turned up the volume. They both watched their recorded progress down the tunnel.

"The kid's voice isn't on there," he said. "I definitely think we should go back."

Belle replayed the clip, turning the volume up to maximum level. Every breath, every noise made by the two of them came across clearly. But the sound of the shadowy figure calling for his mother appeared to be—

"Wait," he said. "Think I heard it. Rewind again."

"Mahhhh—"

"There. It's faint."

"Mahhhh—"

They both froze. This time the voice didn't come from the phone.

Alonzo whispered, "Where did that——?"

"Behind us, back toward the lift."

"How could we have missed him?"

"Could've been in a side tunnel." She activated her walkie. "Anyone hearing this, pick up." After pressing the transmit button, all they heard was static. "Down too deep. Let's head back, check the side tunnels more closely. If we find him on the way, great. If not we ride the lift up and call for reinforcements."

"I'll second that."

Belle took the lead, taking care to skirt the drain chute in the middle of the tunnel floor. They approached the bend.

Crak.

A bullet pinged off the wall ahead of them, and the sound of the shot echoed back and forth across the rocky tunnel walls, seemingly destined never to end.

Ice locked her spine. Another shot, and this time the bullet ricocheted inches from Alonzo's head. The beam from a flashlight moved toward them. She looked over her shoulder to see the elongated shadow of a man moving along the rocky wall, approaching, taking his time.

Alonzo dropped to his knees and pushed Belle behind him. "Where the hell did he come from?"

"Anyone's guess. Narrow passageways honeycomb throughout the mine where the miners dug looking for silver veins. When none were found, they moved on. Most of these exploratory passages are impassable or dead ends, but some connect. He must've come from one of them."

Alonzo fired three quick shots at the shadow, hoping the bullets would bank off the wall and hit the shooter. The shadow stopped but unfortunately didn't fall. Two more shots from the man behind the shadow, both ricocheting inches from their bodies.

"We need to find cover, one of those side tunnels," Alonzo whispered. He grabbed her hand and turned back down the tunnel away from the lift.

They raced down the tunnel toward the dead end, hoping to find an excavation that might offer some protection. Adrenaline softened her ankle pain for the moment, and she was able to keep up with Alonzo. The shooter blocked the way back to the lift and safety. How long would he remain there? Could they wait him out? She'd been shot at before, but it's never something you get used to.

They saw no more side tunnels as they headed toward the dead-end in the distance. *Dead end. Fitting.* She spotted a dark spot on the floor ahead. Another drain shaft. They could keep going and hope for a cut-out closer to the end, but if there wasn't one, they'd be trapped. One option remained, but she knew he wasn't going to like it.

"We have to slide down the shaft."

"No way."

"It'll take us to the next horizontal tunnel. From there we can move back up toward the lift where there should be a power box to toggle the lift down."

"Are you nuts?" he hissed. "I'm not crawling into that shaft. You said the next level could be as much as a hundred feet below us. That's like falling off the roof of a ten-story building."

"The narrowness of the shaft will allow us to control our speed. Expand your arms and legs so they rub against the walls. Scrape your way down." She stuck the flashlight in her pocket and shed the backpack. She couldn't take a chance on it snagging in the shaft.

The next shot smacked into the ceiling directly above them sending a spray of rock chips down on their heads. They flattened out on the floor, and Alonzo fired two more shots back up the tunnel.

Belle slipped her legs down into the shaft feet first, using her elbows to brace herself on the edge.

"You go ahead," Alonzo said. "Hopefully, he'll come around the bend and I can take him out. I'll go back up the tunnel, and we'll meet when you stop the lift at this level."

"I'm not going anywhere without—"

She felt his strong hand on the top of her head.

Belle couldn't see his smile, but she heard it in his voice. "See you soon."

He pushed, and she dropped into the black.

Chapter Twenty-Three

Alonzo doused his flashlight, plunging himself into total darkness.

He shrugged off his backpack and flattened against the cold stone floor, head hovering over the drain hole. Silence. Was the shooter still there? Maybe he'd decided to return to the surface, disable the lift, and leave them down here with no means of escape.

At some point they would be missed and a search and would find their skis under the spruce behind the mine. But would the searchers assume they were in the mine? And once searchers eventually did enter and saw footprints, how long would it take to repair the lift? And when they did eventually repair it, how would they know which tunnel to explore? The more he thought about it, abandoning them and disabling the lift was a smart—

Three shots fired in rapid succession smacked into the rocky walls and ricocheted, hissing in all directions around him like a swarm of deadly bees. The faint glow of a light beam on the tunnel wall softened the blackness and slowly moved toward him, but the shooter remained safely behind the tunnel curve. Alonzo checked his gun. Four rounds left.

Two more shots splintered the rock around him. Then three more, but these came from down the tunnel. *Two shooters!* He was boxed in, caught in a crossfire. *Shit.*

The next barrage slammed into the floor inches from his feet. Instinctively he scooted forward. His shoulders now hovered over the drain hole. *No way I'm going into that hole.* He fired twice down the tunnel into the darkness.

An instant later a light beam from the down-tunnel shooter lit him up like a Christmas tree.

He jammed the gun into his jacket pocket and pulled the zipper tight. He was about to swing his legs around and lower himself into the shaft when a bullet pinged an inch from his knee. He rolled away and found himself with his head and shoulders hovering over the open drain tunnel. Another bullet just missing his hip. No time to scooch. Another nanosecond and he'd be dead. He slipped headfirst into the tunnel and shot straight down the shaft like a torpedo. A fusillade of bullets stitched across the floor above him.

"*Shiiit...!*"

Almost immediately, the tunnel widened. He tried to flare his legs and arms to slow his descent, but the drain water slickening the walls acted as a lubricant. Fear wrenched his gut. He pressed harder against the cold rock with his knees and forearms. At first, his ski coat and jeans offered some protection, but the ragged surface quickly sliced through the fabric and scraped into his skin. After a year of slugging up the rugged mountain trails of the Cheekha Dar with an eighty-pound pack on his back, his abductor outer thigh muscles were well-developed, but they now burned to the bone as he continued to strain against the shaft walls. *Push!* His fall slowed only marginally. He wasn't going to stop. Terror squeezed his lungs. He couldn't breathe. His head would split open like a melon when he hit the tunnel floor eight or ten stories below. *Oh, my God!*

He pushed his limbs outward with every ounce of strength he could muster. But the chute angled steeper. The speed of his descent quickened.

Crak, crak.

One of the shooters fired down into the drain tunnel but because of the angle, the bullets bounced harmlessly off the rocky walls above him.

He was now the bullet in the barrel as his headfirst descent accelerated down the black tube. The sharp rock clawed at his hands, his arms, his legs, his feet, as he pressed every muscle as hard as he could against the slick walls to slow his drop. But he fell faster. Then—

He screamed as his left shoulder smashed into an outcropping, instantly stopping his descent. A million electrified needles shot into every nerve on the left side of his body. First thought, bad news—he must've broken a collarbone. Second thought, good news—he'd stopped falling. The pain brought tears to his eyes. He gasped for breath.

He wiggled the fingers on his left hand and moved his elbow back and forth. Did that mean he hadn't broken a bone? No. He struggled to maneuver his left hand down to the outcrop, pressed it flat, and winced when his raw-scraped palm pressured the cold rock.

Now stationary, he felt the tunnel walls closing in, wrapping him in a thick, black, suffocating robe. A SEAL instructor advised him once to distract from his claustrophobia by self-imposing pain. At the moment he felt plenty of pain, but the slowly enclosing walls continued to encroach. Okay, fight it. *You're in charge of your mind, Longabaugh. Take control. Forget about the tightening walls. Get off the damn outcrop.*

He took a deep breath and counted to himself. *One, two, THREE!* When he pushed up it instantly felt like someone had stabbed an electric cattle prod into his shoulder. He immediately dropped back, panting like a dog tied up for hours under the hot sun.

Again he worked to control his breathing and turned his focus to his right arm, carefully extending it down beyond the outcrop. From patting the walls, the shaft appeared to narrow. If he could get beyond the outcrop the narrower diameter might allow him to control his descent. *If* he could get beyond the outcrop.

He positioned his left hand for a second attempt to push off the outcrop. Hopefully, expecting the pain might make the attempt a bit easier. The stakes were plain. If he remained in his current position, he would die. Another deep breath. *One, two, THREE!* He howled as loud as he could, pushed up hard through the burning needles jabbing deep into his arm, and rolled to his right.

He was free.

His left arm being close to useless, he needed to exert more pressure from his left leg and knee as he skidded down the shaft. His brake pads now consisted almost completely of raw flesh, but for the first time he was able to exert a level of control over his descent and slowed to a stop.

The darkness compressing against him by the tightening tunnel walls seemed almost alive. There was pitch black, and there was beyond black. Inside the shaft, inside the tunnel, inside the mountain, he felt immersed in beyond black. Like being buried alive within a coffin below five hundred feet of rock. His heart quickened, he gulped for air. Sweat beaded on his face—or was that—?

"Alonzo?"

Belle's voice. Barely audible.

He gasped for breath. "You were expecting someone else?"

"I'm—I'm stuck."

Her voice sounded weak, and with the echo effect, he couldn't tell how far down she was.

He struggled to project calm. "What happened?"

He heard her grunt, and the sound of fabric scraping as she shifted in her spot. "Dropped like a stone at first then my jacket caught on an outcrop wall, and that slowed my fall. The walls narrowed, and I was able to scooch my way down by scraping the walls with my boots."

"Can you reach your flashlight?" Did she leave it in her backpack? No, he remembered she'd put it in her pocket.

"Hold on."

He struggled to hide the shakiness in his voice with only marginal success. "Not going anywhere."

"I can put my hands on it, but my arms are pinned so I can't get it out of my pocket."

"Try turning it on anyway." After a few seconds, he saw a muted glow below, much like the very first gray whispers of dawn. "I see it. You're not that far away."

"I heard you yell. I thought you'd been shot."

"I'm fine." He laughed inwardly. *Fine. Right.* He forced himself to slow his breathing then lowered toward the gray light, shimmying his body when the shaft tightened and using his feet and right hand to brake when the shaft opened up. He noticed the trickle of water draining down the shaft appeared to be strengthening. The dull glow from her flashlight gradually brightened. He arrived at a tight area and no longer needed his right arm for braking. He slid his hand up along the trunk of his body, retrieved the flashlight from his pocket, and aimed the light down the shaft. There, maybe fifteen feet away, a brown spot—Belle's hair covered in grime.

Relief surged through his body. "I see you."

"I see your light."

He wiggled closer and the light caught her face tilting up toward him. He saw smudges on her cheeks—could be dirt or blood. Their eyes met, and he was amazed. Did he see fear? Yes, of course. But he also saw a steely determination. He'd only recently met Belle Bannon, but already he felt an attraction triggered by something much more than just another hot female flipping his hormone switch. He wasn't yet sure what that something was, but he felt compelled to find out.

He noticed the water trickle had now increased to a narrow stream, like the flow coming out of a kitchen faucet.

"Where are you stuck?"

"My hips," she responded, sounding slightly embarrassed. "The shaft really narrows."

He could see now. Belle had a body most runway models would envy, but her hips were still too wide for the opening.

"The water's starting to pool here," she said.

He couldn't believe the steadiness of her tone. Anyone else in her position would be hysterical, in full panic mode, but he could only detect the tiniest quaver in Belle's voice.

She struggled to wiggle free, but her body had wedged tight into the rock like a—*oh, shit.* Like a plug.

Chapter Twenty-Four

The water pooled up past Belle's waist, her panic level rising with it.

Alonzo wiggled down closer so the top of his head was nearly touching mine. "How are you doing?"

Fear hardened every cell of her body. She could barely move, and her raspy voice sounded like a gargle. "Just peachy."

"We need to lift you so the water can drain past. Can you wiggle this way?"

She'd tried before without success, but the rising water left her no choice. She found a small outcrop on her left side, barely big enough to place her hand. The right side was smooth, so she pressed her upper arm tight against the wall while pushing as hard as she could with her left hand against the outcrop. She felt the veins along the side of her head bulge out like bloodworms. She drained every ounce of strength she could muster. Nothing. She didn't budge. The water now reached her chest. She released the pressure and gasped for breath. *My God, where is it coming from?*

"Not going to work," she said, now resigned to her fate. During Recon night rescue training fifty miles off the coast of Hatteras, one of her brothers struggled in the heavy waves, dropped below the surface, and didn't come back up. She was the closest and dove down to find him. Got lucky and pulled his unconscious body to the surface. They hauled him into the boat, and she immediately performed CPR. He made it and told her later what drowning felt like. *You hold your breath until you're close to losing consciousness. But your brain won't let that happen and it forces you to take an involuntary breath of water. Your lungs burn and your throat spasms. Your body struggles to remain alive when all you want is for the pain and panic and helplessness to end. It was torture, Belle. Like being waterboarded only worse.*

Belle thought of Alonzo. If it weren't for her, he wouldn't be wedged upside-down inches above her head, moments away from the same fate. "So sorry I got you into this."

"You didn't get me into anything." His voice sounded oddly soothing. Resigned?

"Funny, over in the sandbox if you allowed yourself you could think about dying every second of every day. Will tomorrow be my last day alive? Will I feel anything? Is there anything beyond this life? I never thought drowning in a mine tunnel would be the way I departed this earth."

"No one's going to die," he said. "Not tonight anyway." He pressed his thighs tight against the wall, reached down with his right hand, and slipped it under her armpit. "Maybe if we tried together—"

"Not going to work."

He ignored her and wiggled down farther to gain a little leverage. The crown of his head was now almost touching hers. She could smell his hair, an odd mixture of lavender shampoo and sweat.

"For what it's worth," she said, "I'm kind of disappointed I won't have more time to get to know you better."

"Listen to me, Belle." His voice had an edge to it. "You have a reputation as a fighter. Now's not the time to change your MO."

"News flash. That reputation's bullshit."

"Come on. One more try. We need to create a little opening, that's all, a small passage for the water to drain."

"You'd need both arms, and you injured your shoulder."

"So I dislocated my shoulder. If I drown, it won't make any difference." He reached his left arm under my right shoulder. "On three."

The water reached her mouth. She coughed and tried to spit it out, but the water kept rising. Now lapping against her nose. She twisted her head back as far as it would go, straining for that one last breath of dirty air. *Like being waterboarded only worse.* Their eyes met, and she saw a mix of fear, resistance, and resignation.

"Fight, Belle!" A direct order.

She held her breath. Now or never. She again placed her left hand on the outcrop and pressed her right arm against the wet wall. The water covered most of her face up to her eyes.

"One, two, *THREE!*"

The water covered her ears, but she could still hear his muffled scream. Belle watched him trigger every fiber of upper-body muscle, lifting twisting, turning, then—

She heard a sucking noise.

The greatest sound in the world.

The water dropped below her nose, and she gulped in the wonderful dank, dirty air. In a moment it drained down past both of their heads into a widening space between her left thigh and the wall. Both of them gasped for air as the remainder of the pooled water flushed away. He released her and her body settled back into place.

"Cutting it a little close, Longabaugh," she said, her words interspersed with hacking coughs.

He rubbed the top of his head against the top of mine. But the plug had reset and the water began pooling again.

"So now what?" she asked. He'd have to continue lifting her each time the water pooled, but how long could that last before exhaustion won out?

"Lower your pants."

She blinked. "Takes the phrase 'not the time or place' to a new level."

"Bare skin lubricated by the draining water might allow you to slip through."

Without hesitation, Belle unsnapped her jeans, unzipped the fly, and scooched the jeans and underwear down as far as they would go. He again slipped his hands under her shoulders, and she heard him yelp from the pain. This lift would be harder as she would need use of both hands to completely shrug off her pants.

"Ready?"

She nodded.

No "one, two, three" this time. Only a hard yank and a guttural male scream. Her body rose slightly above the opening.

"Go! Go!" he shouted.

She jammed her pants and underwear down to her lower legs, but the balled-up clothing got caught in the bottleneck.

"Hurry," he rasped.

By compressing the material to her knees, she was able to wiggle the top of her pants through the narrow opening.

Alonzo lowered her back down, and she heard him struggle to catch his breath.

"You okay?" she asked. "Sorry, stupid question."

"Try to squeeze through."

She twisted her hips back and forth, up and down, but even with the water lubricating the rock she couldn't squirm through the bottleneck.

"I have an idea. Are you carrying sunblock?"

Patrollers always carried sunblock since the thinner air at high altitudes increased the danger of sun damage. "Yeah, there's a zipper pocket in the back of my jacket near my left hip."

He slid his hand down, lifted a flap, and found the pocket and the lotion. A couple of moments later, she felt his hand lathering first her left hip, then her right.

"Okay, give it a try."

She wiggled her hips back and forth. The sharp rock scraped against her skin, but there was movement. She squirmed harder, and the blood from the cuts on her bare flesh mixed with the lotion, turning it orange in the yellow flashlight beam.

Then, her hips were through.

"Yes!"

Belle quickly tilted her shoulders, squeezing them past the constriction, and in a moment her entire body had passed through the bottleneck. Alonzo's shoulders were wider than her hips but much more maneuverable. He stretched his right arm high and, biting his lip to mask the pain, he lowered his left arm like a swimmer performing the sidestroke and wiggled through to his waist where his clothing snagged.

"Brace against me," she said.

He wedged his head against her shoulder and neck and used his right hand to reach up and unbuckle his belt. With some more shifting, he was able to slip down out of the jeans. His boots caught on the balled-up clothing above the bottleneck, but she was able to stretch up and loosen the laces on his right boot then pull his foot loose. His other shoe was easier, and in a few moments he was completely free. He pulled his pants through and raised them to his waist so he could spread his legs wide against the chute walls.

Once they were clear of the bottleneck, the shaft opened up. With their heads only inches apart, they tried to use their arms, knees, and feet to control their descent. Except Belle's pants balled up around her ankles made it impossible to stretch her legs wide.

Her flashlight lit the shaft below. In the distance, she could see the mouth opening above what looked like a railroad trestle crossing water.

"Belle—?"

"I see it. The Keetley Tunnel. The trestle was built about five feet above the tunnel floor so water could drain down the tunnel to its mouth."

"If we follow the tracks—"

"The mouth opens above the Jordanelle Reservoir." Originally the trestle had been needed to transport ore carts, men, and machinery to the valley long before the Jordanelle had been created. "The water flows to a treatment plant adjacent to the reservoir, and the trestle's used to service the tunnel."

They no longer had to worry about finding their way back to the lift. A moment of euphoria.

"The shooter could be down there waiting for us," Alonzo cautioned.

Euphoria moment gone. "Maybe. But it would've taken him time to return to the lift, descend, and then trek down the Keetley to the drain. And the rail tracks would've slowed him down. Even with our plug delay, I think we would've beaten him. Besides, if he were down below he'd probably have shot up into the drain opening by now. I'm sure he assumed we're stuck forever, and he went away."

Chapter Twenty-Five

T he shaft widened further, but not enough for Belle to reach down and pull up her pants. She kicked off her boots, then her pants, and stretched her legs wide, pressing hard against the ragged drain chute walls.

They approached the mouth, the chute widened, and they both struggled to maintain even minimal contact with the walls. Alonzo's inability to use his left arm didn't make things easier for him, nor did the fact he happened to be upside down. Despite his best efforts, because of his heavier weight, he plowed into her from above. The shaft spread open even wider. She couldn't stop, and they tumbled through the tunnel mouth to the trestle twelve feet below.

Belle hit hard. A moment later, Alonzo landed on top of her, and for a few seconds, everything went black.

When she regained consciousness, she realized her head had dropped down between two rail ties. The flowing black water below soaked her hair and licked the top of her head. She tried to jerk her head up but was blocked by a stabbing pain in her neck and left shoulder. She moved more slowly on the second try and this time was able to lift back to the top of the trestle and roll onto the thick rail ties toward Alonzo. His head rested at an odd angle across the rail. He wasn't moving. *God—No!*

She did her best to ignore the pain and pulled the flashlight from her jacket pocket. He was breathing.

"Alonzo?" She shook his good shoulder. He winced and a few seconds later opened his eyes. I could tell he was momentarily disoriented then his expression changed as he realized where he was.

"Don't move," she said. "Just tell me what hurts."

"Everything." One by one, he tried to move his four limbs. In addition to his injured left shoulder, his right ankle had slipped between two ties, and he grimaced when he attempted to move it.

Belle probed his ankle. Didn't seem to be broken. "Probably a sprain."

"Help me up." A direct order.

"Not sure that's a good—"

"I said, help me up!"

She crawled to her feet, carefully maintaining her balance on the trestle, slipped her arms under his shoulders, and helped him up. Her walkie floated by, and she grabbed it. They're not waterproof, but she hit the transmit button anyway. Silence. She spotted her pants floating between two rail ties and grabbed them. No sign of their boots. Probably filled with water on the floor of the tunnel. She fished her phone from her jeans pocket and tried to turn it on. "Dead."

"Mine, too, but forget it. The shooter could be coming. We need to get the hell out of here."

Belle couldn't have agreed more. She slipped on her water-soaked jeans. No boots, and no time to search for them. "Let's go. One tie at a time." They aimed their feet squarely on the next tie and struggled to hold each other up. He slipped again, and she pulled him tight to her body. "I have you." Okay, they were in a serious life-threatening situation. Yet when she pulled his hips flush with hers, she had a flash of impure thoughts. She realized then and there that the human body has a mind of its own, quite apart from the reason and logic contained in the space between the ears.

He separated a few inches. "Next tie. Ready? Step."

They tried again, and this time, knowing what to expect, they both kept their balance.

Under the circumstances, there was no way to tell the true extent of his injuries. For that matter, Belle didn't know for sure how badly *she* was hurt. Her ankle sprain from falling through the floor, layered on top of her muscle aches from the Black Lightning incident, left doubt in her mind whether any part of her body remained unaffected. Still, between the two of them she was the more mobile at the moment. She doubted he could go much farther on his injured ankle.

"You can't walk. I think you'll be safer here while I go—"

"Where you go, I go. Remember?"

Got it.

Soon they fell into a rhythm—stepping on one tie, then the next one, then the next.

He sniffed the air. "There's that piss smell again." He spotted something on one of the ties and picked it up. Wet cardboard.

She pointed her light at the object. "What is it?"

"An empty coffee filter box. Must've come from whoever maintains these tracks." The light beam reflected off of a small piece of foil floating in the water. "Looks like a chewing gum wrapper."

"Chewing gum, maybe. But I doubt anyone's actually making

coffee up here in the—"

They both heard a sound coming from far up the track behind us. Belle aimed her light. *Stupid move.*

Crak.

The bullet splashed in the water at their feet. Her flashlight provided the shooter an easy target, and she quickly turned it off. "You still have your weapon?"

Alonzo unzipped a jacket pocket and pulled out his gun. "Right now he can't see us. Unless I get lucky and hit him with the first shot, the gun flash will make it easy for him. You go on ahead while I wait in the water between the ties. If he's using a flashlight I'll have a decent chance of taking him out."

"What happened to I go, you go?"

A deep sigh. "Then let's move."

They hobbled the best they could down the trestle, bending over to reduce the size of the target on their backs. A few more shots didn't come close, pure luck considering they were all inside a tunnel.

They had to perch on each tie and probe a foot out until it touched the next one. Belle flicked her flashlight on for a split second so they could see the tie ahead of them and jump. Periodically they happened upon gaps caused by missing ties. She'd hold on to Alonzo while he stretched out as far as he could to reach the next tie. Then they'd need to coordinate a jump to the tie. Difficult under any circumstances, but especially challenging when they were both restrained by bad ankles.

Fortunately, the tunnel contained several bends that prevented the shooter from having a clear shot, but Belle figured at some point the tunnel would straighten as they moved closer to the mouth.

She urged Alonzo forward. "We need to go faster."

Gaps now appeared every few feet, and the rushing water

below the trestle splashed high enough to lap against the sides of the ties. She knew increasing their speed meant a greater risk they'd lose their balance and trip through missing ties into the black water, but they had to take the chance.

She flicked on her light for the next tie, and Alonzo glanced behind them. "He must be around the bend for the moment. Keep your light on for a bit longer so we can move faster. And be careful of those cables."

Belle trained the beam on two cables dropping from an overhead crossbeam directly in front of them.

Then the cables rattled.

She froze, unable to move. Two Great Basin rattlers. She knew rattlers were mostly inactive during the winter months, only rising when their sense of vibration and infrared vision is triggered. Then they get really pissed. Her eyes widened, and her heart revved up, shooting past redline. She couldn't breathe. Her whole body shook.

The rough, hissing sound of their rattles increased in intensity. The snakes raised their diamond-shaped heads, coiled back on themselves, and bared their yellow fangs, ready to strike. Suddenly the closest snake propelled itself toward Belle, its black eyes flashing red in the light beam. Her piercing scream echoed down the tunnel.

Alonzo didn't hesitate. He fired, and the snake dropped into the water.

She gasped for air, struggling to take deep breaths to calm her heart. She aimed the light on the limp floating body to make sure it was dead. She hated snakes.

Alonzo took a step and lost his balance. She grabbed for him. They both tumbled through a gap in the trestle ties and dropped into the swirling black water.

Her feet found the tunnel floor, and she propelled herself up hard to the surface only to crash her head against one of the ties.

She shifted her body, found a gap between the ties, and poked her head up through the surface. "Alonzo?"

No answer. Belle aimed the beam of her waterproof flashlight in all directions but saw no sign of him. She ducked back underwater and felt the current pushing her down the tunnel.

Where is he?

She emerged again between a gap in the ties.

"Alonzo?"

The only sound came from the shoulder-high water rushing past her. She pointed the light to the top of the tunnel and saw she'd drifted beyond the snakes. She aimed the beam back up the tunnel. The shooter hadn't made the turn.

She heard splashing.

There. Maybe twenty feet down-tunnel she saw movement—an arm sticking up between the ties. She tried to crawl onto the trestle but her ankle and the rushing water rendered her efforts useless. She inhaled a deep breath and swam as fast as she could underwater until she reached him. Probing, she found a gap. They both pushed themselves up through the ties.

"Any sign of the shooter?" he asked between gasps of breath.

"No. Maybe he's gone."

"Doubt it."

Belle figured they could probably manage to crawl back up onto the tracks, but they'd present an easy target. And they might run into more snakes. She tried to remember whether the Great Basin rattlers were swimmers. She didn't think so. "Let's stay in the water." She could hear his teeth chattering and knew they both were looking hypothermia straight in the face.

"Cold water, cold air, doesn't make much difference," he said.

"We can move underneath the trestle and pop up for air whenever we need to. Go."

They walked bent over along the tunnel floor submerged in the swirling water, stopping every thirty seconds or so to lift their heads between the ties for air. Soon they approached the mouth of the tunnel and spotted lights in the distance illuminating the treatment plant. The sight gave them both a small spurt of energy, and they moved more quickly until they finally reached the mouth itself.

The water level lowered to chest height, but they kept their bodies submerged to make it harder for the shooter. Belle checked her watch again. Almost midnight. Had they been in the tunnels that long? The treatment plant appeared deserted.

The trestle curved away from the tunnel, down to a small maintenance station in the distance, over half a mile away. The water poured through the mouth into a dirt ditch fifteen feet below us. She could see the ditch continuing for about sixty feet before funneling the water to a huge pipe, maybe four feet in diameter, leading into the plant itself.

The mouth of the tunnel outcropped over the steep cliff so there was no way to climb down, certainly not in their condition. No walkies and both of their phones were dead inside their pants pockets floating back up the tunnel. They huddled under the water with only their heads showing.

"If we make our way down the track to the maintenance station," Belle said, "it will take us a while. The station's deserted, and we'll be over a half-mile from the plant itself. Not to mention being a sitting duck on the open trestle for the shooter to pick us off. But if we stand up to jump into the ditch we're also fully exposing ourselves to the shooter if he's still back there, just not as long. So we have two choices. One, we wait here in the water until the morning shift arrives and shout for help. The downside is, we might not be able to shout because we'll have turned into ice cubes. Choice two—"

"C'mon!"

He rose, planted his wobbly feet, and half sprang, half fell into the ditch. She watched his head go under, which meant the water was deep enough to cushion his fall.

Crak, crak.

Two bullets whizzed by her ear. She ducked, stumbled, and fell out through the tunnel mouth into the ditch water. Her feet touched bottom, probably ten feet deep, and she propelled back up to the surface.

When her head broke through, she spotted Alonzo. "Stay under!"

This time three shots slapped the water between them. They submerged, and the force of the water pushed them downstream toward the pipe. Belle poked her head up to breathe and risked looking back. In the mouth of the tunnel, she glimpsed a man. Too dark and too far away to make out any features. After a long moment, the shadow retreated back into the tunnel. Alonzo popped his head up next to her and took a breath.

"I think we're safe," she said. "The shooter's gone."

The water tumbled them along toward the pipe leading to the treatment plant. She didn't know what was at the other end of that pipe, but she had no intention of finding out. She swam to the wall of the ditch and tried to climb, but the sides consisted of cold, slick mud, and she couldn't find purchase. The water pushed her toward the open pipe, which now resembled the gaping maw of a sea monster about to swallow them up.

Alonzo swam past her and reached the pipe first. *Oh, my God, he's going to be sucked in.* "Alonzo!"

He spread-eagled his body across the mouth of the pipe like a very porous filter. A moment later Belle crashed into him, almost knocking his grip loose.

"Climb over me! Hurry!"

She understood and crawled up his body, reached the top of the pipe then rolled off onto the dirty snow.

She could see his grip loosening. She pulled off her jacket, wrapped one end around her fist, and tossed the other end to him.

He grasped the jacket with his right hand and clawed his feet against the soft walls of the ditch. She leaned back, pulled with all of her remaining strength, and he was finally able to slither and slide up and over the edge.

He crawled over to her and helped her put her jacket back on. Their whole bodies shook.

Fortunately, the temperature was probably a degree or two above freezing, but with wet clothing and nothing on their feet, they couldn't survive much longer without shelter. They hugged each other close and rubbed each other's backs in a futile attempt to generate heat. She looked over his shoulder to the water treatment plant fifty yards away.

They staggered to their feet and headed toward the building. Her bare feet were numb, and Belle hardly felt the icy cold from the snow. Not a great sign.

She assumed the door would be locked, so they'd need to break a window to gain entrance. She refused to allow Alonzo to die of hypothermia huddled in the doorway of the Jordanelle Water Treatment Plant. They were close now—

"Shit."

"What?"

The building had no windows. Could there be a night watchman? She had no idea.

They staggered to the door. Belle found a rock and pounded it against the locked double doors as hard as she could. No response. Off in the far distance she saw the flickering lights from the highway. She'd have to trek across heavy snow and through a thick stand of pine trees to flag down a car. "Wait here. I'll get help."

"You'll never make it. I'll go."

The truth was, neither of them could make it to the highway in their condition.

Then, from inside the plant, they heard footsteps.

Chapter Twenty-Six

S cout snuggled his big head tighter into the space between Alonzo's lap and the couch arm, nudging him close enough to Belle so their shoulders grazed. Alonzo finished up a call with the Park City police detective.

"I'll be happy to shoo him away," she said, not taking her eyes off her nails, chipped in far too many places to count as a result of their tunnel adventure. She dabbed the nail polish remover onto each one.

Alonzo responded by scratching under the dog's chin, and Scout's eyes closed in blissful pleasure. He was the only one close to experiencing blissful pleasure. Alonzo wore jeans with a wide leather belt and one scuffed tan boot. His other foot, tightly wrapped like hers, rested on her thirdhand coffee table.

Carrie sat on what passed as Belle's one living room chair, and her knees almost touched the coffee table. Alonzo ended the call. "How's the shoulder?" Carrie asked him.

"Little better. No broken bones."

She turned to Belle.

"I'm fine. Really."

"You're the worst liar in the world. Don't ever play poker."

"I told her the same thing," Alonzo added. He nodded toward Belle's hands. "How can you be so concerned about your nails after almost drowning in the tunnel?"

She shrugged. Her aches, pains, cuts, and bruises had been part of her long enough now to qualify as her new normal. But she was not prepared to include her disastrous nails in the new normal category. She nodded toward four nail colors on the table. "So, Carrie, which color do you like?"

Carrie's eye roll signaled she couldn't care less. "I don't know. Maybe that brownish-orange one?"

"Burnt Copper. Good choice. Feels like a burnt copper kind of day."

After finding them drenched and shivering uncontrollably at his door, Belle was sure the watchman's first inclination had been to contact the nuthouse and reserve two rooms. Instead, he kept his composure and offered treatment from the plant's first-aid kit along with some dry uniforms and socks. And most important, two cups of steaming hot coffee. Belle even drank it black.

While waiting for Carrie to pick them up, they went back and forth about alerting the police to the shooters. In the end, they decided to wait until the next morning. Even if they called immediately, by the time the cops arrived and worked their way up the tunnel the shooter would be long gone. They both needed sleep, and neither of them was interested in getting bogged down by police interviews. Her mind remained only sharp enough to know her mind wasn't sharp enough to deal with penetrating questions concerning the reason they were in the mine in the first place. Carrie arrived quickly and transported them to the town's all-night clinic where x-rays determined they both would probably live.

Alonzo spent what was left of the night on her couch. She considered offering him the left side of her bed, figuring they were both too tired and beat up for any accidental connections. But then she remembered what happened down in the mine, facing certain death, when their bodies touched. Not saying the thought of making love to the man never crossed her mind, but her head brain reminded her body brain there's a time and place for everything. And this wasn't it.

When she woke, Alonzo had already been up a few hours, using the time to report their ordeal to the local cops. A few hours later Carrie showed up with fresh bagels, OJ, and a lot of questions. Belle had given her the abridged version. The plastic bag containing the powder residue had survived their tunnel ordeal and Alonzo arranged for testing.

"You think it was Danny Pags in the tunnel?" Carrie asked.

Belle shrugged, wincing as the move sent pain shooting up her neck. "I glimpsed the shooter standing in the mouth of the tunnel but only saw him for a second. Could've been him, but I doubt it. Our decision to check out the mine was spur-of-the-moment. He would have no way of knowing we were going to be there." She turned to Alonzo. "So what did the police say?"

"They sent a team into Keetley soon as daylight broke using one of the maintenance rail cars," he replied wearily. They made it to the lift but found nothing except a dead rattlesnake caught on one of the ties, a couple pairs of jeans, each with a phone in the pocket, and one soggy boot. They figured the other boots were underwater and didn't spend time looking for them. By the way, our stuff will be at the station whenever we want to pick it up."

She didn't care about the phone or the jeans and had no use for a single boot. "No sign of the shooter?"

Alonzo stiffly shook his head. "Not really surprising. Once the shooter saw us escape, I'm sure he didn't stick around."

"Did they check out the other tunnels?"

"Captain wouldn't let them use the lift. He said it was unsafe, and to search every tunnel in that mine, including side-tunnels and passageways, would take a small army."

"What about the drugs in the storeroom?"

"I checked with my boss, and he liked the idea of leaving the coke in place. Hopefully, Pagano will be spooked by the attention and decide to move his stash. When he does we'll nab him."

Belle didn't try to hide her skepticism. "The DEA's going to post a twenty-four-hour stakeout?"

"Don't need to. It's highly unlikely Pagano will try to move the drugs during broad daylight, and only a few lifts are open at night, and we'll have someone monitoring them. But..." He paused.

"But what?"

"But somebody wants you dead. I wish you'd reconsider and leave town for a week or so, just in case."

Belle didn't respond.

"Hopefully the powder sample will show something," Carrie said.

"Even if forensics comes back with a positive finding on the powder," Alonzo said, "connecting that powder to the avalanche, and then linking that with an attempt to kill Belle is way beyond conjecture. Pagano overheard where you were skiing next, that's it. That's all we have. He would've had to make his way back up to Jupiter, set the explosives, and time the explosion to the precise point necessary for triggering the avalanche to hit you. Virtually impossible under the best of circumstances in the short time frame involved. If someone wanted to knock Belle off, there are much easier and more reliable ways to do it. Sorry, but all things considered, we have nothing."

Taking care not to smudge her nails, Belle opened the drawer in the coffee table and pulled out the Grover Cleveland Alexander baseball card. "I disagree. We showed you this card from the judge's jacket. With a Grover reference attached now to three of the four victims, how can you believe there's no connection?"

"And what about Annie Grover?" Carrie asked.

"Alonzo ran the Annie Grover name through his databases this morning," Belle explained.

"We found an eighty-year-old grandmother in Salt Lake with a few parking tickets and a high school cheerleader in Orem who's a youth leader in her church," Alonzo said. "If there really is a woman connected to Pagano with that name here in the area, my guess is she's using an alias." He stood to leave, and Belle helped him slip his boot over the wrapped ankle. "But it's pretty clear Pagano sees Belle snooping around as a threat. It really might be a good idea if you got out of Dodge for a little while."

"As it happens I'm scheduled to take a group of clients from Omaha down to Monroe Mountain for an elk hunt, so I'll be away for a couple of days."

"A couple of days isn't enough," Carrie said, "but I'm glad you're getting away. I'm not glad you're going to murder a defenseless creature. Can't you tell your clients to take a picture of the animal and hang it on their wall?"

"This isn't a photography excursion. They're paying Peabody a lot of money for the hunt."

Carried sighed. "You're hopeless."

Alonzo and Belle hobbled together out to the door then to the porch. She noticed the bulge in his jacket pocket. No doubt his gun. "By the way, I never told you but shooting that wriggling snake down in the mine in low light was pretty impressive."

"It's in the blood. I was serious, you really should stay out of town for a while. If Pagano believes you might interfere with his

- 194 -

business, he'll kill you."

"I can take care of myself."

A half-smile then a strong, gentle hand on her shoulder. "I'm well aware of that, but Danny Pags is different." He locked his gas-flame blue eyes with hers. "Please be careful."

"Promise." *Did her throat catch? Don't think he noticed.*

He made it down a few steps and turned. "One more thing."

"Yeah?"

"You have a great ass."

She smiled. "Ditto."

He chuckled and walked away.

Chapter Twenty-Seven

Belle watched Carrie shuffle in from the kitchen with another cup of tea, apparently suffering from a crazy compulsion to mother her. She was watching an old *Law & Order* episode on TV, but her mind was on Alonzo.

"No more tea. I'll go to the bathroom and never leave."

Carrie ignored her and set the cup down on the coffee table. "Goldenseal. It contains berberine that activates your white blood cells. Critical for fast healing."

Belle sipped the tea and forced herself to swallow. It tasted like she'd just taken a bite out of a dead tree branch, and she coughed to clear her throat.

"Sometimes it can taste a bit bitter," Carrie said.

"You think?" Belle pushed the cup away and leaned back on the couch. "Here's an idea. How about a little vodka? No olives, no lemon or lime, no produce of any kind. Maybe an ice cube or two."

Carrie's expression clouded, and she didn't respond right away.

She sat down beside Belle and hesitated before she spoke. "I've been thinking. And if you tell me to mind my own business, I'll completely understand. But I did a little research online about your IED condition. Apparently, it can be exacerbated by the consumption of alcohol."

Hadn't been expecting that. She was fully aware of the booze-IED connection. Counseled about it in juvie and by the Marine shrinks. Uncle Sal and Aunt Helen might've mentioned it a time or two. Or three. She'd tried to cut back and felt she'd made progress, but she figured a couple of pops now and then weren't going to make any difference. "You think I drink too much?"

"No. I mean, I don't know." Carrie shuffled in her seat. "Is it possible that the euphoria you feel when the IED trips in allows you to momentarily escape the guilt for what happened to your Marine brothers?"

Never thought of that.

She straightened and raised both of her palms outward. "Look, none of my business. I won't bring it up again. Drink your tea."

"Do I have a choice?"

"No, but if you're going to be such a baby, maybe I could put a drop of honey in it."

"Here's a better idea. Bring me a cup of honey with a drop of tea in it." Carrie reached for the mug, and Belle covered her hand with hers. "I really appreciate your concern. You wouldn't have brought up the booze if you didn't care."

She smiled warmly and headed back to the kitchen.

Belle filed away a small promise to think more about the drinking. Maybe cut back to one drink a day. Unless it was a short pour of course.

She turned her attention back to secret agent Alonzo Longabaugh. *"It's in the blood."* Alonzo's strange comment nagged at her. Was his father a government agent? She pulled out her phone and googled "Longabaugh and lawman." She was surprised when the first entry read, "The Sundance Kid." Belle loved the old movie and eagerly read the Wikipedia entry. *Holy shit.* The Sundance Kid's real name was Harry Alonzo Longabaugh. The article showed a photo of Longabaugh posing with Robert Leroy Parker, aka, Butch Cassidy. Maybe she was only seeing what she was looking for, but to her, the resemblance of the real Sundance Kid to Alonzo was striking.

Belle called out with a drop of excitement in her voice. "Hey, get this. I think Alonzo's a descendant of the Sundance Kid."

"What?" Carrie responded from the kitchen. "So a descendant of the Sundance Kid is visiting the film festival named after his famous ancestor. Little weird."

"I know."

"Actually, he does look a little bit like a young Robert Redford," Carrie added.

"He resembles the real Sundance even more." Belle smiled inwardly and looked forward to teasing Alonzo about his famous gunfighter ancestor the next time they met.

She changed the channel. A cable news show was airing a retrospective on the life of Brad Banks. Anything for ratings. A string of photos from his life flashed on the screen—pictures of his parents who'd moved to Park City from Ohio, Brad as a toddler on skis, the typical school pictures, his big break in a comedy about a moose, his rise through Hollywood to stardom, his glamorous wife, his home in Beverly Hills, and then the video of his death. Though she'd seen it many times, she still couldn't pull her eyes from the image of the juggler in the crowd behind Banks.

A few more photos appeared. These must've referenced the handful of controversies in his life because the caption below the picture described disputes with co-stars and showed cell phone footage of a fistfight with a parking attendant who supposedly made an unflattering comment about his wife. Another photo flashed on the screen, and this one looked like a high school photo of a young woman. The caption below the photo read: Annie Kupchak.

Belle grabbed the remote again, turned up the volume, and called out to Carrie. "Listen to this."

The female narrator's voice filled the room. "...Kupchak. Three years ago Annie worked as a waitress at a bar in Park City, Utah. She claimed she'd been impregnated by Brad when he returned home to visit his folks. He vehemently denied the allegations and called Annie another crazy stalker-fan who would say or do anything for her few minutes of fame."

"I think I remember that now," Carrie said. "The mini-scandal made the headlines for about a minute and a half then disappeared into the dustbin of pop news history. The name of the girl never registered."

The narrator continued. "Annie gave birth to the child and was encouraged by her friends to institute a paternity suit against Brad, but she had no money for lawyers. Sadly, Brad's characterization of the girl's mental state proved prophetic as less than a year after the child's birth, Annie tragically took her own life. The next scandal in Brad's life took place only two months ago on the set of—"

Belle turned off the TV and returned to her laptop. Carrie sat down and squeezed next to her so she could see the screen. "Annie Kupchak" was still notorious enough to make the first Google search page. Belle opened a two-year-old article in the *Park City Beacon* where the headline read: *Local Girl Dies of Drug Overdose*. The paper displayed the same high school picture they'd just seen on TV.

The story described Annie as a twenty-two-year-old woman who'd stayed in the area after graduating from Park City High and dreamed of becoming a vet. She worked as a waitress around town to save money for college. She told friends she became starstruck when she'd waited on Brad Banks and he'd asked for her number. A night later, he invited her to his hotel room for a drink before a promised dinner at the hotel's restaurant. She knew he was married, but he told her he was getting a divorce. Annie claimed to her friends that he'd forced himself on her, but she didn't tell the authorities because she blamed herself for going to his room.

Two months later, she discovered she was pregnant and contended the child was his. Banks denied he'd ever had sex with her and brushed her off as an obsessed fan. When the baby girl was born, Annie again approached Banks about providing support. He refused, disputing paternity, but declined a blood test. Annie couldn't afford a lawyer to pursue the matter and, according to her family, she became depressed and started drinking heavily. Social Services removed the child from her, and the baby was handed over to foster care. A few days before the article appeared, Annie combined excessive alcohol with a bottle of Dilaudid and never woke up. Banks couldn't be reached, but his publicist released a statement expressing "condolences to the family for the unfortunate death of an obviously very troubled woman." The article went on to provide details of the funeral.

Carrie leaned back. "So when Banks said, 'Annie' he must've meant Annie Kupchak."

"Right, which means Grover is someone or something separate."

"Do you think maybe the juggler was a friend or family member of Annie's who decided to take revenge against Banks? He whispers Annie's name to Banks moments before he pushes Banks into the truck."

"But what about the others? Could Annie Kupchak be linked to them?"

"I don't know, but we still have the Grover connection linking

Harrison and Maddox—Walt's last words to you, and the judge's baseball card."

"Uncle Sal has lived here all his life. Harrison was from out of town, but Virgil Dodd and Judge Maddox were all local. I'm sure he knew them."

Carrie handed Belle her phone.

Belle rose unsteadily to her feet. "No, we need to talk to Sal in person."

***

Sal ended a call and waved them into his office. Scout stayed with Dora because he knew what was in that bottom desk drawer.

They took a seat in front of Sal's desk, and after Belle assuring him her injuries were entirely manageable, they brought him up to date, ending with their theory about Annie Kupchak.

"It's like we know all of these deaths are connected," Belle said, "but the link isn't continuous. Did you know Judge Maddox and Virgil Dodd?"

"Of course. Didn't know Banks, although I'd met his mother on several occasions. She'd moved here from Ohio, I believe, when Brad was young."

"What about Annie Kupchak?" Carrie asked.

His eyes saddened. "No. When the allegations broke about Banks and Annie I, along with most everyone else in town, took notice because she was from here. But then in a day or two, the story disappeared. I think Annie was the product of a broken home. Apparently, her dad was never in the picture, and the mom lived with Annie in a trailer park north of Heber."

"Any knowledge of a link between Annie and the other victims?" Belle asked.

"No." Sal paused. "I did represent Virgil Dodd in a matter a year or so ago. I can tell you only what you can learn from public records. Virgil was sued by a young woman who worked as a secretary in the county public works department. She alleged that at a going-away party for a co-worker Virgil showed up as the city council's representative. Several people were over-served, and Virgil offered the young woman a ride home. Her name was Lettie Carver. When they arrived—"

Carrie and Belle interrupted in unison. "Lettie?"

Belle leaned forward and tried to tamp down the excitement in her voice. "When we arrived on the accident scene, I noticed scratches in the snow next to where we believe Virgil, not Markie, was supposed to die. Could have been intentional, or the random result of dropping tree branches. I thought it read, Lexi." She pulled out her phone and showed him the photo. Looking at the picture now, She could see it spelled Lettie. "Damn."

"Let me guess," Carrie said. "Virgil forced himself on her, she got pregnant, he denied it."

Sal appeared stunned. "You must've read the court filings."

"No, Belle said. "Just starting to see a pattern."

Sal raised a cautionary finger. "Remember, these are her allegations, they were never proven."

"Why not?" Carrie asked.

"Her lawyer withdrew; Lettie could no longer pay him. The judge on his own could've ordered Virgil to take a blood test, but the case became moot when Lettie failed to post for a hearing. She left town. Sadly I heard later she fell on hard times and was arrested for drugs and prostitution in Laramie." Sal's voice softened to a near whisper. "The baby was taken from her, and she hung herself in a jail cell."

"Is it possible Harrison and Judge Maddox also impregnated someone?" Belle asked.

Carrie continued the thread. "And someone is exacting

revenge?"

"Or a group of someones," Belle said. "Family, friends, maybe even a stranger, a deranged avenger."

"I don't know," Sal said. "I'm not sure there is any way of knowing unless the police undertake an investigation. And frankly, right now you have little more than speculation."

"I don't think we're talking about family members here," Carrie said. "If we assume all the male victims impregnated a young woman and, as they used to say, 'didn't do right by her,' the chances family members of four different girls somehow conspired together to exact revenge seems like a stretch."

"So we might be talking about a deranged avenger," Belle said, "someone who believes he's exacting justice for those women."

Carrie said, "We should assume that the female victims had little money, or they'd be able to assert themselves in a court of law. Which means they probably were forced to deliver the baby at the free clinic."

Belle had an idea. "Molly Hovenden, the bartender at NoName, volunteers there part-time."

"Those records are confidential," Sal said.

She ignored him and checked her contact list. She had Molly's number from back when she took care of Fred the cactus. She dialed and after five rings prepared to leave a voicemail message when Molly picked up.

"Hey, Belle." She sounded chipper. "How are you? Everything okay?"

She was breathing heavily, like she'd just come in from a run. Belle put the phone on speaker. "Hey, Molly. Yeah... well, no, not exactly. Look, this might sound a little weird, but do you still volunteer at the woman's clinic?"

"Part-time. Why do you ask?"

Belle hesitated. "I was wondering if I gave you the names of several women, whether you could check to see if they might've given birth at the clinic."

"No, sorry. Without a subpoena those records are confidential. From the first day, it was drilled into me that under the HIPAA law anyone who released that kind of information would find herself in a lot of trouble."

Belle raised a placating hand then quickly dropped it, feeling silly doing so over a phone call. "Fair enough. So let me ask a hypothetical. If a young woman who became pregnant by a man other than her husband or boyfriend came to the clinic to give birth, would the records state who the woman claimed to be the father? Again, hypothetically."

"Well, hypothetically, yes. But you haven't answered my question. Are you okay? Do you need help?"

Belle forced a lighter tone. "I'm fine. Have to go. Thanks, Molly." She ended the call.

"Without more evidence, how are we going to get a subpoena?" Carrie asked.

Sal answered, "You're not."

Chapter Twenty-Eight

D anny absently dragged his finger lightly across her breast. She could tell his mind was elsewhere.

"Penny for your thoughts?" she teased.

"Business."

"Sure it wasn't Sonja?"

"Ah, little sis is jealous."

She shrugged. "Maybe."

He lightly tweaked her nipple.

She was about to suggest that she hoped they were moving toward a place where there would be no one else, just each other. But she hesitated, sensing this wasn't the time. They were both giving off so much body heat from almost an hour of sex that, instead of snuggling back up to him, she elected to simply trail her fingernail lightly back and forth across his sculpted chest, mirroring his finger on her breasts. "Thanks to you, I bet I just lost ten pounds."

"I think you were so high from your avalanche adventure you would've had the same experience with a broom handle."

"Ewww, that's so gross." She tugged on a tuft of his chest hair.

"Ouch."

She immediately kissed his chest. "Sorry."

"I must admit, I am impressed. The odds of catching your target were close to impossible." His approval elevated her mood even higher. The avalanche had been the final test. The chances of it working without any innocents dying were practically zero. She'd assumed Plan B—an apparent suicide—would have to be initiated. She would've forced Maddox at gunpoint to sit in the driver's seat of his car parked in the garage. She'd make him consume whatever amount of Chivas scotch was necessary to cause him to pass out. After connecting the tailpipe to a crack in the window with a garden hose she'd turn on the ignition. He lived alone so the chances of him expiring before someone found him were very high. But it hadn't been necessary because Plan A, the avalanche, her most difficult test yet for God, had worked.

"God's on my side. 'Be ye afraid of the sword: for wrath bringeth the punishments of the sword, that ye may know there is a judgment.' And of course, I had a backup plan; nothing quite so awesomely spectacular."

He rolled onto his elbow. "How many more on your list?"

Good question. Yaeger, her real daddy—may the flesh on his body sear in hell for all eternity—had raped her mom then dumped her like yesterday's trash. Just like her great-great-grandma, Maria. Powerful men who not only physically assaulted their victims, but also stole their dignity, their reputation, their very essence. Evil scum who ruined lives with no fear of consequences.

As a six-year-old, she'd opened that door in the cheap Vegas whorehouse where they'd been staying. The small black hole in her mom's head and the blood on the filthy shag carpet weren't what she remembered the most. Instead, it was her mom's eyes. Half-open, staring at her, yet not seeing. She'd been too young to know what a vow meant. A few years passed before she truly understood what that monster had done to Nancy Halpin, and she'd made herself a promise to make him pay. And she did. Later, Aunt Lucy, Nancy's sister, told her about her great-great-grandma, Maria Halpin, and how Maria's life also had been ruined by a powerful man.

The forced five-year stay in the hospital—*you mean crazyhouse, don't you?*—had given her plenty of time to think. Despite her best efforts, Yaeger was still alive. And other young women who'd been victimized by powerful men then discarded and forgotten. More lives had been ruined. Something had to be done. Someone needed to say, "No more!" The swift administration of justice was required. God had chosen her to undertake the job, and He fully supported her quest.

Yet Danny's question—how many more?—was not an easy one to answer. She knew her cause was just, but she also knew she couldn't rid the entire world of assholes who victimized and dehumanized women. And that touch of stomach indigestion seemed to increase in intensity with each success. Guilt? *Hell no!* At least she didn't think so. But she sometimes wondered whether Nancy Halpin or Maria Halpin would've supported the Sword of Justice? An image of the familiar photo filled her mind. Taken only a week before Nancy died, it showed her and her mom standing together, Nancy's arm around her daughter's shoulder as she held her birthday present. Would her mom have supported her cause? Truth was, she didn't want to answer that question.

So how many more?

She finally answered. "It's a long list, but the avalanche was so..."

"Your words were 'awesomely spectacular.' "

Her smile broadened. "Right. Anyway, maybe I should consider Maddox the finale. You know, like in a movie they save the big explosions for the end? And while I know God's on my side, I wonder if He thinks it might be time to stop, too. And then there's Belle Bannon. She doesn't seem to want to give up. It might be time to stop."

"Sonja reported to me what Bannon said at the coffee shop. She is an irritant and can easily be dealt with."

Sonja. Molly wondered how long she would have to share him with the scrawny bitch. "So, you and Sonja—"

He smiled. "You have nothing to worry about. From now on, Sonja and I will be just business."

Yes! Her whole body brightened. Finally, he would be hers alone. That is, if the bitch didn't bad-mouth her with lies. She had an idea.

Danny asked, "If you end your mission, will you stay here?"

She hadn't planned to bring up Tuscany quite yet, but maybe this was a good time. She rolled to the edge of the bed, reached down to her backpack on the floor and fumbled through its contents. She found her phone, set it on record, and slipped it just under the bed. If Sonja tried to lie about her to wiggle her way back into Danny's romantic life, she'd now know about it. She found the brochure, rolled back up onto the bed and handed it to him. "I want to move there and... and I was hoping you'd move there with me." There, she said it. She rolled up onto one elbow and faced him, so close their bodies almost touched. She barely realized she was holding her breath. He focused on the brochure and didn't speak for what seemed like forever. Finally, he scrunched closer, his face nearly touching hers.

"I've been to this part of Italy. It's very beautiful. I would love to go to Tuscany with you."

She couldn't speak. She kissed him and pressed her body against his. At that moment there was absolutely nothing in the world she wanted more than to have Danny Pagano inside her. She pulled him on top and wrapped her legs around his hips. She didn't try to hold back the tears. She could honestly say she'd never been so happy.

***

Danny tightened the towel around his waist and opened the door for his sister. She almost bumped into Jello and Sonja about to enter. She reached her hand around Danny's neck and kissed him one last time, as giddy as a schoolgirl. It wasn't lost on him that she did so right in front of Sonja. *Women.*

Sonja and Jello entered and closed the door behind them.

Jello grinned. "Looks like you made her happy, boss."

Danny shrugged. He knew he was an accomplished lover.

"So what's up?" Sonja asked.

He kept his voice even, businesslike. "I'm going out of town, and I've decided to temporarily shut down the local operation while I'm gone. Tell our clients there will be no more deliveries for a while." Danny didn't mention that the appearance of a DEA agent on the scene motivated his move. Why tempt fate?

"But we're right in the middle of Sundance," Jello protested. "I'm getting top dollar, especially for the glass."

"Just a week, maybe two."

Sonja's eyes drifted to the Tuscany brochure resting on the crumpled bedsheets. "Is it Maria? Is she causing trouble?"

Danny had never revealed his sister's real name or their family connection. No reason for the help to be privy to his personal life. "No, but Maria can be a little... crazy. These accidents—the man who fell off the lift, the impaled girl, the judge, the movie star—she's responsible for all of them."

Jello didn't hide his disbelief. "How? Why?"

Danny explained her motive and described how she accomplished each of the murders.

When he finished, Sonja shook her head. "She's not only crazy, but also very clever."

"The problem is, her 'mission' as she calls it is drawing attention from Bannon and her friends, attention that isn't helpful."

"Bannon's a hunting guide who volunteers on the ski patrol," Jello said. "She's not a cop, she's not a fed, she's nothing. Why are you so concerned about her?"

Danny paused. Good question. "I personally encouraged her to back off, yet she continues to track the murders like a bloodhound bitch, not to mention she's now befriended a DEA agent. Longabaugh."

"I met him when they tried to flip me," Sonja said. "Not someone to mess with unless necessary."

"Still don't get why Bannon rattles you," Jello said. "And we've dealt with the feds before with no problem."

Danny's withering stare caused Jello to involuntarily step back. "You should know by now that I don't rattle. Bannon and her friend happened to be present at the time of or soon after each 'accident.'"

"If Maria's caught and charged with a string of murders, it won't be good for any of us," Sonja said.

"Agreed."

Sonja looked away like she was talking to someone else. "Would you like us to arrange Maria's own accident?"

Danny paused before answering. *Would I do that to protect myself and the business? Could I do it to my own family?* "We're not there yet. But that doesn't mean something more can't be done to eliminate the Bannon problem."

Sonja and Jello nodded in unison then headed for the door.

"I'll put the word out we're taking a two-week holiday," Jello said. "Our customers will be pissed, but they'll get over it."

"Tell them if they come back to town any time before March we'll offer a loyalty discount."

"That'll help. Good idea, boss."

"Sonja, why don't you stay a while."

Jello suppressed a smile and closed the door behind him.

Danny dropped the towel around his waist and returned to the bedroom with Sonja following close behind.

***

Danny slumped down into the green swivel chair next to his bed, a film of glistening sweat still covering his naked body. First Molly, then Sonja. Even his voracious sexual appetite had been sated, and he was relaxing, catching his breath when the call had come in.

Felix Ross's gravelly voice coming through the burner phone speaker had sounded reasonable, accommodating. "I can pass on the assignment to someone else, Danny. No blowback from us if you want to walk away from it."

Of course, Danny knew the opposite was the case. "No sir. I can handle it. No problem."

"I have confidence in you. Let us know what you need."

"Absolute—"

Ross ended the call. Both an amazing opportunity and a lethal threat had been dumped into his lap. Vegas wanted someone taken out. Hardly a challenge in a normal case, but this was different. Stetson Davis was the head of the DEA's Organized Crime Task Force. Not only would he be well guarded, but Ross insisted that the hit must be viewed as an accident.

Davis was in town for the festival. Apparently, his favorite niece was appearing in one of the films. Danny had been told taking on the job was voluntary, which of course was bullshit. If he tried and failed and there was even a puff of heat blown back to Vegas, he was as good as dead. Yet if he were successful, his stock would rise considerably in the organization and it was likely they'd reward him with territory expansion, hopefully including the lucrative Denver franchise.

It took him almost an hour spinning back and forth in the green chair to come up with a plan to take out Davis and make it appear like an accident.

A plan that involved his sister and a tent company.

Chapter Twenty-Nine

Revenge.

Belle was virtually certain she'd found the link connecting the four victims—revenge against heartless men who impregnated then abandoned a young woman. Yet so many questions remained, and how was she supposed to connect the dots when the damn dots kept jumping all over the page? Okay, she needed to concentrate on her job. Put the "accident" investigations aside for a while.

She pulled out of the stable parking lot east of Heber and headed toward Main Street. She'd accepted Harlan's offer to guide a two-day hunt, a last-minute fill-in for the rescheduled Omaha trip. Two guys from Baltimore. Maybe a couple of days in the wilderness would clear her mind.

At the intersection of Route 189, she took a left and stopped at the traffic light. A café was open, and she knew from experience it served the best cinnamon rolls in the state.

"You guys interested in a cinnamon roll? I personally recommend them."

"No thanks," Bob replied. We're good."

"Suit yourselves."

The light turned green and she was about to ease down on the gas pedal when she noticed a tall woman exit the café and head for a green car in the lot. A tall woman with red hair. The redhead appeared to fix her gaze on Belle, just for a moment. Belle was ninety percent certain she was the same woman who'd been trailing Danny Pags on the slope, the same woman who'd been eavesdropping at the crappy coffee shop. The redhead turned away and entered the car, an SUV of some sort. But she didn't immediately start the car, instead focusing intently on her rearview mirror.

"You got a green light," Bob said.

"Yeah, sorry."

Belle drove off but kept one eye on her rearview mirror. Sure enough, the green SUV drove out of the parking lot and turned in the same direction. When Belle turned south on I-15 for the three-hour drive down to Monroe Mountain, she couldn't tell whether the redhead was still behind her. She'd accepted Harlan's offer to guide a two-day hunt, a last-minute fill-in for the rescheduled Omaha trip. Two guys from Baltimore. Maybe a couple of days in the wilderness would clear her mind.

Scout had been relegated to the cargo area in the back. Bobby O'Rourke sat in the passenger seat and his buddy, Jim Wilson, stretched out on the back seat. She'd learned their names from Harlan. Both appeared to be in their early forties. Bobby was an inch or two shorter than her. Could be a bodybuilder. Wilson was tall and skinny. She'd detected a slight accent when he said hello but couldn't place it. After loading their gear, neither spoke much. She could hear Wilson dozing in the back.

She forced the redhead from her mind and focused on client relations. From her first day on the job, Harlan had drilled into her the importance of being outgoing and friendly with the guests so they would consider returning for a future hunt, but her attempt at conversation had elicited little more than polite, clipped responses from Bobby. In fairness, they'd mentioned they'd flown in yesterday from Baltimore and with the early wakeup were probably tired. She'd noticed all their clothing from their hats to their boots appeared brand new. Harlan habitually sent all guests a detailed list of what kind of clothing to bring depending on the season. She had a strong suspicion Bob and Jim were greenies.

"So, Bob, you guys hunted elk before?" she asked in her chipper cruise director voice.

"No, but we're really excited."

For some reason, Bob didn't seem particularly excited. Then again, it was hard for most people to sound excited at six-thirty in the morning.

Bob continued. "The trip was a Christmas present from our wives. First time hunting big game, so you'll have to excuse us if we do something wrong."

"Only two things can go wrong: you violate my safety rules, or you don't have fun." She flashed a smile that would make Harlan proud. "I'm sure Harlan warned you this time of year bagging a bull in the mountains will be tough. Almost all of them have moved down to the valley for the winter. But chances are half decent you'll get a shot at an elk cow, and in many ways, particularly now, the cows are wilier than the bulls."

"No problem," Bob said. "We're not interested in a trophy for the den. My old lady would mount my own head on the wall if I brought home a stuffed elk head."

She laughed politely.

"And we wanted to hunt in the mountains, you know, like in the movies."

She could feel Bob's eyes scanning her body. No problem, happened every time.

The next question was expected: "So, ain't girl guides kind of unusual?"

"Actually, there are a lot more of us than you might think."

Bob lowered his voice to a conspiratorial tone. "You ever, you know, have any problems with clients getting a little...? You know."

"Very rarely. On those few occasions when a client forgot his manners, the hunt was cut short, he lost a lot of money, and some even went home with a bone positioned differently than when they arrived."

Bob chuckled, as she hoped he would. Jim didn't say a word from the back seat.

"I'll do my best to see you have a great experience."

"That's all we care about. Right, Jim?"

Silent Jim responded with a noncommittal grunt.

She glanced at her dog in the rearview mirror. Instead of nestling down like normal, his ears remained perked up, and he stared at Bob, fully alert. Maybe Scout sensed Bob wasn't a dog person.

***

Belle made better time than expected, and they reached the town of Monroe, population 2,500, fifteen minutes early. After their brief conversation coming out of Heber, Bobby had joined his buddy and nodded off. She never saw the green SUV with the tall redhead again.

"Hey, guys."

Bob and Jim snapped awake, sat upright, instantly alert. After a few seconds, they realized where they were and relaxed.

Bob asked, "Here already?"

"We're in Monroe, still have about a two-hour drive up the mountain to the trailhead. I wanted to see if you needed to stop for anything. Food, bathroom?"

"Thanks, we're good," Bob replied. He closed his eyes and settled back in the seat again. Silent Jim didn't say a word. Scout would be good for the rest of the ride too.

Strange. She'd guided greenhorns before, and in each case, the men had been so excited they peppered her with questions virtually the entire ride from Park City to the trailhead. On the other hand, she honestly didn't mind the quiet. It allowed her to enjoy the scenery along the drive east up into the snow-covered foothills. No matter how often she'd made the trip, each time the view seemed a little different because of the lighting. Last year a hunter brought along his son, a professional photographer. As the kid explained it, even modest changes in the early morning light due to the season or the weather cast the mountain in different hues, like an artist who painted the same landscape a hundred times, yet by changing a dab of color here or there made each a masterpiece in its own right. Belle didn't know anything about art, but she thought she understood what he was saying.

The county did a decent job keeping the road clear of snow, but ten miles later the paved road ended. From that point on, the surface switched to gravel with a six-inch snow cover. She looked for tire tracks in the snow to make the climb easier, but no such luck. Not surprising. Their destination was government-owned land requiring a limited-access permit, and elk hunts in January were not common. She moved the gear knob to four-wheel-drive mode and continued up the mountain.

Ninety minutes later, the road ended at the trailhead.

"We're here, boys." Again the two men awoke as if they'd been zapped by a cattle prod. Scout hopped up to all fours in the back, his eyes locked on Bob.

"Don't think your dog likes me," Bob said.

"No worries, he's fine." She wasn't sure Scout really was fine and wasn't sure why, but she didn't want a customer complaining to Harlan about an aggressive dog. "It'll take a little bit of time to load up the mule before we can be on our way. You'll find sandwiches and water in the cooler."

She unloaded Louise first. The mule had been a member of Peabody's transportation department for years. When Belle first arrived, it took the two of them a little time to come to an understanding about who was boss—Louise was. Belle tied her to the trailer then positioned the sawbuck pack saddle just below her withers. The sawbuck had two cinches instead of one to help with load distribution and reduce friction on the animal's skin. The design dated back to Genghis Khan and had been used by a range of travelers from Middle Eastern Arabs to early American fur trappers. Newer designs existed, but she preferred the sawbuck for the simple reason Louise preferred it, and she was the one carrying the load.

The panniers—weatherproof containers about the size of a carry-on suitcase—had already been packed with the tents, cooking gear, and food. she tied the panniers and tentpoles onto the saddle and added the H-shaped top-pack with lighter, bulkier items such as extra clothing and sleeping bags. Bob and Jim helped themselves to the food. Jim must've devoured his first sandwich in two bites because he'd already consumed half his second. She wasn't concerned. Simply standing in the cold burned calories, and the ride to base camp and the subsequent hike uphill through the snow would burn thousands more. She always brought enough food.

She unloaded the horses. "Hope you guys read the expedition materials where it explained we'd have to travel by horseback part of the way."

"No problem," Bob said. "We've ridden before. Although these horses don't seem very big. Sure they can carry us?"

"They're cow ponies. We'll be moving along narrow trails overlooking some pretty high cliffs. You want an animal who has the agility to avoid falling."

Bob grinned. "Sounds good to me. Last thing we want is for one of us to fall off a cliff."

Belle rode point, leading them along the trail through a thick stand of limber pine with Louise tethered to her saddle and Scout walking along side. Bob followed, then Jim.

They'd been riding a switchback trail up the mountain for two hours. The temperature hadn't risen much, and a few random snow flurries floated down from a leaden sky. Belle was used to dressing for the elements— thick stocking cap, heavy wool-lined coat, thermal underwear, waterproof wool pants, insulated sorrel boots, heavy gloves—and always carried extra extreme weather gear in the Cherokee for clients in case they arrived unprepared. She was mildly surprised that both Bob and Jim were well equipped, and the extra clothing wasn't needed.

They arrived at a fork in the trail. Belle stopped and dismounted. "This is a good place to take a pee and stretch your legs."

The two men dismounted and stepped off the trail to relieve themselves. She walked a bit deeper into the trees on the other side of the trail and did the same.

When she returned, Bob immediately asked, "How much longer before we make camp?"

"Two choices." She gestured toward the path on the left. "We can take that trail to a good camping spot at this same elevation. Maybe take us half an hour. The second trail leads to a site farther away and requires a more challenging ride up the mountain, but the view is more spectacular, and the chances of finding elk are greater."

Bob didn't even bother to check with his buddy. "Let's go up the mountain."

Chapter Thirty

An hour later they still hadn't reached the campsite. The sun finally made an appearance and the temperature rose to just above freezing. Only a few wispy clouds streaked across a cobalt blue sky. Beautiful, and if Belle had her way, she wouldn't ruin the moment with conversation. But part of her job entailed making friendly with the customers. The trail widened enough for them to ride three abreast, and she slowed to allow Bob and Jim to catch up.

"You guys doing okay?"

Bob responded, "Fine."

I turned to Silent Jim who'd barely said a word since initial introductions back at the stable. "So, Jim, being from Baltimore you must be a big Ravens fan."

"Yeah." His voice was surprisingly high-pitched for such a big man.

"I lived in Pittsburgh for a while and love the Steelers," she said.

"Always a battle between the Steelers and Ravens," Bob said.

Silent Jim said nothing. A bit unnerving, but she'd met people over the years who released words sparingly. Nothing wrong with that.

The trail narrowed up ahead. "We should be at the base camp site soon. From here on up the trail can be a little tricky. Most important thing is to trust your mount. No quick jerk of the reins. These horses have made this ride many times." She rode forward, pulling Louise behind her.

The trail veered away from a thick stand of bristlecone pine. Hardly the most majestic of conifers, the bristlecone was noted for its distinctive yellow-orange bark and its gnarly profile. The trees were extremely hardy and often could be seen curling up from near-vertical surfaces making them a favorite subject of landscape painters and photographers. The juxtaposition of color—orange bark, green needles, white snow, blue sky—usually spurred guests to snap a few pictures. She stopped.

"Pretty view. We can pause for a minute if you want to take a few photos."

"That's all right," Bob said. "Let's keep moving."

"Suit yourself." While there was no cell coverage in the mountains, the phones' photo feature worked fine, and she'd never led a hunting group that didn't pull out their phones and snap photos along the way, particularly greenies. A worrisome feeling sprouted in her gut. Probably nothing. She continued up the trail toward the McConkey Gorge.

After another half hour, they reached the gorge and followed the very narrow trail along the ridge. The gorge might not meet Grand Canyon standards, and the McConkey River at the bottom was little more than a trickling creek. But anyone who fell off the gorge cliff would be a goner.

Bob called from behind me. "Why can't we ride through the

trees?"

"A fair question. Fallen trees and broken limbs are hidden beneath the snow. Too easy for a horse to break a leg."

"Better for the horse to break a leg than for the rider to fall over the cliff," Bob gruffed.

She twisted back in the saddle to face Bob and flashed a wide, reassuring, Harlan-approved smile. "No one's going to fall over the cliff. Pretend you're on a pony ride at the state fair. Let your mount find his way. Haven't lost anybody yet."

Bob seemed satisfied.

A couple of miles later the trail widened again and she led them away from the gorge to a clearing between two stands of limber pine. "We'll set up base camp here." She dismounted and the others followed suit. She found a chunk of beef in one of the food packets and tossed it to Scout then set about untying the panniers. "If you guys want to give me a hand unloading Louise, that would be great."

Neither Bob nor Silent Jim looked particularly happy as the three of them carried the panniers to a level spot she'd used on previous hunts.

"When are we hunting?" Bob asked.

"I figured we'd go out at dawn tomorrow." The sun had disappeared, clouds approached from the west, and the snow flurries swirling through the air had increased. "Only a couple hours of light left, and by the time we pitch the tents—"

"We was hoping we could go out today. Can't we put up the tent later?"

Belle was surprised by Bob's reaction. Most hunters, especially greenies, welcome the opportunity to rest after the trek up the mountain on horseback. That uneasy feeling in her gut was growing. "Uh, sure. Just don't get your hopes up."

She attached three-leg hobbles to all four animals and removed the rifle scabbards. She'd learned her lesson a few months earlier when a two-leg hobble hadn't prevented a horse from bunny-hopping down the trail and almost tripping into the gorge. She would unsaddle them later.

Bob and Jim removed their rifles from the scabbards. Before leaving the stable, She'd checked to make sure their rifles were not loaded. Safety rule number one. Each carried Browning BAR LongTrac .30-06 semi-automatics, both outfitted with Leupold scopes—very good hunting rifles that allowed for rapid-fire without having to pull a bolt between each shot. She found the ammo box in her saddlebag and gave each man four cartridges. The rifles actually held five cartridges—four in the magazine and one in the chamber—but safety rule number two was no hiking with a shell in the chamber. A guest trips, the safety's off, and suddenly one of Harlan's potential return customers is missing a head.

"Two-twenty grain soft points," she explained. "They'll do max damage when they enter the body. In the unlikely event you get a shot, the kill zone's an eighteen-inch circle right behind the shoulder, about eight to ten inches behind the withers. The bullet will explode the heart and lungs, and hopefully, the animal won't go far before he drops."

Bob and Jim loaded their rifles.

Belle strapped on a holster carrying her Stealth just in case she needed to put an animal down then dug out three small backpacks from the top-load pack and handed one to each man. "Throw in a few sandwiches, a flashlight, and an extra pair of socks. You'll find them in the red pannier. Normally I'd say take along a roll of toilet paper but we're not going to be out that long."

The two men did as instructed and they were ready to move out. Belle made sure the safeties were on and instructed the men how to position the rifle sling so they carried the weapon on their backs with the barrel pointed up. She checked her watch. One hour up, one hour back. Two hours. Maybe an extra half hour because the return hike would be faster, but no more. Her watch included a GPS feature, and she marked their location. In an emergency, they'd be able to find their way back in the dark. "All right, gentlemen, follow me. We're at about eight thousand feet. The air's thin so if you need to stop and catch your breath just give the word."

With Scout leading the way they moved up through the trees, taking care to hike in a switchback pattern to make the climb easier. The tightly wrapped Ace bandage and the thick boots acted like a splint on her ankle, and she felt little discomfort trekking through the snow.

Fifteen minutes later, Bob asked, "Can we stop for a minute?"

"Sure." Both men were gassed. No surprise. Time for a little client relations small talk.

"You know, the largest elk ever taken was killed right here on Monroe Mountain."

Bob's grunt was the only response. Interesting. In the past when she'd mentioned this fact to other groups they'd immediately hit her with a barrage of questions about the trophy elk: How big was it? Where was it shot exactly? How many tines in its antlers? What gun and ammo were used? She figured Bob and Silent Jim were probably focused on catching their breath. The thin air affected some people more than others. She pulled a bottle of Gatorade from her pack and handed it to Bob. "Drink this. The electrolytes will help."

"Thanks." The two men split the bottle, and a few minutes later they continued up the mountain. As they moved, Belle searched for three things: tracks, scat, and compacted snow where an elk might have bedded down.

After another twenty minutes, she could hear both men gasping with each step. Time for another—suddenly Scout turned sharply and ran twenty yards to their left. they followed him to a large oval of compacted snow.

"Elk bed, and it's recent," she said. "Size indicates a bull. You boys might get lucky after all. Who knows, you might even get really lucky and bag *Tsoapittsi*."

"What's *Tsoapittsi?*" Bob asked.

"Ute word for Ghost Elk. No one really has ever seen him, but the legend goes there's a white elk, big as a house who roams these mountains. You bag him, and your picture will be on the cover of every hunting magazine in the country. But I wouldn't get your hopes up. I doubt if he's even real."

Usually when she told the story of the Ghost Elk questions would pour out of the clients' mouths. Jim and Bob looked like they couldn't care less. That uneasy feeling in her gut was growing like a weed.

She spotted the tracks heading east and they looked fresh. Bob slipped the rifle from his shoulder. "Not yet," she cautioned. The man hesitated for a moment then slung the rifle back over his shoulder.

They followed the tracks for a few hundred yards. She spotted the pile of scat and bent down for a closer look. "Still steaming. He's close." Any other hunters would hardly be able to control their excitement, but Bob and Jim looked bored out of their minds. She felt an icy chill, and it wasn't because of the weather. *Was it possible? Maybe I should've paid more attention to my dog.*

She stood. "Let's catch our breath for a minute then we'll see if we can bag you an elk."

Without appearing obvious, she maneuvered so both men were in front of her. "I went back to Pittsburgh this year visiting family and had a chance to take in the Ravens-Steelers game. Froze my butt off, but at least the Steelers won."

Bob responded, "Yeah, but we'll get you next year."

The Steelers-Ravens rivalry was the most intense in the league. Even a casual Baltimore fan would know the Ravens swept the Steelers this season.

Shit.

Chapter Thirty-One

Belle figured since her new pals likely intended their happy little group to be a person short on the way down the mountain, it might be a good idea to create a little social distancing.

"Okay, guys, here's what we're going to do. I need you to split up a hundred yards apart and move downwind. I'll circle upwind. He'll catch my scent and hopefully move away from me toward you. Be alert because on rare occasions a bull will charge you. Don't un-sling your weapons or chamber a round until you spot him. Safety first. Decide between yourselves who's taking the first shot. And remember, aim for the kill-zone."

Bob and Silent Jim exchanged nervous glances; they clearly didn't know what to do next.

"Uh, sure," Bob said. "Safety first."

Belle remained in place with Scout hugging close to her legs and watched them trudge through the snow heading east. Bob said something to Jim, but they were eighty yards away, too far for her to hear. She bent down and scratched Scout's head. "Should've paid more attention to you, boy." She was almost certain her Baltimore clients were Pagano's men sent to finish what they started on Black Lightning. That was the problem—*almost* certain. She watched them disappear into the trees. Could she abandon two greenies alone on the mountain based on that single football comment? Lots of guys pretended to know more about sports than they really did. She was probably over—

Crak.

The bullet smashed into a branch just above her head. Guess she wasn't overreacting. She dropped to the snow and rolled behind the tree. Scout stood tall in the clearing, a sitting duck.

"*Corri!*" Run! He fled into the underbrush.

Crak crak.

The bullets skimmed the tree trunk spraying her face with bark chips. Three shots. Between the two of them, they now had only five rounds left. *Unless they carried extra cartridges in their jacket pockets.* Which, of course, they must've done.

The next two shots came from a different direction. Belle glimpsed one of the men moving counter-clockwise. He was circling behind me. Made sense. She fished a small telescope out of her backpack and saw Bob, or whatever his real name was, move closer to the gorge at her nine o'clock. He'd have to expose his head, arms, and shoulder to take another shot. From her three o'clock Jim fired again. He wanted to distract her so his buddy could take dead aim.

Belle remained focused on Bob who moved behind a thick pine. She felt a familiar calm as she trained her Stealth on the left edge of the tree. She recalled Bob was right-handed, so unless he was ambidextrous he'd emerge from that side.

There was the gun... the hands... the shoulder... the head...

She squeezed the trigger. Bob fell and disappeared in the snow.

She wriggled backward to another tree, then another. If she could reach the trail along the gorge rim, she figured she'd be able to make good time back to base camp. It would be too dark to ride a horse down to the trail head, but Jim would freeze up on the mountain, which meant he'd need to head to the base camp as well. She'd be expecting him.

The snow came down heavier now, giving her more cover. She thought about Scout but resisted calling for him. She trusted the dog's survival instincts and assumed he'd be following her on a parallel route through the protective brush. The light was diminishing, so she risked rising from her crouched position. No gunshots. She turned and moved west through the trees as fast as she could.

Ten minutes later, she could see the gorge rim.

"Freeze."

Jim's high-pitched voice came from behind a tree off to the side. *Damn.* He'd anticipated her path and was waiting for her.

"Drop the gun."

Belle considered a drop-and-roll to her left behind a thick pine tree, but at that moment Jim, who now apparently decided to no longer remain silent, emerged from his cover and approached with the rifle trained on her head. She dropped the gun.

He smirked. "You made us, didn't you?"

"Ravens won both games."

Jim shook his head. "Sloppy on our part. Jello and me, we never been to Baltimore."

Jim had turned into a regular Chatty Cathy. "And where *are* you from, *Jim*?"

"Denmark. They call me the Dane."

"I assume Jello is your pal, Bob."

"Real name's Angelo but people call him Jello."

"Cute. So, Dane, can we make a deal here? I can double whatever Pagano's paying you."

"Sorry." His finger tightened on the trigger.

From a spot hidden in the trees, Scout's bark shattered the silence. The Dane glanced up.

The split-second distraction was all she needed. She lunged for the gun barrel and pushed it aside as the Dane fired. With the benefit of leverage, she twisted the barrel toward the man's leg, slipped her finger over Dane's finger on the trigger, and pulled. The heavy round caused the big man's leg to explode in a spray of muscle, ligament, blood, and bone. He screamed and dropped to the snow, writhing back and forth in pain.

This man was at least partly responsible for the deaths of four innocent people. Belle felt the lizard door in the back of her brain crack open. The white light leaked through.

Carrie's image momentarily blocked the door. *Are you crazy! You're in control of the door, Belle. He's no longer a threat to you. Break the cycle....*

Then she saw Markie Dodd, an innocent eighteen-year-old girl skewered on a tree branch, her life snuffed away from her, away from everyone who knew her and would have known her over the next seventy or eighty years. Belle saw her dead eyes staring at her, the snowflakes softly dusting her lashes.

The lizard door flew wide, flooding her mind with blinding white rage. She crashed the gunstock down hard on the Dane's face and vaguely heard the man's cheekbone crack. The next blow pulverized the big man's eye sockets. She felt a rush, an indescribable high as she luxuriated in the white light enveloping her. She pounded the Dane's head again and again until the Dane's face had turned to raw hamburger.

The white light drifted away like an early fog dissipating in the morning sun. And Belle felt—what? Guilt? *You didn't break the cycle of violence, Belle….* Maybe a little. Maybe more than a little. *Shit.*

Given the late hour, she had no choice but to hike down to the base camp. At first light she could ride back to the trailhead and get help. But first, she needed to find her dog.

"Pick him up."

She stiffened and turned to see Jello pointing his rifle at her head. Blood seeped from the left shoulder of his jacket.

She didn't hide the resignation in her voice. "Why, Jello, what an unpleasant surprise."

"You're supposed to be such a tough bitch, pick him up. We're going back to base camp."

"No way. He's too heavy."

"Pick him up or die."

A quick review of her options revealed she had none. She bent down and struggled to boost the body across her right shoulder, then stood, staggering under the heavy weight. She couldn't hold him for long, not in these conditions. She tried a few steps and collapsed.

She stood and brushed the snow from her jacket. "Your pal has gone on to his just reward, so I don't think he'd mind if we left his worldly remains here."

Belle figured his next move would be to fire a bullet into her brain. At first, fear immobilized her. And then, the inevitability of death cloaked her with a strange calm. She gazed at the majestic snow-covered trees surrounding her and decided she would be hard-pressed to come up with a more preferred place to depart this world.

Jello raised his gun, and she took in a last deep breath of the crisp mountain air.

"Then drag him."

She wasn't expecting that.

"You got it."

"Now move."

A few more minutes of life perked her up and allowed a chance, however slight, that she could come up with a miracle. She grabbed the body by the collar and pulled enthusiastically. At first, the snow acted as an impediment, but she discovered if she could maintain a little speed, the body would plane on top of the snow like a motorboat moving across the water. Of course, the faster she moved the sooner she would meet the bullet meant for her head.

Along the way, she stumbled numerous times—some legitimate, some not—as she dragged the Dane's body like a field-dressed whitetail, continually searching for an opportunity to make a break. But Jello never got too close. She had a knife sheathed on her belt; he had a gun. If she made a move, she calculated her survival chances as zero. Of course, they were probably zero anyway.

By the time they approached base camp, full darkness had descended, and she was gassed.

"Use your flashlight," Jello ordered.

She got it. Jello needed both hands to hold the rifle. Belle dropped the Dane and found her flashlight in the backpack. With the light in one hand, she grabbed the Dane's jacket collar with her other hand and kept pulling.

Maybe a little conversation might act as a distraction. "I assume you and the dear departed Dane were the ones shooting at me on Black Lightning."

"Wasn't trying to kill you, just cause a fatal accident."

"And that's supposed to make me feel better? By the way, you almost blew my head off with the first shot."

"Yeah, that was a mistake. Boss didn't want somebody to find you with a bullet in your brain."

"Your boss and I are in agreement on that one. And the mine?"

"That was me. Didn't make no difference if I shot you there 'cause I would've made sure no one found your bodies."

"Except you shot at us after we jumped into the drainage pond."

"I was pissed. Good thing I missed."

Again they we're in agreement.

"Now move, bitch."

She moved.

***

When they eventually reached the edge of the campsite, she could scarcely catch her breath. "Where do you want me to put him?" she gasped. "By the way, sorry about your friend, but in fairness he was trying to blow my head off."

"Not my friend. Partner. Toss me your watch." She did as she was asked. He stepped back to give himself time to react if she tried anything. With his left hand, he removed a phone from his jacket pocket.

"Sat-phone?"

Jello ignored her, pressed a single button, and spoke into the phone. "The Dane's down. Need a pickup." He provided the coordinates of the base camp from her watch and ended the call.

"No one's going to be able to rescue you tonight," Belle said.

Jello glanced up with a tiny smile on his face.

"Helicopter? "You're bringing a helicopter in here?" Actually, the weather was clearing, and spots in the terrain were probably flat enough for a copter to land. "Danny Pags is not going to like you adding the cost of a helicopter to your bill." He ignored her.

She had an idea. A pretty crappy idea, but at the moment, a crappy idea was better than no idea.

"You're losing blood," she said. "I have a first-aid kit in my saddlebag. You're not going to be able to dress the wound yourself.

Who knows how long it'll take for the copter to arrive? Maybe I do a good turn for you, you do a good turn for me. I disappear, change my name. You tell Pagano you left me for dead. Everybody's happy." She saw the tiny smile she was hoping for.

He shrugged. "Sure."

Of course, Jello didn't believe her line of bullshit, and as soon as she dressed the wound she had no doubt he'd kill her.

"Leave the body here, and no funny stuff."

"Don't worry, we have a deal."

Belle walked toward the horses. Fortunately, her horse was the farthest from the Dane, and Louise offered a partial screen. She pocketed the flashlight then reached up and slowly unbuckled her saddlebag. Using her body to block Jello's view of her right hand, she slipped the hunting knife from the scabbard on her belt, reached down, sliced through the hobble, and replaced the knife.

Jello called out, "Hey, what are you doing there?"

Okay, showtime. She jumped on the horse. *"Heeeyahhh!"*

The horse leaped forward. Jello's first shot caught Louise in the flank, and she stumbled to the ground. Belle headed for the rim trail. The beam from Jello's flashlight darted from ground to tree then side to side. Once out of his sightline she figured she could make her way down the trail using her flashlight. Another shot sailed overhead. She reached the rim trail.

The next bullet smacked into her horse's rump. The animal reared up and she struggled for control.

"Whoahh!"

The final shot caught the horse in the neck. Blood spattered back onto her face.

The horse squealed, reared up again then lurched forward, flying over the cliff carrying Belle in the saddle.

Chapter Thirty-Two

*W*hap whap whap...

    Hostiles closing. Fingers drenched in blood trying to plug the hole in his chest. Hang on, Charles, I can hear the copter. So sorry.

Belle's eyes cracked open. Barely a slit. Bright light overhead. Consciousness fading, in and out and in again.

Whap whap whap...

Can't hear the screams. No acrid smell of propellant.

I'm not in the sandbox.

Her eyes transitioned from blur to semi-blur. Another minute—maybe less, maybe more, maybe a lot more—passed before her mind cleared enough to focus. *Helicopter.* It hovered over the campsite then slowly descended, guided by a spotlight mounted to its undercarriage, until it disappeared overhead behind the cliff overhang.

Jello's Ubered helicopter. Made sense. The copter would

remove Jello and the Dane's body to places unknown, leaving her crumpled remains at the bottom of the canyon. When she didn't arrive back in the office, Harlan would send a search team. That Bob and Jim from Baltimore, Maryland, were missing and her horse and pack mule had been shot would trigger an investigation, but discovering the Dane's body with his head smashed to a bloody pulp would amp up the attention paid to the tragic situation exponentially.

For the first time, she sensed her head leaning on something warm and hairy. The horse. She must've landed on the horse instead of the ice-covered rocks at the bottom of the cliff. She looked up to the cliff overhang, trying to judge the depth of her fall. Twenty, thirty feet? Didn't make sense as the gorge dropped a minimum of two-hundred feet from the rim. She wiggled her toes and fingers. Check. One by one she moved her arms and legs and in each case felt pain. She couldn't tell for sure, but nothing appeared broken.

She tried rolling to her left and smacked her head into the trunk of a solitary bristlecone pine. Using the tree to steady herself, she struggled to her feet and took stock. Every muscle in her body screamed, but all things considered, she was in decent shape for a gal who just fell off a cliff. Her pack hung by a single strap from her shoulder. The dead tree broke the horse's fall, and the horse broke her fall. If the tree hadn't been there... She figured the substantial cliff overhang prevented Jello from having a clear line of sight in the darkness, and the big man had every reason to assume she'd fallen to the rocky floor far below.

The problem was the copter. When it lifted off, Jello might spot her with the benefit of the undercarriage light. She'd be an easy target and at that point, Jello might decide her body being discovered with a bullet in the brain was vastly preferred to the alternative. She figured she had two choices: lie down next to the horse and play dead, or press herself under the overhang and hope she wouldn't be discovered. Neither was particularly promising. Her heart moved quickly toward jackhammer mode.

Belle chose option two. Ignoring the pain shooting through her body with every movement, she crawled up the slope to a spot where the overhang seemed to extend out the farthest and pressed herself flat against the cliff wall. A moment later, the copter rose into her sight line. She couldn't make out the shape of the copter itself, but the spotlight lit up everything in its narrow cone.

The edge of the cone skimmed the slope then stopped, lighting up the dead horse like a diva on a Broadway stage. She'd never actually watched a diva on a Broadway stage, but she'd seen pictures. She pressed her body hard against the cliff face, trying to melt into the rocky soil. The light seemed glued in place, its intensity bleaching the dead horse's coat from chocolate to tan. The edge of the spotlight's cone tickled her feet. She held her breath. Her pulse accelerated even faster.

The light flicked off. She could hear the sound of the copter fade as it rose and melted into the darkness above. She released a string of rapid breaths and stepped out from under the overhang.

Her foot slipped out from under her, and she tumbled down the slope, scraping every limb into the rocky soil to gain purchase without success. She shot past the dead horse and stretched her arm out as far as she could. Her fingers brushed the horse's tail and clamped tight. She spun around the horse and stopped. *That's twice the horse has saved my ass.* She ran her hand along its neck and silently offered her thanks.

Now what? The temptation to simply lie there, close her eyes, allow sleep to salve her pain, and never wake up overwhelmed her.

Then she heard a bark.

Belle slowly raised her head. Scout's nose slipped over the crest of the cliff. Her dog was alive. She couldn't abandon him. He'd die if she didn't move.

"*Stai li!* Stay there."

Using the horse's tail, she pulled herself to her feet. Somehow her backpack remained on her shoulder. She fished out a flashlight and aimed the beam in each direction parallel to the rim. The drop to the left appeared shallower. She slipped the pack back over her shoulder, trained the light at her feet, and carefully climbed across the cliff face, moving slightly upward every few feet.

Each step seemed to trigger sharp pain in a different part of her body. *Control your mind, control your pain.* Sir, yes sir! Words from her SERE training—survival, evasion, resistance, escape. *Force yourself to focus on something else.* So she focused on something else—an image of Jello's neck with her fingers wrapped around it—and continued to angle her way upward toward the surface, inch by inch.

Jello had taken her watch so she had no real sense of time, but she figured almost an hour passed before she reached a point directly under the overhang.

Scout had been following her progress, making his way along the edge of the rim and offering an occasional bark of encouragement. She reached her right arm up and over the extending lip, hoping to find a rock, a tree root, something, anything to grab. No luck. She'd seen a movie once where a group of friends out for a sail all jumped overboard for a swim. But there was no ladder to climb back into the boat. There they were, all next to the boat hull, the gunnel barely out of reach. And they drowned. Safety so close, yet so far. She had no interest in drowning.

Belle carefully moved along the cliff face under the rim for forty or fifty feet and extended her arm over the lip until finally, her fingers felt a thick tree root. She tugged hard. The root held firm. She pocketed her flashlight and slipped her belt under the root.

After buckling the belt to create a closed-loop, she inserted her foot and vaulted up, her full weight now on the belt.

The root snapped.

She lurched forward and grasped onto the broken root as her legs flew out into the cold night air.

"Arrahhhh!"

Straining every muscle in her arm, she struggled to hold on. The root was slick with ice. Her grip slipped. Frantic, she swung her body back and forth like a spastic pendulum. First her knee then her leg slid up over the edge. She wiggled and squirmed until her hip, elbow, and the whole left side of her body had rolled up onto the surface. *I made it.* Her heart was about to explode.

She felt herself slipping back down the ice to the cliff edge. The weight distribution was too unbalanced. She clawed at the ice in a futile attempt to slow her speed. Scraping her toes into the ice did nothing. *My knife!* She pulled the knife from its scabbard and stabbed the ice hard, hoping the knife would hold and she'd be able to use it to leverage her body away from the rim. It held, and she held.

For a moment.

Then her body weight loosened the knife, and it scraped a jagged line in the ice as her body resumed its momentum. Her gouging feet then her legs slid over the edge. *No!* This time there would be no dead horse to break her fall.

A viselike grip grabbed her collar. *Scout!*

He held tight, allowing her to shift her weight just enough to roll away from the rim.

Belle lay there for a while, catching her breath then rolled to her knees and hugged her dog. She figured she had just enough energy left to make it back to the campsite and pitch a tent. SERE rule of thumb: first shelter, then heat, then water, then food. They would survive.

She heard a soft intermittent braying. Louise, dying in pain. She remembered the mule had been hit by Jello's bullet, the one meant for her. The mule needed to be put down, but her gun was up on the mountain. She shuddered. She'd have to use her knife.

Belle vowed she would find Danny Pagano and his man, Angelo. And then she would kill them.

Chapter Thirty-Three

H aving crossed the Nevada line ninety minutes earlier, she spotted the Elko exit up ahead and figured she should be getting close to her destination. Westbound 80 had been wide open almost since she'd left Park City, and she could've goosed up the speed of her old rust bucket and arrived sooner. But now wasn't the time to be pulled over by some bored cop anxious to flash his shiny lights and wail his cool siren.

Sonja changed the station to some hip-hop crap and immediately closed her eyes and bounced up and down and back and forth to the beat.

She switched back to country. "Driver chooses."

"We've been listening to that crap for hours."

"I like it."

"Christ, it all sounds the same." She lowered her voice in a poor attempt at parody. "I lost my girl and my truck and my dog and I'm so sad I'm gonna drown myself in beer and cheap whiskey."

"At least it has a melody."

Sonja sighed dramatically, folded her arms, and turned her attention to the bleak passing landscape. Without moving, she said, "You know Danny and I fucked for an hour after you left."

She didn't know but responded with a shrug. The last thing she wanted was this bitch to think she cared. She tried with only partial success to convince herself Danny was just sleeping with Sonja to keep her in line. A morale boost from a boss to his employee, nothing more. "Of course I knew. Danny tells me everything. He and I are going to Tuscany, just the two of us very soon." As soon as the words left her mouth, she regretted them. What if Sonja told the stooges and they told Vegas? *Shit.*

"Well that's not definite, and if we do go it wouldn't be for a long time."

Sonja shook her head and tried to scrunch her body sideways to get more comfortable. She winced then pulled the Glock from her waistband and rested it on the seat between them.

She wished she didn't need her, but someone had to drive the truck back, and in a previous life Sonja had worked as a driver for a construction company. Besides, having a little protection handy was always a good idea.

The previous night Sonja had knocked on her door to deliver a message from Danny—*her* Danny—along with a genealogy chart showing that some government dude named Davis was a direct descendant of President Grover Cleveland. Mind-blowing. At last, a chance to right the horrible wrong Cleveland had visited upon her great-great-grandmother, Maria Halpin.

And yet... Davis himself had done nothing wrong. Was it right to visit the sins of a man upon his great-grandson? For all she knew, Davis was a good person who respected women. Danny also sent along a plan that would allow her to exact revenge against Davis and still have his death appear like the others—a tragic accident.

She couldn't disappoint Danny, and she rationalized that Davis, like all politicians, must have engaged in dirty deeds somewhere along the line. Yet she couldn't escape that sickening feeling in the core of her stomach. She took a sip of the stale takeout coffee from the rest stop. It didn't help.

She had to trust Danny, and his plan was brilliant. His idea would provide a truly spectacular mission finale, a plan even more awesome than the avalanche. Then they'd fly off to Tuscany and their new lives together. She struggled to suppress the smile that was trying to burst across her face at the thought. The last thing she wanted was for the skinny bitch next to her asking why she was so—she grimaced from a quick sharp pain in her belly then a light lingering ache. Nerves. That's all, just nerves.

A green overhead road sign signaled her exit was approaching. She turned off the radio. "I think this is the exit."

Sonja pulled a grimy piece of crumpled paper from her jeans pocket and checked the direction notes. "Yeah, this is right."

"You sure he's expecting us?"

"Vegas gave Danny the contact, and he made the call. If Danny says the guy will be there...he'll be there."

She took the exit and had to slow as she made her way along the old country road east of Elko. She drove by a small motel. Judging by the number of parked vehicles the place looked to be mostly vacant. A mile later she came to an abandoned filling station.

"That's it," Sonja said.

She drove along the cracked pavement to the back of the dilapidated structure. The only illumination came from a streetlight a quarter mile up the road. Sure enough, the truck was there with *GoldChem Corp.* emblazoned on the door in gold and black lettering. Two huge cylindrical ISO tanks lined up on the truck flatbed, each containing 145 tons of liquid. According to Danny, the chemicals were en route from a supply company near Reno to the gold mines in northeast Nevada where they would be used in a process to extract the precious metal from chunks of ore.

The truck cab door opened, and a short fat man stepped down. He waddled toward her. His uniform jacket was too small, barely reaching to the bottom of his rib cage, and she could see the thick rolls of fat around his waist jiggle with every step.

"You go," Sonja said. "I'll wait here." She checked her scrawled notes. "His name's Pinski. Make sure."

She stepped out of the old SUV and from the back seat pulled out a black and silver nylon athletic bag with the Vegas Raiders logo emblazoned on the side. She closed the door and walked up to the fat man. "What's your name?"

"What difference does it make?" The man reeked of stale beer, and he seemed to wheeze with every word. "You got the money in that there bag or don't you?"

She held his gaze. "Need a name."

His eyes rolled. "Pinski. All right? Now if I don't see some cash in the next—"

"I have your money." She unzipped the bag. "Hundred grand. It's all there. You're not going to make me wait while you count it, are you?"

Pinski paused for a moment. "Guess not. But if I find you're short I'm calling the cops and telling them I was robbed. I'll give them a real accurate description."

She didn't hide her impatience. "It's all there."

"Remember, you need to have the truck back in forty-eight hours. That's it."

"Understood." Her eyes narrowed. "Is there going to be a problem when you don't post at the mine on schedule?"

"I already told them I got food poisoning at the last truck stop. They bought it. It's happened to me for real a couple of times before." He patted his ample belly. "I have a delicate digestive system."

A few comebacks popped into her head, but she wisely held her tongue.

"Each tank contains 4600 gallons. You have to leave a thousand gallons in each tank and refill them with water. The pump and hose are in the housing behind the cab. The ignition key will unlock it."

"How long will it take me to refill?"

"Hard to say for certain. That's a strong pump and the hose is as thick as a fire hose. Maybe five, six hours."

She figured she'd have more than enough time to do the refill and make the four-hour trip back to Elko. "The guys at the gold mine won't know it's been diluted?"

"Not for a while, and by then the problem will be chalked up to a bad batch or even the chemistry of the ore itself. No one will test the contents before use."

"Where will you be?"

He pointed up the street. "At that motel. And remember, if by any chance you don't make it back on time —"

"Got it." The idiot didn't realize if she went down, he was going with her.

"One more thing." He gestured for her to follow him to the deep shadows behind the truck, out of Sonja's sight. She had a pretty good idea where this might be heading. He held up the ignition keys to the truck and grinned for the first time. "Figured since I was doing you a big solid I deserved a little tip from a pretty girl like you. Gets mighty lonely on the road if you get my meaning." He rubbed his crotch.

Her already churning stomach tightened in revulsion. *Jesus.* Okay, if she had to blow the asshole to get the truck keys, she figured Danny would understand. Just business.

She heard a soft *click* startling Pinski.

Sonja emerged from the shadows behind Pinski and pressed the barrel of his gun against the fat man's head.

"So, Maria, you want me to kill him?" Sonja asked, her voice and face as smooth as glass. "Or maybe just shoot his balls off?"

Pinski shook so hard the ignition keys jingled. "Please, I got a family. Two kids."

She didn't cause collateral damage unless absolutely necessary. *What about Markie Dodd?* Not her fault.

Her mind snapped forward to Danny's plan for the big finale. Could there be widespread collateral damage? No. Sonja had relayed Danny's promise that maybe a few people might get a little tummy ache, but that was it. She snatched the keys from Pinski's trembling fingers and kicked him hard in the balls.

The fat man screamed in pain and doubled over, gasping for breath.

She had one last question for the asshole. "What's the concentration of the solution in each tank?"

Sonja interrupted Pinski before he could respond. "Thirty percent, right?"

Pinski trembled so hard that his double chin jiggled up and down like a tiny bird was caught in his throat. His wide eyes locked with Sonja, and his voice squeaked. "Right."

"Let's get out of here," she said and tossed the keys to Sonja. They needed to drive four hours back to Park City and find a place to park the truck where it wouldn't stand out. The plan was for Sonja to drain a few gallons of the pale yellow liquid and dump it in the creek next to the tent company.

Tomorrow night was the finale. She'd already planned what would happen next. The following morning she and Danny would drive to Mexico, relax for a few days on a sun-drenched beach then fly to Tuscany and start a new life together, just the two of them. Or, who knows? Maybe a kid someday. They weren't blood relatives so no problem there. She hadn't made up her mind on that part yet. Of course, Danny would have to agree.

But right now all she could think about was getting back to her grungy apartment and falling asleep. And hopefully waking up without feeling like battery acid was slowly dripping into her stomach.

Chapter Thirty-Four

Belle scooched down into the worn couch seat, snuggled under her blanket, and propped her feet up on the coffee table, her quilting pouch on one side of her, and her hero dog on the other. Carrie fussed in the kitchen brewing undrinkable tea while she worked on her Navaho quilt.

By the time she'd pitched a tent and lit the gas heater up on the mountain, she'd been too tired and sore to eat and fell asleep in her sleeping bag with Scout beside her. At dawn, she'd consumed three turkey sandwiches and reassessed her injuries. She pictured anatomy drawings of the human body and tried to identify a single muscle that didn't ache. No luck. She'd twisted her right knee and further aggravated her sore ankle. Still, by some miracle she hadn't broken anything and was able to ride down to the trailhead pulling the second horse behind her with Scout following. She hadn't taken the time to pack the camp gear on the second horse but figured Harlan would understand.

The police detective had just left. He'd brought a thumb drive of mug shots from the FBI database, and she'd identified both the Dane, whose real name was Einar Arnesen, and Angelo Biondi. Accompanying information revealed that Biondi and Arnesen have been doing contract work out of Vegas for years.

Carrie brought in a steaming cup of tea. "Drink this. I added a lot of honey."

Though skeptical, Belle did as she was told. The honey helped. Barely.

Carrie asked, "You sure you don't need a doctor?"

Belle's previous new normal had given way to a more current new normal, a status that included every square inch of her body remaining in a steady state of pain. "I'm fine. Doc in Monroe checked me out and gave me some painkillers."

"They working?"

"Absolutely."

"You're a lousy liar, Bannon."

Belle didn't respond, instead focusing on Bondi and Arneson. "Jello and the Dane didn't look smart enough to act on their own. They had to be working for Pagano. But what possible motive could a major drug dealer have in avenging the honor of a few girls?"

"I've been thinking about it almost nonstop," Carrie said. "I now question if there *is* a link. We could be talking about two separate stories. Danny Pags is trying to run a profitable drug business, and he thinks you're interfering. The second story is our avenger, someone bent on exacting justice against these four men."

"If the cops can find Biondi and arrest him for the attempted murder of one Isabella Bannon—that would be me—maybe under questioning he'll shed light on any connections to the four victims."

"From what you said he's a pro, and the likelihood of him getting caught probably isn't that great."

Belle picked up the baseball card from the side table. Grover

Cleveland Alexander. Carrie wedged between Belle and Scout with her cup of tea and watched while Belle googled Alexander. "Even if we assume there's some crazy avenger out there, that doesn't explain the Grover references." They both read a few articles but found nothing of note.

Carrie said, "So you think maybe Alexander impregnated a girl?"

There was no reference to anything of the sort in the articles they read. Belle was vaguely aware of stories of drunkenness and debauchery among baseball players of that era, so she modified her search to "Grover Cleveland Alexander scandals." Again they found no articles. She was about to close the page when Carrie put a hand on her arm.

"Wait. Look at the next entry."

It read, "Grover Cleveland Paternity Scandal." Belle opened the link and they each read silently to themselves. After the first article, they read three more. *Holy shit.*

"Grover Cleveland is one of those run-together presidents between Jackson and Lincoln and Lincoln and Roosevelt," Carrie said. "For the life of me, I couldn't tell you one thing he's known for."

"Well if these accounts are correct, a woman named Maria Halpin, a widow with two children, in a sworn affidavit accused him of rape and fathering her third child then later conspiring with a doctor friend to have her committed to a mental institution so she wouldn't derail his political career."

"Says here she claimed they pressured her to give up the child. God, can you imagine the reaction if that happened today?"

"He denied the rape," Belle said, "and who knows what really happened? Given how women were treated back then, my guess is rape meant something different than it does now."

"So our avenger is calling his victims 'Grovers' in reference to Cleveland."

"But we still don't know what set him off, or why he picked these four men."

"You're right," Carrie said. "Sadly, women become impregnated by jerks every day. And by the way, who's to say the avenger's a man?"

Why hadn't I thought of that? Belle opened several more articles then froze.

"What?"

"Cleveland's victim, Maria Halpin. Check out her maiden name."

Carrie followed her finger to the second paragraph. "Maria Hovenden. Why does that name sound familiar?"

Belle responded with stunned disbelief. "Molly."

"Molly the bartender Molly?"

"Molly Hovenden." She googled the name, found a few matches, and checked out the images. None were Molly the bartender Hovenden.

"Try Halpin."

Belle changed the search term and again received several hits, but not the right ones. "Maybe Molly's not her real name." She seemed to recall Molly mentioning she was from Arizona, so Belle googled "Halpin" in Arizona. She opened the link to an article from the *Arizona Republic* seven years earlier. "Check this out."

The story reported a minor scandal involving the former mayor of Hastings, a small town in the northwest corner of the state near the Nevada border. Sixteen years earlier, then-Mayor John Yaeger allegedly impregnated a young woman named Nancy Halpin who did housecleaning for him. She claimed rape, he denied it, said the encounter was consensual. A typical he-said-she-said situation—except here the "he" was the mayor whose brother happened to be the part-time prosecutor. No charges were brought. He refused a voluntary blood test to determine paternity, and Nancy had neither the money nor the political clout to challenge him.

The cleaning service agency fired her, and because of her minor notoriety no one else would give her a job. She gave birth to a baby girl and moved to Las Vegas, less than two hours away, where she fell on hard times—drugs, booze, prostitution. Two days before her thirtieth birthday, her six-year-old daughter found Nancy's naked body in the seedy flophouse where they were living, sprawled out on the floor with a bullet in her brain. Whether the gunshot was self-inflicted or the result of a dispute with a customer was never determined. "It says Nancy's sister who lived back in Hastings, took custody of the little girl."

Carrie was a faster reader. "Look at this last paragraph. Ten years later, at three a.m. someone set fire to former Mayor Yaeger's home. He almost died. Nancy's daughter was charged as an adult with arson; apparently, the girl blamed Yaeger for her mother's downfall. Because the daughter was a juvenile, the newspaper didn't provide her name. Could the daughter be Molly?"

"Sounds like it. And I wouldn't be surprised if Nancy Halpin was a descendant of Maria Halpin. Remember, the first article said Maria had two children when she was assaulted by Cleveland."

"So Molly learns about Maria, her ancestor. She sees the same thing happen to her mother; a powerful man takes advantage of Nancy then discards her like yesterday's garbage. Molly decides to exact revenge against the man she believes is responsible—Mayor Yaeger."

Belle followed the thread. "Presumably she went to jail. Now she's out, assumes the maiden name of her ancestor, and takes on a quest to avenge girls who've been victimized by powerful men. Her work at the women's clinic gives her the perfect opportunity to find targets."

"We've got to call the police," Carrie said. "For all we know she could be planning her next hit."

Belle didn't respond right away, trying to sort it all out in her mind. "Here's the problem. We have a nice theory, but we have no evidence that Molly Hovenden is Nancy Halpin's daughter, the girl who tried to kill the mayor. Or, what if Molly says, 'Yeah, that was me, I was young and stupid and I paid my dues and now I'm citizen of the year?' It all comes back to the accidents. We need something concrete to first prove they were murders, and then link Molly as the murderer. And we haven't considered what role if any Danny Pags played in the deaths."

"Now I'm feeling the case for Molly acting alone is even stronger," Carrie said. "Yeah, she might've used drugs from Pagano to push Harrison, but I can't see any link between Pagano and..." She gasped. "Oh, my God."

"What?"

"Check out the sister's name."

"Lucy Halpin Pagano."

"Molly is Danny Pags's step-sister?"

Belle ran Lucy Halpin Pagano's name through Google and found a dated wedding announcement." She read out loud from the article. "Lucy Halpin Smith, the widow of Horace Smith of Phoenix, will wed Ralph Pagano of Hastings October 15 at Our Lady of Saints Catholic Church. Mr. Pagano has a son from a prior marriage, and Ms. Smith is the guardian of her late sister's daughter. The couple intends to make their home in Hastings."

"The son has to be Danny."

"So Molly and Danny are what? Step siblings? Step cousins? Definitely not blood relatives." Belle pushed the blanket away and struggled to her feet.

"Where do you think you're going?" A scolding tone from her new mother hen.

"To NoName. It's so hard to believe Molly's responsible. If we're right, she's not an indiscriminate killer. She views herself as some kind of a feminist superhero who's exacting justice against bad guys, the ultimate #MeToo revenge. Her brother, not Molly, is the one trying to knock me off. I want to confront her face-to-face, surprise her. Maybe make her say something we can give to the police."

Carrie frowned. "There have already been three attempts on your life. I don't think you should tempt fate."

Belle ignored her and shuffled toward the door.

Chapter Thirty-Five

As expected, NoName was jammed, so Belle told her trusty dog to wait outside. She and Carrie entered, and Belle stopped short. There at one of the front tables, she saw the tall redheaded woman enjoying a beer and burger. She was smiling at a good-looking guy with shaggy brown hair. Both wore wedding rings. Between them sat a rambunctious toddler in a high chair rubbing ketchup all over his face. *Got that one wrong.* She sent a silent apology to the young mom then turned to the bar. Molly wasn't there.

She and Carrie squeezed between two Woodies wearing their official head-to-toe black outfits and waved to the bartender.

"Where's Molly?" Belle asked.

"Doing a private gig," the guy responded impatiently.

The Woodies shouted drink orders. The bartender pressed, "You want a drink or not?"

In the mirror behind the bar, Belle caught the reflection of the front window, and through that the street, and beyond that... "No, thanks." She headed back toward the door.

Carrie hesitated. "Where are you going?"

"We need hard evidence, right? Maybe the best place to find it is in Molly's apartment across the street. If she's out working a private party, she won't be home." Belle led her out the door.

Carrie stopped on the sidewalk. "Uh, Belle, what you're contemplating constitutes breaking and entering."

"Right. You should wait here." She and Scout left Carrie on the sidewalk and crossed the street.

"Wait." Carrie dodged several cars and caught up with them in front of Molly's apartment building.

"It's really best if I go in alone," Belle said. "Doesn't make sense for you to get yourself in hot water. Stay outside with Scout and act as a lookout. If you see her coming, text me. That way if anything breaks bad, you're in the clear."

She pushed Belle toward the door. "You're wasting time talking. Let's get this over with."

The three of them entered the building and climbed the stairs to the second floor. Belle pointed out her apartment. "Hopefully, the extra key's still where she kept it when I was taking care of her cactus, but that's been a while." She hurried to a potted fake ficus tree at the end of the hall and found the key underneath the decorative white pebbles surrounding the trunk of the tree. The key worked, and in a moment they were inside the apartment of Molly Halpin, aka Molly Hovenden.

Carrie's eyes widened. "My God."

Belle followed her gaze to the dirty blue wall by the door. Someone had written in lipstick, *This is not the blue room!!!!*

Carrie asked, "In the time you've known her, did she seem, I don't know..."

"Crazy?"

"Yeah."

"Not really."

"Not sure what blue room means, but normal people don't write stuff in lipstick on their walls."

The efficiency apartment was sparsely furnished. A cheap unmade bed, a rickety table, an old TV. Small bathroom, smaller kitchen.

Carrie opened a door to the single closet. A few clothes, some ski gear. Scout sniffed a cardboard box resting on the closet floor. Belle opened the box and found a hoodie, silver face paint, and juggling knives.

"Bingo."

Carrie pulled out her phone and snapped pictures.

The fridge held a couple of beers, small plastic carry-out containers from NoName, and a bottle of vodka. Empty microwave dinner boxes were stuffed into the trashcan. Belle lifted the boxes and rummaged through the rest of her trash. At the bottom she found a crumpled envelope addressed to Molly Halpin and handed it to Carrie. "Return address is someone named ASH in Phoenix." Carrie photographed the envelope, and Belle replaced it in the trashcan.

"We need to officially confirm Molly is the one who attempted to murder her father, her 'Grover,'" Carrie said. "Can we call the Arizona prosecutor? Should be public information."

"Probably be better if I can persuade Sal to do it. He's a lawyer and knows the lingo." She checked her watch. "He should still be in his office. With the juggler costume and the letter addressed to Molly Halpin, once Sal confirms Molly was the girl convicted of attempted murder hopefully there'll be enough for a search warrant."

"You realize we'll be putting ourselves in jeopardy for a possible B&E charge," Carrie said anxiously.

"Don't worry, I'll take full responsibility."

Belle spotted a large plastic freezer bag resting on a tiny bedside table. Inside the bag was a small book. "Looks like a diary. Maybe Molly confessed in her diary." She was about to open the bag when Carrie put her hand on Belle's arm.

"Fingerprints."

They'd probably already left fingerprints in the apartment, but just in case Belle found a paper towel roll on the kitchen counter, tore off a piece, and used it to open the plastic. She pulled out the diary and immediately saw that the book was very old. The faded brown cover looked like it might've been red when new, and the edges were frayed. Using the towel, she opened the book and read a short inscription on the inside cover written in flowery cursive:

What Really Happened. Maria Hovenden Halpin. Jan-Feb. 1902.

Below her words, another inscription, this one in different handwriting:

At my insistence, the truthful account outlined in this diary was written by my mother, Maria Halpin, in the days leading up to her death of pneumonia on February 6, 1902. Frederick Halpin.

Without either of them saying a word, they sat down on Molly's couch and read the words of Maria Halpin:

To whom it may concern:

I know I have only weeks left, maybe less. Much has been made of my role in the presidential election of 1884, a time when I was called a drunk, a whore, and a lunatic. At my son's insistence, I'm using my last ounces of strength to write these words. Not to tell "my side," not to offer my "version" of what happened, but to tell the unvarnished truth.

After my husband's death, I needed to find employment and moved from New York City to Buffalo where I'd been offered work in the collar-making department at Flint & Kent, an established dry goods store on Main Street. I could not work and care for both of my children so I left my youngest, Ada, with my in-laws in New Jersey and took young Freddie to Buffalo with me. The store catered to the city's upper classes, and I soon became friendly with many in Buffalo's social circles.

I was introduced to Grover Cleveland, the sheriff of Erie County, and he soon made his feelings known that he would like to court me. I remained friendly but gave him no encouragement.

Time passed. I was promoted to head of the cloak department. I developed a group of friends, mostly through my affiliation with St. John's Episcopal Church.

At about five-thirty in the evening on December 15, 1873, I left my room at the boarding house on Swan Street and walked toward Main where I intended to join a birthday party at the Tifft House Hotel for a friend. I ran into Grover coming in the opposite direction. Over six feet tall, he cut an imposing figure in his black broadcloth coat and top hat. We exchanged pleasantries. I was a grown woman, not a child, and recognized the look of a man bent on turning on the charm. But I wanted to move on. The wind blowing off the lake was particularly bitter, and I was anxious to reach my destination.

He invited me to dinner at the Oyster House. I declined and told him about the birthday party. Grover was charmingly persistent. I found him fascinating. His ambition for higher office was hardly a secret, and at thirty-seven, his future seemed bright. Finally I gave in.

It was the most disastrous decision I ever made and changed my life forever.

"We know how this story ends," Carrie said. "But hearing it from her point of view...wow."

Belle turned the page, careful not to damage the brittle paper.

The dinner was delicious, the conversation very pleasant. Grover could not have been more respectful and gracious. He walked me back to my living quarters at the boarding house. After greeting Freddie, he walked me to my bedroom and, to my mild surprise, closed the door behind him. I suspected he didn't want Freddie to witness his efforts to extract a goodnight kiss. He offered a chaste kiss, and I didn't resist. I could smell the whiskey and tobacco on his breath, but I didn't mind as the same could be said for any man in town. I thanked him again for dinner and led him to the door.

Suddenly, he pulled me tight to his body and groped my breasts. I was about to scream, but he covered my mouth with his hand and roughly tossed me on my bed. I struggled violently against his considerable weight to no avail. A moment later he pulled up my skirt and yanked open my lace drawers. I wanted to scream for help, but doing so would bring Freddie into the room. I could not allow my son to witness what was happening and feared what Grover might do to him.

I thrashed back and forth and through my tears whispered harshly, "Please don't."

His animal passion consumed him, and he continued to have his way with me.

After he accomplished his purpose, I tearfully threatened to report his crime to the police. He went into a rage and threatened to ruin me. He reminded me he was the county sheriff, and his allegation that the encounter was wholly consensual would be believed. I commanded him to leave my room and told him I never wanted to see him again.

Six weeks later I discovered I was pregnant. I considered swallowing poison or snakeroot to induce an abortion but couldn't bring myself to do it. I did what I promised myself I would never do—I contacted Grover Cleveland. He was apoplectic and called me a blubbering baby. Later, he calmed down and offered to send me a stipend to help care for the child. I resigned from my position at Flint & Kent. Were I to stand behind the counter with my protruding belly, I would've been the top subject of gossip in the city, an unmarried fallen woman.

His stipends barely sustained me over the months leading to the delivery date. Grover made arrangements to have the child delivered by his close friend, Dr. James E. King. My son was born September 14, 1874, at St. Mary's Lying-In Hospital, the city's only hospital for unwed mothers. I named him Oscar.

Two years later, on the night of July 10, 1876, my son was taken from me.

The events of that night seared into my brain forever. I was reading by the open window trying with little success to find relief from the oppressive humidity. Oscar played on the floor. I heard footsteps coming up the stairs. I couldn't tell how many people, but definitely more than one. The door burst open and a burly man who identified himself as Detective Watts entered, followed by Dr. King, the man who delivered Oscar.

Dr. King scooped up my child and moved to leave. The baby shrieked in terror. I jumped in front of the door and pulled Oscar away from him. Detective Watts wrapped his arms around me from behind, and Dr. King ripped my son from my arms and hurried down the stairs. I tried to chase after them, but Detective Watts forcibly held me in his grasp and dragged me down the stairs. I was hysterical and shrieked in agony as I heard Oscar's pitiful cries. On the street, I saw two waiting carriages. Detective Watts hauled me into one of them where another officer awaited to help restrain me. Dr. King took Oscar to the second carriage and pulled away. I sobbed uncontrollably for the next hour as the carriage transported me to the outskirts of the city where it turned into the entranceway of the Providence Lunatic Asylum. Both men, one on each side, escorted me into the lobby, and I was assigned patient number 1050. I felt I was experiencing a horrible nightmare. I watched in stunned disbelief as the duty physician wrote my diagnosis on the medical chart: dementia and onomania, a now archaic medical term meaning I suffered from paroxysms of excess, violence, indecent acts, a peculiar form of insanity.

To protect Grover's political career, Dr. King had certified that I was insane.

Belle leaned back and slowly exhaled. "My, God. That poor woman."

Carrie pointed to the page. "Notice how her handwriting is loosening."

"Hardly surprising. Remember, she wrote this account in the days leading up to her death."

They continued reading.

The events that followed are of little moment. I eventually was released from the asylum, but Grover and Dr. King saw to it that I lost custody of Oscar. Dr. King and his wife ultimately adopted the boy and changed his name to James E. King, Jr. Young James ultimately followed in his adoptive father's footsteps and became a respected gynecologist.

In the presidential election of 1884, Grover's opponents discovered what happened to me and tried to use this sordid experience against him. They even came up with a disgusting slogan: "Ma, ma, where's my pa? Gone to the White House ha ha ha!" Grover's campaign responded by painting me as a drunken lunatic whore. I was humiliated, reviled. I moved back to New Jersey with Freddie, reunited with my daughter, and ultimately remarried. My new name offered me some protection, but for the rest of my life I carried the pain and anguish of what Grover Cleveland had done to me. Like a cancer that could not be excised.

I feel the specter of death approaching now, and I welcome it. I am weary of this life and am anxious to pass on to a world free of pain. Perhaps at some point, I will meet up with Grover Cleveland again, this time with the just eye of God on my side.

Let us see what happens then.
MH

Belle closed the diary. "Only two people know the truth of what happened that night, but Maria makes a credible case. After reading her account, it's hard not to feel some sympathy for Molly. Whether or not Maria Halpin was raped by Grover Cleveland, Molly believes it to be true. In her mind, not only her ancestor, but her own mother fell victim to the callous treatment of a powerful man."

"My God, just think if this happened today. The *#MeToo* movement would string Cleveland up from the highest tree. We need to take the diary to the police."

"Not sure we can do that seeing as how we're not exactly invited guests here. We need to make everything look undisturbed." She photographed the book, the cover, the inscriptions, and a few pages then inserted the diary back inside the freezer bag and replaced it on the table, approximating as best as she could its exact position. "Let's get out of here."

They moved quickly to the door. Carrie stopped, her eyes trained on another book, this one resting on a table near the front window next to Fred the cactus. She crossed the room and retrieved the book—a Holy Bible.

A faded photo marked a page in the Book of Job. The picture showed a young woman, maybe late twenties, and a young girl, five or six. The little girl held a small potted cactus. On the back of the photo were scratch notes, mostly numbers.

Belle glanced at the barrel-shaped cactus in the corner of the room that looked to be about Carrie's height, just over five feet. "Fred. That must be Molly and her mom in the photo." They both checked out the marked page and saw an underlined passage from the Book of Job: *Be ye afraid of the sword: for wrath bringeth the punishments of the sword, that ye may know there is a judgment.*

"It all fits," Carrie said. "She sees herself as exacting fatal justice—the wrath of the sword—on behalf of girls who've been victimized by Grovers, men like her own father."

"Let's go see Sal."

Carrie reinserted the slip of paper and photo back into the Bible, and they headed for the door. She again stopped in her tracks.

"What?"

"Those scratch notes, they're triggering something in my brain."

Before Belle could respond, Carrie hurried back into the apartment and grabbed the Bible.

"Uh, remember what I said about leaving things undisturbed?"

Chapter Thirty-Six

"Y ou did *what?*"

Belle couldn't really blame Sal for being pissed. "I take full responsibility."

"I went along willingly," Carrie said. "And we didn't break in. Molly gave Belle the location of the key so she could read to her cactus."

"Fred," Belle added.

"A cactus named Fred. Of course." Sal walked back and forth behind his desk deep in thought, pausing only to step over Scout. Finally, he plopped down in his desk chair.

He exhaled slowly and shook his head. "I don't even know where to begin." First, the unauthorized entry. The fact she'd given you the location of the key is marginally helpful, but the passage of time is a big problem. The issue would be, was it reasonable for you to believe you had her permission to enter her home without an invitation, and the answer to that question is an emphatic no.

The good news is, you didn't take anything, so——"

Belle held up Molly's Bible. "Don't worry, we're only borrowing it." She showed him the photo. "Carrie thinks the picture and the numbers on the back might be important."

Sal sighed. "Not helpful. But even though your entry was illegal, because you weren't sent there by the police, any information you discovered could still be used to justify a warrant. And as a practical matter, I don't see the DA prosecuting you *if* your wrongful act results in stopping a serial killer. But that's still a big 'if.' "

Belle said, "It all fits."

"Maybe. You've discovered Molly Hovenden's real name might be Halpin, and, based on a quick read of an old diary, you believe she might be a descendent of a woman who was

allegedly assaulted by President Cleveland. You've also uncovered evidence raising the suspicion Molly's the same young woman who tried to kill her father, the man who impregnated and abandoned her mother. But motive in and of itself is not enough."

"We also know she works at the women's clinic," Carrie said. "She had access to the names of men who impregnated and abandoned young women who didn't have the resources to pursue a paternity claim. Of the four victims, we have first names of women associated with two—Brad Banks said, 'Annie,' and someone scratched 'Lettie' in the snow where Virgil was supposed to die. We don't know their last names and we don't know the names of the women Harrison and Maddox impregnated."

"*Might've* impregnated," Sal said.

Belle kept her voice steady. "Do you know anything about Judge Maddox getting someone pregnant?"

Sal hesitated then slumped back in his chair. "There was a rumor, but that's all it was. A rumor."

"We're listening," Carrie said. Sal shifted uncomfortably.

"We think the judge was murdered," Belle pressed. "If he did impregnate someone, that information could lead us to his killer."

Another long moment, then a sigh, then a short nod. "Judge Maddox lives—lived—on a small ranch outside of Kamas. His wife passed away several years ago and he lived alone. He hired a housekeeper—"

"A young woman," Carrie interrupted.

"Don't know how young. Only met her once when I had to swing by on a Sunday for a signature to have a client released from custody. She opened the door. Early twenties, I'd guess. Latina. Pretty. I asked the judge about her, just making conversation, and he seemed flustered, which I remember finding unusual. Judge Maddox never got flustered. He mumbled something about her moving to L.A., and that was it. Her name escapes me."

"I'll bet she got pregnant," Carrie said, "and didn't want an abortion."

Belle continued the narrative. "So she goes to the women's free clinic where Molly finds out about her. She doesn't press paternity because she has no money and probably is afraid of the judge. Might've even been undocumented. If the story came out, the judge would've had to resign."

"A lot of supposition," Sal said without conviction.

"All the victims were public figures," Belle said, "like Grover Cleveland. Isn't there enough to subpoena the clinic's records for any patient who might have identified one of the victims as the man who impregnated her?"

"Not that easy. You're talking about a local judge, a man with an impeccable reputation. I'm sure his family will fight to keep any dirt about him from surfacing. Because of the conflict, our local prosecutor would have to go to a judge in another circuit to seek a subpoena, and she's not going to do that if the probable cause is thin. The big obstacle is, other than motive, which is hardly airtight, you don't have any evidence actually linking Molly to these deaths—no eyewitnesses, no forensic evidence, nothing."

"What about the juggler costume in her apartment?" Carrie asked.

"But there's no footage showing the juggler pushing the bodyguard into Banks. *Could* Molly have given Harrison the meth with the goal of causing him to have a fatal accident? *Could* she have positioned the tree branch to kill Virgil? *Could* she have triggered the avalanche? Sure, but 'could' ain't enough."

Belle didn't try to hide her frustration. "So what the hell are we supposed to do? Wait around while she kills someone else on her list?"

"I understand how you feel. And the information you've uncovered is probably enough to justify the cops searching Molly's apartment. That will allow them to show she wore the juggler costume. The Brad Banks-Annie Kupchak relationship fits with the revenge motive, so there should be no problem in bringing Molly in for questioning. But unless she says something stupid, I don't see how they can hold her. You need more evidence, a real provable connection." He glanced at his watch and stood. "I have to head home or your Aunt Helen will have my head, but I'll call the lead prosecutor in Phoenix on the way. Maybe he can shed some light on Molly that could be helpful." He opened the office door. "Want to come to dinner? Your aunt always loves to see you, and I'm sure she'd enjoy meeting Carrie."

Belle's voice deflated. "Not tonight, thanks."

"Suit yourself. I'll let you know if I hear back from Phoenix tonight. They're an hour behind us, so you never know." He held her gaze. "And Isabella, don't do anything stupid."

"Why does everyone keep telling me that?"

Sal smiled, left the office, and a few moments later they heard the front door open and close.

Neither Belle nor Carrie spoke as they processed what Sal told them. Carrie studied the notepaper from Molly's Bible.

"There's something about these numbers," Carrie said.

Belle glanced at the markings. "Looks like a bunch of doodles. Are those swords?"

"Remember the Bible quote. It all ties in. Molly believes she's on a righteous mission of vengeance."

Belle pointed to "ac/ft" after the number 320. "What's that mean?"

"Probably acre-feet. A unit of volume. One acre of surface area to a depth of one foot. I tell my students to picture a deck of cards."

"Never heard of it."

"It's mostly used to measure the volume of large bodies of water. The k after three hundred twenty probably means three hundred and twenty thousand acre-feet."

"Sounds like a lot."

"It is a lot."

"Why would Molly be doing acre to feet calculations?"

"What's the largest body of water around here?"

"The Jordanelle Reservoir, I guess."

Carrie jumped up, moved to the other side of Sal's desk, and tapped on his keyboard. After a minute, she said, "Guess how many acre-feet of water are in the Jordanelle?"

"Three hundred twenty thousand?"

She nodded. "Oh, my God. I know this sounds crazy, but is it possible Molly intends to poison the water supply?"

Belle's blood turned ice cold, and she struggled to fight the suspicion Carrie was right. "But that doesn't fit our profile of her as the avenging heroine. She would be responsible for possibly killing hundreds of innocent people, not a single jerk who impregnated a girl and didn't take responsibility."

"We need to tell the police, Belle."

"Not sure what we'd tell them. You heard Sal."

"You're saying we do nothing?"

"I'm saying we need more."

Carrie huffed in frustration. "More what?"

"What if we take a little drive around the Jordanelle? We spot anything unusual, we call the police."

"And if we don't?"

"We still call the cops. I'm just hoping to find something to make our case stronger."

"Okay, but all we do is observe. If we see something—"

Belle raised a forestalling hand. "I know. Don't do anything stupid."

Chapter Thirty-Seven

B elle felt on edge and she wasn't the only one. Even Scout sat up, alert, in the back seat. Carrie unwrapped a piece of gum, popped it into her mouth, and chewed ferociously. Belle turned onto Deer Hollow Road and headed into the state park on the western side of the Jordanelle. The gum wrapper reminded Belle of the wrapper and coffee filter she and Alonzo happened upon in the mine. She glanced at Carrie. "Can you think of any reason why a coffee filter might be floating in the mine tunnel?"

"Not offhand. Why do you ask?"

"We saw the filter along with a thin piece of foil we assumed was a gum wrapper."

It only took a moment for her eyes to light up. "Pfed."

"Excuse me?'

"Pfed foil packaging."

"And Pfed is a drug?"

"Pseudoephedrine. Commonly found in decongestant pills like Sudafed. The coffee filters are used to filter out red phosphorus as part of the process to make—"

"Methamphetamine. Damn. And the urine odor?"

"Makes sense. Pagano's cooking meth in the mine tunnels, and the process can emit an odor that some say smells like cat pee."

In the absence of Pagano's neck, Belle tightened her grip on the steering wheel. "He stores a few bricks of coke in the ore bucket at the top of the mine for easy access while the real business is going on hundreds of feet below. And I'm betting big that Molly's the one who provided Harrison with Pagano's's meth before the earthquake intervened. If we find even a shred of evidence to prove our water-poisoning theory, the police won't be able to ignore us."

"That along with the foil and filter should be more than enough for a full-scale search of the mine," Carrie declared.

"We keep wondering about Molly's affiliation with Danny Pags. Maybe it's as simple as he could provide her the meth to take out Harrison."

"Which would mean he had nothing to do with the deaths of the Grovers."

"Don't forget the money," Belle countered. "The cost of chemicals in quantities sufficient to poison a body of water the size of the Jordanelle would be very expensive. Where would Molly find that kind of money? She certainly isn't living lavishly. Maybe Pagano's bankrolling her. Who knows? He might be in the Halpin family tree, or they could be having a personal relationship."

"If there's a personal relationship between Molly and Danny, he could be the one pushing her beyond the righteous avenger stage. The question is, why? How would Pagano benefit from poisoning the town's drinking water?"

"My head's about to explode," Belle groaned, grinding the heel of her hand into her throbbing brow.

They passed through the camping park and saw a few tents clustered together near the shore. A group of men with beer cans in their hands gathered around a campfire. Belle could smell fried fish and hear their hearty laughter even through the closed windows. Lights flickered from three nearby tents out on the ice. "Doubt if Molly would stage anything here. Too many people."

"What's that over there?" Carrie pointed across the reservoir to a light flickering in the far distance.

"Another ice fisherman. Probably convinced himself he's found a secret fishing spot far
away from the regulars here in the park."

"Or?"

She got it. "Let's check it out."

***

It took over forty-five minutes to circle to the eastern shore of the Jordanelle on the narrow, two-lane road. The road was little-used except for employees of PC Tents, the tent manufacturing company up on the hill.

During the drive, Belle didn't bother Carrie while she concentrated on deciphering Molly's scratch notes. Heading south, Belle wound her way back and forth on a gravel road through thick pine trees. On each side of the road, snow draped the tree branches like heavy white bunting, and she had the sense she was proceeding along a macabre parade route right out of a Stephen King novel. Now and then the trees parted and she could spot the dim lights flickering from the camps in the distance across the water.

Carrie mumbled, "Seventy-three."

"Seventy-three what?"

"Seventy-three kilograms equates to 160 pounds, about the size of an average man. So Molly could be multiplying 1.52 of something times the weight of a human and arrives at 111 mg."

"What's the 'something'?"

"I don't know. But let's say 1.52 mg of this chemical—call it X—is a lethal dose per kilogram of body mass."

"Then it would take 111 mg. of X to kill a 160-pound man."

"But she's not feeding our average man a straight dose of X. The poison would be diluted in water. And the "thirty pc" here probably means the chemical itself is at a thirty percent concentration."

Belle rounded a bend and saw a small snowy beach off to the right leading down to the ice-covered reservoir. Someone had pitched an ice-fishing tent a short distance from the shoreline. A weak interior light source—probably a single battery-powered lantern—lit the tent in a soft orange glimmer.

She doused the headlights. No use taking any chances. The moon slipped out from behind a cloud, and its light reflecting off the snow cast the frozen reservoir in an eerie glow.

Carrie, intently focused on Molly's notes, didn't notice. "The dilution, that's what I think the 3L/d refers to. The average person consumes three liters of water per day, so she's calculated it would take thirty-seven mg. of X per liter of water for a fatal dose. When she says 5mg/L for 7, she's figuring it would take a dosage of 5 mg of X at a thirty percent concentration per liter of water over seven days to kill an average man."

"If I'm understanding you, those notes mean she's calculated the amount of X she needs to dump into the reservoir to kill a sizable portion of the town's population in a week. And by the time that happened, Molly and Pagano would be long gone, the act untraceable to them."

"Or the notes could mean something else entirely. Or nothing.

Why calculate for seven days? Once people began getting sick someone would figure it out and treat the poisoned water with an appropriate antidote. Now, if someone has heart or respiratory problems, they're particularly susceptible and could succumb much more quickly to smaller doses."

"I don't know. I keep alternating between how brilliant we are to we're so far out on a limb a light puff of fresh air will snap the branch."

Carrie grimaced. "I'm now leaning toward the limb option because I just realized the only way she could transport that tonnage of liquid would be in a tanker truck."

Belle felt her phone vibrate. Sal. She put the phone on speaker and answered, not bothering with a greeting. "Did you reach the Phoenix DA?" The windows were closed, but she didn't take a chance and turned down the volume.

"Just got off the phone with him," Sal said. "He was very familiar with Molly Halpin, whom he confirmed was Nancy Halpin's daughter. There were early police reports that Mayor Yaeger beat Nancy Halpin and threatened her daughter, whom Nancy claimed was fathered by the mayor. Nothing ever came of the allegations. Nancy couldn't get a job in town, went to Vegas looking for work and soon turned to drink and prostitution. She died under suspicious circumstances in Vegas, and Nancy's sister Lucy took custody of the girl. When she grew older, Molly held the mayor responsible for her mom's death. She burned down his house, and the mayor almost died. Molly confessed, and as part of a plea deal she was charged as a juvenile and confined to a mental institution until release on her twenty-first birthday."

Something clicked in Belle's mind. "Did the DA happen to provide the name of the mental institution?"

"Yeah. Arizona State Hospital. Why?"

Carrie saw where Belle was going and responded. "ASH. The

return address on the envelope you found in her apartment. Arizona State Hospital. That confirms our Molly is the Molly Halpin who was institutionalized."

"I assume Molly wasn't completely cured of her disorder," Belle said.

"The DA told me Molly was very manipulative. She studied the Bible, mechanics, chemistry, math, any book she could get her hands on. According to him, the girl has a near-genius IQ."

"So *now* do we have enough to go to the police?" Carrie asked.

"Yeah," Sal responded. "At least enough to pick her up for questioning. I'll make the call. Where are you two sleuths at the moment?"

"On the gravel road east of the reservoir," Belle said. "I stuck the photo of Molly and her mom in my pocket in case we connected with the police and they needed a face for a BOLO."

Carrie read Sal the calculations on the back of the notepaper, explaining her theory of what they meant.

"Sit still until the police arrive. Poisoning the town's water supply doesn't fit her MO, but we can't be too careful." He ended the call.

Belle spotted something up ahead and slowed. A flatbed truck carrying two large cylindrical tanks was parked up ahead of them.

Carrie gasped. "Chemical tanks. Dear God."

Belle's throat turned dry. "Looks deserted." She parked short of the truck where the Cherokee couldn't be seen by anyone out on the ice then disabled the overhead light and quietly opened the driver's side door.

Carrie whispered, "Where are you going?"

"I need to confirm what's in the truck. Then we'll call the cops. Wait here, I'll be right back."

"Don't you want a flashlight?"

"They might see it. I'll be fine."

"What happened to, 'Don't do anything stupid'?"

Chapter Thirty-Eight

Belle weaved her way through the dark piney woods bordering the road. The uneven terrain strained her sore ankle, but she feared walking on the crunchy gravel, even with a light snow cover, might signal her approach to anyone inside the truck cab.

When she reached the trunk of a thick spruce directly opposite the cab, she waited a moment but heard nothing. Either no one was there, or they saw her coming and were lying in wait. She peeked around the tree and was able to see inside the cab. Empty. She waited in place a few minutes, but again heard nothing and observed no movement.

She needed to learn what was in those tanks. The moon lit the ice-covered reservoir but fortunately didn't penetrate the trees lining the gravel road. There was a good chance she wouldn't be seen by whoever was inside the tent out on the ice. She made her way toward the front of the truck, stepped over a thick tree root, and confirmed no one was inside the cab. Whoever drove the truck was likely inside the tent.

The truck held two chemical tanks secured by a steel frame attached to the truck bed. Each tank looked to be about twenty feet in diameter. After making a mental note of the markings on the back of the tanks, she turned to head back to the Cherokee and tripped over the tree root.

"Shit."

She looked up quickly. *Did somebody hear me?* Sound traveled over water, and she assumed the same principle applied to ice. She pressed herself against the truck body trying to melt into the shadows. Thirty seconds passed and no one emerged from the tent. She didn't realize she'd been holding her breath and exhaled slowly. Then she saw it.

What tripped her hadn't been a tree root, but a thick hose running from one of the tanks, across the gravel road, then down a short embankment, then disappearing in the darkness. She scanned the ice where it met the embankment. Was that the hose extending across the ice toward the tent? *My God*, someone— Molly?—at that very moment was inside the tent emptying the contents of the tank into the reservoir through a hole in the ice.

Belle crawled up onto the truck bed. The hose was affixed to the tank with a hex attachment, just like a garden hose—a garden hose that happened to be six inches in diameter. She'd need a special wrench to uncouple it. The hose itself appeared to be made of multiple plies of polyester tire cord wrapped in heavy steel mesh. No knife could cut it, but maybe if she hammered a screwdriver through the mesh, she could puncture the hose. Still, even if successful she'd only cause a small leak at best. The chemicals would flow uninterrupted into the reservoir.

A steel housing box attached to the back of the truck cab emitted a low humming sound. A pump—had to be. If she could disable the pump, the flow would stop. She ran her fingers over the housing looking for a way to open it and near the bottom found a lock. Damn. The engine wasn't running, so the power for the pump must be coming from batteries. She found a rock and bashed in the driver's side window. Fortunately, whoever was inside the tent didn't hear the glass break, although at that moment she didn't really care. Somehow she needed to cut off the poison pouring into the town's drinking water. She unlocked the door.

Many truck models housed the battery under the seat. Belle felt along the floor and behind the seats. Again nothing. She suspected the batteries were contained in the same housing as the pump. She imagined she could see the thick stream of liquid poison gushing through the black hose, fast and powerful, destined to kill innocent men, women, and children in town. She had only one alternative.

When she returned to the Cherokee, Carrie rolled down the passenger-side window.

"Took you long enough."

"NaCN. That's what's in those tanks."

Her eyes widened. "Sodium cyanide. I can't tell you how lethal that can be."

"Wouldn't the treatment plant filter it out?"

"Probably not. As long as the amount of cyanide dissolved in the water doesn't exceed the solubility limit."

"So everyone who drinks the water over the next few days will die?"

"Molly's calculations indicate a concentration of thirty percent."

Her gaze blanked, and she rubbed her temples. Belle assumed she was calculating the math in her head.

"At that soluble level, widespread mortality would be unlikely. Cyanide is unstable, and by this time tomorrow all traces of it will probably be gone."

"Why not just pump it directly into the water here at the

shoreline?"

"Speed. If the poison's pumped closer to the center of the reservoir it will spread more quickly."

"There has to be an antidote," Belle said, projecting a certainty based on wish, not knowledge.

"There is if it's ingested in time. But some people—mostly children, the elderly, and those with a heart or respiratory condition—could die. And it's a horrible death. Your body convulses then your mouth fills with a mixture of saliva, vomit, and blood. Your body screams for oxygen that isn't there. You pass out and die."

"How long does it take?"

"Depends on a lot of factors. Remember those 900 people who died of cyanide poisoning at the Jonestown massacre?"

"Sure. 'Don't drink the Kool-Aid.'"

"Some of them died within minutes. Many of them children."

"Jesus."

She held up a thin sheet of paper and handed it to Belle. "While I was waiting, I thumbed through Molly's Bible looking for more underlined passages and found another tightly folded piece of paper. It's an excerpt from a genealogy chart showing a man named Stetson Davis is a direct descendant of President Grover Cleveland. I googled the name. The head of DEA's organized crime unit is a guy named Stetson Davis. And apparently, he's been very successful."

"Unusual name. Given Pagano's chosen profession, it has to be him, the perfect target. He's both the ultimate Grover and a likely sharp thorn in Pagano's side, or the sides of whoever Pagano's working for. What about these other two names, Bill and Laura?"

Bill and Laura's the name of a Sundance movie. I saw an ad for the film posted in a shop window on Main Street. And according to Dr. Google, guess who's starring as Laura?" She answered her own question. "Jessica Davis."

"Stetson's daughter?"

"Or niece or some beloved relative."

"So he's in town for the film, and doesn't realize he's been targeted by Molly and Danny."

"Call Sal right away," Belle ordered, "and tell him what we've found. Davis needs to be warned immediately."

"Where are you going?"

"To drag the nozzle end of that damn hose out of the water."

Belle hurried back along the road behind the Cherokee looking for a spot on the embankment that wasn't so steep. One thing nagged at her. What if Davis didn't drink water from the spigot? Maybe he only drank bottled water. And even if he did, the likelihood of a near-instant death was low unless he suffered from a heart or respiratory condition. Assuming he didn't have such a condition, might he succumb to the diluted poison over a period of days? Maybe. But presumably by that time he'd receive treatment. Something didn't add up.

Belle's phone dinged. She checked the screen. A text from Alonzo: *Lab says avalanche sample positive for explosive powder residue. Call me.*

She needed to tell him about the threat to Davis. She was about to punch in his number when she heard a bark then a low growl.

"Belle!"

She turned back and hissed, "Shhh, someone might hear—"

Angelo Biondi, aka Jello, stood outside the open passenger-side window of the Cherokee with a gun pointed at Carrie's head. A wide grin spread across his ugly face.

Chapter Thirty-Nine

J ello pressed the gun barrel hard against Carrie's temple, his eyes locked on Belle.

"Okay, bitch, first thing I want you to do is call off your dog or I'll put a bullet in his brain."

Scout was still in the back seat, but by the time he lunged into the front seat, jumped across Carrie, and attacked through the window he'd be dead. *"Stai gui!"* Stay down. Scout didn't move. Jello's finger tightened on the trigger. Belle raised her voice and repeated the command. Fortunately, the dog complied.

"Now, pull out your gun with two fingers and throw it into the woods."

"Don't have a gun. Your old pal, the Dane, may he not rest in peace, forced me to leave it in the snow up on Monroe Mountain."

"Your phone. Toss it into the woods." He screwed a suppressor into the barrel.

"Sure, whatever you want, just please don't hurt her." Belle threw her phone into the trees where it disappeared beneath a heavy blanket of snow.

"Gimme your phone too, sweetheart."

From where Belle was standing, it was too dark to see whether the big man was leering, but the tone of his voice definitely suggested a leer. Carrie handed Jello her phone; he threw it into the woods and opened the car door.

"Out."

Carrie did as she was told, leaving the dog inside.

"Now, both of you, we're going for a little stroll. Move."

Belle had a pretty good idea where they were headed but figured she'd make sure.

"Where to?"

"The tent."

She was right. Carrie walked toward her, and they found an easy slope down to the ice-covered reservoir then made their way carefully toward the tent with Jello following close behind.

Carrie whispered, "Why is he taking us to the tent?"

"I don't know." Actually, she had a pretty good idea that if Jello had his way they'd both soon be taking a cyanide bath under the ice.

"Shut up, both of you. And Bannon, I admit you're a resilient bitch. I thought for sure you were buzzard meat up on the mountain, and yet here we are together again. You try anything, she's the first to get a bullet in the brain. *Capiche*?"

"*Capisco*." Speaking Italian to a thug with a goofy name, Belle felt like she was on the set of a cheap Mafia movie. Maybe if she rattled him a little bit he'd give her an opening. "By the way, how are you getting along without your pal? The big dog was clearly the brains of the outfit." She slowed her pace to narrow the distance between them. "Feeling a little lonely? Hey, we all must overcome life's obstacles and soldier on, am I right?"

"I said shut up," he growled.

"And what kind of stupid name is Jello?"

Pffft.

The muffled bullet smacked next to Carrie's foot, and she tripped to the ice. Unfortunately, there was no chance the fishermen on the other side of the reservoir could hear it.

Jello grunted. "Next time I aim for her head."

Belle raised her arms in supplication. "Okay, okay. Just trying to have a friendly conversation." She helped Carrie to her feet, taking her time, and whispered, "At the tent try to distract him, even for a second." She turned back to Jello. "So, how did you acquire the huge quantities of cyanide? Not something you buy at the local Home Depot."

"His girl brought it in from Nevada."

"Molly?"

"Don't know no Molly. Maria. Bartender in town."

"And when you say 'his' girl, you're referring to—?"

Jello responded with a silent grin.

"Look, you've done your job. Hundreds, maybe more, will become very ill from cyanide poisoning. The police are on the way." Sal said he'd call them, but when they'd arrive was an open question. "It will take time for you to roll up the hose and drive off. Leave us alone. We can't tell the cops any more than they already know. You want to escape, I'd suggest you get moving. I see flashing lights coming along the road." She was hoping if he looked over his shoulder she'd have the opening she needed. He stepped back, too far away to make a move, and took a quick glance. The guy was a pro.

"Don't see no lights. Now move." Belle was close enough to see him flash a cold smile.

"And Bannon, those people you was talking about? They ain't gonna just get sick."

Carrie stopped in her tracks. "What do you mean? Molly's calculations are based on about thirty percent cyanide concentration, and at those soluble levels—" Her voice lowered to just above a whisper. "But that's wrong, isn't it?"

Jello's smile widened. "Try eighty percent."

Carrie's jaw dropped. "Oh, my God. Belle, at that level, even diluted by reservoir water, a lot of people are going to die."

Jello prodded her with his gun. "Move!"

Belle wondered why he didn't just shoot them when they were back at the truck and dump their bodies in the woods. Only thing she could think of was Molly wanted to make their demise look like an accident, just as she'd done with the other victims. Even the cyanide poisoning would be made to look accidental. Many people would drink the water and likely die. By the time the cause was discovered, the last traces of the poison in the reservoir would be long gone. Two bodies, each with a bullet in the brain, would change everything.

Tomorrow, someone would find the abandoned Cherokee and spot the tent on the ice. Inside the tent, they'd discover an ice-fishing hole, and the assumption would be the two young women fell into the water and drowned. Probably drank too much hooch; it had happened before. Sal would lay out the theory of a serial killer bent on revenge against powerful men who'd taken advantage of young women, and his theory would be investigated. But in the end, there would be no hard evidence, only suspicion. Davis would die from cyanide poisoning, and Danny Pags would be long gone. Then one spring day the ice would melt and the bodies of Carrie Palmer and Isabella Bannon would be discovered. Molly Halpin would have split the scene.

"So, Jello—mind if I call you Jello?—is Davis Danny's target?" Belle didn't know what she expected him to answer, but his response sent chills down her spine.

"You mean the dude with the bad heart condition?" He grinned, his words almost casual.

Molly and Pagano were going to murder top DEA agent Stetson Davis, and in the process kill many people in Park City, visitors, and townies alike, including innocent children.

Belle couldn't let that happen.

"Open the tent flap," Jello ordered. Carrie did what he asked. "Now, both of you, inside."

Carrie froze. "No, please, I won't tell anyone. I promise."

"I said, get inside."

She fell to her knees and burst into tears. "Please, I don't want to die."

Belle figured part of her performance was acting, but only part. Jello glanced over his shoulder. Still no flashing lights, but at least she had him thinking. He did what she'd hoped he would do and stepped forward to jam the gun barrel into the back of her head, taking his eye off Belle for a split second.

A split second was all she needed.

Belle shot out both hands to grab the gun and levered it from his grip. But before she could re-aim the weapon, Jello chopped his hand down hard on her wrist. The gun flew across the ice into the darkness. Instead of attacking her as she expected, the big man grabbed Carrie around her neck. Her scream was abruptly cut off as he tightened his chokehold and flashed a stupid smile.

"In the tent, or I break her neck."

"Okay, okay." The clouds passed, and as Belle entered the tent the full light of the moon leaking through the tent flap allowed her to see the thick black hose running from the truck, under the tent, to a hole in the ice close to three feet in diameter. The truck pump caused the hose to pulse giving the impression it was alive, like a giant python bent on inflicting death.

"Look, Jello, we're not stupid, we know you intend for us to take a dip in the pool. But here's your problem. You have no weapon and there's no way you're going to be able to force us into that liquid poison."

"If you don't go in voluntarily I'll break her neck." A simple, direct response. But effective.

"And if I do as you ask, will you let her go?"

"Sure. I give you my word. Although we might have a little quick fun first." He lowered his hand to her crotch.

Big mistake.

By loosening his grip, he allowed Carrie to lower her chin. She bit down hard on his hand. He yelped. Belle sprang forward and crushed a hard right fist into his temple. He didn't fall, but he let go of Carrie, staggered, and turned toward Belle. She prepared to block his right arm, the one connected to the huge right fist she knew was coming. Instead, the man charged at her like an NFL linebacker and tackled her into the tent wall. The tent fell, she fell, and Jello fell, all in a heap. Unfortunately, she was at the bottom of that heap.

Jello wrapped his meaty hands around Belle's throat and dragged her to the ice hole. She tried hitting him, but he dodged her swings. Carrie jumped onto his back and rode him to the hole, punching him in the face and head to no effect. He flipped Belle onto her back and shoved her forward so her head hovered over the ice hole. She could smell the bitter almond odor of the cyanide. Jello fired a sharp elbow back, hitting Carrie in the face; she screamed and rolled off his back to the ice, stunned.

Jello was a pro, but even pros make mistakes, and Belle watched him make a big one: A man should never straddle someone he's trying to choke for the simple reason doing so positions his testicles over his adversary's knees. She crushed her knee into his balls, and he immediately loosened his grip. She rolled away and whipped her legs hard across his ankles, knocking him onto his back, and wrapped her hands around his neck. Using thumb pressure to his throat, she pushed him forward so now *his* head was over the ice hole. Turnabout's fair play.

She pressed his head down, rubbing it hard against the slimy black hose, still pulsing as it pumped the deadly liquid into the water. The lizard door opened and the white light flooded her brain.

"Belle—"

This giant piece of shit had tried to kill Carrie. And caused the death of Louise, an ornery mule with whom she'd developed a special connection. She pushed his head lower.

He bucked up and down like a crazed rodeo bull, but she held tight. The white light warmed her, infusing every cell in her body with an indescribable sense of pleasure. This son of a bitch was going to die. She eased his face closer to the hose and the cyanide-laced water—

"Belle!"

The white light was in control, and it felt so good—

"Belle, stop!"

Carrie?

"Please, you promised!"

Why would I want to stop feeling so good?

"You promised..."

Remember, I'm in control. I'm the doorkeeper. Focus, focus... Okay, deep breaths. I'm the doorkeeper. Pushing the light back behind the door now... I'm the doorkeeper...

The lizard door closed.

She took another deep breath and felt a shiver run down her entire body. She slackened her grip on Jello's throat. The big man, semi-conscious, coughed violently and gasped for air. Then his head lolled back and forth on the ice, and he emitted a low guttural moan.

Carrie put her hand on Belle's shoulder and whispered in her ear, "I'm proud of you."

Belle nodded her thanks, and part of her was proud of herself.

Then there was the other part.

"Molly's not here," Belle said. "There's a good chance she and Pagano are together and about to kill Davis. We need to find them. He knows where they are. What do you want me to do?"

Belle saw the indecision on Carrie's face and felt a little sorry for her. How does a pacifist choose when violence is necessary to save a life?

After a long beat, she whispered, "Just try not to hurt him."

Belle slapped Jello hard and his eyes flew open. "Where's Molly...or Maria?"

He grinned. She shoved his head over the water and held it there, using her leverage to resist his violent thrashing.

"Where is she?" Belle growled.

He tried to spit in her face and struggled to wrench free. She tightened her grip on his throat and pushed his head down so everything but his face was under water.

His eyes bulged and he rasped, "Movie...party."

"For Jessica Davis's movie," Carrie said. "Has to be."

"Where?" Belle pressed.

"H-hotel Park City."

"We have to warn Davis," Carrie said. "Heck, we have to warn the whole city not to drink the water!"

Jello's chest heaved, and he gasped for air. Belle searched his pockets and found his phone. "Make the call." She tossed the phone toward Carrie.

With a roar, Jello swatted the phone in midair, and it sailed into the open ice hole. He bucked Belle off his body, and she rolled onto the ice. He attempted to crawl to his feet, but fumes from the poison had significantly weakened him. She swept her feet across his legs, tripping him. His head slapped hard against the ice, and he was out cold.

The cyanide fumes made her eyes water as she yanked the hose out of the water. Now it really looked alive as it whipped back and forth across the ice like an angry viper, spewing puddles of deadly poison. She needed to turn off the pump. She searched his pockets and found the trucks ignition keys.

"Carrie, if we leave him alive, when he wakes up he'll find a way to contact Pagano, warn him, and there's a good chance Pagano will immediately kill the Davis. He was willing to murder both of us, help poison a town full of innocent people, and is a professional killer."

Carrie wiped her eyes and stared down at Jello, mounded on the ice like a huge bloated fish. She swallowed hard. "He has no phone and no quick way to gain access to one," she said, her voice weak with indecision. "After we call to warn the Davis, we'll notify the police and they'll pick him up. He'll face justice in our court system under the law. That's the way it's supposed to work."

Belle glanced across the ice where the faint flickering lights signaled the fisherman were still there. "If he wakes up, he could crawl toward those fishermen, get their attention, make up some bullshit story, and borrow a phone. By choosing to save this professional killer you could be sentencing Davis to death. How does that break the cycle of violence?"

"All I know is, if we kill him, we're no better than he is."

Belle wasn't sure she agreed with her, but there was no time for a lengthy philosophical discussion. She found a line used to attach the tent grommets to the ice stakes and hogtied Jello so he couldn't crawl or walk then cut a piece of the tent material and gagged the son of a bitch.

"Thank you," Carrie said.

Belle nodded. Did Carrie's approval make her feel better? *Yeah, a little.* "We have to turn off the pump at the truck then we need to find a phone to warn Davis. Let's go." They hurried toward shore.

Belle asked herself, *would I have left Jello alive on the ice were it not for Carrie Palmer?* She answered her own question.

No.

Chapter Forty

Alonzo felt a familiar jolt as the wheels of the CRJ900 touched down. The usual two-hour SkyWest flight from Rapid City to Salt Lake had extended by almost two extra hours due to heavy weather. He'd been in South Dakota meeting with prosecutors, preparing his testimony for an upcoming trial. He was anxious to return to Utah for two reasons. First, his boss, Stetson Davis, happened to be in Park City and wanted to meet with him for a status update on the Danny Pagano investigation. Second was Belle Bannon. He'd spent most of the time on the flight thinking about her—beautiful, troubled, funny, enigmatic, tough, tender—the most interesting woman he'd ever met. He wanted to get to know her better.

The plane rolled out and headed toward its gate. Along with the seventy other passengers on board, Alonzo pulled out his phone. Immediately a string of texts filled the screen. He opened the one from Belle first.

We think Stetson Davis targeted by DP. He's in P.C. at PC hotel. Recommend added security. Call me for details. B

Alonzo immediately tapped in Belle's number. After four rings, no answer. He left a message to call him back immediately. His next call would be to Davis's security detail.

He was worried about Belle. For her information to be accurate, she had to be deep in the middle of some dangerous shit. He needed a helicopter to take him up the mountain to Park City, and he needed it now.

***

They'd managed to shut off the pump, and Belle now drove as fast as she could back toward town looking for a phone to call in the cavalry. From the rear seat, Scout licked the back of her neck to let her know he was okay.

"We're still missing something," Carrie said. "There wouldn't have been enough time for the cyanide to reach the hotel, and even at eighty percent, if it did, the impact on Davis would be unpredictable. He'd have to drink tap water, not bottled water, and a sip or two probably wouldn't be enough."

"Remember what Jello said. Davis has a heart condition. He would be more susceptible."

Carrie sagged in her seat. "You're right, and there are other factors that can affect the cyanide's potency. For example, drinking the chemical with a soft drink can accelerate and enhance its lethal effect. But still, even with a heart condition, the timing is way too uncertain."

"Something else. Molly views herself as a hero exacting revenge on those she sees as hurting young women and children. Even if Davis is a descendant of Grover Cleveland, I have trouble seeing her putting the lives of innocent people, especially children, at risk."

"Her calculations assumed thirty percent concentration," Carrie reminded. "I bet she doesn't know the poison's true potency. Pagano could be using Molly to help take out the Davis without telling her about the true threat to the whole town."

"Jello confirmed she has a personal relationship with Danny that goes beyond being raised in the same household. But I'm still not sure how he'd get her to go along. In her mind, she protects the innocent, she doesn't threaten them."

Both of them remained silent for the next few minutes, their minds churning.

Molly was the key, Belle concluded. "Molly must believe no one will die except Davis. So maybe the water poisoning's a cover, something to explain away Davis's death as an accident. The hotel water's contaminated, as is the water throughout the town. Because of his heart condition, the conclusion would be Davis died because he's particularly susceptible to the diluted contamination."

"If the citywide contamination's a cover, that would mean they'd need to poison him directly," Carrie said. "And it would have to be fast and final since he'll have security with him at all times. Think of the cyanide tablets used in books and movies. The speed of death might be exaggerated a bit for dramatic purposes, but in real life, if the cyanide concentration is high enough, the result would be irreversible. Death would occur in a few minutes."

"Like Jonestown." Belle drummed her fingers on the steering wheel. "Okay, but how would cyanide in the reservoir be explained away? If the contamination is their cover, there has to be a plausible non-sinister explanation. Were the authorities to believe the cyanide was intentionally dumped in the water, the FBI would swarm the town and leave no stone unturned. So far, Molly's been too smart to leave a trail, making the other murders all appear as accidents, and I doubt if Pagano would intentionally open himself

Mike Pace

up to a full assault from the nation's law enforcement community."

They covered a few more miles in silence before Carrie spoke.

"The tent company," she blurted.

"PC Tents, okay, so what?"

"I took my junior chem class there on a field trip a few months ago," she explained. "The company's been in the same location up on the hill there for over eighty years. Half of the facility manufactures the tent fabric, and the other half assembles the tents."

Belle thought she saw where Carrie was heading. "And cyanide's used in the manufacturing process?"

"Acrylonitrile is a key ingredient in the manufacture of acrylic filament."

And this acrylonitrile is—"

"Vinyl cyanide."

"So with no other reasonable explanation, the cyanide would be blamed on groundwater contamination from the tent company."

"Except we happened on the scene and spoiled the party."

"But Molly and Danny don't know that yet." She pointed to a 7-Eleven. "Pull in there. We need to call the police."

Belle kept the car running, and they rushed inside. Other than the clerk, the place was deserted.

"Quick, I need to use your phone, it's an emergency."

The clerk, a kid barely out of his teens, looked them over, and his eyes widened. Belle couldn't blame him. Two women, wet, dirty, bloody, smelling of chemicals, bursts into his store and demands his phone. Without saying a word, the kid ran into what Belle assumed was a storage room and locked the door.

Belle leaped over the counter and put her face close to the storeroom door. "Listen to me. Call the cops and send them to the Hotel Park City. Tell them DEA agent Stetson Davis is in danger. And don't drink the water!"

They returned to the Cherokee, and Belle pulled out of the lot, heading toward the hotel. "There has to be a bar, a restaurant, someplace we can find a phone."

"My apartment's two blocks away," Carrie said. "Drop me off, I'll use the landline. You go on to the hotel. I'll drive over soon as I make the calls."

Belle sped into the apartment parking lot and barely stopped long enough for her to jump out and run to the front door of her building. "Meet me at the hotel!"

***

Sonja Valek pulled into the apartment parking lot and watched Bannon speed away after dropping Palmer off. No doubt Bannon was headed for the hotel.

She'd arrived at the cyanide pumping site from the south side of the reservoir in time to see Bannon and Palmer drive away. Jello's body lay sprawled on the ice. After confirming a steady pulse, he checked the big man's pockets for a phone, found none, then dragged his body over to the ice hole and left it there with Jello's head submerged in the poisoned water.

Bannon probably took the truck keys with her so he couldn't restart the pump. Sonja decided to follow Bannon at a safe distance.

The wide chemical truck had taken up most of the narrow road, but she was able to squeeze past, only sacrificing a side mirror in the process. She had to assume Jello told Bannon about targeting Davis. The question was, what happened to Jello's phone, and did he strip Bannon and Palmer of their phones? If not, the feds would soon be swarming the hotel.

She'd followed Bannon and Palmer to the 7-Eleven and watched from across the street. The moment they left, she entered to see the young clerk emerge from a storage room, tapping on his phone screen. She snatched the phone out of the boy's hand and used her gun to escort the kid back into the storeroom. The blubbering clerk told her Bannon wanted to use his phone, but he escaped to the safety of the storeroom without giving her a chance. Good news: Security hadn't been alerted yet. Sonja had popped the kid with a single muffled shot through the forehead and hid the body behind stacked boxes of soda.

But at this moment, Palmer was on the way up to her apartment and a phone.

Sonja parked the car and entered the apartment building.

***

Belle intentionally ran a red light on Park Avenue both to save time and hoping she'd get pulled over. Didn't happen. Where's a cop when you need one? She hung a left onto Thaynes Canyon Drive then another left past a giant snow-covered moose sculpture and drove into the circular drive leading to the hotel's main entrance.

A cheerful young fellow in a snappy red uniform opened her car door and said something, but the loud dance music blaring from a second-floor window made it difficult to hear. She cupped her hand around her ear, and he raised his voice over the music. "Are you checking in, ma'am, or are you here for the film party?"

"Film party." She left Scout in the car and rushed past the kid into the lobby, ignoring his direction to move the Cherokee to an adjoining lot.

Hotel Park City was one of the most expensive hotels in the area. The interior smelled of money featuring rich mahogany-colored leather furniture, heavy ceiling beams, low lighting, and two-story windows overlooking the snow-covered golf course. She ran to the front desk. A tastefully dressed young woman, not a hair out of place, asked how she could help.

"Where's the film party?"

Understandably wary based on Belle's appearance and the urgency of her tone, the clerk hesitantly responded, "Upstairs in the Aspen Room."

"Listen to me. The tap water's been poisoned. Alert the security staff and instruct all guests to only drink bottled water. And call the cops." The woman's cool demeanor cracked wide open. Belle couldn't really blame her; not the normal comment from a patron. "Stairs?" Still too stunned to speak, she pointed to her left.

Belle climbed the stairs three at a time and on the second floor hurried toward the sound of the band. The small brass sign at the door to the Aspen Room listed the capacity as 125, but there had to be more than two hundred people jammed inside. Like the lobby, the room reeked of money—vaulted ceiling with thick mahogany beams, gold walls, pine green chair rail, and patterned green carpet. Some couples up near the bandstand tried to dance but kept bumping into people in the crowd. Others just bobbed up and down to the beat of the music.

Belle jumped up onto a chair leaning against the wall to get a better view of the room. No sign of Molly at the bar. She hurried to the bar where a young blonde woman in a pine green jacket bearing an aspen leaf logo poured water from a pitcher into a tumbler half-filled with scotch for a twenty-something Woodie.

"Don't drink that."

The kid looked at Belle like she'd lost her marbles. She couldn't blame him. "I received word that the hotel's water might be contaminated. I'd recommend using bottled water. Just in case."

He raised his brows and changed his order. "Gimme a beer."

The bartender eyed her suspiciously, complied, and the guy left to mingle.

"I'm looking for Molly Hovenden."

"Molly's working the bar with me. She's in the ladies' room at the moment. So what's the deal with the water?" She gave Belle the once-over. "You're not from the hotel."

Brilliant observation, Belle noted. "What about Jessica Davis?" She figured Stetson would be near Jessica. "Have you seen her?"

"Jess was at the bar here a minute ago," she replied, her eyes grazing the crowd for a second or two. "She said her uncle didn't like the noise and went outside for a walk. His bodyguards are with him."

"Did Molly serve Mr. Davis any beverage?"

"Who are you?"

Belle bore her eyes into the young woman. "People are going to die unless you answer me."

She gasped, and looked around wide-eyed for help, but saw none. "I...I think Jess ordered a draft beer for herself and a Diet Coke to take out to her uncle. I poured the beer, Molly poured the Coke. So like, what's the deal with the water?"

Belle recalled Carrie saying the combination of cyanide with a soft drink would intensify and accelerate the effects of the poison. But the Coke wouldn't—

The ice.

"What ice did she use to make his drink?"

The bartender took a step back. The bar was positioned so with Belle blocking one side she was effectively penned in.

"I'm not going to hurt you," Belle assured her. Please, just tell me, what ice did she use?"

"Molly brought up a fresh container of spherical ice cubes, the ones we use when a customer asks for a single cube. Like for a good brandy or a single-malt scotch. I remember her using that instead of our regular ice because it was unusual. She said something about Mr. Davis being a VIP, and he should get the fancy ice."

"Show me the special ice."

She nodded toward the bar sink. "After Molly made the Secretary's drink, she dumped the rest of the ice. I thought it was kind of weird at the time, but before I could ask her about it she left."

Belle looked in the sink and saw a half dozen spherical ice cubes melting. She grabbed a glass and scooped up the ice. "She said the ice came from your normal source?"

"She didn't say, I just assumed—"

Now it made sense. Molly had prepared ice cubes heavily fortified with a dose of cyanide that would be instantly lethal. The sweet soft drink would likely mask the poison's taste and almond odor. Davis would drink his Coke, die, and the contaminated reservoir, and ultimately the tent company, would be blamed. Belle handed the bartender the glass with the poisoned ice. "The cops will be here very shortly. Keep this for them and tell them what you told me. Now, do you have any idea where Mr. Davis went for his walk?"

"No. Look, could I please see some—?"

Belle was out the door.

She exited the hotel and shouted to the kid in uniform. "Where did Davis go?"

He ignored her question and pointed to a nearby dimly lit parking lot where she saw the Cherokee parked in the corner. "I moved your vehicle to the front lot, ma'am, but you'll—"

She grabbed him by the front of his jacket and pulled him close enough to kiss. "Jessica Davis's uncle's in danger. I need to know where he is."

She heard the kid's sharp intake of breath. He pointed to the snow-covered golf course across the street from the hotel.

Belle ran to her car, climbed up to the roof, and scanned the area. There. Maybe sixty yards away.

A man she assumed was Davis walked away from the hotel, heading farther in the opposite direction. Her message must've gotten through because he was accompanied by two bodyguards—

One of the bodyguards was *Alonzo!* He must've received her text and arrived in time to provide personal protection to his boss. The men stopped to wait for a young woman—had to be Jessica. The young woman carried a beer in one hand and a glass in the other, no doubt containing the cyanide-laced ice.

Belle jumped up and down on the roof, waved her hands, and screamed, "*Stop! Don't drink the Coke! Alonzo!*"

They didn't hear her; the music drowned out her voice. If she had a gun she could fire a warning shot, but her Stealth was buried under the snow up on Monroe Mountain.

***

Carrie couldn't take her eyes off the gun.

"Drop the phone," Sonja ordered. The young woman's voice was rough, scratchy, like a heavy smoker. She used the gun to gesture Carrie toward the bedroom.

"Please—"

Sonja pressed the gun barrel against Carrie's temple. "Move."

Carrie shuffled out of the kitchen and slowly walked down the narrow hallway to her bedroom, twice having to brace against the walls to keep from collapsing to the floor.

They entered her bedroom. Carrie turned and raised her hands, placating. "Please..." She backed up to the bedside table, unable to pull her eyes away from the gun in Sonja's hand, and struggled with only limited success to calm her voice. "Listen, Sonja, you don't have to do this. I understand how drugs have clouded your reasoning and how a world of violence might seem exciting now. And I know you and Danny—"

"Shut the fuck up."

Sonja screwed a suppressor into the gun barrel. Her face remained without expression, and her dead eyes didn't blink. Like she was a monster on one of those TV zombie shows. Hopefully, she didn't happen to be hopped up on something at the moment. Maybe Carrie could reason with her.

"I can assure you it's never too late to break the cycle of violence. And I promise that if you lay down that gun—"

Pffft.

The force of the bullet knocked her to the floor. It took a full second to feel the fire burning inside her chest. Another couple of seconds later a pool of red surrounded her, the bright color almost festive in its slowly expanding free-form design painted on the white rug.

Two or three seconds later the black curtain began to descend.

Oh, Lilly...

Chapter Forty-One

S tetson Davis and his guards, now about seventy yards away, had stopped to admire a life-size ice sculpture of an elk. Even running as fast as she could there was no way Belle could reach them before Davis drank the cyanide. She considered sending Scout, but there was a strong likelihood that the bodyguard, seeing a 150-pound animal emerge out of the darkness and charge Davis, would shoot him before Alonzo could intervene. She saw no options. Unless...

She jumped down, opened the driver-side door, and leaned on the horn. They had to hear the blast. The bodyguard turned first, then Alonzo, then Jessica and her uncle. Belle continued to honk, but after a quick glance they turned back. They couldn't see her and probably figured a car alarm had gone off in the parking lot. They kept walking farther away. *Shit.*

She spotted her bow. Another idea, this one ranking at the top of her craziest-ideas-ever hit list. She pulled out the bow and a target arrow.

She nocked the arrow and took aim for the ice sculpture, a difficult shot at thirty or forty yards, a near-impossible shot at twice that distance. Davis paused, put his arm around his niece, leaned up against the sculpture, and lifted the glass toward his lips.

Belle pulled back on the string, and the eccentrics at the top of the Hoyt tripped in, allowing her to take advantage of a sixty-five-pound pull. The bow wasn't sighted for anywhere near the correct distance, so she was relying solely on feel. She released the arrow and immediately lost sight as it disappeared into the dark.

A moment later Davis dropped the glass. Alonzo pushed him to the ground and covered him with his own body while simultaneously whipping a gun from his shoulder holster and aiming it her way. With her hands in the air, she ran toward them.

"Alonzo, the ice is poisoned! The ice is poisoned!" As she got closer he recognized her.

"Belle?" Then to the other agent. "Don't shoot, she's with me!"

A glance revealed the arrow had struck the ice elk dead in the heart, inches from where Davis had been standing.

Alonzo holstered his weapon. "Belle, what the hell?"

"The ice in that drink is laced with cyanide!" She turned to Davis, sitting on the ground. "There was no time for a warning, sir. The arrow was the only way to get your attention and keep you from drinking the poison."

She found the dropped glass and used it to scoop up the remaining chunks of ice from the snow. She handed the glass to the flummoxed agent who had yet to holster his weapon. "Keep this for testing." The agent looked like he was about to strangle her.

Alonzo helped Davis to his feet. "Sir, this is Isabella Bannon. She's on my team."

Well, not exactly, but given the scowl on the agent's face, at that moment Belle welcomed being considered a member of any team captained by Alonzo Longabaugh. The agent took the glass.

"Again, Mr. Davis, I'm very sorry. You were about to drink the poison, and I had no other alternatives at the moment."

Davis spoke for the first time. "Miss, if what you say is true, you saved my life. If it's not true and that arrow was meant for me, I'm afraid you're going to be spending a long time behind bars."

***

Molly Halpin had received a message from Danny instructing her to meet Sonja in the 7-Eleven parking lot. She was to leave her car in the lot where she'd meet Sonja and the conniving bitch was supposed to take her to connect up with Danny.

Molly had retrieved her phone from under Danny's bed and listened to the recording. Her worst fears had been realized. Danny and Sonja had screwed just minutes after Molly had left the apartment, obviously because Sonja had enticed Danny to bed. Molly had shuddered with each moan and groan, but there was no doubt in her mind to Danny it had been just sexual release. They hadn't made *love*, that was the difference. And very soon Sonja would be out of their lives forever. Molly also had also heard a phone conversation between Danny and some guy named Felix, but that was Danny's business.

She pulled into the lot and parked. Maybe while she was there she'd take a moment and buy some antacids. That feeling in the pit of her stomach hadn't gone away; it felt like an acid-soaked knot the size of a softball. She got out of her car and was about to enter when Sonja pulled in next to her and gestured for her to enter the car. Carrie sighed and slid into Sonja's passenger seat.

Sonja was speaking into her phone. "Okay, I'll ask her." She ended the call, turned to Molly and paused, scrutinizing Molly's face in the dim light. "Is something wrong?"

"No, why?" Molly wasn't going to give the bitch the bitch the satisfaction of thinking she cared about the woman rutting with her man. And then, of course, there was the fact that she'd just poisoned a man who, to the best of her knowledge, had done nothing wrong, simply because of what his ancestor did 140 years ago. *For wrath bringeth the punishments of the sword, that ye may know there is a judgment.* Was she still the Sword of Justice? Or would God's wrath now turn that sword on her?

"You look...I don't know, troubled."

"I'm fine." She tamped down her discomfort and struggled to force a smile. "The plan worked like a charm."

"Danny will be pleased." Sonja continued to study Molly's face with a skeptical eye.

"Sure there's no problem?"

"Absolutely." Get on with it, bitch.

Sonja held up her phone. "I just finished talking to Danny, and by the way, he's very supportive of you completing your mission."

"My mission's over." She spoke more forcefully than she intended, but there was no longer any doubt in her mind. She was laying down the sword forever.

"We have a situation," Sonja said. "Bannon and Palmer showed up at the reservoir. They pulled the hose, and I think made Jello sing."

"Too late. When I left, Davis was out walking the grounds, and his daughter was taking him a drink with the bad ice."

"Good job, Maria."

I couldn't care less what you think, bitch. She offered a weak smile.

"But the problem is the cover to make it appear Davis's death was an accident has been blown. We need to get you out of Dodge. Also, Danny's worried about Bannon. He says she's like a bulldog and will never let go. He wants her to disappear, or you both will be on the run for the rest of your lives. But out of respect and affection for you, he said you have to approve."

Approve? Approve what? The murder of Belle Bannon? "There has to be another way. Can I talk to Danny?"

"Not now. He wants me to take you to the lab. He'll meet us there. His car's parked at Little Cottonwood Canyon. The two of you are to take off tonight for Mexico."

Tonight? But she needed to pack. She'd insist they swing by her apartment so she could at least pick up her Bible and the photo of her mom. She'd known all along she couldn't take Fred. She'd kept the cactus all these years, and it had grown almost as tall as she was. Maybe she could cut off a small piece, wrap it in wet soil, and tuck it in a suitcase. She had no doubt the cutting would survive. Fred, like her, was a survivor. She could repot the cutting when they arrived in Tuscany.

"We need to get moving. There's always a chance Bannon could follow us to the lab."

"What makes you think that?" Looked like she wasn't going to have time to buy the antacids.

Sonja glanced down the street, and her eyes seemed to pause at an apartment building in the distance.

"Just a feeling."

***

Carrie still hadn't shown up. Belle had borrowed Holly's phone to call her repeatedly, but she never answered. Something was wrong. Belle heard her name and saw Stetson Davis waving her over. Alonzo stood nearby. She'd told him everything we'd learned about Molly.

Davis greeted her. "Ms. Bannon, I've been further briefed by

Agent Longabaugh. I don't know for certain who would've instructed Pagano to take my life, but I have several potential suspects and they happen to reside in Las Vegas, Nevada. I promise you we'll find the people behind this attempt and bring them to justice, an attempt that would've been successful were it not for you. I owe you my life." He extended his hand. "Thank you."

Belle shook his hand, and Jessica, who hovered nearby, hugged me. "Actually, the person you should thank is my friend, Carrie Palmer. She's the one who figured out the cyanide formula."

"The soonest I have a chance, I'll do just that."

"May I ask you a question, sir?"

"Anything."

"Are you a descendant of President Cleveland?"

"I understand from Agent Longabaugh why you ask that question, but no. My wife's spent a great deal of time tracing our family roots, so I'm certain."

She glanced at Jessica. "One more thing, but it's kind of personal." Holly quickly took the hint and stepped out of earshot. "From Agent Longabaugh you've learned that you were about to be poisoned by the bartender, a young woman named Molly Halpin, who sees herself as an avenger exacting retribution against powerful men who impregnate women and then abandon them. I hate to ask you, sir, but could there have been some incident in your past when—"

"Never. Don't get me wrong, I'm no saint. But I've never, er, impregnated a woman other than my wife, and if I had, I would've owned up to it."

Belle believed him. "Thank you."

Davis waved Alonzo closer. "Agent Longabaugh, what do you think of recruiting Ms. Bannon?"

His face lit up. "An excellent idea, sir."

"Belle, we could use a woman like you."

A woman like me?

"Thanks, but I'm a hunting guide, not a secret agent. I'll pass."

"If you change your mind, let us know," Davis said. "And whenever you see Ms. Palmer, please tell her I'm looking forward to thanking her personally."

I'd love to give Carrie your message if I only knew where the hell she was.

Belle stepped away and asked to borrow Alonzo's phone to call Molly then realized she couldn't remember her phone number. After a few taps, he provided her number. A nice government agent perk. She dialed; no answer. She was switched to voicemail and spoke with a tinge of genuine sympathy in her voice.

"Molly, it didn't work. Stetson Davis is alive, and we now know you were behind all of the deaths. I believe you were doing what you thought was right. We read Maria Halpin's diary and understand your urge to exact revenge. I promise if you turn yourself in, I'll do everything in my power—" I glanced at Alonzo and he nodded in agreement. "—to see you receive the help you need. Molly, please."

Belle ended the call and stared at the phone hoping for an answer.

"I doubt if she'll reply," he said.

She tried Carrie's landline. Nothing. "I'm worried about Carrie. I dropped her off at her place to use the phone. Haven't heard from her since. I'm heading over there."

He led the way toward a Secret Service car with a flashing red light on the dash. "I'll drive."

***

Sonja Valek drove through Little Cottonwood Canyon and pulled into an arroyo behind the small copse of gnarly pine covering a secret entrance into the mine on the other side of the ski resort.

Molly reached for the door latch when her phone buzzed. She checked the screen.

"Longabaugh. Who's Longabaugh?"

Sonja snatched the phone from her hand.

"Hey—"

Sonja ignored her and waited for the call to roll over to voicemail then held the phone to her ear and listened.

Molly didn't hide her agitation. "Who is it? What the hell's going on?"

"Davis is alive." Sonja's eyes bore into her. "You fucked up."

The blood drained from Molly's face. "What? I don't understand."

Sonja snarled and lowered her voice to a harsh whisper. "Thanks to Bannon."

Molly felt relieved but struggled not to show it, responding dutifully, "Danny's not going to be happy."

Chapter Forty-Two

A lonzo had called ahead and used his Fed creds to arrange for the apartment manager to meet them.

Belle knocked hard and when there was no immediate response didn't bother to knock a second time. The manager unlocked the door and followed Alonzo's instructions to wait in the hallway.

The apartment was quiet. Too quiet. She'd been there once before and as far as she could tell, nothing was out of place.

"Carrie?" No response.

"She probably tried to drive over to the hotel and got caught up in the security blockade," Alonzo said. "No cellphone, so no way to notify you."

"I bet you're right."

Belle scanned the living room and kitchen. Again, everything seemed normal. But there was something about the kitchen—

She froze.

The handset of the phone in the kitchen dangled to the floor.

Oh, God. She rushed into the bedroom. At first, nothing unusual. Then she heard a barely perceptible moan from the other side of the bed. Two long strides and Belle saw her.

Oh, Jesus. Oh, God!

She lay there sprawled out on the floor with her head propped up awkwardly against the leg of the bedside table. A bright red pool of blood stained the front of her shirt and spread wide on the white carpet.

"Call an ambulance! Now!"

Carrie was fading in and out of consciousness.

Belle crouched down. "It's Belle. Don't worry, you're going to be okay. You're going to be fine."

Belle lowered Carrie's head gently to the carpet and ripped open her bloody shirt. A single bullet wound, large caliber, near the center of her chest. Belle grabbed a pillow from the bed, yanked the pillowcase free, folded it quickly, and pressed it hard against the wound. Reaching around her back, she searched for the bullet's exit. Nothing. Carrie's clammy skin had paled almost to white.

"Carrie?" Belle tried with little success to block the panic from her voice. "Carrie, can you hear me?" Carrie moaned. Alonzo entered the bedroom. Belle screamed, "Where the hell's the ambulance?"

"On its way."

"You're a goddamn federal agent! Get it here faster!"

"I'll go out to the front and wait for them." He took Carrie's hand. "Hang in there. Help will be here very soon." He hurried out of the room.

Belle felt so helpless. Nothing she could do but wait. She sat on the floor and rocked her friend in her arms. Carrie murmured something, and Belle lowered her ear to Carrie's lips.

"Belle?"

"I'm here. Don't worry, you're going to be—"

Her eyes fluttered open, just a slit really, but Belle thought Carrie could see her. "Did...?"

"Shhh, don't talk."

"Davis?"

"You did good. Thanks to you he's fine. Got there in time. And the town's been warned about the water. Now, who—?"

"Belle, you're the one who saved Davis and many others. Children in the town... Those lives...all those lives... You no longer have to feel guilty about your three brothers."

Belle pressed harder on the wound to stench the blood flow. Didn't help. "Shhh, you need to conserve—"

"You know I love—"

"Yeah, me too. Who did this?"

"Sonja. Belle, tell Lilly... Mommy loves her."

"No more talking." Belle bit her lip. "You have to save your strength so you can tell her yourself."

"And Dad..."

Her body shivered, and Belle pulled her tighter.

"Belle, promise you'll find Pagano and—"

She turned her face and brushed Belle's lips with hers. Then she closed her eyes and stopped breathing.

"No!"

Belle rolled her onto her back, breathed hard into her mouth then straddled her and rhythmically pushed her interlocked hands hard down on Carrie's chest to the beat of the BeeGees song, "Stayin' Alive." Tears poured down her face. *Please, God, not her. Stayin' alive, stayin' alive. Kind, generous, peaceful, loves everyone, even the assholes of the world. Stayin' alive, stayin' alive. Turns the other cheek. Jesus! Isn't that what the hell you want! Sorry, God. Stayin' alive, stayin' alive...*

Three young men in crisp blue shirts arrived and pulled Belle off of her. All sense of time disappeared. Belle floated in the air, invisible, observing a surreal presentation of a stage play. It couldn't be real, of course. Carrie Palmer couldn't actually be gone. Belle didn't move and watched dispassionately as they did their thing and eventually took her away.

Alonzo sat on the floor with her, put his arm around her shoulders, and pulled her close.

Belle wasn't a crier, but she bawled her eyes out, and her mind spun through the times she'd spent with Carrie. Like binge-watching reruns at warp speed. They were so different from each other—Carrie was Belle's reflection in a mirror where everything appeared opposite. Yet the core remained the same. A sister? In some ways, more than that. That blood on the carpet was also Belle's blood.

Belle didn't know how long she remained curled up in Alonzo's arms. He didn't say a word, which she appreciated.

She didn't hear the ping, but Alonzo did and fished his phone from his pocket. He showed her the screen. From Molly. Belle grabbed it and tapped for the text message.

"Too bad about your friend. You want me, come get me. Bring A.L. No one else. One
    below K. D.P."

The word spit out of Belle's mouth. "Pagano."

"One below K?"

A switch tripped—her face hardened, her eyes flared. A seething rage permeated every cell in her body. Her mind whirred, now fully engaged. She was in warrior mode. "K must mean Keetley. He knows we were in the mine and that we'd understand what 'K' meant. One below K means the tunnel below Keetley."

Alonzo took his phone back and was about to tap a number.

She rested a firm restraining hand on his arm and held his gaze. "No. Anyone other than you and me shows up, we'll lose him. He's responsible for Carrie's death." She gritted her teeth.

"Did you see what he said? *Did you see what he fucking said?* 'Too bad about your friend'?"

"He's obviously baiting you. He holds you responsible for saving Davis, and he wants you to come for him so he can exact revenge."

"He's asking for you, too."

"Killing a DEA agent might not be the same as Stetson Davis, but he's probably hoping it might smooth over whatever is about to befall him for botching Davis's murder. Look, I can post five men at each entrance."

"Remember, the tunnel system in these mountains is like a beehive—a maze of narrow sloping passageways interconnecting with the main tunnels. Most all of them are probably no longer passable, but it's certainly conceivable Pagano found his way to an alternative outside exit, one you'll never find in time. So, please, no."

"Then I'm going alone. You're a civilian, Belle. There's an excellent chance whoever goes up there won't be coming back. This isn't your fight."

Her mind drifted to the image of the EMTs slowly zipping up the black body bag, starting at Carrie's feet. As the zipper moved up her body, every inch came closer to extinguishing her, until the beautiful, serene face of Carrie Palmer was all that remained exposed. Then the zipper went all the way.

Belle bit her lip. No more tears. Not now. "You don't understand," she whispered. "This is my *only* fight."

Chapter Forty-Three

For a while, neither Belle nor Alonzo spoke as they hiked from the Jordanelle Treatment Plant maintenance station up toward the mouth of the Keetley tunnel. Scout followed close behind. Her mind was overrun with only one thought—exacting revenge for the death of Carrie Palmer.

She could tell something was on Alonzo's mind. Finally, he broke the silence.

"If we both happen to be alive tomorrow morning, I wish you'd reconsider joining up."

Belle was irritated that he would bring up any subject other than assuring Pagano and his skanky assistant suffered a long, painful death. "Not interested in talking about that now. Besides, you don't want someone like me. I have certain...issues."

"We're well aware of your IED and the Zagros incident. It's not a problem." He paused then lowered his voice to a near whisper. "In combat, shit happens."

Something about his tone and expression suggested he wasn't only talking about her. She filed his comment away to maybe ask him about it later. If they happened to have a later.

But apparently, he wanted to talk about it now. "I killed a seven-year-old boy, Belle. I aimed at his head and pulled the trigger." He stopped, closed his eyes, and dropped his head. "Jesus."

Maybe the prospect of impending death loosens a compulsion to confess one's sins. She could relate to that. But at the moment, she didn't have time to think about anything other than Pagano. A look at Alonzo's face changed her mind. He needed to unburden, and she needed his mind clear as fast as possible. "What happened?"

His words flowed freely, the sinner in the confessional. "We were in Ghazni manning a roadblock. From around the corner, this boy appears wearing a suicide vest. The vest was so big and heavy it almost reached the ground. He continued to walk toward us with his hand on the detonator. We all shouted at him to stop. Tears were rolling down his cheeks. That's what I'll always see, those huge brown eyes and the tears pouring out. But he kept coming. Anything other than a headshot would've triggered the device. I was the best shot. I took it. God help me."

She didn't know what to say, so she said nothing. They both had issues from their days in the sandbox. Probably not much different from most everyone else who's served there. If they survived the next hour or so, there would be plenty of time to hopefully deal with those issues.

He looked relieved. "Sorry, didn't mean to unload all that on you. Never really talked about it with anybody else before. Weird, I know, but although we haven't known each other very long, I feel a connection to you I haven't felt in a long time." He chuckled. "True confessions as the condemned man marches to the gallows."

Belle felt the same connection, but this wasn't the time or place to tell him. "Nothing to be sorry about. Have you considered quilting?"

He smiled. "Maybe you can teach me."

She squeezed his shoulder, and they continued climbing the hill toward the tunnel with no more confessions, true or otherwise.

Soon they reached a spot about a hundred yards away from their destination. They decided to crawl up the curving maintenance car trestle rather than attempting to scale the cliff to reach the tunnel. As accomplished rail tie jumpers, they had no problem and soon found themselves entering the tunnel mouth.

They left the moonlight behind, and each used flashlights to guide their path. Belle led the way along the rail tracks up through the tunnel with Alonzo and Scout jumping from tie to tie behind her. She noticed the water level below the rail ties had lowered since she and Alonzo had last visited.

She'd left a text message for Sal—She and Alonzo were exploring a few leads. Nothing to worry about. But if he hadn't heard from them in an hour he needed to send the cops up to the mine with a full posse. He immediately called back, but she didn't answer. Belle knew he'd tell them to wait. Not happening.

She scanned her light beam around the tunnel ceiling. "Up ahead should be the vertical drain chute we fell through."

"I'm having an unpleasant flashback," Alonzo said.

"Copy that. When we see the drain, I'll have an idea how far we are from the lift."

He pulled a gun from his side holster. "Just in case we see any more snakes."

For the first time in her life, she didn't care about snakes. She didn't care about anything except finding Pagano and Sonja.

They reached the vertical drain shaft. "Probably less than an hour from here to the lift," she said.

As they moved up the tunnel, the tension increased

exponentially, threatening to encase her entire body. She felt a tightness in her chest. She was walking through wet cement and could barely move. Her stride shortened to the point where she was taking baby steps. All caused not by fear, but bubbling anger so powerful it threatened to paralyze her. Belle could actually feel Carrie's weight in her arms as she lay dying, and Carrie's last faint breath lightly brushing Belle's cheek. Her sluggish pace didn't go unnoticed.

"Belle? We don't have to do this. I can call—"

"No. I'm fine." She knew she needed a mental distraction or she'd never make it. She could ask Alonzo more about the Ghazni incident, but she was afraid that might cause too intense a distraction. Her eyes fell on Alonzo's gun. A Colt .45 SAA revolver. The single-action Army revolver had been very popular at the end of the nineteenth century, used by good guys and bad guys alike. Maybe a little light conversation about family would help.

"So, the Sundance Kid was your what? Great-grandfather?"

"Great-great."

"You ever get teased about it?"

"Few people know about the connection. This is his gun, by the way. Before that final shootout, he sent my great-great-grandma, Etta Place, home from Bolivia to the States with a baby in her belly and a gun—this gun—for protection. If we happen to get out of this alive, I'll tell you the whole story."

For some reason, the image of Alonzo Longabaugh instead of a young Robert Redford wearing a black cowboy hat, Paul Newman at his side, guns blazing, jolted her with an infusion of adrenaline. She wanted to shoot somebody. She wanted her Stealth, long gone on the mountain. No, she wanted—she *needed* to strangle Danny Pagano slowly, with her bare hands. Her gait quickened, and Alonzo struggled to catch up. They actually made it to the lift in twenty minutes.

"How do we call for the lift?" Alonzo asked. "Is there a power box?"

A piercing *screech* of rusty interlocking gears interrupted him. The lift rose then stopped in front of them, vibrating up and down before coming to a complete rest.

"They know we're here," Belle said. "The moment we descend he'll likely open fire, and that lift car offers no protection."

She hopped onto the lift platform, and Scout followed. "I'm going down. You coming?" He sighed and stepped aboard. She toggled down.

As soon as the lift floor reached the top of the first horizontal tunnel, she inserted the lit flashlight into her jacket pocket, substantially dimming the beam, and hit "stop."

"No use giving Veshenko a big target. I suggest we lie flat." Without objection, Alonzo assumed a prone position on the wood plank floor and steadied his gun in both hands. She wondered about his claustrophobia and noticed a glistening of sweat covering his face. "You okay?"

He reached up from his knees and toggled down.

They saw a faint light coming from farther down the tunnel. She took over and lowered the lift a bit more to provide him a sightline then flattened herself to the floor.

After waiting a couple of minutes and not drawing fire, she reached up and toggled the lift down another few feet. They again waited. The tunnel curved away from us, and the light source appeared to be located around the bend. They spotted several crags and cutouts where Veshenko or his man could be lying in wait.

"Maybe he's not waiting for us," she whispered.

"Or maybe he has more patience than we do."

This time Belle lowered the lift to the tunnel floor. They quickly stepped off and immediately pressed their bodies tight against the wall. Using a hand command, she positioned Scout behind her then took the lead while Alonzo covered their backs.

They tried to avoid tripping on the rocks and other debris scattered along the floor, but she was hesitant to shine her light for fear it would serve as an easy target. Instead, she kept the light in her pocket where its muted glow barely registered.

They moved carefully, each sliding their lead foot forward, much like a blind man's cane, probing for obstacles hidden by the dark. Their efforts were only partially successful as each of them stumbled over rocks on the uneven floor.

"Where the hell's Pagano?" Alonzo whispered.

"Maybe he left."

Crak.

The noise from the pistol shot echoed through the tunnel, amplifying to the level of a shotgun blast. They dove to the rocky floor.

"Where did it come from?" Alonzo whispered.

"I don't know. Up ahead, I think." For a few moments, the tunnel was deathly quiet. Then a female voice up ahead broke the silence.

"Hey, bitch, thanks for stopping by. And so glad you brought your boyfriend."

"Sonja Valek," Belle whispered. "Maybe twenty yards ahead."

"Not quite that far." Her words mixed with a wheezy giggle. "Remember, these tunnels amplify sound."

"You fuck! You didn't have to kill her!"

"No time to tie her up. It was the most efficient alternative. Just business."

Alonzo extended his foot and kicked Belle to get her attention. He held a rock in his hand and simulated throwing it. She understood. Just like in those old cowboy TV shows—the good guy throws the rock, the bad guy shows himself, the good guy shoots the bad guy, cut to a commercial for Cocoa Puffs. She found a rock that fit her hand near where the floor intersected with the tunnel wall. After checking to make sure Alonzo was ready, she heaved the rock down the tunnel along the right wall. The moment the rock hit the floor, Alonzo raised and fired. The sound of his gun was immediately trumped by another gunshot. He yelped and fell back, holding his leg.

Belle slithered across the ragged tunnel floor on her belly, snatched the Sundance Kid's famous revolver from Alonzo's hand, and blindly fired three shots down the tunnel. Unfortunately, she didn't hear anyone say "ouch," and a moment later they heard footsteps running away. She pulled her flashlight free to check on Alonzo's wound. His face twisted in pain, and she could see a dark stain spreading across the jeans on his right thigh.

He grimaced and spoke through clenched teeth. "I'm okay. Can still shoot."

The blood was seeping, not spurting, signaling the femoral artery wasn't hit. "I need to check the wound and stop the bleeding. Pull down your pants."

"What is it about being in dark tunnels that makes us want to take each other's clothes off?"

"Not funny." She unbuckled his belt, unzipped his fly, and pulled his jeans down to his knees. The bullet had entered his outer thigh. Lucky. A few inches inside and it would've cut the femoral artery, and there probably would've been no way to save him before he bled out. She reached around to the back of his thigh. "Feels like a clean exit." she helped him out of his jacket and shirt. Using her knife, she cut off both shirtsleeves. She ripped one sleeve in half, folded the two pieces, and pressed them against the entry and exit wounds. "Hold these tight." He complied, and she used the second sleeve to tie the two compresses in place. "You'll be fine."

He slipped his jacket back on and tried to struggle to his feet.

"We need to move."

"You're not going anywhere," she ordered. "I can't be focusing on the hostiles if I'm worried about you. Stay here. I'll pick you up on the way back."

"You're outnumbered. You can't go down there alone."

"Yes, I can."

He knew she was right and slumped back down against the wall. He handed her the Colt. "Take this."

"Think she's gone?"

"Stay low. Could be she moved to a different position down the tunnel and is lying in wait."

The wheezy voice, teasing from farther away. "Still heeere." She giggled. "C'mon back, bitch. We can't wait to see you."

Chapter Forty-Four

B elle slipped away and inched along the tunnel wall with Scout following close behind. After covering about thirty yards, she slid around a curve and saw a dim light coming from a cutout maybe another fifty or sixty yards farther ahead. They moved down the tunnel until they reached a spot just outside the cutout. She hand-signaled Scout to stay put and peeked around the edge, her finger tight on the trigger.

At first, the space appeared deserted. Several large battery-powered lanterns lit the front of the opening. Deep shadows running irregularly along each side of the cutout suggested additional nooks, some likely leading to other connectors in the beehive, but most probably dead-ends.

Three long folding tables lined up against the side walls. On the tables and the floor beneath them were various glass and plastic bottles with wide, easily readable labels—muriatic acid, kerosene, ammonia, iodine, rubbing alcohol, and gun cleaner. A copper gas line ran from three propane tanks in one corner to two burners on one of the tables. Boxes of kitchen matches, lithium batteries, aluminum foil, coffee filters, tubing, and Pyrex dishes were scattered on and under the tables. The whole place smelled like piss and kerosene. Danny Pags had established what looked like a fairly sophisticated meth lab.

The flickering shadows made seeing difficult. She stepped inside and moved toward the back.

"Freeze." Molly's hesitant voice behind me.

Belle turned slowly.

"I said stop!"

The light from the lantern reflected off her eyes. She seemed nervous, uncertain. Scared. She held a gun pointed at Belle in a shaking hand.

Belle kept her voice low, unthreatening. "I don't think you'll shoot me."

Her humorless smile faded as fast as it appeared. "Sorry, Belle, but if I have to choose between you and Danny, you lose." She nodded to the center of the lab. "Now stand over there where I can see you. And, Belle, I know you're an expert in all that kung-fu shit, so even the slightest move, and I'll shoot. Please don't make me do that."

Something in Molly's eyes raised a question in Belle's mind whether she would actually pull the trigger, but Belle couldn't tell for certain and moved to the center of the space.

She spotted a small mound of plastic gallon bottles on the floor under one of the tables. The bottles rested on a wooden box. On the side of the box was stenciled: *Dynamite. Danger. Explosive Material.* She had a bad feeling where this might be going and raised her hands in a calm-down gesture. "Molly, listen to me. I know in your heart you're not a cold-blooded killer. You believed you were doing the right thing. You need help, and I promise you if you let us go—"

"No!" Her eyes widened, and the shriek in her voice sounded as if it were grounded in fear as much as aggression. "Just...stop. I don't need 'help.' I don't need anything. You want me to go back to the blue walls. I'll never do that. Never. Now drop your gun on that table over there."

Belle hesitated, instantly calculating her options—measuring the distance between her and the gun, Molly's line of sight, the closeness of the quarters—and decided she couldn't take a chance. She stepped over to the table.

"Two fingers, just like on TV."

Belle did as she asked. "I have to hand it to you. Your ability to make the murders look like accidents—"

The hand holding the gun seemed to steady. "Not murders, justice."

"Still, pretty amazing. We saw the juggler costume in your apartment so we know you were the one who shoved Brad Banks."

Panic flared in her voice. "You were in my apartment? How did you..." Her eyes widened in realization. "Fred."

"You hooked Harrison on meth," Belle ventured, "and sent him up to ski a suicide run down Black Lightning."

"But God intervened with the earthquake."

"Why Harrison?"

Molly's lip curled in disgust. "Last year, he and his pals got an eighteen-year-old girl named Sally Hawthorne drunk at NoName and took her back to their hotel room where he screwed her when she was barely conscious. Two months later at the clinic, she confided in me she was pregnant and told me what happened. She contacted Harrison, he denied it. Her parents lived in Florida and were some kind of bullshit fundamentalists. She said they would've blamed her and disowned her if they found out. She had her own issues with abortion, so she gave birth to a baby boy at the clinic but couldn't care for him and put him up for adoption. Later, she tried to get the kid back. Didn't work. A few months ago she overdosed on fentanyl down in Heber and died."

Belle wanted her to keep her talking. "What about Markie Dodd?"

Molly's expression clouded. "She wasn't the target. It was her lying scumbag father. Their tradition of him leading her down the last run had become common knowledge among the locals, and then it was in the newspaper. But the asshole decided to stop and adjust his boot mid-run. I mean who does that? I'm really sorry about Markie, I really am, but her father's to blame, not me. And now Danny says Virgil will suffer for the rest of his life."

"Speaking of Danny Pags, where is your partner in crime and his idiot bitch?"

"I wouldn't be in too big a rush to see him because once he arrives we're out of here and, sorry, maybe you're not." She glanced at the dynamite.

"I see. So, what about the judge? You had to know triggering the avalanche would put lots of innocent people in jeopardy, including the judge's grandson."

She tilted her head side to side like she was rattling her reasoning around between her ears. "To tell you the truth, I'd gone back and forth on that one. The likelihood of success was very uncertain, but the challenge was too tempting. Besides, there are very few beginners who night ski. I had a remote detonator and was monitoring the run. You should know, Belle, I almost aborted when I saw you and Carrie on the run. But I had faith you would survive, and I was right. I knew God was on my side, and I proved it with every case by stacking the odds against myself higher and higher. And each time He came through. Justice, Belle, not murder."

"But why Maddox?"

"He was as bad as the rest. He impregnated Rita Sanchez, his housekeeper, and she couldn't do anything about it. She had no money and was in the country illegally."

"I understand she moved to L.A."

"More lies. She gave birth to Maddox's kid at the clinic. Her family effectively disowned her, and she moved to Arizona. Almost immediately she was recruited into a gang. Two months ago, she and Stella—that's what she named her baby—were both shot and killed by a rival gang."

"My God. Look, when you explain what motivated you, I'm sure a court—"

"I will only be judged by God." She took her eye off Belle and looked heavenward. "God has been my guiding—"

Belle dove for her gun hand, and they both crashed to the floor. The gun flew from her grip. Belle crawled over her body and reached for it.

"Freeze!"

Belle looked up, and Sonja Valek stepped out from one of the shadowy nooks with a gun pointed at Belle's head.

"Where's Danny?" Molly asked.

"On his way."

Belle tried bluffing. "Both exits to the mine are covered by cops. There's no way you'll escape."

Sonja smiled. "There are lots of exits, bitch."

Belle tried to focus her eyes on the shadowy area in the back of the cutout. "So, I assume there's an exit back there?"

"Danny picked this place for many reasons. One was it had a back door," Sonja said.

"Where does it lead?"

"Little Cottonwood Canyon, but that's not something you need to worry about seeing as how you ain't leaving." She picked up Molly's gun, handed it to her, and stuck her weapon in her belt.

"Keep an eye on her, Maria, while I string the fuse."

"Maria?"

"I took her name when I was exacting justice," Molly said.

Belle forced herself to keep her eyes away from Alonzo's gun resting on the table maybe three long strides away, and focused on Molly. The core of Molly Halpin's heart was pure. She was Belle's only hope. "Molly, please. While I can't agree with your methods, there's no doubt your mission was honorable. Those men deserved punishment, just like Grover Cleveland deserved to be punished. And Maria Halpin deserved justice, which she never received."

"You read Maria's diary?"

Belle nodded. "But the world doesn't know what happened. Things are so much different now. Her story needs to get out. History must be corrected. I promise you together we can help make that happen. You've done what you believed you had to do. Your mission is now over."

Belle had another thought and pulled the faded photo of Molly and her mom from her pocket. "And what about Nancy? What about your mom?"

"Where did you get that?" Her eyes brimmed with tears.

"What Yaeger did to her was unspeakable, and you made him pay. But what would your mom think of you now if you pull that trigger? Killing me would be murder, not justice." The indecision on her face signaled Belle might be getting through. Something else occurred to her. Was it possible she didn't know? "Just like Danny ordering Sonja here to murder Carrie Palmer in cold blood."

"What?"

Belle knew she'd hit a nerve.

Molly glanced at Sonja, but not long enough for Belle to disarm her. She backed up a few steps so Belle and Pags were both in her sightline. "Is that true?"

Her question was to Sonja, but Belle answered it. "She followed her to her apartment and shot her through the heart in her bedroom. Carrie was the most passive person either of us will ever know and couldn't have posed a threat."

"She was about to use the phone to warn Davis," Sonja said.

Belle had to somehow nudge Molly over the line to the good-guy side. "All she had to do was tie her up. Or, hell, even wound her in the leg."

"Shut up," Sonja said. "Or I'll shoot you now, although the boss thought it might be more fun if you stuck around long enough to watch the fuse burn. Then boom!" She laughed. "But think of the positive side. You and your hot boyfriend lying alone up the tunnel will die in the same instant. Who knows? Maybe you'll reunite in Hell."

She ran the fuse under and around the tables and equipment. It seemed like she was using much more fuse line than needed. Of course. They needed to delay the explosion until they had time to escape.

Belle heard footsteps coming from what Sonja called the back door.

Danny Pagano stepped into the center of the space and a cold grin creased his face.

"Sorry I'm late."

Chapter Forty-Five

Alonzo gripped a rough edge of the hacked rock wall with his fingertips and pulled himself to his feet. His leg throbbed and standing increased the pain. He knew trying to walk could dislodge the compresses and increase the bleeding, but he'd be damned if he was going to wait while Belle put her life on the line against Pagano. That was *his* job.

He attempted a single step. An electric jolt shot up his leg, and he stumbled hard to the floor. Again he crawled to his feet and leaned against the wall, panting like a dog, trying to catch his breath with only partial success.

He shuffled forward, scraping his body against the wall. After a few more steps he fell into a spastic rhythm—forward with his left leg, drag his right. Step, drag, step, drag.

Belle's voice. Down at the light source. Then the sound of others. He needed a weapon, anything.

He scooped a rock the size of a softball from the floor.

***

Molly threw herself into Pagano's's arms, but the man didn't respond; instead he stood rigid, his eyes burning into Belle.

Molly stepped back. "Sorry, baby, but Belle stopped Jello at the Jordanelle." She glanced at Belle. "And she saved Davis before he drank the cyanide."

The blood drained from Pagano's face. Seething, he glanced at Sonja but remained silent.

Molly's voice quickened. "I know you're mad because your plan didn't work, but don't worry. We're going to blow the lab, and then you and I can escape, and there'll be no evidence, and no one will chase us. We'll fly to Mexico then catch a plane to Italy. Rome, I think. Wouldn't Rome be the closest?' Her words sped up even faster. "We rent a car and drive north to Tuscany, and then we can live there together forever." Again she wrapped her arms around him.

Pagano shoved her away, and his voice rose, the anger easily seeping through. "You're the one who fucked this up. Do you *realize*, do you have any *idea,* what Vegas will do to me when they hear Davis is alive? *Jesus.* You were a nice piece of ass, sis, that's it. You're crazier than a shithouse rat and I can't believe I allowed myself to rely on you."

Molly's face froze in shock. "I...I know you don't mean that."

"You killing those people made it harder for me to make a living. I was stupid to keep you around. But you were family, and I thought I could take advantage of your 'mission' to get Davis. My mistake."

Belle figured the wider the distance between Molly and Danny the better. "By the way, your brother there faked the genealogy chart. Secretary Davis is not a descendant of President Cleveland."

"Shut the fuck up," Sonja ordered.

Molly's expression blended surprise and confusion. "I don't understand. Why would you lie to me?"

Belle interjected again. "Because he needed you to kill Davis and make it look like an accident. He wanted his hands clean. If you got caught, with your record of attempted murder in Arizona and your stay in a juvenile mental institution, he figured anything you said that might implicate him wouldn't be believed."

Molly spoke as much to herself as to Danny. "The phone call I recorded between you and that guy named Felix. He was hiring you to kill Davis."

"You recorded?"

"By the way," Belle added, "he also lied to you about the cyanide concentration."

"Thirty percent," Molly said with forced conviction. "The driver confirmed, thirty percent. No one would get hurt. A few tummy aches, that's all. It was only a way to make Davis's death look accidental."

Sonja smirked. "You dumb bitch. Pinski said that because I goaded him into saying that."

"The concentration was eighty percent," Belle said.

Molly's jaw dropped.

"We needed people to die to make sure the cover for Davis's death held up," Danny said.

"And you set up the tent company to take the fall," Belle added.

Danny sighed impatiently. "Who gives a shit about the fucking tent company? Who gives a shit about a bunch of rich Hollywood assholes? Fuck. I got to get out of here."

"But what about the children?" Molly asked. "Children would've died."

"Christ, children die every day."

Molly's whole body appeared to deflate. Her eyes glazed over, and her gun hand drooped. Belle saw the opening and tensed.

Sonja noticed. "Don't try it or you're dead. Well, you're gonna be dead anyway, but Danny has this idea about you lying here wounded as the dynamite fuse burns as sort of a prolonged mental torture. Me? I'd just put a slug in your brain. But he's the boss."

Molly turned so she was facing her step-brother. "Why do we have to kill them? How about this? We tie her and Alonzo—"

"Where is he?"

"Wounded out in the tunnel," Sonja said.

Molly continued. "So we tie them up and leave them in one of the lower tunnels. When we're safely away, we make an anonymous call and—"

"Give me the gun."

Molly hesitated then reluctantly handed it to him.

Pagano used his left hand to pull a cigarette lighter from his pocket. Without taking his eyes off Belle, he walked to the edge of the cutout and dislodged a thin piece of fuse from a crack in the wall. "The dynamite is covered in bottles of chemicals. If there's any attempt to cut the fuse a blasting cap will explode and the dynamite will detonate instantly." He lit the fuse and the flame almost immediately disappeared.

"Let me guess," Belle said. "The fuse is threaded inside the wall."

Belle understood. Over eons of time, water had carved a widespread capillary system in the rock creating transit pathways for the groundwater found in the tunnels. "And it's waterproof."

Danny glared at Belle. "As Sonja said, a bullet to the brain is too kind for you, so I will shoot you but not enough to kill you. I want you to lie here, shitting your pants, waiting for that flame to move slowly toward the dynamite."

She saw his finger tighten on the trigger.

Then she saw a familiar black-and-white blur.

With a roar, Scout leaped through the cutout entrance from the tunnel shadows and sank his teeth deep into Pagano's right arm. He screamed in rage and fumbled the gun, sending it skidding behind the equipment under a table.

Sonja trained her gun on Scout. Belle crashed into her as she pulled the trigger. The bullet grazed Scout's flank, and he let out a howl. The gun flew from Sonja's hand.

"Scout, *corri!*" Belle ordered, and the dog hobbled back into the tunnel.

Belle straddled the woman and wrapped her fingers around her throat.

The lizard door flew open and the white light swamped her brain. This was the bitch who'd murdered Carrie Palmer in cold blood, the most passive, gentle person Belle had ever met. Sonja's eyes bulged and the veins in her neck ballooned. She tried to talk but couldn't breathe.

The fuse... Alonzo...no time...

Belle slid her hands up to Sonja's head and violently wrenched it, snapping her neck like a chicken.

She glanced up to see Pagano staggering toward Alonzo's gun on the table. Belle sprang to her feet and lunged for the gun. Out of the corner of her eye she saw Pagano pull something from his jacket pocket. *A fork?* He screamed in rage as he swung the grilling fork down hard toward her hand. She tried to yank it away but one of the fork tines pierced clean through the outside of her left hand near the pinkie, pinning the hand to the table. She howled in pain.

Pagano snatched Alonzo's gun. His eyes reflected his barely controlled rage. He pointed the gun at Belle's knee.

Molly shouted. "My God! You're no different from all the others." Tears flowed down a face wracked in agony as she realized she'd also become a #MeToo victim and had experienced the ultimate betrayal. "You used me, and now I'm nothing to you."

Danny ignored her and his trigger finger tightened.

"No!" Molly jumped in front of her brother and swung her arm to knock the gun away.

Too late. The gun fired, and the bullet caught Molly flush in the chest. She slumped to the rocky floor.

Belle gritted her teeth and jerked her hand away. The fork ripped through her flesh, triggering a scream that ricocheted off the tunnel walls.

Danny instantly jumped back to create space between him and Belle. His glistening eyes widened, and his expression flashed a toxic mix of both rage and fear. "Do you have any idea...do you have any *clue* what will happen to me now?"

This time he aimed at her head.

"Hey!"

Alonzo.

Pagano turned and was rewarded with a chunk of black rock flying through the air and smashing into his face. He yelped and buckled as he fired. The bullet flew over Belle's head, smacking into the tunnel wall. He dropped the gun and crumpled to the floor. Dazed, blood streaming from his face, he stretched for the gun.

Belle yanked the fork from the table and plunged it into his neck. She didn't hit the carotid artery, but he was bleeding steadily.

Alonzo limped in, and Belle gave him a quick embrace. "Nice throw."

"Thanks."

He noticed the blood flowing from her hand to the floor. "Your hand!"

"I'm fine." She pointed to the dynamite. "Can't pull the fuse. We need to get out of here. Fast." She scooped up Alonzo's gun.

They hurried toward the entrance to the main tunnel. When they passed Sonja, Alonzo paused. "What about them?"

"She's dead."

"C'mon, we gotta go!"

Danny's voice came out in truncated rasps. "....ease, you can't...eave me!" He was crying now, his tears mixing with the snot and blood oozing down his face and neck. He pointed to Alonzo. "You...cop...have to save me..."

They ignored him and checked on Molly. Her chest rose rapidly up and down. Covered in blood, she was still alive. Barely.

"I'll get her," Alonzo said.

"You can hardly walk."

Belle lifted Molly into her arms. She coughed, and Belle saw the dark blood bubble out onto her shirt.

"Leave me—"

Carrie Palmer wouldn't allow Belle to consider such a thing. But what about Pagano? Would Carrie have approved of leaving him conscious to suffer the terror of waiting for the rock to come crashing down upon him? Belle sure as hell wasn't going to try to save the asshole.

But, she was willing to compromise.

She fired a bullet into Danny Pagano's brain.

Alonzo wrapped his arm around Belle's shoulder. Belle pulled Molly tight to her body, grimacing from the pain in her hand, and the three of them, like contestants in a Fourth of July sack race, shuffled as fast as they could out into the main tunnel.

Chapter Forty-Six

"Scout!"

He wasn't there.

Belle could feel Molly's heart beating fast, pressed against her body. Alonzo used his flashlight to show them the path ahead toward the lift. At any moment Belle expected a huge explosion would release untold tons of rock crashing down on them.

The light beam reflected off the lift up ahead. They tried to move faster.

"Scout!" She shouted. No sight of him. The bullet that had grazed him might've been more serious than when first realized.

They reached the lift and stepped on board. "Scout? *Scout?*" Nothing.

"Belle, we gotta go!" Alonzo shouted.

You don't understand. Scout's my pal. He saved my life. "Scout!"

"Belle!"

Holding Molly tight with one arm, Belle maneuvered her body around so her wounded hand could reach the toggle switch and flipped the toggle up. *Please work, please work...*

It didn't move.

Maybe a reboot. She tugged the toggle and the lift moved down. *If it only goes down, we're dead.* She moved the switch to "stop," then toggled back up. This time the lift moved upward. *Yes!*

"Belle!"

Alonzo pointed down the tunnel where a familiar black and white dog burst through the darkness and ran with a pronounced limp toward the lift.

Her heart lept. "C'mon, baby! C'mon boy!"

She grabbed the toggle to stop the lift. *What if I stop it and it doesn't start up again?* "Scout, *corri!*"

He jumped just as the lift approached the ceiling. His front paws made it. The rest of his body didn't.

Alonzo dropped flat on the floor, reached out and dragged the dog on board. Scout screeched as the ceiling shaft edge scraped across the wound on his back. Belle cringed, feeling his pain, and hugged him close with her bloody hand while balancing Molly against the dirty plywood wall with the other.

"Think we'll make it in time?" Alonzo asked.

"No problem." *No way. Not unless the fuse didn't ignite the explosives.*

Alonzo must've read her mind. "Dynamite's tricky. Sometimes it doesn't explode."

After rising about fifty feet Belle felt a little better. "The dynamite should've gone off by now. Just two more levels to go."

Alonzo offered a hopeful smile. "Looks like the dynamite was a dud."

"You better knock on wood."

"I don't believe in that—"

The shape of the tunnel below amplified the sound of the explosion. The lift shook so violently there was little doubt at any moment it would break away from the two supporting cables and send them all crashing to oblivion.

Fortunately, Molly was unconscious and wouldn't have to experience these last seconds of terror before death.

The rock wall shaft housing the lift rumbled then split, shooting rock shards through the open sides of the lift compartment. Alonzo ducked, covering his head with his arms while Belle protected Molly the best she could. Scout lay low.

Snap.

The lift cantered to one side.

"A cable broke!" Alonzo shouted over the din.

The volume of the sound below increased steadily as if a giant freight train barreled toward them full speed, and they were tied to the tracks.

Wait. The concussion field. Was it possible?

The runaway train felt like it was nearly upon them. The booming sound of the explosion crescendoed. Alonzo pointed his light down through the crack between the lift and the chute walls, and Belle saw a giant ball of rock chunks and dust hurtling up the lift shaft toward them.

"Hold on!" She shouted.

Snap.

The last cable!

The lift dropped hard and fast. She held Molly tight. Alonzo wrapped his arm around both of them and shouted in Belle's ear. "Sorry we never got to—"

The concussion ball smacked hard up into the lift floor, knocking them off their feet. The force of the explosion acted as a propellant, shooting the lift up the shaft along with dust and rocky debris. In moments it approached the top level. Now the deafening sound made it impossible to be heard, so Belle crawled to her knees and made a diving motion with her hand. Alonzo nodded. She picked Molly back up into her arms.

They'd only have one chance, one split second before the lift would fall again, carrying them a thousand feet down to their rocky coffin.

The lift shot up above the entrance floor. Belle shouted, *"Now!"* but didn't think Alonzo heard her. With Molly in her arms, she dove left. Scout followed right behind her, and they landed hard on the dusty floor of the main building. Alonzo dove right, then waved his arm frantically. "Belle!"

She realized her leg still hung over into the lift shaft. Like a spurting fountain, the concussive force dissipated, and the lift dropped. She jerked her foot back as the lift car fell, shearing off the sole of her boot.

They had no time to catch their breath. The blast had blown away part of the outer wall, and the old wooden structure was on fire. They crawled to their feet and stumbled through the opening, collapsing in the snow. Without a sole on the bottom of her boot, the ice penetrated her sock immediately. She barely noticed and plunged her bleeding hand into the snow.

"You okay?" Belle wheezed.

He nodded. "How's your hand?"

"I'll live."

"How's Molly?"

She could feel her heart fluttering. "Not good. She scooped snow into her hand and pressed it against Molly's wound. Scout nuzzled up close to her and focused his eyes on Molly. Belle rubbed snow against his wound as well.

Alonzo pulled out his phone and was about to tap a speed dial when he pointed down the mountain. "Lights!" A half-dozen headlights headed toward us.

The cavalry.

They heard a muffled boom and looked back to see a fireball exploding through the mine building. The flames quickly consumed the old wooden structure. After almost 150 years, the Silver Moon mine was finally gone, now only an underground mausoleum for Sonja Valek and Daniel Pagano.

Molly stirred. She opened her eyes barely more than a slit, and Belle could see she was trying to talk.

"Shhh. Help's almost here."

"Belle."

Her voice was barely a whisper. Belle bent her ear close.

"Belle?"

"Right here."

The corners of her mouth struggled to form a smile. "Always the hero to save the day."

"Molly—"

"The Sword of Justice has completed her mission. It's time to sleep."

Molly Halpin had been responsible for four deaths and intended to kill Stetson Davis, not to mention sicken a whole town. But if Carrie were sitting here with them there was no doubt in Belle's mind what she would do. Belle still had the photo of Molly, her mom, and Fred, the cactus, in her pocket. She pulled it out and wrapped Molly's fingers around it.

Belle spoke as if the words were coming directly from Carrie Palmer's mouth. "No. You will *not* sleep. You will *not* die. You will live. You will receive treatment, and maybe someday..."

Molly's eyes flickered open.

Chapter Forty-Seven

T he midmorning air was unusually warm for a sunny March day in the Wasatch Mountain Range.

Belle and Alonzo hiked through the heavy snow. They didn't say much. He knew her thoughts were filled with memories of Carrie, and he respected her need for quiet.

She hadn't known Carrie that long, not really. They weren't lovers, although Belle sensed Carrie had romantic feelings for her that she couldn't reciprocate. They were just friends. But Belle had come to believe "just friends" could be the strongest bond of all.

Images of Markie Dodd also weighted her thoughts. She could still see her bouncing as she walked. So full of life. And in an instant, gone.

And Molly. She'd survived and was recovering at a level 1 trauma center in Salt Lake. Everyone expected that when she was able she'd plead not guilty to the Grover murders by reason of insanity, and the prosecutor had already indicated he was favorably disposed to that outcome. Hopefully, she would receive the treatment she needed. With Carrie's spirit whispering in Belle's ear, she intended to speak on Molly's behalf in support of that happening.

Molly's phone recording along with her testimony appeared like they might be what was needed to nail this Vegas dude Felix Ross. Belle and Alonzo would be witnesses if it ever reached trial, which was fine with her.

Molly killed as an act of vengeance. And Pagano almost murdered hundreds of innocents. Again, motivated by a perverted sense of revenge. But didn't she act in a fit of revenge when she almost twisted Sonja Valek's head off her neck? She concluded that in some ways human beings were all too predictable.

Belle and Alonzo had traveled to Wyoming for Carrie's funeral. They were pleasantly surprised by the turnout. She supposed the tragic death of a vibrant young woman can act as a big eraser, wiping away, at least for a little while, the biases and prejudices that a few days earlier, when everything was "normal," seemed so routine.

Her parents were devastated, particularly her father whom Belle had come to learn had been the strongest voice to banish her from the family. Belle told him his daughter's last words were to tell her dad she loved him. It was like watching a mountain crumble. His legs gave out and he fell back into a chair shaking, barely able to breathe, then a river of tears. Belle thought, if nothing else, maybe Carrie's death might have a positive effect on changing attitudes in Carrie's family. She hoped so.

Belle met Carrie's former husband and his new wife and fully expected to hate them both. But truth be told, they were very nice, and she could tell he was heartbroken. After all, he'd loved Carrie once. Maybe he still did.

Carrie's daughter, Lilly, was amazing and the spitting image of her mother. Belle spent a little time alone with her and told her how brave her mommy was, how she'd saved Belle's life, and how her mommy told Belle to tell Lilly how much her mommy loved her. Belle showed her a picture of Scout and told her maybe when she got older her daddy would let her come and visit them in Park City. Before they left, Lilly wrapped her arms around Belle and gave her a big hug. Belle had bit her lip to keep from crying. Hadn't worked.

A week later, Belle received a package in the mail from Carrie's parents. Inside was a small wooden box taped shut along with a note. Her dad had sent Belle part of Carrie's ashes, telling her that he was sure she'd know an appropriate place to scatter them.

She'd stared at the box for weeks before deciding the best place was here in the Wasatch wilderness. Alonzo had volunteered to join her.

His leg was on the mend. She'd offered him the opportunity to stay with her while he recuperated. While they both recuperated. Belle's hand had benefitted from twenty-one stitches and a strong regimen of pain killers. The wound hadn't completely healed yet, but the doctor had assured her that day would come soon.

During his stay, Belle had been surprised how much she enjoyed mothering him. She never thought that was her thing. She even forced him to drink some of Carrie's god-awful tea. At night they'd enjoy a cocktail together. She hadn't forgotten Carrie's concern about the effects of alcohol on her IED, and she had reduced her intake somewhat. But not completely.

After a week off, Belle was going stir crazy and returned to her routine—taking hunting guide gigs when she could get them and working ski patrol at night. Her bum hand meant she couldn't shoot a bow quite yet, but she could grip a ski pole with her thumb and three fingers. She had a hog hunt scheduled down near Amarillo coming up and after the hunt, she intended to visit her little sister who attended college in nearby Canyon. Belle's sister was only a few years older than Markie Dodd and pregnant. Belle had a strong yearning to hug her close and never let go.

Alonzo spent most of his time at the kitchen table doing government agent stuff on his secure computer. He'd received a call asking him to join some hush-hush international government unit. Sounded like secret agent bullshit right out of the movies. He'd be returning to Washington to meet with whoever was honcho'ing it. She could tell he was interested, which was fine. His life. Except selfishly she'd kind of hoped he'd stay in the area. He was scheduled to depart the next day.

At night they'd talk. She even showed him some rudimentary quilting stitches. He said he found it interesting...probably just being polite. Sometimes he'd provide more information about the Ghazni City incident. He seemed more comfortable discussing it. And sometimes she'd talk about the three wonderful young men who died because of her. Unlike Alonzo, talking about that didn't relieve her guilt. Although Carrie's words—that stopping Davis's murder at least partially atoned for her sins—did offer some comfort.

He slept on the couch. She didn't invite him to her bed, and he didn't press. She couldn't articulate a reason other than it just didn't feel like the time was right.

They continued to trek through the trees. So far, she'd found several beautiful locations, but nothing perfect.

They climbed for another half hour and approached the edge of a sun-dappled clearing surrounded by majestic pines. God's cathedral, the perfect place. She slipped off her bow and backpack, ready to pull out the box containing Carrie's ashes when she heard rustling in the underbrush.

A moment later a huge white elk stepped into the clearing.

She froze, not believing her eyes, and whispered, *"Tsoapittsi."*

Alonzo gasped, and she couldn't blame him. The animal was

magnificent. Over six feet at the withers, close to 2,000 pounds, and a rack that had to extend seventy-five inches.

The huge white elk must've seen them, yet he didn't flinch. She pulled out her phone. Did the animal's eyes meet hers and momentarily hold her gaze? *No, that would be ridiculous, right?* She snapped a picture. Taking his own good time, he turned and disappeared into the trees.

"This is the place." They both stood there for a while, not saying a word. Then she slipped her hand around his neck and kissed him. He returned the kiss, and they gently embraced.

Belle opened the box of ashes, and they stepped into the center of the clearing. She thought maybe she should say something, but couldn't find words sufficient to describe her feelings. So Belle held the box high in the air and let the crisp breeze float Carrie's ashes into the clearing, into the trees, into the snow that in a few months would allow her remains to nourish the soil beneath.

A few minutes later they headed back down the mountain. As soon as Belle returned home, she planned to call her family and tell them what she'd done. She'd send a picture of the white elk to Lilly and tell her the elk represented her mom's spirit.

When Belle returned from Texas she'd need to alert Harlan not to schedule her for a hunt where the client was looking to kill *Tsoapittsi,* although she had a strong hunch the animal would never be found unless it wanted to be found.

Belle brushed up against Alonzo and folded her hand into his. "So, how's the couch on your back?"

"Not bad."

"Tonight's your last night before you run off to play secret agent."

"Yeah."

"There may be another alternative."

"Been waiting for you to offer. And by the way, I didn't think it was right to say anything at the time, but at the funeral, you really looked great."

"Thanks."

"First time I've seen you in a skirt."

"I own skirts. Lots of—"

His kiss cut her off, and she melted into his arms.

AUTHOR'S ACKNOWLEDGEMENTS AND NOTES

Many thanks to Steve Soderquist, Laura Ranger, and all of the amazing folks at Foundations Book Publishing. Their motto "Where the Author Comes First" isn't just an empty slogan—they live it in every decision they make.

Thanks to Steve Keithley for teaching me about bow hunting and for allowing me to tour his house full of hunting trophies. I felt like I was visiting the Museum of Natural History.

Thanks to Bill Thurber whose detailed chemical advice educated me on how to poison a town's drinking water with cyanide. (Don't worry, key information was intentionally withheld.)

Thanks to outside editors John Paine, Stacey Donovan, and Carol Rosenberg for their outstanding contributions in helping to bring Belle Bannon and her adventures to life. And to my official first editor, Anne Pace.

Thanks also to my agent, Linda Langton and her great staff at Langtons International, for their assistance.

And a special thank you to the Park City Resort ski patrollers who were kind enough to educate me on their often-perilous job.

Now a few words about what's real and what's fiction.

Maria Halpin's little red diary is totally fictional. However, that Grover Cleveland fathered a child out of wedlock with Maria is undisputed. Was it rape? The two parties are the only ones who ever knew the truth. However, in his book, *A Secret Life: The Lies and Scandals of President Grover Cleveland* (Skyhorse 2011), author

Charles Lachman makes a rather convincing case that Maria did not succumb willingly to Grover's advances. I recommend the book to anyone interested in this fascinating sidebar to American history.

To skiers who love the slopes of Park City, I know I didn't accurately describe the ski runs or overall geography of the mountain. Artistic license and all that.

Dolly's fudge is very real and very delicious. Atticus is a great coffee shop.

My description of the mine is pretty close. The Keetley tunnel is real and does empty into the general area of the Jordanelle Reservoir (although the drop from the tunnel outlet is only a few feet.)

The No Name saloon is real as are their delicious buffalo burgers. Peabody Outfitters is fictional, and if you're looking for the law office of Attorney Sal Marino or Frannie's Nail Salon you won't find them. The Summit Restaurant is a great place for lunch on the slopes.

The Sundance Film Festival is very real and provides a huge economic shot in the town's arm every January. Descriptions of the craziness along Main Street were based on first-hand observations. Yes, the locals hate the traffic and the California invasion but love the big bucks. (Real estate prices are soaring.) "Woodies" is my creation, but the locals do have nicknames for the Hollywood types and can pick them out in large crowds because, in a bold assertion of their artistic individuality, they all seem to wear black from head to toe.

Tsoapittsi is Shoshone for ghost, and albino elks, while exceedingly rare, do exist.

The fictional Molly is portrayed as a descendant of Maria Halpin. I have no idea whether descendants of Maria exist, but if so, any resemblance, physical or mental, is purely coincidental.

Harry Alonzo Longabaugh, aka the Sundance Kid, was very real. Speculation about his love, Etta Place, abounds, and she seems to have disappeared into the mist of history. Could she have left Bolivia with a baby in her belly? Why not? But Belle's Alonzo is pure fiction.

Finally, of course, any and all mistakes are mine and mine alone.

Mike Pace
Belleair, Florida, January 2021

About the Author

Born in Pittsburgh, Mike Pace received a B.F.A. degree in painting from the University of Illinois and a law degree from Georgetown University where he served on the editorial board of the prestigious Georgetown Law Journal.

He taught art in a Washington D. C. inner-city public school before being appointed Assistant U.S. Attorney for Washington. After a stint as a commercial litigator, he served as General Counsel to an environmental services company before resigning to practice law part-time, thereby allowing him to focus on his first love, creative writing.

Mike lives in Florida and when not writing or practicing his sax loves long beach walks with his parti-standard poodle, "Handsome Jack."

Other Titles Available from Foundations Book Publishing

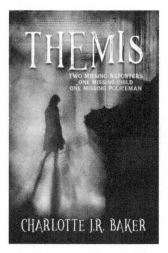

Where do the lines blur between justice and sacrifice?

Run by the beautiful and charismatic woman known only as Bow, Themis is an organization created with the sole purpose of doling out justice—justice that picks up where the law fails. When fifteen-year-old Liberty begins questioning what she'd been taught all her life, the decision to either continue to give her protection or seal her fate within its walls is at stake. **One young woman holds the key, but will she turn the locks of Themis?**

Sherman Lancaster has lived 119 years. The only thing he fears is living 119 more.

Sherman has sent legions of demons back to hell. He's killed enough men to decimate a small country—but the odds are stacked against him this time. Before an apprentice can be named, Sherman must confront an enemy who threatens to unravel everything.

Sherman's two great-grandsons are coming to stay with him. The boys believe it's because their mother can't afford daycare. Sherman knows the truth—one of the boys will become his apprentice.

Sherman lives by a simple code to which there are no exceptions: The Guilty must pay.